Monkey is a sixteenth-century Chinese novel which combines beauty with absurdity, profundity with nonsense. Folk-lore, allegory, religion, history, anti-bureaucratic satire and pure poetry are the diverse elements that make up the novel.

Wu Ch'êng-ên (c 1505–80) had some reputation as a poet, but only a few of his rather commonplace verses survive. Of his life little is known.

Arthur Waley C.B.E., F.B.S. was a distinguished authority on Chinese language and literature. He was honoured many times for his translations from the Chinese and received the Queen's medal for poetry in 1953. He died in 1966. His many books include *Chinese Poems*, *Japanese Poetry*, *The Tale of Genji*, *The Way and Its Power*, *The Real Tripitaka* and *Yuan Mei*.

Translations by Arthur Waley

ANALECTS OF CONFUCIUS
THE BOOK OF SONGS
CHINESE POEMS
JAPANESE POETRY THE 'UTA'
THE LIFE AND TIMES OF PO CHU-I
THE NO PLAYS OF JAPAN
THE OPIUM WAR THROUGH CHINESE EYES
THE PILLOW BOOK OF SEI SHONAGON
THE POETRY AND CAREER OF LI PO
THE REAL TRIPITAKA
THE TALE OF GENJI
THREE WAYS OF THOUGHT IN ANCIENT CHINA
THE WAY AND ITS POWER
YUAN MEI: EIGHTEENTH CENTURY POET

Monkey

WU CH'ÊNG-ÊN

Translated by ARTHUR WALEY

London
UNWIN PAPERBACKS
Boston   Sydney

This translation first published in Great Britain by George
Allen & Unwin 1942
Reprinted six times
First published in Unwin Paperbacks 1979

UNWIN ® PAPERBACKS
40 Museum Street, London WC1A 1LU

This translation © George Allen & Unwin (Publishers) Ltd 1942, 1979

British Library Cataloguing in Publication Data

Wu Chêng-ên
Monkey.
I. Title
895.1'3'4'   PL2697.M/

ISBN 0-04-823173-8

Typeset in 10 on 11 point Times
and printed in Great Britain by
Hunt Barnard Printing Ltd, Aylesbury, Bucks.

To
Beryl and Harold

Introduction

This story was written by Wu Ch'êng-ên, of Huai-an in Kiangsu. His exact dates are not known, but he seems to have lived between A.D. 1505 and 1580. He had some reputation as a poet, and a few of his rather commonplace verses survive in an anthology of Ming poetry and in a local gazetteer.

Tripitaka, whose pilgrimage to India is the subject of the story, is a real person, better known to history as Hsüan Tsang. He lived in the 7th century A.D., and there are full contemporary accounts of his journey. Already by the 10th century, and probably earlier, Tripitaka's pilgrimage had become the subject of a whole cycle of fantastic legends. From the 13th century onwards these legends have been constantly represented on the Chinese stage. Wu Ch'êng-ên had therefore a great deal to build on when he wrote his long fairy tale. The original book is indeed of immense length, and is usually read in abridged forms. The method adopted in these abridgements is to leave the original number of separate episodes, but drastically reduce them in length, particularly by cutting out dialogue. I have for the most part adopted the opposite principle, omitting many episodes, but translating those that are retained almost in full, leaving out, however, most of the incidental passages in verse, which go very badly into English.

Monkey is unique in its combination of beauty with absurdity, of profundity with nonsense. Folk-lore, allegory, religion, history, anti-bureaucratic satire and pure poetry – such are the singularly diverse elements out of which the book is compounded. The bureaucrats of the story are saints in Heaven, and it might be supposed that the satire was directed against religion rather than against bureaucracy. But the idea that the hierarchy in Heaven is a replica of government on earth is an accepted one in China. Here as so often the Chinese let the cat out of the bag, where other countries leave us guessing. It has often enough been put forward as a theory that a people's gods are the replica of its earthly rulers. In most cases the derivation is obscure. But in Chinese popular belief there is no ambiguity. Heaven is simply the whole bureaucratic system transferred bodily to the empyrean.

As regards the allegory, it is clear that Tripitaka stands for the ordinary man, blundering anxiously through the difficulties of life, while Monkey stands for the restless instability of genius. Pigsy, again, obviously symbolizes the physical appetites, brute strength, and a kind of cumbrous patience. Sandy is more mysterious. The commentators say that he represents *ch'êng*, which is usually translated 'sincerity', but means something more like 'whole-heartedness'. He was not an afterthought, for he appears in some of the earliest versions of the legend, but it must be admitted that, though in some inexplicable way essential to the story, he remains throughout singularly ill-defined and colourless.

Extracts from the book were given in Giles's *History of Chinese Literature* and in Timothy Richard's *A Mission to Heaven*, at a time when only the abridgements were known. An accessible, though very inaccurate account of it is given by Helen Hayes, in *A Buddhist Pilgrim's Progress* (Wisdom of the East Series). There is a very loose paraphrase in Japanese by various hands, with a preface dated 1806 by the famous novelist Bakin. It has illustrations, some of them by Hokusai, and one of the translators was Hokusai's pupil Gakutei, who admits that when he undertook the work he had no knowledge of Chinese colloquial. I lost my copy of this Japanese version years ago and am grateful to Mr Saiji Hasegawa, formerly head of the London branch of the Domei Press Agency, who generously presented me with his copy. The text I have used for translation was published by the Oriental Press, Shanghai, in 1921. It has a long and scholarly introduction by Dr Hu Shih, now Chinese ambassador in Washington.

Chapter 1

There was a rock that since the creation of the world had been worked upon by the pure essences of Heaven and the fine savours of Earth, the vigour of sunshine and the grace of moonlight, till at last it became magically pregnant and one day split open, giving birth to a stone egg, about as big as a playing ball. Fructified by the wind it developed into a stone monkey, complete with every organ and limb. At once this monkey learned to climb and run; but its first act was to make a bow towards each of the four quarters. As it did so, a steely light darted from this monkey's eyes and flashed as far as the Palace of the Pole Star. This shaft of light astonished the Jade Emperor as he sat in the Cloud Palace of the Golden Gates, in the Treasure Hall of the Holy Mists, surrounded by his fairy Ministers. Seeing this strange light flashing, he ordered Thousand-league Eye and Down-the-wind Ears to open the gate of the Southern Heaven and look out. At his bidding these two captains went out to the gate and looked so sharply and listened so well that presently they were able to report, 'This steely light comes from the borders of the small country of Ao-lai, that lies to the east of the Holy Continent, from the Mountain of Flowers and Fruit. On this mountain is a magic rock, which gave birth to an egg. This egg changed into a stone monkey, and when he made his bow to the four quarters a steely light flashed from his eyes with a beam that reached the Palace of the Pole Star. But now he is taking a drink, and the light is growing dim.'

The Jade Emperor condescended to take an indulgent view. 'These creatures in the world below,' he said, 'were compounded of the essence of heaven and earth, and nothing that goes on there should surprise us.' That monkey walked, ran, leapt and bounded over the hills, feeding on grasses and shrubs, drinking from streams and springs, gathering the mountain flowers, looking for fruits. Wolf, panther and tiger were his companions, the deer and civet were his friends, gibbons and baboons his kindred. At night he lodged under cliffs of rock, by day he wandered among the peaks and caves. One very hot morning, after playing in the shade of some pine-trees, he and the other monkeys went to bathe in a mountain stream. See how those waters bounce and tumble like rolling melons!

There is an old saying, 'Birds have their bird language, beasts have their beast talk.' The monkeys said, 'We none of us know where this stream comes from. As we have nothing to do this morning, wouldn't it be fun to follow it up to its source?' With a whoop of joy, dragging their sons and carrying their daughters, calling out to younger brother and to elder brother, the whole troupe rushed along the streamside and scrambled up the steep places, till they reached the source of the stream. They found themselves standing before the curtain of a great waterfall.

All the monkeys clapped their hands and cried aloud, 'Lovely water, lovely water! To think that it starts far off in some cavern below the base of the mountain, and flows all the way to the Great Sea! If any of us were bold enough to pierce that curtain, get to where the water comes from and return unharmed, we would make him our king!' Three times the call went out, when suddenly one of them leapt from among the throng and answered the challenge in a loud voice. It was the Stone Monkey. 'I will go,' he cried, 'I will go!' Look at him! He screws up his eyes and crouches; then at one bound he jumps straight through the waterfall. When he opened his eyes and looked about him, he found that where he had landed there was no water. A great bridge stretched in front of him, shining and glinting. When he looked closely at it, he saw that it was made all of burnished iron. The water under it flowed through a hole in the rock, filling in all the space under the arch. Monkey climbed up on to the bridge and, spying as he went, saw something that looked just like a house. There were stone seats and stone couches, and tables with stone bowls and cups. He skipped back to the hump of the bridge and saw that on the cliff there was an inscription in large square writing which said,

'This cave of the Water Curtain in the blessed land of the Mountain of Flowers and Fruit leads to Heaven.' Monkey was beside himself with delight. He rushed back and again crouched, shut his eyes and jumped through the curtain of water.

'A great stroke of luck,' he cried, 'A great stroke of luck!' 'What is it like on the other side?' asked the monkeys, crowding round him. 'Is the water very deep?' 'There is no water,' said the Stone Monkey. 'There is an iron bridge, and at the side of it a heaven-sent place to live in.' 'What made you think it would do to live in?' asked the monkeys. 'The water,' said the Stone Monkey, 'flows out of a hole in the rock, filling in the space under the bridge. At the side of the bridge are flowers and trees, and there is a chamber of stone. Inside are stone tables, stone cups, stone dishes, stone couches, stone seats. We could really be very comfortable there. There is plenty of room for hundreds and thousands of us, young and old. Let us all go and live there; we shall be splendidly sheltered in every weather.' 'You go first and show us how!' cried the monkeys, in great delight. Once more he closed his eyes and was through at one bound. 'Come along, all of you!' he cried. The bolder of them jumped at once; the more timid stretched out their heads and then drew them back, scratched their ears, rubbed their cheeks, and then with a great shout the whole mob leapt forward. Soon they were all seizing dishes and snatching cups, scrambling to the hearth or fighting for the beds, dragging things along or shifting them about, behaving indeed as monkeys with their mischievous nature might be expected to do, never quiet for an instant, till at last they were thoroughly worn out. The Stone Monkey took his seat at the head of them and said, 'Gentlemen! "With one whose word cannot be trusted there is nothing to be done!"[1] You promised that any of us who managed to get through the waterfall and back again, should be your king. I have not only come and gone and come again, but also found you a comfortable place to sleep, put you in the enviable position of being

[1] *Analects* of Confucius, II. 22.

householders. Why do you not bow to me as your king?'

Thus reminded, the monkeys all pressed together the palms of their hands and prostrated themselves, drawn up in a line according to age and standing, and bowing humbly they cried, 'Great king, a thousand years!' After this the Stone Monkey discarded his old name and became king, with the title 'Handsome Monkey King'. He appointed various monkeys, gibbons and baboons to be his ministers and officers. By day they wandered about the Mountain of Flowers and Fruit; at night they slept in the Cave of the Water Curtain. They lived in perfect sympathy and accord, not mingling with bird or beast, in perfect independence and entire happiness.

The Monkey King had enjoyed this artless existence for several hundred years when one day, at a feast in which all the monkeys took part, the king suddenly felt very sad and burst into tears. His subjects at once ranged themselves in front of him and bowed down, saying, 'Why is your Majesty so sad?' 'At present,' said the king, 'I have no cause for unhappiness. But I have a misgiving about the future, which troubles me sorely.' 'Your Majesty is very hard to please,' said the monkeys, laughing. 'Every day we have happy meetings on fairy mountains, in blessed spots, in ancient caves, on holy islands. We are not subject to the Unicorn or Phoenix, nor to the restraints of any human king. Such freedom is an immeasurable blessing. What can it be that causes you this sad misgiving?' 'It is true,' said the Monkey King, 'that today I am not answerable to the law of any human king, nor need I fear the menace of any beast or bird. But the time will come when I shall grow old and weak. Yama, King of Death, is secretly waiting to destroy me. Is there no way by which, instead of being born again on earth, I might live forever among the people of the sky?'

When the monkeys heard this they covered their faces with their hands and wept, each thinking of his own mortality. But look! From among the ranks there springs out one monkey commoner, who cries in a loud voice 'If that is what

12

troubles your Majesty, it shows that religion has taken hold upon your heart. There are indeed, among all creatures, three kinds that are not subject to Yama, King of Death.' 'And do you know which they are?' asked the Monkey King. 'Buddhas, Immortals and Sages,' he said. 'These three are exempt from the Turning of the Wheel, from birth and destruction. They are external as Heaven and Earth, as the hills and streams.' 'Where are they to be found?' asked the Monkey King. 'Here on the common earth,' said the monkey, 'in ancient caves among enchanted hills.'

The king was delighted with this news. 'Tomorrow,' he said, 'I shall say good-bye to you, go down the mountain, wander like a cloud to the corners of the sea, far away to the end of the world, till I have found these three kinds of Immortal. From them I will learn how to be young forever and escape the doom of death.' This determination it was that led him to leap clear of the toils of Re-incarnation and turned him at last into the Great Monkey Sage, equal of Heaven. The monkeys clapped their hands and cried aloud, 'Splendid! Splendid! Tomorrow we will scour the hills for fruits and berries and hold a great farewell banquet in honour of our king.'

Next day they duly went to gather peaches and rare fruits, mountain herbs, yellow-sperm, tubers, orchids, strange plants and flowers of every sort, and set out the stone tables and benches, laid out fairy meats and drinks. They put the Monkey King at the head of the table, and ranged themselves according to their age and rank. The pledge-cup passed from hand to hand; they made their offerings to him of flowers and fruit. All day long they drank, and next day their king rose early and said, 'Little ones, cut some pine-wood for me and make me a raft; then find a tall bamboo for pole, and put together a few fruits and such like. I am going to start.' He got on to the raft all alone and pushed off with all his might, speeding away and away, straight out to sea, till favoured by a following wind he arrived at the borders of the Southern World. Fate indeed had favoured him; for days on end, ever since he set foot on the raft, a strong south-east wind blew and carried him at last to the north-western bank, which is indeed the frontier of the Southern World. He tested the water with his pole and found that it was shallow; so he left the raft and climbed ashore. On the beach were people fishing, shooting wild geese, scooping oysters, draining salt. He ran up to them and for fun began to perform queer antics which frightened them so much that they dropped their baskets and nets and ran for their lives. One of them, who stood his ground, Monkey caught hold of, and ripping off his clothes, found out how to wear them himself, and so dressed up went prancing through towns and cities, in market and bazaar, imitating the people's manners and talk. All the while his heart was set only on finding the Immortals and learning from them the secret of eternal youth. But he found the men of the world all engrossed in the quest of profit or fame; there was not one who had any care for the end that was in store for him. So Monkey went looking for the way of Immortality, but found no chance of meeting it. For eight or nine years he went from city to city and town to town till suddenly he came to the Western Ocean. He was sure that beyond this ocean there would certainly be Immortals, and he made for himself a raft like the one he had before. He floated on over the Western Ocean till he came to the Western Continent, where he went ashore, and when he had looked about for some time, he suddenly saw a very high and beautiful mountain, thickly wooded at the base. He had no fear of wolves, tigers or panthers, and made his way up to the very top. He was looking about him when he suddenly heard a man's voice coming from deep amid the woods. He hurried towards the spot and listened intently. It was someone singing, and these were the words that he caught:

> I hatch no plot, I scheme no scheme;
> Fame and shame are one to me,
> A simple life prolongs my days.
> Those I meet upon my way
> Are Immortals, one and all,

Who from their quiet seats expound
The Scriptures of the Yellow Court.

When Monkey heard these words he was very pleased.
'There must then be Immortals somewhere hereabouts,' he
said. He sprang deep into the forest and looking carefully
saw that the singer was a woodman, who was cutting brushwood. 'Reverend Immortal,' said Monkey, coming forward,
'your disciple raises his hands.' The woodman was so
astonished that he dropped his axe. 'You have made a mistake,' he said, turning and answering the salutation, 'I am
only a shabby, hungry woodcutter. What makes you address
me as an "Immortal"?' 'If you are not an Immortal,' said
Monkey, 'why did you talk of yourself as though you were
one?' 'What did I say,' asked the woodcutter, 'that sounded
as though I were an Immortal?' 'When I came to the edge of
the wood,' said Monkey, 'I heard you singing "Those I meet
upon my way are Immortals, one and all, who from their
quiet seats expound the Scriptures of the Yellow Court."
Those scriptures are secret, Taoist texts. What can you be
but an Immortal?' 'I won't deceive you,' said the woodcutter. 'That song was indeed taught to me by an Immortal,
who lives not very far from my hut. He saw that I have to
work hard for my living and have a lot of troubles; so he
told me when I was worried by anything to say to myself the
words of that song. This, he said, would comfort me and get
me out of my difficulties. Just now I was upset about something and so I was singing that song. I had no idea that you
were listening.'

'If the Immortal lives close by,' said Monkey, 'how is it
that you have not become his disciple? Wouldn't it have
been as well to learn from him how never to grow old?' 'I
have a hard life of it,' said the woodcutter. 'When I was eight
or nine I lost my father. I had no brothers and sisters, and it
fell upon me alone to support my widowed mother. There
was nothing for it but to work hard early and late. Now my
mother is old and I dare not leave her. The garden is neg-
lected, we have not enough either to eat or wear. The most I

15

can do is to cut two bundles of firewood, carry them to market and with the penny or two that I get buy a few handfuls of rice which I cook myself and serve to my aged mother. I have no time to go and learn magic.' 'From what you tell me,' said Monkey, 'I can see that you are a good and devoted son, and your piety will certainly be rewarded. All I ask of you is that you will show me where the Immortal lives; for I should very much like to visit him.'

'It is quite close,' said the woodcutter. 'This mountain is called the Holy Terrace Mountain, and on it is a cave called the Cave of the Slanting Moon and Three Stars. In that cave lives an Immortal called the Patriarch Subodhi. In his time he has had innumerable disciples, and at this moment there are some thirty or forty of them studying with him. You have only to follow that small path southwards for eight or nine leagues,[1] and you will come to his home.' 'Honoured brother,' said Monkey, drawing the woodcutter towards him, 'come with me, and if I profit by the visit I will not forget that you guided me.' 'It takes a lot to make some people understand,' said the woodcutter. 'I've just been telling you why I can't go. If I went with you, what would become of my work? Who would give my old mother her food? I must go on cutting my wood, and you must find your way alone.'

When Monkey heard this, he saw nothing for it but to say goodbye. He left the wood, found the path, went uphill for some seven or eight leagues and sure enough found a cave-dwelling. But the door was locked. All was quiet, and there was no sign of anyone being about. Suddenly he turned his head and saw on top of the cliff a stone slab about thirty feet high and eight feet wide. On it was an inscription in large letters saying, 'Cave of the Slanting Moon and Three Stars on the Mountain of the Holy Terrace'. 'People here,' said Monkey, 'are certainly very truthful. There really is such a mountain, and such a cave!' He looked about for a while, but did not venture to knock at the door. Instead he jumped up into a pine-tree and began eating the pine-seed and playing

[1] A league was 360 steps.

16

among the branches. After a time he heard someone call; the door of the cave opened and a fairy boy of great beauty came out, in appearance utterly unlike the common lads that he had seen till now. The boy shouted, 'Who is making a disturbance out there?' Monkey leapt down from his tree, and coming forward said with a bow, 'Fairy boy, I am a pupil who has come to study Immortality. I should not dream of making a disturbance.' *'You* a pupil!' said the boy laughing. 'To be sure,' said Monkey. 'My master is lecturing,' said the boy. 'But before he gave out his theme he told me to go to the door and if anyone came asking for instruction, I was to look after him. I suppose he meant you.' 'Of course he meant me,' said Monkey. 'Follow me this way,' said the boy. Monkey tidied himself and followed the boy into the cave. Huge chambers opened out before them, they went on from room to room, through lofty halls and innumerable cloisters and retreats, till they came to a platform of green jade, upon which was seated the Patriarch Subodhi, with thirty lesser Immortals assembled before him. Monkey at once prostrated himself and bumped his head three times upon the ground, murmuring, 'Master, master! As pupil to teacher I pay you my humble respects.' 'Where do you come from?' asked the Patriarch. 'First tell me your country and name, and then pay your respects again.' 'I am from the Water Curtain Cave,' said Monkey, 'on the Mountain of Fruit and Flowers in the country of Ao-lai.' 'Go away!' shouted the Patriarch. 'I know the people there. They're a tricky, humbugging set. It's no good one of them supposing he's going to achieve Enlightenment.' Monkey, kow-towing violently, hastened to say, 'There's no trickery about this; it's just the plain truth I'm telling you.' 'If you claim that you're telling the truth,' said the Patriarch, 'how is it that you say you came from Ao-lai? Between there and here there are two oceans and the whole of the Southern Continent. How did you get here?' 'I floated over the oceans and wandered over the lands for ten years and more,' said Monkey, 'till at last I reached here.' 'Oh well,' said the Patriarch, 'I suppose if you came by easy stages, it's not altogether impossible.

But tell me, what is your *hsing*?'[1] 'I never show *hsing*,' said Monkey. 'If I am abused, I am not at all annoyed. If I am hit, I am not angry; but on the contrary, twice more polite than before. All my life I have never shown *hsing*.'

'I don't mean that kind of *hsing*,' said the Patriarch. 'I mean what was your family, what surname had they?' 'I had no family,' said Monkey, 'neither father nor mother.' 'Oh indeed!' said the Patriarch. 'Perhaps you grew on a tree!' 'Not exactly,' said Monkey. 'I came out of a stone. There was a magic stone on the Mountain of Flowers and Fruit. When its time came, it burst open and I came out.'

'We shall have to see about giving you a school-name,' said the Patriarch. 'We have twelve words that we use in these names, according to the grade of the pupil. You are in the tenth grade.' 'What are the twelve words?' asked Monkey. 'They are Wide, Big, Wise, Clever, True, Conforming, Nature, Ocean, Lively, Aware, Perfect and Illumined. As you belong to the tenth grade, the word Aware must come in your name. How about Aware-of-Vacuity?' 'Splendid!' said Monkey, laughing. 'From now onwards let me be called Aware-of-Vacuity.'

So that was his name in religion. And if you do not know whether in the end, equipped with this name, he managed to obtain enlightenment or not, listen while it is explained to you in the next chapter.

[1] There is a pun on *hsing*, 'surname', and *hsing*, 'temper'.

Chapter 2

Monkey was so pleased with his new name that he skipped up and down in front of the Patriarch, bowing to express his gratitude. Subodhi then ordered his pupils to take Monkey to the outer rooms and teach him how to sprinkle and dust, answer properly when spoken to, how to come in, go out, and go round. Then he bowed to his fellow-pupils and went out into the corridor, where he made himself a sleeping place. Early next morning he and the others practised the correct mode of speech and bearing, studied the Scriptures, discussed doctrine, practised writing, burnt incense. And in this same way he passed day after day, spending his leisure in sweeping the floor, hoeing the garden, growing flowers and tending trees, getting firewood and lighting the fire, drawing water and carrying it in buckets. Everything he needed was provided for him. And so he lived in the cave, while time slipped by, for six or seven years. One day the Patriarch, seated in state, summoned all his pupils and began a lecture on the Great Way. Monkey was so delighted by what he heard that he tweaked his ears and rubbed his cheeks; his brow flowered and his eyes laughed. He could not stop his hands from dancing, his feet from stamping. Suddenly the Patriarch caught sight of him and shouted, 'What is the use of your being here if, instead of listening to my lecture, you jump and dance like a maniac?' 'I am listening with all my might,' said Monkey. 'But you were saying such wonderful things that I could not contain myself for joy. That is why I may, for all I know, have been hopping and jumping. Don't be angry with me.' 'So you recognise the profundity of what I am saying?' said the Patriarch. 'How long, pray, have you been in the cave?' 'It may seem rather silly,' said Monkey, 'but really I don't know how long. All I can remember is that when I was sent to get firewood, I went up the mountain behind the cave, and there I found a whole slope covered with peach trees. I have eaten my fill of those

19

peaches seven times.' 'It is called the Hill of Bright Peach Blossom,' said the Patriarch. 'If you have eaten there seven times, I suppose you have been here seven years. What sort of wisdom are you now hoping to learn from me?' 'I leave that to you,' said Monkey. 'Any sort of wisdom – it's all one to me.'

'There are three hundred and sixty schools of wisdom,' said the Patriarch, 'and all of them lead to Self-attainment. Which school do you want to study?' 'Just as you think best,' said Monkey. 'I am all attention.' 'Well, how about Art?' said the Patriarch. 'Would you like me to teach you that?' 'What sort of wisdom is that?' asked Monkey. 'You would be able to summon fairies and ride the Phoenix,' said the Patriarch, 'divine by shuffling the yarrow-stalks and know how to avoid disaster and pursue good fortune.' 'But should I live forever?' asked Monkey. 'Certainly not,' said the Patriarch. 'Then that's no good to me,' said Monkey. 'How about natural philosophy?' said the Patriarch. 'What is that about?' asked Monkey. 'It means the teaching of Confucius,' said the Patriarch, 'and of Buddha and Lao Tzu, of the Dualists and Mo Tzu and the Doctors of Medicine; reading scriptures, saying prayers, learning how to have adepts and sages at your beck and call.' 'But should I live forever?' asked Monkey. 'If that's what you are thinking about,' said the Patriarch, 'I am afraid philosophy is no better than a prop in the wall.' 'Master,' said Monkey, 'I am a plain, simple man, and I don't understand that sort of patter. What do you mean by a prop in the wall?' 'When men are building a room,' said the Patriarch, 'and want it to stand firm, they put a pillow to prop up the walls. But one day the roof falls in and the pillar rots.' 'That doesn't sound much like long life,' said Monkey. 'I'm not going to learn philosophy!' 'How about Quietism?' asked the Patriarch. 'What does that consist of?' asked Monkey. 'Low diet,' said the Patriarch, 'inactivity, meditation, restraint of word and deed, yoga practised prostrate or standing.' 'But should I live forever?' asked Monkey. 'The results of Quietism,' said the Patriarch, 'are no better than unbaked clay in the kiln.'

'You've got a very poor memory,' said Monkey. 'Didn't I tell you just now that I don't understand that sort of patter? What do you mean by unbaked clay in the kiln?' 'The bricks and tiles,' said the Patriarch, 'may be waiting, all shaped and ready, in the kiln; but if they have not yet been fired, there will come a day when heavy rain falls and they are washed away.' 'That does not promise well for the future,' said Monkey. 'I don't think I'll bother about Quietism.'

'You might try exercises,' said the Patriarch. 'What do you mean by that?' asked Monkey. 'Various forms of activity,' said the Patriarch, 'such as the exercises called "Gathering the Yin and patching the Yang", "Drawing the Bow and Treading the Catapult", "Rubbing the Navel to pass breath." Then there are alchemical practices such as the Magical Explosion, Burning the Reeds and Striking the Tripod, Promoting Red Lead, Melting the Autumn Stone, and Drinking Bride's Milk.' 'Would these make me live forever?' asked Monkey. 'To hope for that,' said the Patriarch, 'would be like trying to fish the moon out of the water.' 'There you go again!' said Monkey. 'What pray do you mean by fishing the moon out of the water?' 'When the moon is in the sky,' said the Patriarch, 'it is reflected in the water. It looks just like a real thing, but if you try to catch hold of it, you find it is only an illusion.' 'That does not sound much good,' said Monkey; 'I shan't learn exercises.' 'Tut!' cried the Patriarch, and coming down from the platform, he caught hold of the knuckle-rapper and pointed it at Monkey, saying, 'You wretched simian! You won't learn this and you won't learn that! I should like to know what it is you do want.' And so saying he struck Monkey over the head three times. Then he folded his hands behind his back and strode off into the inner room, dismissing his audience and locking the door behind him. The pupils all turned indignantly upon Monkey. 'You villainous ape,' they shouted at him, 'do you think that is the way to behave? The Master offers to teach you, and instead of accepting thankfully, you begin arguing with him. Now he's thoroughly offended and goodness knows when he'll come back.' They were all very angry and poured abuse on

21

him; but Monkey was not in the least upset, and merely replied by a broad grin. The truth of the matter was, he understood the language of secret signs. That was why he did not take up the quarrel or attempt to argue. He knew that the Master, by striking him three times, was giving him an appointment at the third watch; and by going off with his hands folded behind his back, meant that Monkey was to look for him in the inner apartments. The locking of the door meant that he was to come round by the back door and would then receive instruction.

The rest of the day he frolicked with the other pupils in front of the cave, impatiently awaiting the night. As soon as dusk came, like the others, he went to his sleeping place. He closed his eyes and pretended to be asleep, breathing softly and regularly. In the mountains there is no watchman to beat the watches or call the hours. The best Monkey could do was to count his incoming and outgoing breaths. When he reckoned that it must be about the hour of the Rat (11 p.m.– 1 a.m.) he got up very quietly and slipped on his clothes, softly opened the front door, left his companions and went round to the back door. Sure enough, it was only half-shut. 'The Master certainly means to give me instruction,' said Monkey to himself. 'That is why he left the door open.' So he crept in and went straight to the Master's bed. Finding him curled up and lying with his face to the wall, Monkey dared not wake him, and knelt down beside the bed. Presently the Patriarch woke, stretched out his legs and murmured to himself:

Hard, very hard!
The Way is most secret.
Never handle the Golden Elixir as though it were a mere toy!
He who to unworthy ears entrusts the dark truths
To no purpose works his jaws and talks his tongue dry.

'Master, I've been kneeling here for some time,' said Monkey, when he saw the Patriarch was awake. 'You wretched Monkey,' said Subodhi, who on recognising his voice pulled off the bedclothes and sat up. 'Why aren't you asleep in your own quarters, instead of coming round behind to mine?' 'At the lecture today,' said Monkey, 'you ordered me to come for instruction at the third watch, by way of the back gate. That is why I ventured to come straight to your bed.' The Patriarch was delighted. He thought to himself 'This fellow must really be, as he says, a natural product of Heaven and Earth. Otherwise he would never have understood my secret signs.' 'We are alone together,' said Monkey, 'there is no one to overhear us. Take pity upon me and teach me the way of Long Life. I shall never forget your kindness.' 'You show a disposition,' said the Patriarch. 'You understood my secret signs. Come close and listen carefully. I am going to reveal to you the Secret of Long Life.' Monkey beat his head on the floor to show his gratitude, washed his ears and attended closely, kneeling beside the bed. The Patriarch then recited:

> To spare and tend the vital powers, this and nothing else
> Is sum and total of all magic, secret and profane.
> All is comprised in these three, Spirit, Breath and Soul;
> Guard them closely, screen them well; let there be no
>   leak.
> Store them within the frame;
> That is all that can be learnt, and all that can be taught.
> I would have you mark the tortoise and snake, locked in
>   tight embrace.
> Locked in tight embrace, the vital powers are strong;
> Even in the midst of fierce flames the Golden Lotus may
>   be planted,
> The Five Elements compounded and transposed, and put
>   to new use,
> When that is done, be which you please, Buddha or
>   Immortal.

By these words Monkey's whole nature was shaken to the foundations. He carefully committed them to memory; then humbly thanked the Patriarch, and went out again by the back door.

A pale light was just coming into the eastern sky. He retraced his steps, softly opened the front door and returned to his sleeping place, purposely making a rustling noise with his bedclothes. 'Get up!' he cried. 'There is light in the sky.' His fellow pupils were fast asleep, and had no idea that Monkey had received Illumination.

Time passed swiftly, and three years later the Patriarch again mounted his jewelled seat and preached to his assembled followers. His subject was the parables and scholastic problems of the Zen Sect, and his theme, the tegument of outer appearances. Suddenly he broke off and asked, 'Where is the disciple Aware-of-Vacuity?' Monkey knelt down before him and answered 'Here!' 'What have you been studying all this time?' asked the Patriarch. 'Recently,' said Monkey, 'my spiritual nature has been very much in the ascendant, and my fundamental sources of power are gradually strengthening.' 'In that case,' said the Patriarch, 'all you need learn is how to ward off the Three Calamities.' 'There must be some mistake,' said Monkey in dismay. 'I understood that the secrets I have learnt would make me live forever and protect me from fire, water and every kind of disease. What is this about three calamities?' 'What you have learnt,' said the Patriarch, 'will preserve your youthful appearance and increase the length of your life; but after five hundred years Heaven will send down lightning which will finish you off, unless you have the sagacity to avoid it. After another five hundred years Heaven will send down a fire that will devour you. This fire is of a peculiar kind. It is neither common fire, nor celestial fire, but springs up from within and consumes the vitals, reducing the whole frame to ashes, and making a vanity of all your thousand years of self-perfection. But even should you escape this, in another five hundred years, a wind will come and blow upon you. Not the east wind, the south wind, the west wind or the north wind; not flower wind, or willow wind, pine wind or bamboo wind. It blows from below, enters the bowels, passes the midriff and issues at the Nine Apertures. It melts bone and flesh, so that the whole body dissolves. These three calamities you must be able to avoid.' When Monkey heard this, his hair stood on end, and prostrating himself he said, 'I beseech you, have pity upon me, and teach me how to avoid these calamities. I shall never forget your kindness.' There would be no difficulty about that,' said the Patriarch, 'if it were not for your peculiarities.' 'I have a round head sticking up to Heaven and square feet treading Earth,' said Monkey. 'I have nine apertures, four limbs, five upper and six lower internal organs, just like other people.' 'You are like other men in most respects,' said the Patriarch, 'but you have much less jowl.' For monkeys have hollow cheeks and pointed nozzles. Monkey felt his face with his hand and laughed saying, 'Master, I have my debits, but don't forget my assets. I have my pouch, and that must be credited to my account, as something that ordinary humans haven't got.' 'True enough,' said the Patriarch. 'There are two methods of escape. Which would you like to learn? There is the trick of the Heavenly Ladle, which involves thirty-six kinds of transformation, and the trick of the Earthly Conclusion, which involves seventy-two kinds of transformation.' 'Seventy-two sounds better value,' said Monkey. 'Come here then,' said the Patriarch, 'and I will teach you the formula.' He then whispered a magic formula into Monkey's ear. That Monkey King was uncommonly quick at taking things in. He at once began practising the formula, and after a little self-discipline he mastered all the seventy-two transformations, whole and complete. One day when master and disciples were in front of the cave, admiring the evening view, the Patriarch said, 'Monkey, how is that business going?' 'Thanks to your kindness,' said Monkey, 'I have been extremely successful. In addition to the transformations I can already fly.' 'Let's see you do it,' said the Patriarch. Monkey put his feet together, leapt about sixty feet into the air, and riding the clouds for a few minutes dropped in front of the Patriarch. He did not get more than three leagues in the whole of his flight. 'Master,' he said, 'that surely is cloud-soaring?' 'I should be more inclined to call it cloud-crawling,' said the Patriarch laughing. 'The old saying runs, "An Immortal wanders in the morning to the Northern Sea, and the same evening he is in Ts'ang-wu.'" To take as long as you did to go a mere league or two hardly counts even as cloud-crawling.' 'What is meant by that saying about the Northern Sea and Ts'ang-wu?' asked Monkey. 'A real cloud-soarer,' said the Patriarch, 'can start early in the morning from the Northern Sea, cross the Eastern Sea, the Western Sea and the Southern Sea, and land again at Ts'ang-wu. Ts'ang-wu means Ling-ling, in the Northern Sea. To do the round of all four seas in one day is true cloud-soaring.' 'It sounds very difficult,' said Monkey. 'Nothing in the world is difficult,' said the Patriarch, 'it is only our own thoughts that make things seem so.' 'Master,' said Monkey, prostrating himself, 'you may as well make a good job of me. While you're about it, do me a real kindness and teach me the art of cloud-soaring. I shall never forget how much I owe to you.' 'When the Immortals go cloud-soaring,' said the Patriarch, 'they sit cross-legged and rise straight from that position. You do nothing of the kind. I saw you just now put your feet together and jump. I must really take this opportunity of teaching you how to do it properly. You shall learn the Cloud Trapeze.' He then taught him the magic formula, saying, 'Make the pass, recite the spell, clench your fists, and one leap will carry you head over heels a hundred and eight thousand leagues.'

When the other pupils heard this, they all tittered, saying, 'Monkey is in luck. If he learns this trick, he will be able to carry dispatches, deliver letters, take round circulars – one way or another he will always be able to pick up a living!'

It was now late. Master and pupils all went to their quarters; but Monkey spent all night practising the Cloud Trapeze, and by the time day came he had completely mastered it, and could wander through space where he would.

One summer day when the disciples had for some time been studying their tasks under a pine tree, one of them said, 'Monkey, what can you have done in a former incarnation to merit that the Master should the other day have whispered in your ear the secret formula for avoiding the three calamities? Have you mastered all those transformations?' 'To tell you the truth,' said Monkey, 'although of course I am much indebted to the Master for his instruction, I have also been working very hard day and night on my own, and I can now do them all.' 'Wouldn't this be a good opportunity,' said one of the pupils, 'to give us a little demonstration?' When Monkey heard this, he was all on his mettle to display his powers. 'Give me my subject,' he said. 'What am I to change into?' 'How about a pine tree?' they said. He made a magic pass, recited a spell, shook himself, and changed into a pine tree.

The disciples clapped and burst into loud applause. 'Bravo, Monkey, bravo,' they cried. There was such a din that the Patriarch came running out with his staff trailing after him. 'Who's making all this noise?' he asked. The disciples at once controlled themselves, smoothed down their dresses and came meekly forward. Monkey changed himself back into his true form and slipped in among the crowd, saying, 'Reverend Master, we are doing our lessons out here. I assure you there was no noise in particular.' 'You were all bawling,' said the Patriarch angrily. 'It didn't sound in the least like people studying. I want to know what you were doing here, shouting and laughing.' 'To tell the truth,' said someone, 'Monkey was showing us a transformation just for fun. We told him to change into a pine tree, and he did it so well that we were all applauding him. That was the noise you heard. I hope you will forgive us.' 'Go away, all of you!' the Patriarch shouted. 'And you, Monkey, come here! What were you doing, playing with your spiritual powers, turning into – what was it? A pine tree? Did you think I taught you in order that you might show off in front of other people? If you saw someone else turn into a tree, wouldn't you at once ask how it was done? If others see you doing it, aren't they certain to ask you? If you are frightened to refuse, you will give the secret away; and if you refuse, you're very likely to be roughly handled. You're putting yourself in grave danger.' 'I'm terribly sorry,' said Monkey. 'I won't punish you,' said the Patriarch, 'but you can't stay here.' Monkey burst into tears. 'Where am I to go to?' he asked. 'Back to where you came from, I should suppose,' said the Patriarch. 'You don't mean back to the Cave of the Water Curtain in Ao-lai!' said Monkey. 'Yes,' said the Patriarch, 'go back as quickly as you can, if you value your life. One thing is certain in any case; you can't stay here.' 'May I point out,' said Monkey, 'that I have been away from home for twenty years and should be very glad to see my monkey-subjects once more. But I can't consent to go till I have repaid you for all your kindness.' 'I have no desire to be repaid,' said the Patriarch. 'All I ask is that if you get into trouble, you should keep my name out of it.' Monkey saw that it was no use arguing. He bowed to the Patriarch, and took leave of his companions. 'Wherever you go,' said the Patriarch, 'I'm convinced you'll come to no good. So remember, when you get into trouble, I absolutely forbid you to say that you are my disciple. If you give a hint of any such thing I shall flay you alive, break all your bones, and banish your soul to the Place of Ninefold Darkness, where it will remain for ten thousand aeons.' 'I certainly won't venture to say a word about you,' promised Monkey. 'I'll say I found it all out for myself.' So saying he bade farewell, turned away, and making the magic pass rode off on his cloud trapeze, straight to the Eastern Sea. In a very little while he reached the Mountain of Flowers and Fruit, where he lowered his cloud, and was picking his way, when he heard a sound of cranes calling and monkeys crying. 'Little ones,' he shouted, 'I have come back.' At once from every cranny in the cliff, from bushes and trees, great monkeys and small leapt out with cries of 'Long live our king!' Then they all pressed round Monkey, kowtowing and saying, 'Great King, you're very absent-minded! Why did you go away for so long, leaving us all in the lurch, panting for your return, as a starving man for food and drink? For some time past a demon has been ill-using us. He has seized our cave, though we fought desperately, and now he has robbed us of all our possessions and carried off many of our children, so that we have to be on the watch all the time and get no sleep day or night. It's lucky you've come now, for if you had waited another year or two, you'd have found us and everything hereabouts in another's hands.' 'What demon can dare commit such crimes?' cried Monkey. 'Tell me all about it and I will avenge you.' 'Your majesty,' they said, 'he is called the Demon of Havoc, and he lives due north from here.' 'How far off?' asked Monkey. 'He comes like a cloud,' they said, 'and goes like a mist, like wind or rain, thunder or lightning. We do not know how far away he lives.' 'Well, don't worry,' said Monkey; 'just go on playing around, while I go and look for him.' Dear Monkey King! He sprang into the sky straight northwards and soon saw in front of him a high and very rugged mountain. He was admiring the scenery, when he suddenly heard voices. Going a little way down the hill, he found a cave in front of which several small imps were jumping and dancing. When they saw Monkey, they ran away. 'Stop!' he called, 'I've got a message for you to take. Say that the master of the Water Curtain Cave is here. The Demon of Havoc, or whatever he is called, who lives here, has been ill-treating my little ones and I have come on purpose to settle matters with him.' They rushed into the cave and cried out, 'Great King, a terrible thing has happened!' 'What's the matter?' said the demon. 'Outside the cave,' they said, 'there is a monkey-headed creature who says he is the owner of the Water Curtain Cave. He says you have been ill-using his people and he has come on purpose to settle matters with you.' 'Ha, ha,' laughed the demon. 'I have often heard those monkeys say that their king had gone away to learn religion. This means that he's come back again. What does he look like and how is he armed?' 'He carries no weapon at all,' they said. 'He goes bare-headed, wears a red dress, with a yellow sash, and black shoes – neither priest nor layman nor quite like a Taoist. He's waiting naked-handed outside the gate.' 'Bring me my whole accoutrement,' cried the demon. The small imps at once fetched his arms. The demon put on his helmet and breastplate, grasped his sword, and going to the gate with the little imps, cried in a loud voice, 'Where's the owner of the Water Curtain Cave?' 'What's the use of having such large eyes,' shouted Monkey, 'if you can't see old Monkey?' Catching sight of him the demon burst out laughing. 'You're not a foot high or as much as thirty years old. You have no weapon in your hand! How dare you strut about talking of settling accounts with me?' 'Cursed demon,' said Monkey. 'After all, you have no eyes in your head! You say I am small, not seeing that I can make myself as tall as I please. You say I am unarmed, not knowing that these two hands of mine could drag the moon from the ends of Heaven. Stand your ground, and eat old Monkey's fist!' So saying he leapt into the air and aimed a blow at the demon's face. The demon parried the blow with his hand. 'You such a pigmy and I so tall!' said the demon. 'You using your fists and I my sword – No! If I were to slay you with my sword I should make myself ridiculous. I am going to throw away my sword and use my naked fists.' 'Very good,' said Monkey. 'Now, my fine fellow, come on!' The demon relaxed his guard and struck. Monkey closed with him, and the two of them pommelled and kicked, blow for blow. A long reach is not so firm and sure as a short one. Monkey jabbed the demon in the lower ribs, pounded him in the chest, and gave him such a heavy drubbing that at last the demon stood back, and picking up his great flat sword, slashed at Monkey's head. But Monkey stepped swiftly aside, and the blow missed its mark. Seeing that the demon was becoming savage, Monkey now used the method called Body Outside the Body. He plucked out a handful of hairs, bit them into small pieces and then spat them out into the air, crying 'Change!' The fragments of hair changed into several hundred small monkeys, all pressing round in a throng. For you must know that when anyone becomes an Immortal, he can project his soul, change his shape and perform all kinds of miracles. Monkey, since his Illumination, could change every one of the eighty-four thousand hairs of his body into whatever he chose. The little monkeys he had now created were so nimble that no sword could touch them or spear wound them. See how they leap forward and jump back, crowd round the demon, some hugging, some pulling, some jabbing at his chest, some swarming up his legs. They kicked him, beat him, pommelled his eyes, pinched his nose, and while they were all at it, Monkey slipped up and snatched away the Demon's sword. Then pushing through the throng of small monkeys, he raised the sword and brought it down with such tremendous force upon the demon's skull, that he clove it in twain. He and the little monkeys then rushed into the cave and made a quick end of the imps, great and small. He then said a spell, which caused the small monkeys to change back into hairs. These he put back where they had come from; but there were still some small monkeys left – those that the Demon had carried off from the Cave of the Water Curtain. 'How did you get here?' he asked. There were about thirty or forty of them, and they all said with tears in their eyes, 'After your Majesty went away to become an Immortal, we were pestered by this creature for two years. In the end he carried us all off, and he stole all the fittings from our cave. He took all the stone dishes and the stone cups.' 'Collect everything that belongs to us and bring it with you,' said Monkey. They then set fire to the cave and burnt everything in it. 'Now follow me!' said Monkey. 'When we were brought here,' they said, 'we only felt a great wind rushing past, which whirled us to this place. We didn't know which way we were coming. So how are we to find the way home?' 'He brought you here by magic,' said Monkey. 'But what matter? I am now up to all that sort of thing, and if he could do it, I can. Shut your eyes, all of you, and don't be frightened.' He then recited a spell which produced a fierce wind. Suddenly it dropped, and Monkey shouted, 'You may look now!' The monkeys found that they were standing on firm ground quite close to their home. In high delight they all followed a familiar path back to the door of their cave. They and those who had been left behind all pressed into the cave, and lined up according to their ranks and age, and did homage to their king, and prepared a great banquet of welcome. When they asked how the demon had been subdued and the monkeys rescued, he told them the whole story; upon which they burst into shouts of applause. 'We little thought,' they said, 'that when your Majesty left us, you would learn such arts as this!' 'After I parted from you,' said Monkey, 'I went across many oceans to the land of Jambudvipa, where I learnt human ways, and how to wear clothes and shoes. I wandered restless as a cloud for eight or nine years, but nowhere could I find Enlightenment. At last after crossing yet another ocean, I was lucky enough to meet an old Patriarch who taught me the secret of eternal life.' 'What an incredible piece of luck!' the monkeys said, all congratulating him. 'Little ones,' said Monkey, 'I have another bit of good news for you. Your king has got a name-in-religion. I am called Aware-of-Vacuity.' They all clapped loudly, and presently went to get date-wine and grape-wine and fairy flowers and fruit, which they offered to Monkey. Everyone was in the highest spirits. If you do not know what the upshot was and how he fared now that he was back in his old home, you must listen to what is related in the next chapter.

Chapter 3

Monkey, having returned in triumph, after slaying the Demon of Havoc and snatching the demon's huge cutlass, practised sword-play every day and taught the small monkeys how to sharpen bamboos with spears, make wooden swords, and banners to carry; how to go on patrol, advance and retreat, pitch camp, build stockades, and so on. They had great fun doing this; but suddenly, sitting in a quiet place, Monkey thought to himself, 'All this is only a game; but the consequences of it may be serious. Suppose some human king or king of birds or beasts should hear what we are at, he may well think that we are hatching a conspiracy against him and bring his armies to attack us. Bamboo spears and wooden swords wouldn't help you much then. You ought to have real swords and lances and halberds. How are we to get hold of them?' 'That's an excellent idea,' they said, 'but there's nowhere we can possibly get them from.'

At this point four old monkeys came forward, two red-bottomed horse-apes and two tailless apes with plain behinds. 'Great king,' they said, 'if you want to get weapons made, nothing could be easier.' 'Why do you think it so easy?' asked Monkey. 'East of our mountains,' they said, 'there are two hundred leagues of water. That is the frontier of Ao-lai, and at that frontier there is a king whose city is full of soldiers. He must certainly have metalworks of all sorts. If you go there, you can certainly buy weapons or get them made for you. Then you can teach us to use them, and we shall be able to defend ourselves. That is the way to protect us against extinction.' Monkey was delighted with this idea. 'You stay here and amuse yourselves,' he said, 'while I go off and see what can be done.'

Dear Monkey! He set out on his cloud-trapeze, and in a twinkling he had crossed those two hundred leagues of water, and on the other side there was indeed a city with walls and moat, with wards and markets, and myriad streets where men walked up and down in the happy sunshine. He thought to himself, 'In such a place there are sure to be ready-made weapons. I'll go down and buy some. Or better still, I'll get some by magic.' He made a magic pass, recited a spell and drew a magic diagram on the ground. He then stood in the middle of it, drew a long breath and expelled it with such force that sand and stones hurtled through the air. This tempest so much alarmed the king of the country and all his subjects that they locked themselves indoors. Monkey lowered his cloud, made straight for the government buildings, and soon finding the arsenal he forced open the door, and saw a vast supply of swords, lances, scimitars, halberds, axes, scythes, whips, rakes, cudgels, bows and crossbows – every conceivable weapon. 'That's rather more than I can carry,' he said to himself. So, as before, he changed his hairs into thousands of small monkeys, who began snatching at the weapons. Some managed to carry six or seven, others three or four, till soon the arsenal was bare. Then a great gale of magic wind carried them back to the cave. The monkeys at home were playing in front of the cave door, when suddenly they saw a great swarm of monkeys in the sky above, which scared them so much that they all rushed into hiding. Soon Monkey lowered his cloud and turned the thousands of little monkeys into hairs. He stacked the weapons on the hillside and cried, 'Little ones, all come and get your arms!' To their astonishment they found Monkey standing all alone on the ground. They rushed forward to pay homage, and Monkey explained to them what had happened. When they had congratulated him on his performance, they all began to grab at swords and cutlasses, pick up axes, scramble for spears, drag off bows and crossbows. This sport, which was a very noisy one, lasted all day.

Next day they came on parade as usual, and the roll-call disclosed that they numbered forty-seven thousand in all. All the wild beasts of the mountain and demon kings of every kind, denizens of no less than seventy-two caves, came to pay homage to Monkey, and henceforward brought tribute every year and signed on once in every season. Some supplied labour and some provisions. The Mountain of Flowers and Fruit became as strong as an iron bucket or wall of bronze. The demon kings of various districts also presented bronze drums, coloured banners, helmets and coats of mail. Day after day there was a tremendous bustle of drilling and marching. Everything was going well, when suddenly one day Monkey said to his subjects, 'You seem to be getting on well with your drill, but I find my sword very cumbersome, in fact not at all to my liking. What is to be done?' The four old monkeys came forward and said, 'Great King, it is quite natural that you, being an Immortal, should not care to use this earthly weapon. Do you think it would be possible for you to get one from the denizens of the sea?' 'Why not, pray?' said Monkey. 'Since my Illumination I have mastery of seventy-two transformations; greatest wonder of all, I can ride upon the clouds. I can become invisible, I can penetrate bronze and stone. Water cannot drown me, any more than fire can burn me. What's to prevent me getting a weapon from the Powers of the Sea?' 'Well, if you can manage it,' they said. 'The water that flows under this iron bridge comes up from the palace of the dragon of the Eastern Sea. How about going down and paying a call upon the dragon-king? If you asked him for a weapon he would no doubt be able to find you something suitable.' 'I'll certainly go,' said Monkey. He went to the bridge-head, recited a spell to protect himself from the effects of water, and jumped in, making his way along the water-course till he came to the bottom of the Eastern Sea. Presently he was stopped by a Yaksha who was patrolling the waters. 'What deity is that,' he asked, 'pushing along through the water? Give me an account of yourself and I will announce your arrival.' 'I am the monkey-king of the Mountain of Flowers and Fruit,' said Monkey. 'I am a near neighbour of the Dragon King, and consider that I ought to make his acquaintance.' The Yaksha brought in the message, and the Dragon King rose hastily and came to the door of his palace, bringing with him his dragon children and grandchildren, his shrimp soldiers and crab generals. 'Come in, High Immortal, come in,' he said. They went into

35

the palace and sat face to face on the upper seat. When they had taken tea, the dragon asked, 'How long, pray, have you been Illumined, and what magic arts have you learned?' 'I have led a religious life since my infancy,' said Monkey, 'and am now beyond birth and destruction. Recently I have been training my subjects how to defend their home; but I myself have no suitable weapon. I am told that my honoured neighbour within the shell-portals of his green jade palace certainly has many magic weapons to spare.' The Dragon King did not like to refuse, and ordered a trout-captain to bring out a huge sword. 'I'm no good with a sword,' said Monkey. 'Can't you find something else?' The Dragon King then told a whitebait-guardsman with the help of an eel-porter to bring out a nine-pronged fork. Monkey took hold of it and tried a few thrusts. 'It's much too light,' he said. 'And it does not suit my hand. Can't you find me something else?' 'I really don't know what you mean,' said the Dragon King. 'The fork weighs three thousand six hundred pounds.' 'It doesn't suit my hand,' said Monkey, 'it doesn't suit my hand.' The Dragon King was much upset, and ordered a bream-general and a carp-brigadier to bring out a huge halberd, weighing seven thousand two hundred pounds. Monkey seized it and after making a few thrusts and parries tossed it away saying, 'Still too light!' 'It's the heaviest weapon we've got in the palace,' said the Dragon King. 'I have nothing else I can show you.' 'The proverb says "It's no use the Dragon King pretending he's got no treasures," ' said Monkey. 'Just look again, and if you succeed in finding something suitable, I'll give you a good price.' 'I warn you I haven't got anything else,' said the Dragon King.

At this point the Dragon Mother and her daughter slipped out from the back rooms of the palace and said, 'Great King, we can see that this Monkey Sage is of no common capacities. In our treasury is the magic iron with which the bed of the Milky Way was pounded flat. For several days past it has been glowing with a strange light. Was this not perhaps an omen that it should be given to the Sage who has just arrived?' 'This,' said the Dragon King, 'is the thing that

36

was used by the Great Yü, when he subdued the Flood, to fix the depth of the rivers and seas. It's only a piece of holy iron. What use could it be to him?' 'Don't worry about whether he uses it or not,' said the Dragon Mother. 'Just give it to him, and if he can cope with it, let him take it away with him.'

The Dragon King agreed, and told Monkey. 'Bring it to me and I'll have a look at it,' said Monkey. 'Out of the question!' said the Dragon King. 'It's too heavy to move. You'll have to go and look at it.' 'Where is it?' asked Monkey. 'Show me the way.'

The Dragon King accordingly brought him to the Sea Treasury, where he at once saw something shining with innumerable beams of golden light. 'There it is,' said the Dragon King. Monkey respectfully tidied himself and approached the object. It turned out to be a thick iron pillar, about twenty feet long. Monkey took one end in both hands and raised it a little. 'A trifle too long and too thick!' he said. The pillar at once became several feet shorter and one layer thinner. Monkey felt it. 'A little smaller still wouldn't do any harm,' he said. The pillar at once shrunk again, Monkey was delighted. Taking it out into the daylight he found that at each end was a golden clasp, while in between all was black iron. On the near end was the inscription 'Golden Clasped Wishing Staff. Weight, thirteen thousand five hundred pounds'. Splendid!' thought Monkey. 'One couldn't wish for a better treasure than this.' But as he went along, he thought to himself, fingering the staff, 'If only it were a little smaller, it would be marvellous.' And sure enough, by the time he got outside it was not much more than two feet long. Look at him, how he displays its magic, making sudden thrusts and passes on his way back to the palace. The Dragon King trembled at the sight, and the Dragon Princes were all in a flutter. Tortoises and turtles drew in their heads; fishes, crabs and shrimps all hid themselves away. Monkey, with the treasure in his hand, sat down by the Dragon King. 'I am deeply grateful for my honoured neighbour's kindness,' he said. 'Pray don't mention it,' said the Dragon King. 'Yes, it's a useful bit of iron,' said Monkey, but there is just one more thing I should like to say.' 'Great Immortal,' said the Dragon King, 'what else have you to say?' 'Before I had this iron,' said Monkey, 'it was another matter, but with a thing like this in my hand, I begin to feel the lack of anything suitable to wear with it. If you have got anything in that line, please let me have it. I should really be grateful.' 'I have nothing at all,' said the Dragon King. 'You know the old saying,' said Monkey, ' "one guest should not trouble two hosts." You won't get rid of me by pretending you haven't got any.' 'You might try another sea,' said the Dragon King, 'it's just possible they would be able to help you.' ' "Better sit in one house than run to three," ' said Monkey. 'I insist on your finding me something.' 'I assure you I don't possess anything of that sort,' said the Dragon King. 'If I did you should have it.' 'All right,' said Monkey. 'I'll try my iron on you, and we shall soon see whether you can give me one.' 'Steady, steady, Great Immortal,' said the Dragon King. 'Don't strike! Just let me find out whether my brothers haven't got anything that you could have.' 'Where do they live?' asked Monkey. 'They are the dragons of the southern, northern and western seas,' said the Dragon King. 'I am not going as far as that,' said Monkey. ' "Two in hand is better than three in bond." You must find me something here and now. I don't mind where you get it from.' 'I never suggested that you should go,' said the Dragon King. 'We've got an iron drum and a bronze gong here. If anything important happens, I have them sounded, and my brothers come immediately.' 'Very well,' said Monkey. 'Look sharp and sound the drum and gong.' A crocodile accordingly beat the drum and a turtle sounded the gong, and in a twinkling the three dragons arrived. 'Brother,' said the Dragon of the South, 'what urgent business has made you beat the drum and sound the gong?' 'You may well ask,' said the Dragon King. 'A neighbour of mine, the Sage of the Mountain of Flowers and Fruit, came to me today asking for a magic weapon. I gave him the iron with which the Milky Way was pounded. Now he says he must have clothes. We have nothing of that sort here. Couldn't one of you find me something, so that we can get rid of him?' The Dragon of the South was furious. 'Brothers,' he cried, 'let us summon men-at-arms and arrest the rascal.' 'Out of the question!' said the Dragon King. 'The slightest touch of that iron is deadly.' 'It would be better not to tamper with him,' said the Dragon of the West. 'We'll give him some clothes, just to get rid of him, and then we'll complain to Heaven, and Heaven will punish him.' 'That's a good idea,' said the Dragon of the North. 'I've got a pair of cloud-stepping shoes made of lotus-fibre.' 'I've got a cap of phoenix-plume and red gold,' said the Dragon of the South. 'I've got a jerkin of chain-mail, made of yellow gold,' said the Dragon of the West. The Dragon King was delighted and brought them in to see Monkey and offer their gifts. Monkey put the things on and, with his wishing-staff in his hand, strode out. 'Dirty old sneaks,' he called out to the dragons as he passed. In great indignation they consulted together about reporting him to the powers above.

The four old monkeys and all the rest were waiting for their king beside the bridge. Suddenly they saw him spring out of the waves, without a drop of water on him, all shining and golden, and run up the bridge. They all knelt down, crying 'Great King, what splendours!' With the spring wind full in his face. Monkey mounted the throne and set up the iron staff in front of him. The monkeys all rushed at the treasure and tried to lift it. As well might a dragon-fly try to shake an ironwood-tree; they could not move it an inch. 'Father,' they cried, 'you're the only person that could lift a thing as heavy as that.' 'There's nothing but has its master,' said Monkey, lifting it with one hand. 'This iron lay in the Sea Treasury for I don't know how many hundred thousand years, and only recently began to shine. The Dragon King thought it was nothing but black iron and said it was used to flatten out the Milky Way. None of them could lift it, and they asked me to go and take it myself. When I first saw it, it was twenty feet long. I thought that was a bit too big, so I gradually made it smaller and smaller. Now just you watch while I change it again.' He cried 'Smaller, smaller,

smaller!' and immediately it became exactly like an embroidery needle, and could comfortably be worn behind the ear.

'Take it out and do another trick with it,' the monkeys begged. He took it from behind his ear and set it upright on the palm of his hand, crying 'Larger, larger!' It at once became twenty feet long, whereupon he carried it up on to the bridge, employed a cosmic magic, and bent at the waist, crying 'Tall!' At which he at once became a hundred thousand feet high, his head was on a level with the highest mountains, his waist with the ridges, his eye blazed like lightning, his mouth was like a blood-bowl, his teeth like sword-blades. The iron staff in his hand reached up to the thirty-third Heaven, and down to the eighteenth pit of Hell. Tigers, panthers, wolves, all the evil spirits of the hill and the demons of the seventy-two caves did homage to him in awe and trembling. Presently he withdrew his cosmic manifestation, and the staff again became an embroidery needle. He put it behind his ear and came back to the cave.

One day when Monkey had been giving a great banquet to the beast-monarchs of the neighbourhood, after seeing them off and giving presents to the leaders great and small, he lay down under a pine tree at the side of the iron bridge, and fell asleep. In his sleep he saw two men coming towards him, bearing a document on which was his name. Without giving him time to say a word, they brought out a rope and binding Monkey's dream-body, they marched him away, presently bringing him to the outskirts of a walled city. Coming to himself and looking up, he saw that on the wall of this city was an iron placard saying 'Land of Darkness'. 'Why,' said Monkey to himself, suddenly realising with an unpleasant shock where he had got to, 'that's where Yama, the King of Death, lives. How did I get here?' 'Your time in the World of Life is up,' said the two men, 'and we were sent to arrest you.' 'But I have got beyond all that,' said Monkey. 'I am no longer compounded of the Five Elements, and do not come under Death's jurisdiction. What's all this nonsense about arresting me?' The two men took no notice, and continued to drag him along. Monkey now became very angry, snatched the needle from behind his ear, changed it to a formidable size, and pounded the two messengers into mincemeat. Then he freed himself from his bonds, and swinging his staff strode into the city. Bull-headed demons and horse-faced demons fled before him in terror. A mass of ghosts rushed to the palace, announcing that a furry-faced thunder-god was advancing to the attack. In great consternation the Ten Judges of the Dead tidied themselves and came to see what was afoot. Seeing Monkey's ferocious appearance, they lined up and accosted him in a loud voice: 'Your name, please!' 'If you don't know who I am, why did you send two men to arrest me?' asked Monkey. 'How can you accuse us of such a thing?' they said. 'No doubt the messengers made a mistake.' 'I am the Sage from the Water-curtain Cave,' said Monkey. 'Who are you?' 'We are the Ten Judges of the Emperor of Death,' they said. 'In that case,' said Monkey, 'you are concerned with retribution and rewards, and ought not to let such mistakes occur. I would have you know that by my exertions I have become an Immortal and am no longer subject to your jurisdiction. Why did you order my arrest?' 'There's no need to lose your temper,' they said. 'It's a case of mistaken identity. The world is a big place, and there are bound to be cases of several people having the same name. No doubt our officers have made a mistake.' 'Nonsense,' said Monkey. 'The proverb says "Magistrates err, clerks err, the man with the warrant never errs." Be quick and bring out the registers of the quick and the dead, and we'll soon see!' 'Come this way, please,' they said, and took him to the great hall, where they ordered the official in charge of the record to bring out his files. The official dived into a side room and came out with five or six ledgers, divided into ten files and began going through them one by one – Bald Insects, Furry Insects, Winged Insects, Scaly Insects . . . He gave up in despair and tried Monkeys. But the Monkey King, having human characteristics, was not there. Not however being subject to the unicorn, he did not come into any animal category, and as he was not subject to the phoenix, he could not be classed as a bird. But there was a separate file which Monkey insisted on examining himself, and there, under the heading 'Soul 3150,' he found his own name, followed by the words 'Parentage: natural product. Description: Stone Monkey. Lifespan: 342 years. A peaceful end.' 'I haven't got a lifespan at all,' said Monkey. 'I'm eternal. I shall cross my name out. Give me a brush!' The official hastened to provide a brush, soaked in heavy ink, and Monkey put a stroke not only through his own name, but through those of all the monkeys named in the Monkey File. Then throwing down the ledger, 'There's an end of the matter,' he exclaimed. 'Now at any rate you've got no hold over us!'

So saying he picked up his staff and forced his way out of the Palace of Darkness. The Ten Judges dared not protest; but all went off at once to the Kshitigarbha, Guide of the Dead, and discussed with him the advisability of laying a complaint about the matter before the Jade Emperor in Heaven. As Monkey rushed naked out of the city, his foot caught in a coil of creeper and he stumbled. He woke with a start, and found that it had all been a dream. Sitting up, he heard the four old monkeys and the others who were mounting guard over him saying, 'Great King, isn't it time you woke up? You drank so heavily that you've been sleeping here all night.' 'I must have dozed off for a time,' said Monkey, 'for I dreamt that two men came to arrest me.' And he told them his dream. 'I crossed off all our names,' he said, 'so the fellows won't be able to interfere with us any more.' The monkeys kowtowed and thanked him. From that time onward it has been noticed that many mountain monkeys never grow old. It is because their names were crossed out from the registers of the King of Death.

One morning when the Jade Emperor was sitting in his Golden-doored Cloud Palace, with all his ministers civil and military, an officer announced, 'Your majesty, the Dragon of the Eastern Sea is outside, with a plea to lay before you.' The Dragon was shown in and when he had paid his respects, a fairy boy presented a document, which the Jade Emperor began to read. 'This small dragon of the Eastern Sea informs your Majesty that a certain counterfeit Immortal from the Water-curtain Cave has maltreated your servant, forcing a way into his watery home. He demanded a weapon, using gross intimidation, and forced us to give him garments, by violence and outrage. My watery kinsmen were dismayed, tortoises and turtles fled in panic. The Dragon of the South trembled, the Dragon of the West was appalled, the Dragon of the North collapsed. Your servant was obliged to part with a holy iron staff, a phoenix-plume hat, a coat of mail and a pair of cloud-stepping shoes, before we could get rid of him. But even then he threatened us with arms and magic, and called us dirty old sneaks. We are ourselves quite unable to deal with him, and must leave the matter in your hands. We earnestly beg that you will send soldiers to control this pest and restore peace to the World Below the Waves.'

Having read the document, the Jade Emperor gave judgement. 'The Dragon,' he said, 'is to return to his sea, and I will send officers to arrest the criminal.' The Dragon King bowed and retired. Whereupon another officer immediately appeared, announcing that the First Judge of the Dead, supported by Kshitigarbha, the Advocate of the Dead, had arrived with a petition. With them was a fairy girl, who presented a document which read as follows: We respectfully submit that Heaven Above is for spirits, and the Underworld is for ghosts. Darkness and Light must have their succession. Such is the way of Nature, and cannot be changed. But a counterfeit Sage from the Water-curtain Cave has violently resisted our summons, beating to death our emissaries and menacing the Ten Judges. He made an uproar in the Palace of Death, and erased names from our books, so that in future monkeys and apes will enjoy improper longevity. We therefore appeal to your Majesty to show your authority by sending spirit soldiers to deal with this monster, restore the balance of Dark and Light and bring back peace to the Underworld.

The Jade Emperor gave judgement, 'The Lords of Darkness are to return to the Underworld, and officers shall be sent to arrest this pest.' The First Judge of the Dead bowed and retired.

'How long has this pernicious monkey been in existence?' the Jade Emperor asked of his ministers, 'and how comes it that he acquired Illumination?' At once the Officer of the Thousand League Eye and the Officer of the Down the Wind Ear stepped forward. 'This monkey,' they said, 'was emitted three hundred years ago by a stone. At first he displayed none of his present powers; but since then he has managed somehow to perfect himself and achieve Immortality. He now subdues dragons, tames tigers and has tampered with the Registers of Death.' 'Which of you deities will go down and deal with him?' asked the Jade Emperor. The Spirit of the Planet Venus came forward. 'Highest and Holiest,' he said, 'all creatures that have nine apertures are capable of achieving Immortality. Small wonder then that this monkey, produced by the natural forces of Heaven and Earth, nurtured by the light of the sun and the moon, fed by the frost and dew, should have achieved Immortality and subdue dragons and tigers. I suggest that an indulgent course should be followed. Let us send a rescript, commanding him to appear in Heaven. We will then give him official work of some kind, so that his name will appear on our rolls, and we shall be able to keep an eye on him here. If he behaves well, he can be promoted, and if he misbehaves, he must be put under arrest. This course will save us from military operations and will add to our numbers an undoubted Immortal.'

This suggestion pleased the Jade Emperor. He ordered the Spirit of the Book Star to draw up a summons and bade the Planet Venus deliver it. He went out at the southern gate of Heaven, lowered his magic cloud and soon reached the Water-curtain Cave, where he said to the crowd of monkeys, 'I am a messenger from Heaven, bearing a command that your king is to proceed at once to the Upper Realms. Tell him of this immediately.' The little monkeys outside the cave sent word to the interior that an old man had come with some writing in his hand. 'He says he is a messenger from Heaven, sent to ask you to go with him.' 'That's very

44

convenient,' said Monkey. 'I have been thinking lately of making a little trip to Heaven!'

Monkey hurriedly tidied himself and went to the door. 'I am the Spirit of the Planet Venus,' the messenger said, 'and I bring an order from the Jade Emperor that you are to come up to Heaven and receive an Immortal appointment.' 'Old Star,' said Monkey, 'I am much obliged to you for your trouble,' and he told the monkeys to prepare a banquet. 'With the sacred command about me, I dare not linger,' said the Star. 'After your glorious ascension we shall have ample opportunity for conversation.' 'I will not insist,' said Monkey. 'It is a great honour for us that you should have paid this visit.' Then he called the four old monkeys to him. 'Don't forget to put the young monkeys through their paces,' he said. 'I'll have a look round when I get to Heaven, and if it seems all right there, I'll send for the rest of you to come and live with me.' The old monkeys signified their agreement, and the Monkey King, following the Star Spirit, mounted the cloud and soared up. If you do not know what rank it was they gave him, you must listen to the next chapter.

Chapter 4

When they had mounted together for a little while, Monkey forgot all about the Star Spirit and soon left him far behind; and when he reached the southern gate of Heaven, the Spirit was out of sight. He was just going in when a number of Guardian Deities, armed with daggers, swords and halberds, barred his path. 'What an old swindler that Planet is!' exclaimed Monkey. 'Fancy letting these cut-throats hold me up like this, after inviting me to come!' At this point the Planet arrived, quite out of breath. 'You old fraud,' said Monkey, confronting him, 'you said you had come with an invitation from the Jade Emperor. Why are these people barring the gate?' 'Don't be angry,' said the Planet. 'As you haven't been to the Hall of Heaven before and haven't yet been given a name, the Guardians don't know who you are, and are quite right not to let you pass. When you have seen the Emperor and received your appointment, they'll let you go in and out as you please.' 'That's as may be,' said Monkey, 'but at the present moment I can't get in.' 'You can if you come with me,' said the Planet, and he called in a loud voice, 'Guardians of the Gate of Heaven captains great and small, make way! This is an Immortal from earth below, whom the Jade Emperor commissioned me to bring here.' The Guardians then withdrew their weapons and retired. Monkey, his confidence in the Planet now quite restored, walked slowly by his side through the gates and on into the palace. Without waiting to be announced, they went at once into the August Presence. The Planet immediately prostrated himself, but Monkey stood erect by his side, not showing any sign of respect, but only pricking his ears to hear what the Planet would say. 'I beg to report,' he said, 'that I have carried out your command; the pernicious Immortal is here.' 'Which is he?' asked the Emperor, peeping over the top of his screen-of-state. At this point Monkey bowed, saying, 'It's me.' The assembled ministers turned pale with horror. 'This barbarous monkey!' they cried. 'When brought into the Presence he did not prostrate himself, and now, without being addressed, he has ventured to say "It's me." Such conduct is worthy of death.' 'He comes from earth below,' said the Jade Emperor, 'and only recently learned human ways. For the present we must not be too hard on him if he does not know how to behave at Court.'

The celestial ministers all congratulated the Emperor on his clemency, and Monkey shouted 'Bravo!' at the top of his voice. Officials were then ordered to look through the lists and see what appointments were vacant. 'There is no vacancy at present in any section of any department,' one of them reported. 'The only chance is in the Imperial Stables, where a supervisor is wanted.' 'Very well then,' said the Jade Emperor, 'make him *Pi-ma-wên* in the stables.' Accordingly he was taken to the stables and the duties of this department were explained to him. He was shown the list of the horses, of which there were a thousand, under the care of a steward, whose duty it was to provide fodder. Grooms who combed and washed the horses, chopped hay, brought them their water and cooked their food. The superintendent and vice-superintendent helped the supervisor in the general management. All of them were on the alert night and day. In the daytime they managed to get a certain amount of fun; but at night they were on the go all the time. The horses all seemed either to go to sleep just when they ought to be fed, or to start galloping when they ought to be in their stalls. When they saw Monkey, the heavenly horses pressed round him in a surging mob, and ate the food he brought them with such appetite as they had never shown before. After a week or two the other officers of the stables gave a banquet to celebrate Monkey's appointment. When the feast was at its height, he suddenly paused, and cup in hand he asked, 'What does it really mean, this word *Pi-ma-wên*?' 'It's the name of the rank you hold,' they said. 'What class of appointment is it?' Monkey asked. 'It doesn't come in any class,' they said. 'I suppose it's too high to count as being in any class?' said Monkey. 'On the contrary,' they said, 'it's too low.' 'Too low!' exclaimed Monkey. 'What do you mean?' 'When an officer doesn't manage to get classed, they put him to mind the horses. There's no salary attached. The most you'll get for fattening up the horses as you've done since you were here, is a casual "Not bad!" But if any of them had gone a bit lame or out of condition, you'd have caught it hot. And if any of them had come to real harm, you'd have been prosecuted and fined.'

Flames leapt up in Monkey's heart when he heard this. He ground his teeth and said in a great rage, 'So that's what they think of me! Don't they know that on the Mountain of Flowers and Fruit I was king and patriarch? How dared they swindle me with coming and looking after horses? If looking after horses is a job for the lowest riff-raff of all, what do they want to put me into it for? I won't stand it? I'm going at once!'

With a sudden cry of rage, he pushed over the official desk, took his treasure from behind his ear and rushed out to the Southern Gate. The deities on guard, knowing that he was now an official and authorised to go in and out, did not attempt to stop him. Soon he lowered his cloud and landed on the Mountain of Flowers and Fruit. 'Little Ones,' he cried, 'Old Monkey has come back.' They gave him a great banquet of welcome, saying, 'As your Majesty has stayed away in the upper regions for ten years, we may surely presume that you have had a great success there?' 'I've been away about a fortnight,' said Monkey. 'What do you mean by ten years?' 'In Heaven,' they said, 'you did not notice how the time was going. One day in heaven is a year below. Tell us, please, what rank they gave you.' 'Don't talk of it!' said Monkey, 'or I shall die of shame. The Jade Emperor has no idea how to make use of one. He saw what I am; but all he could do with me was to make me into something they call a *Pi-ma-wên*. I was told to look after his horses – just a menial post to which no rank attaches at all. I didn't realise this when I took the job, and didn't have a bad time playing about in the stables. But today I asked some of the others, and discovered what sort of post it was. I was furious and

48

gave up the job at once. So here I am!' 'And a good thing too,' they said. 'With an enchanted spot like this to rule over, what sense is there in going away to be a groom? Little ones, prepare a banquet, to cheer our great king.'

They were just beginning to drink, when someone announced that two one-horned demon kings were outside, asking to see the Monkey King. 'Show them in,' said Monkey. The demons tidied themselves and hastened into the cave, prostrating themselves deeply. 'What has brought you here?' asked Monkey. 'We have known for a long time,' they said, 'that you appreciate good qualities, but no suitable occasion presented itself for us to pay you our respects. However, hearing that you had secured a post in Heaven and returned triumphant, we thought you would not object to receiving a little present. Here is a red and yellow rug, which we hope you will accept. And if you will deign also to take into your service such humble folk as ourselves, we are ready to perform the most menial of tasks.' Monkey wrapped the rug round himself in high glee, and all his subjects lined up and did homage. The demon kings were made Marshals of the Vanguard, and when they expressed their gratitude, they asked what position Monkey had held in Heaven. 'The Jade Emperor,' said Monkey, 'has no regard for talent. He made me a groom in the stables!' 'With magic powers like yours,' they said, 'why should you stoop to look after horses? "The Great Sage, Equal of Heaven," – that is the title for such a one as you.' Monkey was delighted with the sound of this, and having exclaimed 'Good, good, good!' many times, he ordered his generals to set up a banner with 'Great Sage, Equal of Heaven' written on it in large letters. Henceforward, he said, he was to be addressed by no other name, and instructions to this effect were to be given to all fiends that acknowledged his sway.

When the Jade Emperor held his court next day, the head of the Stable appeared kneeling on the steps of the throne, announcing that the newly appointed groom had complained that the job was not good enough for him and had returned to earth. 'Very good,' said the Jade Emperor, 'you may return to your duties. I will send heavenly soldiers to arrest him.' At once Vaiśravana and his son Natha came forward and volunteered for this service. They were put in command of the expedition, and appointed the Mighty Magic Spirit to lead the way, the Fish-Belly general to bring up the rear, and the captain of the Yakshas to drive the troops on. Soon they were out of the southern gate of Heaven, and on their way to the Mountain of Flowers and Fruit. They then chose a piece of flat ground, where they encamped, and the Mighty Magic Spirit was chosen to provoke battle. He buckled on his armour and, brandishing his great axe, he strode towards the mouth of the Water-curtain Cave. Outside it were gathered together a band of monsters – wolves, tigers and so on – prancing about, flourishing spears and swords, leaping and noisily brawling. 'Accursed creatures,' cried the spirit, 'go quickly and tell the groom that a great commandant from Heaven has come by order of the Jade Emperor to receive his submission. Tell him to be quick about it, or you will all of you pay with your lives.' The monsters came helter-skelter into the cave. 'A terrible thing has happened,' they announced. 'What's the matter?' asked Monkey. 'There's a heavenly commandant at the gate,' they said, 'declaring that he has been sent by the Jade Emperor to receive your submission. If you don't submit at once, he says we shall all pay for it with our lives.' 'Bring me my arms,' cried Monkey. He put on his bronze helmet, his golden corselet and cloud-stepping shoes, and with his magic staff in his hand, he led out his followers and arrayed them for battle.

When the Mighty Magic Spirit saw him, 'Wretched monkey,' he cried, 'do you know me or not?' 'What scurvy deity are you?' asked Monkey. 'I have never set eyes on you. Tell me your name at once.' 'Vile trickster!' cried he, 'how dare you pretend you do not know me? I am the leader of the vanguard of Vaiśravana's heavenly host, the Mighty Magic Spirit. I come by command of the Jade Emperor to receive your submission. Disarm at once and throw yourself on Heaven's mercy, or all the denizens of this mountain will be put to the sword. Breathe so much as half of the word

"No", and you will instantly be sliced to pieces.' 'Scurvy deity,' cried Monkey, very angry, 'stop your bragging. If I were to strike you dead with one blow of my staff, you could not carry my message. So I shall spare your life, that you may go back to Heaven and tell the Jade Emperor that he does not know how to use a good man when he finds one. I have innumerable arts of magic. Why should I be put to mind the horses? Look what is written on this banner. If he admits my right to this title, I will leave him in peace. But if he refuses, I will come up at once and strike such a blow at his palace as will tumble him from his dragon couch.' Looking about, the spirit saw the banner, with its inscription, and laughed aloud. 'The impudence of this vile monkey!' he cried. 'Call yourself "Equal of Heaven" if you please, but first swallow a good dose of this axe of mine!' and he struck at Monkey's head. But Monkey was not ruffled, and met the blow with his staff. It was a good fight that followed. At last the spirit could withstand no longer. Monkey aimed a smashing blow at his head, which he attempted to parry with his axe. The axe split in two, and he was obliged to run for his life. Back in the camp he went straight to Vaiśravana and kneeling before him panted out, 'The groom has magic powers that are too great for us. I was unable to stand up to him and have come to plead for mercy.' 'This wretch,' said Vaiśravana, looking contemptuously at the spirit, 'has humiliated me. Take him away and cut off his head!' But his son, prince Natha, slipped forward and said, bowing profoundly, 'Father, do not be angry. Spare the spirit for a while, and let me do battle, so that we may know how things really stand.' Vaiśravana accepted this offer, and ordered the spirit to go back to his camp and await trial.

The prince, having buckled on his armour, sprang from the camp and rushed to the Cave of the Water Curtain. Monkey was just disarming himself, but now came to the gate and said, 'Whose little brother are you and why have you come gatecrashing here?' 'Nauseous ape,' cried Natha, 'why pretend you do not know me? I am Vaiśravana's third son. The Jade Emperor has sent me here to arrest you.'

51

'Little prince,' laughed Monkey, 'you have not yet lost your milk-teeth, your womb-down is not yet dry. How dare you talk so big? For the moment I'll spare your life, provided that you look at what is written on that banner, and tell the Jade Emperor that if he will give me *that* rank he need send no more armies; I will submit of my own accord. But if he will not agree, I shall come and batter down his Jewel Palace of the Magic Mists.'

Natha looked up and saw the inscription: 'Great Sage, Equal of Heaven'. 'You must think yourself a wonder-worker indeed, that you dare lay claim to such a title! Don't worry! One stroke of my sword will settle you,' said Natha. 'I'll stand my ground,' said Monkey, 'and you can break as many swords upon me as you like.' 'Change!' roared Natha, and he at once changed into a deity with three heads and six arms. 'So this little brother,' said Monkey, 'knows some tricks! I'll trouble you to look at my magic.' So saying, he too assumed three heads and six arms, and at the same time changed his cudgel into three cudgels, each of which he grasped with two hands. The battle that followed was one that shook the earth and rattled the hills. Truly a good fight! Each displayed his terrifying powers, and they battled as many as thirty times. The prince turned his six weapons into a thousand thousand weapons. Monkey followed suit. The sparks fell like falling stars as they fought half-way up in the sky and still neither gained advantage.

But Monkey was very swift of hand and eye. Just at the height of the fray, he changed back into his proper shape and, cudgel in hand, closed with Natha. In his own shape he moved with greater freedom; getting behind the prince's head, he brought down a mighty blow on his shoulder. Just as Natha was preparing a new magic, he heard the swish of Monkey's cudgel as it clove the air. He had no time to dodge, and so great was his pain that he at once took to his heels, changed into his true form, and returned ignominiously to his father's camp. Vaiśravana had been watching the battle, and was just thinking of going to his son's assistance, when Natha suddenly appeared before him and, trembling from head to foot, said: 'My father and king! The groom has indeed stupendous powers. Even such magic as mine could not withstand him, and in the end he wounded my shoulder.' 'If a fellow has such powers as this,' said Vaiśravana dismayed, 'how are we to bring him to heel?' 'Outside his cave,' said the prince, 'he has put up a banner, upon which is written "Great Sage, Equal of Heaven."' He had the insolence to say that if you would acknowledge his right to this title he would give no more trouble. Otherwise, he will batter down the Jewel Palace of Magic Mists.' 'If that is so,' said Vaiśravana, 'we had better leave him alone for the present. I will report this to the Jade Emperor and ask for heavenly reinforcements, that we may hem him in while there is still time.' 'Am I to believe,' said the Jade Emperor, when the situation was explained to him, 'that one monkey is so powerful that reinforcements are needed to deal with him?' Natha then stepped forward. 'Great One,' he said, 'though I know that I deserve death at your hands, I beg you to hear me. That Monkey possesses an iron cudgel with which he first defeated the River Spirit and then wounded my shoulder.' 'Take the whole army,' said the Emperor, 'and slay him immediately!' At this moment the Spirit of the Planet Venus stepped forward. 'That Monkey,' he said, 'flings his words about recklessly, and there is no reason to suppose that he can do all he threatens to do. But if soldiers are sent to deal with him, it will mean a long and exhausting campaign. It would be better if your Majesty were to pursue a policy of mercy. Say that you desire a peaceful solution and are quite willing to let him be "The Sage, Equal to Heaven." There will be no harm in his having a nominal post under that title, of course without salary.' 'I don't think I quite understand,' said the Jade Emperor, 'what you are proposing that his position should be.' 'He could be called by that title,' said the Planet, 'without having any special duties or any salary. The advantage would be that living on celestial ground he would soon turn from his depravity, cease his mad tricks, and the Universe would have a chance to settle down quietly.' 'Agreed!' said the Emperor. And the

Planet was sent to convey the peace offering.

He left Heaven by the southern gate and went straight to the Cave of the Water Curtain. Things were very different this time. The place bristled with weapons; every sort of wild ogre was on guard, and they were armed with lances, swords, staves, which they brandished fiercely, leaping this way and that. Seeing the star-spirit, they all rushed forward. 'Come chieftains,' said the spirit, 'I'll trouble you to tell your master that I am here. I am a heavenly messenger sent by God on High, and am come with a summons to your king.' 'Welcome to him,' said Monkey, when he heard that a messenger had come. 'It must be the Spirit of the Planet Venus, who came to fetch me before. That time, although the job I got was not worthy of me, my time in heaven was not entirely wasted. I ran round a good deal, and got to know my way about. No doubt he has come this time to offer me something better.'

And he ordered the chieftains to lead the spirit in, with a great waving of flags and rattle of drums. Monkey received him at the mouth of the cave in full panoply surrounded by hosts of lesser apes. 'Step in, old star,' he called, 'and forgive me for not having come to meet you.' 'Your colleagues,' said the planet, 'informed the Jade Emperor that you were discontented with your appointment in the Stables, and had absconded. "Everyone has to start with something small and work his way upward," said the Emperor. "What has he got to complain of?" And armies were sent to subdue you. When your magic powers proved superior to theirs, and it was proposed to band together all the forces of heaven and dispatch them against you, I put in a word, suggesting that you should be accorded the title you have assumed. This was accepted, and I have come to fetch you.' 'I am much obliged to you for your trouble this time and last,' said Monkey. 'But I don't know whether there is such a rank in heaven as "Great Sage, Equal of Heaven!" ' 'My proposal was that you should have this rank,' said the Planet, 'and it was accepted; otherwise I should never have dared to come with the message. If anything goes wrong, I am ready to take the responsibility.'

Monkey wished to detain the planet and give a banquet in his honour. But the planet would not stay; and they both set off together for the Southern Gate of Heaven. When the 'monkey groom' was announced the Jade Emperor said, 'Come forward, Monkey. I hereby proclaim you Great Sage, Equal of Heaven. The rank is a high one, and I hope we shall have no more nonsense.' Monkey gave a great whoop of delight and thanked the Emperor profusely.

Heavenly carpenters were ordered to build the office of the Great Sage to the right of the Peach Garden. It had two departments, one called Peace and Quiet and the other Calm Spirit. In each were Immortal Officers who attended Monkey wherever he went. A star spirit was detailed to escort Monkey to his new quarters, and he was allowed a ration of two jars of Imperial wine and ten sprays of gold-leaf flowers. He was begged not to allow himself to get in any way excited or start again on his pranks.

As soon as he arrived, he opened both jars and invited every one in his office to a feast. The star spirit went back to his own quarters, and Monkey, left to his own devices, lived in such perfect freedom and delight as in earth or heaven have never had their like.

And if you do not know what happened in the end, you must listen to what is told in the next chapter.

Chapter 5

Monkey knew nothing about official matters, and it was fortunate that all he had to do was to mark his name on a list. For the rest, he and his subordinates ate their three meals, slept soundly at night, had no worries, but only perfect freedom and independence. When there was nothing else going on, he went round and made friends with the other denizens of heaven. He was careful to address the members of the Trinity as 'Venerable', and the four Emperors as 'Majesty'; but all the rest, Planets, Lunar Mansions, spirits of the Hours and Days, he treated as equals. Today he wandered east, tomorrow rambled west; his goings and comings were unhampered as the passage of the clouds. One day at Court an Immortal stepped forward and made the following petition: 'I submit that the Sage, Equal of Heaven has no duties to perform. He spends all his time going round and making friends. All the stars of heaven, high and low, are now his cronies. Trouble will come of it, unless some way is found of employing his time.' The Jade Emperor accordingly sent for Monkey, who arrived in high glee, asking, 'What promotion or reward has your Majesty sent for me to announce?' 'I hear,' said the Emperor, 'that you have nothing in particular to do, and I am going to give you a job. You are to look after the Peach Garden; I wish you to devote the greatest attention to this work.'

Monkey was in wild delight, and unable to wait for a moment he rushed off to take over his new duties in the Peach Garden. Here he found a Local Spirit, who cried out to him, 'Great Sage, where are you going?' 'To take charge of the Peach Garden,' he said. 'I've been appointed by his Majesty.' The spirit bowed low, and called to Hoe-earth, Draw-water, Peach-tender and Leaf-sweeper, the strong men who worked the garden, to come forward and kowtow to Monkey.

'How many trees are there?' Monkey asked of the local

spirit. 'Three thousand six hundred,' he said. 'On the outer side, one thousand two hundred, with inconspicuous flowers and small fruit. They ripen once in three thousand years. Whoever eats them becomes a fairy, all-wise; his limbs are strong and his body light. In the middle of the garden are one thousand two hundred trees, with double blossom and sweet fruit. They ripen once in six thousand years. Whoever eats them can levitate at will, and never grows old. At the back of the garden are one thousand two hundred trees. The fruit has purple markings and the stones are pale yellow. They ripen once in nine thousand years. Whoever eats them outlasts heaven and earth, and is the compeer of sun and moon.' Monkey was delighted, and began at once inspecting the trees and listing the arbours and pagodas. Henceforward he amused himself only once a month, on the day of the full moon, but otherwise saw no friends and went nowhere. One day he saw that high up on some of the trees many of the peaches were ripe, and he made up his mind to eat them before any one else got a chance. Unfortunately he was closely watched by his followers, and to shake them off he said, 'I am feeling tired and am going to take a short rest in that arbour. Go and wait for me outside the gates.' When they had retired, he took off his court hat and robes, and scrambled up on to a high tree, and began to pluck the ripest and largest fruit he could see. Sitting astride a bough, he regaled himself to his heart's content, and then came down. He put on his hat and robes, and called to his followers to attend him while he returned in state to his lodging. After a few days, he did the same thing again.

One morning her Majesty the Queen of Heaven, having made up her mind to give a Peach Banquet, told the fairy maidens, Red Jacket, Blue Jacket, White Jacket, Black Jacket, Purple Jacket, Yellow Jacket and Green Jacket to take their baskets and pick peaches in the Peach Garden. They found Monkey's followers barring the gate. 'We have come,' they said, 'by command of her Majesty to pick peaches for a banquet.' 'Halt, my fairy beauties,' said one of the guards. 'Things have changed since last year. This garden

57

has been put in charge of the Great Sage, Equal of Heaven, and we must get his permission, before we can let you in.' 'Where is he?' they asked. 'He's feeling rather tired,' a guardian spirit said, 'and is having a nap in the arbour.' 'Very well then,' they said, 'go and look for him, for we must get to work at once.' They consented to go and tell him, but found the arbour empty, save for Monkey's hat and robe. They began looking for him, but he was nowhere to be seen. The fact was that Monkey, after slipping away and eating several peaches, had changed himself into a little fellow two inches long, and was curled up asleep under a thick leaf high up on the tree. 'We must carry out our orders,' said the fairy maidens, 'whether you find him or not. We can't go back empty-handed.' 'Quite right, fairy beauties,' said an officer, 'we must not keep you waiting. Our master has been used to going about a great deal, and probably he has gone to look up some of his old friends. Just you go and pick your peaches, and we'll tell him when he comes back.'

So they went into the garden, and first they picked three basketsful from the trees in the near part of the garden, then three from the trees in the middle. But when they came to the trees at the back, they found nothing but snapped stalks. All the peaches had been taken. However, when they had looked about for some time, they did succeed in finding one solitary peach that was not quite ripe, hanging on a southwards facing bough. Blue Jacket pulled the bough towards her and picked the peach, then let go. This was the very bough where Monkey was sleeping in his diminutive form. The jerk awoke him, and rapidly changing himself back again, he cried out, 'Where have you come from, monsters, and how comes it that you have the audacity to pick my peaches?' The terrified fairy maidens with one accord fell upon their knees, crying, 'Great Sage, don't be angry! We are not monsters; we are seven fairy maidens sent by the Queen of Heaven to pick peaches for her Peach Banquet. When we came to the gate, we found your officers on guard. They looked everywhere for you, but couldn't find you. We were afraid to keep her Majesty waiting, so as you could not be found we came in and began to pick. We beseech you to forgive us!' Monkey became all affability. 'Rise from your knees, fairies,' he said. 'Tell me now, who is invited to this banquet?' 'It is an official banquet,' they said, 'and certain deities are invited as a matter of course. The Buddha of the Western Heaven will be there, and the Bodhisattvas and Lo-hans; Kuan-yin too, and all the Immortals of the Ten Islands. Then there will be the five spirits of the Pole Star, the Emperors of the Four Quarters, the gods and immortals of the seas and hills – all of them will come to the banquet?' 'Shall I be asked?' enquired Monkey. 'I haven't heard it suggested,' one of them said. 'But I am the Great Sage, Equal of Heaven,' said Monkey. 'I don't see why I shouldn't be invited.' 'We can only tell you who is invited according to the rules,' they said. 'What will be done this time, we don't know.' 'Quite right, my dears,' said Monkey. 'I'm not blaming you. Just you wait here while I go off and scout round a little, to see whether I'm to be invited or not to be invited.'

Dear Monkey! He recited a magic formula and cried to the maidens, 'Stay, stay, stay,' This was a fixing magic, and the fairies in consequence of it remained rooted to the spot where they stood. Monkey set off on his magic cloud, sailed clear of the garden, and hastened towards the Pool of Green Jade. On the way he ran straight into the Red-legged Immortal. At once he thought of a plan by which he might trick the Immortal and attend the feast himself. 'Old Wisdom, where are you going?' he asked. 'I have been invited to the Peach Banquet,' the Immortal answered. 'You probably haven't heard . . .' said Monkey. 'I've been asked by the Jade Emperor, because I get about so fast on my cloud, to go round to all the guests and tell them there's going to be a rehearsal of ceremonies first, in the Hall of Penetrating Light.' The Immortal was a guileless soul, and was completely taken in. 'Other years we've always had the rehearsal at the same place as the banquet,' he said. 'However, I'm much obliged,' and turning his cloud he made towards the Hall of Penetrating Light.

Then, reciting a spell, Monkey changed himself into the

59

exact image of the Red-legged Immortal and went straight to the Green Jade Pool. After a little while he came to the Treasure Tower, and stepped softly in. Everything was set out for the feast, but no one had yet arrived. Monkey was gazing at the scene, when suddenly a smell of brewing assaulted him. He turned round and in a gallery on the right saw a number of fairy ministrants making wine. Some were carrying the mashed grain, others bringing water. Boys were keeping up the fire, jugs were being washed and jars swept. The wine that had already been made was exhaling a delicious perfume. Monkey's mouth watered, and he would have gone and drunk some at once, had it not been for the presence of all these servants. He was obliged to employ his magic powers. Pulling out a handful of his finest down, he tossed it into his mouth and bit it into ever smaller pieces; then he spat it out, crying 'Change!' and the hairs changed into so many Drowsy Insects, which flew towards the servants and settled on their cheeks. Look at them, how their hands fall to their sides and their heads sink down, their eyes close and they fall asleep.

Monkey then snatched up some of the finest viands, the daintiest dishes, ran into the gallery, seized a jug, tilted a jar, set to and drank deeply.

When he had been drinking for some time and was already pretty drunk, he thought to himself, 'Bad! bad! The guests will soon be arriving, and I shall get into trouble. It's no good staying here; I'd better go and have a sleep in my own quarters.' Dear Monkey! Staggering and blundering along, very much the worse for liquor, he lost his way and instead of getting home he arrived at the Tushita Palace. Suddenly he came to himself and realized where he was. 'Why, this is where Lao Tzu lives,' he said to himself. 'How did I get here? Well, I've always wanted to meet that old man and have never had the chance. It wouldn't be a bad idea, as I *am* here, to go and have a look at him.' So he tidied his clothes and went in. But there were no signs of Lao Tzu or any one else. Actually Lao Tzu was in an upper room with Dīpān-kara, Buddha of the Past, expounding the Way to an audience of Immortal officers, pages and officials.

Monkey went straight into the alchemical laboratory. There was no one there, but a brazier at one side of the hearth was burning, with five gourds arranged round it, and in these gourds was finished elixir. 'This,' said Monkey to himself in high glee, 'is the highest treasure of the Immortals. Since my Illumination I have solved the secret of the identity of Inside and Outside, and was on the verge of producing a little elixir on my own account, when unexpectedly I came home and was busy with other things. I think I'll try a pill or two.' He tilted the gourds and ate up the contents for all the world as though it had been a dish of fried beans.

After a while, full of elixir, and the effects of the wine now wearing off, he again took stock of the situation, and said to himself, 'Bad! Bad! This escapade of mine is even more unfortunate than the last. If the Jade Emperor gets to hear of it, I am lost. Run! Run! Run! I was better off as a king in the world below.'

He rushed out of the Tushita Palace, not going his usual way, but making for the Western Gate of Heaven. Here he used a magic that made him invisible, and lowered his cloud till he was back on the borders of the Mountain of Flowers and Fruit. A flash of banners and gleam of spears told him that his followers were practicing the arts of war. 'Little ones, I am here,'. he cried aloud. They all flung down their weapons and fell upon their knees. 'Great Sage,' they said, 'you're very neglectful of your subjects. Fancy going off all this while without a thought about what becomes of us!' However, they made a great banquet to welcome him, and brought him a huge stone bowl full of date-wine. After drinking a mouthful, he made a very wry face, saying, 'What horrible stuff! I can't drink this.' Two of his generals rushed forward. 'Great Sage,' they said, 'no doubt in the Palace of Heaven you have been drinking the wine of the Immortals, and for that reason cannot stomach this date-wine. But the proverb says: "There is no water like home water!" ' 'And it goes on: "There are no folk like home folk," ' said Monkey 'When I was enjoying myself at the Pool of Green Jade I

61

saw flagon after flagon of jade-juice and ruby-extract, such as you have never in your lives tasted. I'll go back and steal some for you. Half a cup each, and you'll none of you ever grow old.'

All the monkeys were delighted, and the Sage went out to the cave door, turned his somersault, made himself invisible and returned to Heaven. He found the makers of wine, carriers of dregs and water and lighters of fire all still snoring heavily. Taking a couple of large flagons, one under each arm, and two more, one in each hand, he turned his cloud and came back. A great assembly of monkeys was held and each got a cupful or two. There was a rapturous scene.

Meanwhile the seven fairy maidens remained spell-bound a whole day. When at last they could move, they took up their flower-baskets, and going back to the Queen of Heaven they told her that the Sage, Equal of Heaven had held them back by magic, that was why they were so late. 'How many peaches did you pick?' she asked. We got two baskets of small peaches and three baskets of middling peaches. But when we came to the back of the garden we found that half the big peaches were already gone. It seems that the Great Sage has eaten them. While he was being looked for, he suddenly appeared in our midst, made a fearful scene, and asked who had been invited to the banquet. We told him about the usual arrangements for such feasts, whereupon he bound us by a spell and went off we didn't know where. We have only just managed to break the spell and come back.'

The Queen of Heaven went straight to the Jade Emperor, and was telling him what had happened, when a crowd of wine-makers and other celestial officials came pouring in, announcing that someone had made a mess of all the arrangements for the banquet, stolen the wine and eaten up all the dainties. At this moment the Supreme Patriarch of Tao was announced. The Emperor and his consort went out to meet him. 'I am sorry to have to report to your Majesties,' said Lao Tzu, 'that the Elixir which I was concocting for the next Cinnabar Banquet has been stolen.' Presently one of Monkey's celestial attendants arrived, and reported that the Great Sage had been missing since the day before and no one knew what had become of him. The Jade Emperor's suspicions were now confirmed. At this point the Red-legged Immortal appeared before the Throne. 'I was on my way to the banquet,' he said, 'in response to her Majesty's invitation, when I met the Great Sage, Equal to Heaven, who told me that he had been asked to inform all guests that they were to go first to the Hall of Penetrating Light and rehearse the ceremonies of the banquet. I did as he said. But when I got there, I saw no sign of your Majesties having arrived, and thought it better to come at once to Court.' The Jade Emperor was more outraged and astounded than ever. 'So the rogue counterfeits Imperial orders and deceives my ministers!' he exclaimed. 'Tell the Celestial Detective to get on to his tracks at once.' After an exhaustive enquiry, the Detective reported that the disturbances in Heaven had been caused by the Great Sage.

The Jade Emperor then commanded the Kings of the Four Quarters and Vaiśravana and his son to marshal the twenty-eight Lunar Mansions, the Nine Planets, the Twelve Hours and all the Stars, together with a hundred thousand heavenly soldiers, and draw a cordon round the Mountain of Flowers and Fruit, so that Monkey should have no escape.

When this had been done, the Nine Planets were called upon to issue the challenge. Monkey and his generals were drinking wine from Heaven, and when he was told that the Planets were at the door, he refused to worry himself.

If today you have wine, get drunk today;
Pay no heed to what is at the door, be it good or ill.

he quoted. A small imp now scurried up saying that these nine fierce deities were raging at the gate, flinging battle-taunts. Monkey only laughed. 'Don't pay any attention to them!' he said:

Poetry and wine are enough to make this day glad;
High deeds must take their turn, glory can afford to wait.

63

But while he was speaking, another imp rushed in. 'Father,' he cried, 'those nine fierce deities have broken down the gates and are advancing to the attack.' 'Have those scoundrels no manners!' cried Monkey. 'I've never interfered with them. Why should they come here worrying me?' And he ordered the One Horned Ogre to lead out the kings of the seventy-two caves to battle, while he and his four generals came in the rear. The ogre and his followers could get no further than the Iron Bridge. Here the Planets barred their path. 'Make way!' cried Monkey, and he strode through their midst, brandishing his cudgel. The Planets dared not oppose him, and beat a hasty retreat. When they had re-formed their ranks a little way back, their leader cried, 'Insensate groom! What crime is there that you have not committed? You have stolen peaches and stolen wine, upset the high feast, purloined Lao Tzu's elixir, and then taken more wine for your banquet here. You have piled up sin upon sin; do you not realize what you have done?' 'Quite true,' said Monkey, 'all quite true. What are you going to do about it?' 'We have been sent by the Jade Emperor,' they said, 'to receive your submission. If you surrender at once, you will be spared; if not, we shall stamp on your mountain till it is flat, and smash your cave to bits.' 'And where are you going to get the strength from,' asked Monkey, 'to do that? How dare you talk such nonsense! Stand your ground and take Old Monkey's cudgel.' The Planets leapt at him; but Monkey was no whit afraid. He brandished his cudgel, parrying here and thrusting there, till the Planets were quite worn out and one by one slunk away trailing their weapons after them, to seek refuge in their tents. 'That Monkey King is a valiant fighter indeed,' they said to Vaiśravana. 'We were unable to overcome him, and have had to give up the fight.' The Kings of the Four Quarters and the Twenty-Eight Lunar Mansions were then ordered to advance. But Monkey did not quail, but bade the One Horned Ogre, the kings of the seventy-two caves and his four valiant generals to take their stand outside the cave.

The combat began at dawn, and lasted till the sun sank

behind the western hills. The One Horned Ogre and all the kings of the seventy-two caves were captured and carried away. Only the four generals and the monkeys escaped and hid in the far recesses of the cave. But Monkey all alone, cudgel in hand, held back the kings of the Four Quarters, Vaiśravana and Natha, warring with them half way up the sky. At last, seeing that dusk was at hand, he plucked a handful of his hairs, tossed them into his mouth, chewed them up small and spat them out, crying 'Change!' Whereupon they changed into thousands of monkeys each armed with a metal-plated cudgel. They drove back Vaiśravana, Natha and the four kings. Then Monkey, at last victorious, withdrew the hairs and returned to his cave. At the Iron Bridge, he was met by the four generals and all the host of monkeys. On seeing him they wailed three times, and laughed, hee-hee, ho-ho, three times. 'What made you wail three times and laugh three times when you saw me?' asked Monkey. 'We wailed,' they said, 'because the One Horned Ogre and the seventy-two kings were defeated and captured, and because we had to fly for our lives. We laughed with joy because you have come back victorious and unharmed.'

'There is always defeat in victory and victory in defeat,' said Monkey. 'There is an old saying "To slay ten thousand costs three thousand". In this case the chieftains captured were all tigers, leopards, wolves and the like. Not one of our monkey-kind was taken or hurt; so there is nothing to worry about. By the art of self-division I have put them to flight. But it is certain that they have encamped at the foot of our mountain. We must keep strict guard and husband our strength. Tomorrow you shall see me use my most potent magic against those divinities, and avenge the captured.'

Then the four generals and all the monkeys drank a cup or two of date-wine and went quietly to sleep.

After the retreat of the kings of the Four Quarters, all the celestial warriors told of their deeds. Some had captured tigers and leopards, some deer, some wolves and foxes. But not one of them could boast that he had taken a monkey.

5

They did indeed, as Monkey had foretold, set up a camp, surrounding it with a great palisade. Here the meritorious were rewarded, and the troops who formed the cordon round the caves were instructed to give warning by bell or cry and be ready for the great battle that would begin at dawn.

How they fared after day broke, you will hear in the next chapter.

Chapter 6

So the great Sage quietly rested, while the hosts of Heaven encompassed him. Meanwhile the Great Compassionate Bodhisattva Kuan-yin had come at the invitation of the Queen of Heaven to attend the great feast. With her she brought her chief disciple, Hui-yen, and on arriving they were astounded to find the banqueting halls in utter desolation and confusion. The couches were broken or pushed aside, and although there were a good few Immortals, they had not attempted to take their places, but were standing about in noisy groups, protesting and disputing. After saluting the Bodhisattva they told her the whole story of what had occurred. 'If there is no banquet and no drinks are going,' she said, 'you had better all come with me to see the Jade Emperor.' On the way they met the Red-legged Immortal and others, who told them that a heavenly army had been sent to arrest the culprit, but had not yet returned. 'I should like to see the Emperor,' said Kuan-yin. 'I must trouble you to announce my arrival.' Lao Tzu was with the Emperor, and the Queen of Heaven in attendance behind the throne. 'What about the Peach Banquet?' Kuan-yin asked, after the customary greetings had been exchanged. 'It has always been such fun, year after year,' said the Emperor. 'It is terribly disappointing that this year everything has been upset by that terrible ape. I have sent 100,000 soldiers to pen him in, but the whole day has passed without news, and I don't know whether they have been successful!'

'I think you had better go down quickly to the Mountain of Flowers and Fruit,' said the Bodhisattva to her disciple, Hui-yen, 'and investigate the military situation. If hostilities are actually in progress, you can give a hand. In any case let us know exactly how things stand.'

When he arrived, he found a close cordon many soldiers deep, with sentries on watch at every exit. The mountain was completely surrounded, and escape impossible. Day was just breaking when Hui-yen, who was the second son of Vaiśravana and had been called Prince Moksha before his conversion, was shown into his father's tent. 'Where do you come from, my son?' asked Vaiśravana. 'I have been sent to see how things are going on,' he said. 'We camped here yesterday,' said Vaiśravana, 'and I sent the Nine Planets as challengers, but they were unable to stand up against this rogue's magic and returned discomforted. Then I led an army myself and he marshalled his followers. We were about 100,000 men, and fought with him till dusk, when he used some magic method of self-multiplication, and we had to withdraw. On examining out booty we found we had captured a certain number of tigers, wolves, leopards and other animals, but not a single monkey. Today the fight has not yet begun.'

While they were speaking a messenger rushed in and announced that the Great Sage and all his host of monkeys were outside, shouting their battle cries. The kings of the Four Quarters, Vaiśravana and his son Natha had just agreed to go out and meet him, when Hui-yen said, 'Father, I was sent by the Bodhisattva to obtain information. But she said that if hostilities were in progress I was to lend a hand. I confess I should like to go and have a look at this Great Sage of yours.' 'My son,' said Vaiśravana, 'you cannot have studied with the Bodhisattva for so many years without having learnt some form of magic. Don't forget to put it into practice.'

Dear prince! Girding up his embroidered cloak and brandishing his iron cudgel with both hands, he rushed out to the campgate, crying in a loud voice, 'Which of you is the Great Sage Equal to Heaven?' Monkey held up his wishing-staff and answered, 'I am he. Who are you, that you so rashly dare enquire for me?' Hui-yen said, 'I am Vaiśravana's second son, Moksha. Now I am pupil and defender of the Bodhisattva Kuan-yin, and stand before her throne. My name in religion is Hui-yen.' 'What then are you doing here?' asked Monkey. 'I was sent,' said he, 'to get news of the battle. And as they are having so much trouble with you, I have come myself to arrest you.' 'How dare you talk so big?' said Monkey. 'Stand your ground and taste Old Monkey's cudgel.' Moksha was not at all afraid, but advanced flourishing his iron cudgel. Those two stood face to face at the foot of the mountain, outside the gate of the camp. It was a grand fight. They closed fifty or sixty times, till at last Hui-yen's arms and shoulders were aching, he could resist no more and fled from the battlefield. Monkey too withdrew his monkey troops, and bade them rest outside the cave.

Moksha, still gasping and panting, tottered into his father's camp. 'It's only too true,' he said. 'That Great Sage is indeed the most formidable of magicians! I could do nothing with him and have had to come back leaving him in possession of the field.' Vaiśravana was very astonished. He saw nothing for it but to write out an appeal for further help. This he entrusted to the demon-king Mahābāli and his son Moksha, who at once passed through the cordon and soared to Heaven. 'How are you people down below getting on?' asked Kuan-yin. 'My father told me,' said Hui-yen, 'that in the first day's battle they captured a number of tigers, leopards, wolves and other animals, but not a single monkey. Soon after I arrived, the battle began again, and I closed with the Great Sage some fifty or sixty times, but could not get the better of him and was obliged to retire to the camp. My father then sent the demon-king Mahābāli and me to ask for help.' The Bodhisattva Kuan-yin bowed her head and reflected.

When the Jade Emperor opened Vaiśravana's missive and saw that it contained an appeal for help, he said laughing. 'This is preposterous! Am I to believe that a single monkey-spirit is so powerful that a hundred thousand heavenly troops cannot deal with him? Vaiśravana says that he must have help, but I don't know what troops he expects me to send.' Before he had finished speaking, Kuan-yin pressed together the palms of her hands and said, 'Your Majesty need not worry. I know of a divinity who can certainly catch this monkey.' 'Whom do you mean?' asked the Emperor. 'Your nephew, the magician Erh-lang,' she said. 'He lives at the mouth of the River of Libations, and there receives the incense that is burnt in the world below. In old days he once overcame six ogres. He has his brothers with him and one thousand plant-headed deities of very great magical powers. Though he would not come if ordered to, he would listen to an appeal. If you send an appeal to him for troops, with his assistance we could effect a capture.'

The demon-king Mahābāli was sent as messenger, and in less than half an hour the cloud he rode on reached Erh-lang's temple. He came out with his brothers, and after burning incense, read the appeal. 'Let the heavenly messenger go back,' he said, 'and announce that I will help to the utmost of my power.'

So he called together his brothers and said, 'The Jade Emperor has just asked us to go to the Mountain of Flowers and Fruit, and receive the submission of a troublesome monkey. Let's be off!' The brothers were delighted, and they at once marshalled the divinities in their charge. The whole temple set out, falcon on wrist, or leading their dogs, bow in hand, carried by a wild magic wind. In a trice they had crossed the Eastern Ocean and reached the Mountain of Flowers and Fruit. Having announced their mission they were led through the cordon and shown into the camp. They asked how matters stood. 'I shall certainly have to try a transformation,' Erh-lang said. 'Keep the cordon closely drawn, but don't worry about what goes on overhead. If I am getting the worst of it, do not come to my assistance; my brothers will look after me. If I conquer him, do not try to bind him, but leave that to my brothers. All I ask is that Vaiśravana should use an imp-reflecting mirror, standing with it half way up the sky. If he tries to run away and hide, watch his reflection in the mirror, so that we don't lose sight of him.' The heavenly kings then took up their places, and Erh-lang and his brothers went out to give the challenge, telling their fellows to form a circle, keeping their falcons tethered and their dogs on leash. When he reached the door of the cave, Erh-lang found a host of monkeys drawn up in coiling dragon formation. In their midst was a banner with

'The Great Sage Equal to Heaven' inscribed upon it. 'How dare the cursed monster call himself equal to Heaven?' snarled Erh-lang. 'Don't worry about that,' said the brothers, 'but go and challenge him at once.'

When the small monkeys at the entrance to the camp saw Erh-lang coming, they scuttled inside and made their report. Monkey seized his metal-bound cudgel, donned his golden breastplate, put on his cloud-treading shoes and golden cap and rushed out to the gate, glaring about him. 'What little captain are you and where do you hail from,' shouted Monkey, 'that you dare come here and challenge me to battle?' 'Have you eyes with no eyeballs, that you fail to know me?' shouted Erh-lang. 'I am the Jade Emperor's nephew. I have come now by his Majesty's command to arrest you, rebellious groom-ape that you are! Your hour has come.' 'I remember,' said Monkey, 'that some years ago the emperor's sister fell in love with a mortal of the world below, became his consort and had a son by him, who is said to have split the Peach Mountain with his axe. Are you he? I am half minded to give you a bit of my mind, but you are not worth it. I should be sorry to strike you, for one blow of mine would be the end of you. Go back where you came from, little fellow, and tell the four kings of Heaven to come instead.' Erh-lang was furious. 'Keep a civil tongue in your head,' he cried, 'and taste my blade.' Monkey dodged aside and swiftly raising his cudgel struck in his turn. They closed over three hundred times without reaching a decision. Erh-lang exerted all his magic power, shook himself hard and changed into a giant figure a hundred thousand feet high. His two arms, each holding aloft a magic trident, were like the peaks that crown Mount Hua, his face was blue and his teeth stuck far out, the hair on his head was scarlet and his expression malignant beyond words. This terrible apparition advanced upon Monkey, aiming a blow straight down upon his head. But Monkey, also using his magic powers, changed himself into an exact counterpart of Ehr-lang, save that he held above him a single gigantic cudgel, like the solitary pillar that towers above Mount K'un-lun, and with this he fended off Ehr-lang's blow. But Monkey's generals were completely discomfited by the giant apparition, and their hands began to tremble so much that they could not wave their banners. His other officers were in panic and could not use their swords. At a word from the brothers the plant-headed divinities rushed in, letting loose their falcons and dogs, and bow in hand all charged into the fray. Also, Monkey's four generals fled and two or three thousand of the creatures they commanded were captured. The monkeys threw down their weapons and rushed screaming, some up the mountain, some into the cave. It was just as when a cat at night disturbs roosting birds and their panic fills the starry sky.

When Monkey saw his followers scatter, his heart fluttered, he abandoned his giant form and fled as fast as his feet could carry him. Ehr-lang strode after him with huge steps, crying, 'Where are you off to? Come back this minute, and I will spare your life.' But Monkey fled faster than ever to his cave, where he ran straight into the brothers. 'Wretched monkey, where are you running to?' they cried. Monkey, trembling in every limb, hastily turned his cudgel into an embroidery needle, and hiding it about his person, changed himself into a fish, and slipped into the stream. Rushing down to the bank, Erh-lang could see nothing of him. 'This simian,' he said, 'has certainly changed himself into a fish and hidden under the water. I must change myself too if I am to catch him.' So he changed himself into a cormorant and skimmed hither and thither over the stream. Monkey, looking up out of the water, suddenly saw a bird hovering above. It was like a blue kite, but its plumage was not blue. It was like a heron, but had no tuft on its head. It was like a crane, but its feet were not red. 'I'll be bound that's Erh-lang looking for me . . . ' He released a few bubbles and swam swiftly away. 'That fish letting bubbles,' said Erh-lang to himself, 'is like a carp, but its tail is not red; it is like a tench, but there are no patterns on its scales. It is like a black-fish, but there are no stars on its head; it is like a bream, but there are no bristles on its gills. Why did it make off like that when it saw me? I'll be bound it's Monkey, who has changed himself into a fish.' And swooping down, he opened his beak and snapped at him. Monkey whisked out of the water, and changed himself into a freckled bustard, standing all alone on the bank. Seeing that he had reached the lowest possible stage in transformation, for the freckled bustard is the lowest and most promiscuous of creatures, mating at hazard with any bird that comes its way, Erh-lang did not deign to close with him, but returned to his true form, and fetching his sling, shot a pellet that sent Monkey rolling. Taking advantage of his opportunity, Monkey rolled and rolled down the mountain side, and when he was out of sight he changed himself into a wayside shrine; his mouth wide open was the door-opening, his teeth he turned into door flaps, his tongue into the guardian Bodhisattva. His two eyes were the two round windows; he didn't quite know what to do with his tail, but sticking up straight behind it looked like a flag-pole. When Erh-lang arrived at the bottom of the slope, he expected to find the bustard that he had toppled over, but instead he only found a small shrine. Examining it closely he noticed the 'flag-pole' sticking up behind and laughed, saying 'That's Monkey, that is! He's trying his tricks on me again. I have seen many shrines, but never one with a flag-pole sticking up behind. No doubt about it, this animal is playing one of his games. He hopes to lure me up close to him, and then he will bite me. He won't get me that way. I'll clench my fist and bang in the windows first. Afterwards I'll kick down the door.' When Monkey heard this he was horrified. 'That's a bit too much,' he said to himself. 'The doors are my teeth and the windows are my eyes. If he kicks my teeth and bangs my eyes, that won't be nice.' So saying, he made a tiger-spring and disappeared into the sky. Erh-lang was just getting tired of the vain pursuit, when his brothers arrived. 'Well, have you caught the Great Sage?' they asked. 'He has just been trying to dodge me,' said Erh-lang, 'by turning into a shrine. I was just going to hit his windows and kick down his doors, when he suddenly disappeared. It's a queer business.' They all began peering helplessly about in every direction, but could find nothing. 'You stay here and keep a look-out,' said Erh-lang, 'while I go up and search for him.' He mounted the clouds, and half-way up the sky came across Vaiśravana, who was holding the magic mirror, his son at his side. 'Have you seen the Monkey King?' he asked. 'He has not been up here,' said Vaiśravana. 'I can see him in my mirror, you know.' When Erh-lang had told him about the capture of the lesser monkeys and the Great Sage's repeated transformations, he added, 'Then he changed into a shrine, and when I hit at him he suddenly disappeared.' Vaiśravana looked in his mirror and burst out laughing. 'Make haste, Erh-lang, make haste,' he cried. 'That monkey has made himself invisible, decamped and made straight for your River of Libations.' When Erh-lang heard this he picked up his magic lance and fled towards the River of Libations as fast as he could.

Now as soon as Monkey reached the river, he changed himself into the exact image of Erh-lang and went straight into Erh-lang's shrine. The guardian demons of the shrine could not tell the difference and bowed low as he came in. He examined the incense-smoke, and was looking at the votive paintings round the walls, when someone came and announced 'Another Erh-lang has arrived.' The guarding deities rushed out, and could hardly believe their eyes. 'Has a creature calling himself the Great Sage Equal to Heaven been here?' the real Erh-lang asked. 'We've seen nothing of any Great Sage,' they said, 'but there's another holy Erh-lang inside, examining the incense-smoke.'

He rushed in, and as soon as Monkey saw him he changed into his true form and said, 'Erh-lang, I don't mind telling you the surname of that shrine was Sun.'[1]

Erh-lang raised his three-pronged, two-bladed magic lance and struck at Monkey's cheek. Monkey dodged, and the two of them, cursing and fighting, edged towards the shrine-gate and out into the mists and clouds, struggling as they went, till at last Monkey was driven to the Mountain of Flowers and Fruit, where the kings of the Four Quarters were keep-

[1] Monkey.

ing strait guard. The brothers came to meet Erh-lang and surrounded Monkey, pressing about him on every side.

Meanwhile in Heaven everyone was wondering why a whole day had passed without any news from Erh-lang. 'Would your Majesty,' asked Kuan-yin, 'permit me and the Patriarch of Tao to go down in person and see how things are going on?' 'Not a bad idea,' said the Jade Emperor, and in the end he and the Queen of Heaven as well as Kuan-yin and Lao Tzu all went to the Southern Gate of Heaven and looked out. They saw the great cordon of heavenly troops, and Vaiśravana standing half way up the sky, holding a mirror, while Erh-lang and his brothers pressed round Monkey, tussling fiercely with him. 'That Erhlang, whom I proposed, hasn't done so badly,' said Kuan-yin. 'He has hemmed the Great Sage in, though he has not yet taken him prisoner. With a little help, I think he could manage it.' 'What weapon do you propose to use, how are you going to help him?' asked Lao Tzu. 'I shall throw my vase and willow spray down on to his head,' said Kuan-yin. 'That won't kill him; but it will make him lose his balance, and Erh-lang will easily be able to catch him.' 'Your vase,' said Lao Tzu, 'is made of porcelain. If it fell in just the right place, it might be all right. But if it misses his head and falls on his iron cudgel, it will get broken. You had better leave him to me.' 'Have you got a weapon?' asked Kuan-yin. 'I certainly have,' said Lao Tzu, and he produced from his sleeve a magic snare. 'This,' said he, 'is called the Diamond Snare. In old days, when I left China, converted the barbarians of the West and became a god, I owed my success entirely to this snare. It comes in handy for keeping off all manner of dangers. Let me throw it down on to him.' Standing at the gate of Heaven, he cast his snare, and it went rippling down straight on to Monkey's head. Monkey was busy warring with Erh-lang and his brothers, and did not notice that a weapon was falling upon him out of the sky. It hit him just on the crown of the head, and toppled him over. He scrambled to his feet and fled, pursued by Erh-lang's dogs, who went for his calves, so that he stumbled again. Lying on the ground, he cursed, saying, 'That has done for me! Why can't you go and trip up your own master, instead of coming and biting Old Monkey's legs?' He twisted and turned, but could not rise, for the brothers were holding him down. Soon they had bound him tightly with ropes, and severed his lute-bone with a knife, so that he could not transform himself.

Lao Tzu drew in his snare, and begged the Emperor, Kuan-yin, the Queen of Heaven and all the Immortals to go back to the palace. On earth below the kings of the Four Quarters and Vaiśravana, and all the heavenly host sheathed their swords and plucked up their palisades. Then they came up to Erh-lang and congratulated him, saying, 'We owe this victory to you.' 'Not at all,' said Erh-lang. 'It was entirely due to the Founder of Tao and the gallant performances of the heavenly contingent. I can claim no credit at all.' 'Elder brother,' said the brothers of Erh-lang, 'you have said enough. What we must do now is to hoist this fellow up to Heaven and get a ruling from the Jade Emperor as to how he is to be disposed of.' 'Brothers,' said Erh-lang, 'you are not on the roll of Immortals, and cannot appear before the Emperor. Heavenly troops must be told to carry him up, and Vaiśravana and I will go up and report. The rest of you had better search the mountain, and when you can report that all is clear, come to the River of Libations and let me know. Meanwhile I will claim the reward due for my services, and then come back to make merry with you.' The brothers bowed their assent. Erh-lang mounted the clouds, chanting songs of victory, and made his way to Heaven. Here he sent in a message, saying, 'The Great Sage has been captured by the hosts of Heaven, and I have come to receive your instructions.' The Jade Emperor accordingly told the demon-king Mahābāli and a contingent of heavenly troops to hoist Monkey up and bring him to the executioner's block, where he was to be cut into small pieces.

If you do not know what now became of this Monkey King, listen to what is told in the next chapter.

Chapter 7

Monkey was brought to the place of execution, where heavenly soldiers bound him to a pillar and began to hew him with axes, stab him with spears, slash him with swords. But all this had no effect whatever, and presently the Southern Pole-star sent for the spirits of the Five Stars to come and set him alight; but they were quite unable to burn him. The thunder spirits hurled thunderbolts at him; but this had even less effect. 'I don't know where the Great Sage got this trick of inviolability,' said Mahābāli to the Jade Emperor. 'Neither weapons nor thunderbolts have the least effect on him. What are we to do?' 'Yes, indeed,' said the Jade Emperor, 'with a fellow like that, what line *can* one take?' 'It's not surprising,' said Lao Tzu. 'After all, he ate the peaches of Immortality, drank the wine of Heaven and stole the Elixir of Long Life; five bowls full, some raw, some cooked, are all inside him. No doubt he has worked on them with Samadhi fire and fused them into a solid, that makes his whole body harder than diamond, so that he is very difficult to damage. The best thing would be to bring him to me. I'll put him in my Crucible of the Eight Trigrams and smelt him with alchemic fire. In a little while he will be reduced to ashes, and I shall recover my elixir, which will be left at the bottom of the crucible.' So Monkey was handed over to Lao Tzu, and Erh-lang was rewarded with a hundred golden flowers, a hundred jars of heavenly wine, a hundred grains of elixir, along with a great store of jewels, pearls, brocades and embroideries, which he was asked to share with his brothers. He thanked the Emperor, and went back to the River of Libations.

When Lao Tzu got back to the Tushita Palace, he untied Monkey's ropes, removed the blade that was stuck through his lute-bone, pushed him into the crucible, and told his servant to blow up a good fire. Now this crucible was in eight parts, each representing one of the eight trigrams. Monkey wriggled into the part corresponding to the trigram *sun*. Now *sun* is wind, and wind blows out fire; but wind raises smoke, and Monkey's eyes smarted and became red; a condition from which he never recovered, which is why he is sometimes called Fiery Eyes. Time passed, and at last the forty-ninth day came, and Lao Tzu's alchemical processes were complete. When he came to the crucible to take off the lid, Monkey was rubbing his eyes with both hands, so hard that the tears fell. When he heard the lid being moved, he looked quickly up, and the light that came in hurt him so much that he could not bear it and jumped straight out of the crucible, uttering a piercing cry and kicking over the crucible as he jumped. He rushed out of the room pursued by Lao Tzu's servants, all of whom he tripped up, and when Lao Tzu clutched at him, he gave him such a push that he went head over heels. Then he took his cudgel from behind his ear and, armed once more, ran amok in Heaven, frightening the Nine Planets so much that they locked themselves in, and the kings of the Four Quarters vanished from the scene. This time Monkey hit out recklessly, not caring whom he struck or what he smashed. No one could stop him, and he would have broken up the Hall of Magic Mists, had not the divinity Wang Ling-kuan rushed forward with his great metal lash. 'Halt, cursed Monkey!' he cried. 'See who stands before you, and cease your mad pranks!' Monkey did not deign to parley with him, but raised his cudgel and struck. Ling-kuan faced him with his whip aloft. It was a great fight that the two of them had, in front of the Hall of Magic Mists, but neither gained the advantage. At last the thirty-six thunder deities came to Ling-kuan's aid, and Monkey found himself beset on every side by swords, lances, spears, whips, axes, hooks, sickles. He thought it time to transform himself, and took on a form with three heads and six arms, and wielded six magic cudgels which he whirled like a spinning-wheel, dancing in their midst. The thunder deities dared not approach him.

The noise of the combat reached the Jade Emperor who in great consternation sent two messengers to the Western Region to see if Buddha could not come and help. When they had recounted Monkey's misdeeds and explained their mission, Buddha said to the Bodhisattvas who surrounded him, 'You stay quietly here in the Hall of Law, and don't relax your *yoga* postures. I've got to go and deal with this creature who is making trouble at the Taoist court.' But he called on his disciples Ānanda and Kāśyapa to follow him. Arriving in Heaven, they heard a fearful din and found Monkey beset by the thirty-six deities. Buddha ordered the deities to lower arms and go back to their camp, and called Monkey to him. Monkey changed into his true form and shouted angrily, 'What bonze are you that you ask for me in the middle of a battle?' 'I am the Buddha of the Western Paradise. I have heard of the trouble you have been giving in Heaven. Where do you come from, and how long ago did you get your Illumination, that you should dare behave like this?'

Born of sky and earth, Immortal magically fused,
From the Mountain of Flowers and Fruit an old monkey
    am I.
In the cave of the Water-curtain I ply my home-trade;
I found a friend and master, who taught me the Great
    Secret.
I made myself perfect in many arts of Immortality,
I learned transformations without bound or end.
I tired of the narrow scope afforded by the world of
    man,
Nothing could content me but to live in the Green Jade
    Heaven.
Why should Heaven's halls have always one master?
In earthly dynasties king succeeds king.
The strong to the stronger must yield precedence and
    place,
Hero is he alone who vies with powers supreme.

So Monkey recited; at which Buddha burst out laughing. 'After all,' he said, 'you're only a monkey-spirit. How can you delude yourself into supposing that you can seize the Jade Emperor's throne? He has been perfecting himself for 1750 kalpas, and every kalpa is 129,000 years. Just see how long it takes to achieve such wisdom as his! How can you, an

79

animal, who have only in this incarnation received half-human form, dare make such a boast? You exceed yourself, and will surely come to a bad end. Submit at once and talk no more of your nonsense. Otherwise I shall have to deal sharply with you, and there won't be much left of the longevity you crave.' 'He may have begun young,' said Monkey, 'but that is no reason why he should keep the throne forever. There is a proverb that says "This year, the Jade Emperor's turn; next year, mine." Tell him to clear out and make room for me. That is all I ask. If he won't, I shall go on like this, and they will never have any peace.' 'What magic have you got,' asked Buddha, 'that would enable you to seize the blessed realms of Heaven?' 'Many,' said Monkey. 'Apart from my seventy-two transformations, I can somersault through the clouds a hundred and eight thousand leagues at a bound. Aren't I fit to be seated on the throne of Heaven?'

'I'll have a wager with you,' said Buddha. 'If you are really so clever, jump off the palm of my right hand. If you succeed, I'll tell the Jade Emperor to come and live with me in the Western Paradise, and you shall have his throne without more ado. But if you fail, you shall go back to earth and do penance there for many a kalpa before you come to me again with your talk.'

'This Buddha,' Monkey thought to himself, 'is a perfect fool. I can jump a hundred and eight thousand leagues, while his palm cannot be as much as eight inches across. How could I fail to jump clear of it?' 'You're sure you are in a position to do this for me?' he asked. 'Of course I am,' said Buddha.

He stretched out his right hand, which looked about the size of a lotus leaf. Monkey put his cudgel behind his ear, and leapt with all his might. 'That's all right,' he said to himself. 'I'm right off it now.' He was whizzing so fast that he was almost invisible, and Buddha, watching him with the eye of wisdom, saw a mere whirligig shoot along.

Monkey came at last to five pink pillars, sticking up into the air. 'This is the end of the World,' said Monkey to himself. 'All I have got to do is to go back to Buddha and claim

80

Chapter 10

On the banks of the river Ching there lived two worthies, a fisherman named Chang Hsiao and a woodman named Li Ting. Neither of them had passed any of the official examinations; they were what is known as lettered countrymen. One day, when they had been to the Capital, Li with his load of firewood, Chang with his basket of carp, they went into a wineshop and had a few drinks. Then, somewhat tipsy, they set off for home, rambling jug in hand along the banks of the Ching. Reciting song-words and linking verses as they went, they reached the place where their ways parted, and stood bowing ceremoniously to each other. 'Look after yourself, brother Li,' said Chang. 'If a tiger comes along, I may, as the saying goes "have one friend less in the street." ' 'That's not the way to talk to a friend,' said Li. 'It's unlucky to speak of such things – and anyway you're just as likely to capsize in your boat and get drowned.' 'So you say,' said Chang, 'but as a matter of fact I should know if anything was going to happen to me. In West Gate Street there is a fortune-teller. Every day I bring him a carp and he consults the little sticks. He has not been wrong once in a hundred times. Today he told me to set my nets to the east of the big bend of the Ching river and to cast my line from the western bank. I shall certainly get a good catch, which I shall sell in the City, and with the money I get we'll pay for another drink and finish our talk.'

But there is a proverb: 'What is said on the road is heard in the grass.' A yaksha patrolling the river overheard this conversation and reported it to the dragon king. 'If he's never once wrong in a hundred times,' said the yaksha, 'work it out for yourself – it won't be long before our whole watery tribe is extinct.' The dragon king was for seizing his sword and rushing off at once to slay the soothsayer. But his dragon children and grandchildren and all his fish ministers and fish generals restrained him, saying, 'Your Majesty had better

103

find out first if it is true. If you rush off like this, the clouds will follow you and the rains go at your side. Great damage will be done to the people of Ch'ang-an, who will complain of you in their prayers, and Heaven will intervene. Why don't you make use of your magic powers? Disguise yourself as a scholar, and make an investigation on the spot. If anything of this kind is really going on, destroy the fellow at once. If the story is untrue, it would be a pity to slay an innocent man.'

Arriving at West Gate Street, disguised as his councillors had suggested, the dragon saw a noisy crowd thronging round someone who was holding forth to them on the conjunctions of planets and stars. The dragon king pushed through the crowd, and having exchanged civilities with the soothsayer, said he particularly desired to know what the weather was going to be like. The soothsayer handed him a slip on which was written:

> Mists hide the tree-tops
> Clouds veil the hill.
> If you want rain tomorrow
> You shall have your fill.

'At what hour will it rain and how much will fall?' asked the dragon king. 'At the hour of the dragon,' said the soothsayer, 'clouds will gather. At the hour of the snake there will be a peal of thunder, at noon rain will fall, and continue till the hour of the sheep. The total quantity will be 3.048 inches.' The dragon king laughed. 'However, it is no laughing matter,' he said. 'If rain come tomorrow exactly in the quantity and under the circumstances you have described, I shall reward you with fifty weights of gold. But if there is no rain, or any of the particulars given by you fail to come true, I shall come and tear down your shop-sign and drive you out of the city, lest you should continue to impose on the ignorant.' 'Make any conditions you please,' said the soothsayer affably. 'Good-bye for the present. I shall see you again tomorrow after the rain has fallen.'

The dragon returned very agitated to his people, but they only laughed at him. 'Your Majesty,' they said, 'is Supreme Regent of the Eight Rivers; all the rain dragons are under your control. It is for you to decide whether it shall rain or not! Why let yourself be imposed upon by such nonsense? In such a wager as this the soothsayer hasn't a chance.'

Suddenly a voice in the sky called upon the Dragon King to receive a command from on high. They all looked up, and saw a messenger dressed in gold. The king hastily burned incense and tidied himself. When the message was handed to him it turned out to be an order from the Jade Emperor to go next day with all his thunder and lightning to Ch'ang-an, and give the city a heavy deluge of rain. Detailed instructions followed, coinciding exactly with what had been promised by the soothsayer.

The Dragon King was completely overcome by his surprise. 'I should never have believed,' he gasped, 'that in the mortal world there could exist such a magician. He has mastered the principles of Heaven and Earth. There can be no question of winning against *him*.' 'Calm yourself, great king,' said a fish general. 'You can easily get the better of him. I've got a little plan that will easily stop his mouth. All you have to do is to make a trifling alteration in the time and quantity of the rain. Then you can claim that his prediction was false and can proceed to pull down his shop-sign and drive him out into the street. It's all quite simple.'

Next day the king summoned the lords of the wind and of thunder, the rain-boys and the mother of lightnings, and took them with him to the sky above Ch'ang-an. He waited till the hour of the snake before spreading the clouds, at noon he thundered, at the hour of the sheep he released the rain. The rain stopped at the hour of the Monkey, and there was only 3.04 inches of it. He had altered the times by an hour and the quantity by eight points. When all was over he disguised himself again as a scholar and went to the soothsayer's house. Here, without allowing any time for discussion, he smashed the shop-sign, brushes, ink-stone and everything else.

The soothsayer sat all the while in his chair, utterly unperturbed. Then brandishing one of the door-boards that he had wrenched off, the Dragon King bawled, 'You lying quack, you impostor! You've swindled all these people long enough! Your divining is a fraud and all your talk is lunatic twaddle. You were utterly wrong the time of the rain and all the other particulars into which you entered so rashly. Yet there you sit looking as if the world belonged to you! Clear out this minute, or you shall pay for it with your life!' The soothsayer showed not the slightest sign of perturbation, but on the contrary threw back his head and laughed. 'I am not afraid,' he said. 'It is you, not I, who have committed a mortal offence. You may deceive others, but you can't deceive me. I know quite well that you are not a student, but the dragon of the Ching river in disguise. You have disobeyed the orders of the Jade Emperor, changed Heaven's appointed times and measures. There is a special block designed for the execution of dragons, and I fear that is where you will meet your end. Yet you come here and rail at me!' When the dragon heard this, his scales stood on end with fright, the board fell out of his hand and he flung himself on his knees before the soothsayer. 'Good sir,' he cried, 'I assure you I was only joking. I had no idea that my harmless imposture could really be taken as an affront to the Powers above. I implore you to do what you can for me. If you let me die, my ghost will give you no peace.'

'I can't myself do anything for you,' said the soothsayer, 'but I can give you a hint how to save yourself. You are to be executed tomorrow at noon by the minister Wei Chêng. If you want to escape with your life you must go at once to the great Emperor of T'ang by whom this minister is employed. If the Emperor appeals to him to show mercy, you are saved.' The dragon went away, weeping bitterly.

That night, at the hour of the rat, the Emperor dreamt that he went out of his palace to walk under the blossoming trees by moonlight. Suddenly someone knelt before him saying, 'Save me, your Majesty, save me!' 'Who are you?' asked the Emperor. 'Of course I'll help you.' 'Your Majesty, said the dragon king, 'is a True Dragon. I am but a dragon by karma. I have disobeyed Heaven's instructions and am to be executed by your minister Wei Chêng. I have come to ask you to help me.' 'If it is Wei Chêng who is to execute you,' said the Emperor, 'I can certainly put things right. You needn't worry.' The dragon thanked him profusely and went off.

Scanning the ranks of his ministers at Court next morning, the Emperor noticed that Wei Chêng was not in his usual place. 'You must get him to come here at once, and keep him occupied all day,' said one of the other ministers, when he heard the Emperor's dream. 'That is the only way to keep your promise and save the dragon.'

Meanwhile Wei Chêng, sitting in his house at night, surveying the constellations and burning rare incense, suddenly heard the cry of a crane high up in the sky, and in a moment there alighted a heavenly messenger, bearing instructions from the Jade Emperor that Wei Chêng was in dream to execute the dragon king of the Ching River at noon next day. Wei Chêng accordingly purified himself, tested the sword of his intelligence and the free fling of his soul, and kept away from Court. But when the Emperor's summons came he dared not delay, and hastily robing himself he went back to Court at once with the messenger, and apologised for his absence. 'I am not complaining,' said the Emperor, and when they had discussed State affairs for a while, he sent for a draughts board and invited Wei Chêng to a game of draughts. Just before noon, when there were still a good many pieces on the board, Wei Chêng's head suddenly nodded, he began to snore heavily, and was evidently fast asleep. The Emperor smiled. 'No wonder he is tired,' thought the Emperor, 'when one thinks of all the public business he has on his shoulders,' and he did not attempt to wake him.

When at last Wei Chêng woke up, he was appalled to find that he had dozed in the Imperial presence, and flung himself at the Emperor's feet, saying, 'I deserve death a thousand times, I suddenly felt tired; I don't know why it happened. I beg your Majesty to pardon me for this gross disrespect.'

'Get up,' said the Emperor, 'you've done nothing disrespectful.' Then emptying the remaining pieces off the board he suggested that they should start a new game. They were just setting the pieces, when in rushed two captains, carrying a dragon's head dripping with blood. They flung it at the Emperor's feet, crying, 'Your Majesty, we have heard of seas becoming shallow and rivers running dry. But of so strange a thing as this we have never heard tell.' 'Where does this thing come from?' Wei Chêng and the Emperor exclaimed in chorus. 'To the south of the Thousand Steps Gallery, at the top of Cross Street,' they said, 'it fell from the clouds, and we thought it right to inform you at once.' 'What does all this mean?' asked the Emperor, turning much perturbed to Wei Chêng. 'It is the head of the dragon that I killed in dream just now, when I fell asleep,' he said. 'But while you were asleep,' said the Emperor, 'you never moved hand or foot, nor had you a sword. How can you have beheaded this dragon . . . ?' The Emperor was very sad. He had undertaken to save the dragon, and failed to keep his promise. At last he composed himself, and gave orders that the dragon's head should be hung in the market, as a spectacle for the people of Ch'ang-an. That evening in his palace he continually thought of how the dragon had begged for his help, and felt utterly wretched at having failed entirely to protect it from its fate. He worried so much that in the end he began to feel quite ill.

At the second watch a sound of weeping was heard outside the palace gates, and the Emperor became more agitated than ever. A moment later there appeared before him the figure of the dragon king, carrying his gory head in his hand. 'Give me back my life!' the head cried. 'Yesterday you promised faithfully that you would save me; yet when the time came, you set your minister to cut off my head. Come back with me. I am going to impeach you, impeach you before Yama, king of Death.' And he laid hands on the Emperor, who tried again and again to shake him off. He tried too to cry for help, but the cry stuck in his throat. So violent was his struggle that sweat flowed over all his frame.

When at last he came to himself, the apparition had vanished. 'A ghost, a ghost!' he cried, and neither he nor his queens and concubines, in fear and trembling, could sleep a wink for all the rest of the night. At dawn his ministers waited in vain for the Emperor to appear at Court, and the sun was well up when at last a messenger informed them that the Emperor was indisposed, and the Court would not be held. News came that the Court physician had been summoned, and when he came out of the palace the waiting courtiers asked him anxiously what kind of sickness it was. 'His Majesty's pulse is irregular,' he said. 'It misses beats, and then is over-frequent. He talks wildly of seeing a ghost. The pulse showed one intermission to every ten beats. There is no humour in the five entrails. I fear the disease will prove fatal within seven days.'

His verdict caused consternation among the assembled officials. In the midst of the confusion came a message from the Emperor, summoning Hsü Mao-kung and other ministers to his bedside. Addressing them in a firm voice, his Majesty said: 'Wise counsellors, from my nineteenth year I waged war on four frontiers, and for years on end took part in fierce campaigns. In all that time I was never once assailed by spirits of the dead; yet now I have begun to see ghosts.' 'In your conquests,' said his minister Wei-ch'ih, 'you took countless lives. Why should you begin now to fear ghosts?' 'Believe me or not,' said the Emperor, 'as soon as night comes on, bricks and tiles hurtle about just outside my room, and ghosts or goblins scream in a manner truly terrible. If it were in the daytime, I could make shift to put up with it, but on dark nights it is unendurable.' 'Your Majesty need not be disquieted,' said the minister Ch'in Shu-pao. 'I and my colleague Hu Ching-tê will tonight mount guard outside the palace gates, and will find out what spirit it is that is haunting you.' The offer was accepted, and the two ministers, in full armour and axe in hand, took up their position outside the palace gates. But dawn came without the slightest sign of any apparition. The Emperor had a good night's rest, and in the morning sent handsome rewards to the two

109

watchers. The same precaution was taken for several nights in succession, with the same result. But the Emperor was able to take very little nourishment, and his condition became more and more grave. At the end of this period, the Emperor sent for the two ministers and said that he could not bear the idea of their being put to this inconvenience any longer. 'I shall send for a clever painter,' he said, 'to make your portraits and fasten them up on each side of the gate. Would not that be a good plan?' The ministers accordingly dressed up in armour, and posed for the painter. Their portraits were fastened up on the gate, and nothing happened all night. However, when this had gone on for several nights, a great din was suddenly heard at the back gate of the palace, tiles again hurtled through the air, and in the morning the news came that the Emperor had been as badly disturbed as ever. 'We seem to have dealt successfully with the front gate,' said Hsü Mao-kung. 'The best thing would be to get Wei Chêng to guard the back gate.'

So when night came, Wei Chêng donned his armour, and, with the sword with which he had beheaded the dragon in his hand, he took his stand outside the back gate. Nothing happened all night, but in the morning the Emperor was much worse. During the day the Empress, despairing of his recovery, summoned the ministers and discussed with them the details of the Imperial interment. The Emperor himself gave final instructions upon vital points of national policy, and named the Prince of Ch'u as his successor. He was then washed, put into fresh clothing, and lay awaiting his end. Wei Chêng now approached the bed, and pulling at the Imperial bedclothes whispered, 'Your Majesty, have no anxiety. I have a plan which will ensure that you will yet live many years.' 'The sickness has entered the marrow of my bones,' said the Emperor. 'I am at the very point of death. How can you hope to save me?' 'I have a letter,' said Wei Chêng, 'which I shall give you to take with you to the realms of death. It is addressed to Ts'ui Chio, one of the Judges of the Dead.' 'I have never heard of him,' said the Emperor. 'He was a minister of the founder of our

110

dynasty,' said Wei Chêng, 'and rose to be vice-president of the Board of Rites. He was held in great estimation, and when he died he was put in charge of the archives of the Court of Death. He often appears to me in dreams, and if you take this letter as an introduction to him, he will certainly oblige me by sending you back.'

The Emperor took the letter and put it in his sleeve. Then his eyes grew dim and he died. His wives and concubines, his heir and all his ministers, mourned for him with exemplary piety, and the body was duly laid in state in the Hall of the White Tiger.

If you do not know how the Emperor came to life again, you must read what is told in the next chapter.

Chapter 11

Everything was dim and blurred; but it seemed to the Emperor that he was standing outside the Tower of the Five Phoenixes. A little way off he saw a groom holding his war-charger and motioning to him to come and ride to the hunt. The Emperor gladly accepted the suggestion, and set off in that direction. But when he had gone some way, he suddenly became aware that horse and groom had both vanished. He was in wild country, walking all alone. He was looking about for some path or track, when he heard a voice shouting at him: 'This way, great Emperor of T'ang, this way!' Going in the direction of the voice, he found a man kneeling down and crying, 'Forgive me, great King, for having come only this far to meet you.' 'Who are you,' asked the Emperor, 'and why did you come out to meet me?' 'About half a month ago,' said he, 'in the Halls of Death I came across the Dragon of the Ching River, who complained that your Majesty first promised to save him, and then had him be-headed, and that the Senior Judge of the Dead had sent demons to arrest you and bring you to trial. That is why I expected that you would be coming this way. My name is Ts'ui Chio, and I was once vice-president of the Board of Rites. Now I am an assistant judge at the Courts of the Dead.' 'This is indeed a fortunate meeting,' said the Emperor, motioning Ts'ui to rise from his knees. 'I have a letter for you from my minister Wei Chêng. And he took the letter out of his sleeve.

This was what Ts'ui Chio read: Your junior, Wei Chêng, unworthy of your love, bows his head and salutes his vener-able bond-brother Ts'ui. Looking back upon our meetings in old days, I seem to see you before me, and hear the sound of your voice. But years have sped since I received the benefit of your advice. At stated times and seasons I make offerings to your soul, but do not know whether you receive them. You have indeed been kind enough to inform me in dreams of your high promotion; but the worlds of Light and Darkness lie far apart, and we cannot meet face to face. It occurred to me, when his Majesty the Emperor suddenly passed away, that he would certainly come across you at the tribunal of the dead. I beg of you, in remembrance of our friendship while you were alive, to put in a word for his Majesty, in case there is any question of his being allowed to return to life. Thanking you again, I must now close.

'I heard about Wei Chêng killing the dragon in a dream,' said Ts'ui Chio. 'A remarkable feat! I know that he has been very kind in looking after my descendants. Your Majesty may rest assured that, having received this letter, I shall see to it that your Majesty returns to the World of Light, and to your Palace!'

At this point two servants carrying a huge umbrella-of-state, with long streamers, arrived crying, 'The King of Death requests your presence!' The Emperor let them take charge of him, and he soon arrived at a gate above which was the inscription 'Tribunal of the Realms of Darkness,' written in letters of gold. Going in, he came to a street at the side of which stood his predecessor Li Yüan, his elder brother Li Chien-chêng and his deceased younger brother Li Yüan-chi. They came forward crying, 'Here is Shih-min!' His brothers clutched at him, imploring him to save them. He tried to slip past, but they barred his path. At last Ts'ui Chio told a hook-tusked, blue-faced demon to drive them back, and the Emperor was able to proceed. Soon they came to a high, green-tiled platform. There was a tinkle of girdle-jades, a waft of strange perfume, and a number of torch-bearers arrived, followed by the ten Judges of the Dead, who advanced towards the Emperor, bowing low. He did not dare accept their homage, and stood hesitating. 'We are kings of the dead in the World of Darkness, you are a king of men in the World of Light. We and you each have our sphere, and need not stand on overmuch ceremony.' 'I come here to answer for a crime,' said the Emperor, 'and it is not for me to stand upon my rights as a sovereign of the living.'

When they had taken their seats in the Hall, and the

8

Emperor had been motioned to his proper place as defendant, the First Judge addressed him as follows: 'The dragon of the Ching River accuses your Majesty of having promised to save him, and having then beheaded him. What have you to say?' 'It was with the express intention of saving him,' said the Emperor, 'that I invited Wei Chêng to play draughts with me. Unfortunately Wei Chêng fell asleep, and in his dream he executed this dragon. What happened was due to a momentary nervous breakdown which incapacitated my minister, and in any case the dragon was guilty of a mortal offence. I can't see that I am to blame.' 'We are quite aware,' said the Judge, 'that even before this dragon was born it was already entered in the Book of Fate that he was to be beheaded by a human official. But as he made this complaint about you we were under an obligation to bring your Majesty here, and investigate the charge. We shall now submit him to the action of the Wheel of Incarnation and he will enter upon a new existence. It only remains to ask your Majesty to step down, and forgive us for the inconvenience to which you have been put.' He then ordered the records to be brought, that he might see how long the Emperor had still to live. Ts'ui, whose duty it was to keep the archives, hurried off to the office where they were kept, and taking out the file where the dossiers of all the kings in the world were kept, he turned up that of the king of T'ang, and found that he was destined to die in the thirteenth year of the period Chêng-kuan. He quickly seized a brush and added three strokes. Then he presented the papers. The First Judge glanced at them, and saw that the Emperor was to die in the thirty-third year of Chêng-kuan. 'How long have you been on the throne?' he asked. 'Thirteen years,' said the Emperor. 'That gives you twenty more years to live,' said the Judge. 'There is no need to detain you any further.' Ts'ui and a captain-ghost called Chu were detailed to escort him back to life. As he was going out, he turned and asked whether he might feel happy about the various members of his family, or whether any of them was in danger. 'They are all quite safe,' said the Judge, 'except your younger sister. It does not look as though she has long to live.' The Emperor thanked him, and added, 'I should very much like to send you a little present of some kind when I get back. How about some melons?' 'We have plenty of western melons and eastern melons,' said the Judge. 'But we are very badly off for southern melons.' 'I'll make a point of sending you some,' said the Emperor. Then, guided by Chu, who led the way with his ghost-guiding banner, and Ts'ui escorting him in the rear, the Emperor set out for the Realm of Light.

They crossed the River of Death and came presently to the City of the Slain. As he entered, the Emperor's ears were assailed by a hubbub of clamouring voices. He could clearly distinguish the words 'Li Shih-min has come!' A moment later a throng of pitiable ghosts, some headless, some with mangled limbs or bodies deformed by the rack, pressed about him shouting, 'Give us back our lives!' He tried to evade them, crying to Ts'ui for help. 'Those,' said Ts'ui, 'are the ghosts of brigands and robbers who were caught and put to death. Here there is no one to receive them, and they are cut off from Salvation. They have no money or belongings, and are indeed what is known as *pretas* or hungry ghosts. If you gave them some money you would soon be rid of them.' 'I came here empty-handed,' said the Emperor. 'How am I to get money?' 'Among the living,' said Ts'ui, 'there is one who has credit with us for great sums of silver and gold. You can borrow from him on my guarantee, and scatter alms among these ghosts. Then they will let you pass.' 'Who is this man?' the Emperor asked. 'He is called Hsiang Liang,' said Ts'ui. 'And there are thirteen casks of silver and gold to his credit here. You can repay him what you borrow when you get back to life.' So the Emperor borrowed silver and gold, and Captain Chu flung it among the ghosts. 'Divide it fairly between you and let his Majesty pass,' Ts'ui cried to them. 'When he gets back, he will have a great mass said for you, and you shall all be saved.'

Setting out again, they came presently to a gate where Ts'ui said, 'This is almost the end of your journey. I shall now leave you in the hands of Captain Chu, who will escort you on the short remaining stage. Don't forget to celebrate the Great Mass for the salvation of the souls of the hungry. A king against whom no tongue clamours in the underworld for vengeance, will rule long years in peace.' He parted from Ts'ui and followed Chu through the gate. At the far side they found a dappled palfry, ready saddled. Chu helped him to mount it, and in a single, short gallop the Emperor came to the banks of the Wei River, which ran to the south of his capital. In the river were two golden carp sporting together and leaping in and out of the waves. The Emperor found them delightful to look at and, reining in his horse, he watched them attentively. 'There's no time to lose,' cried Chu, coming up from behind. 'You must press on to the City.' But the Emperor continued to gaze at the river. Suddenly, with a loud cry, Chu pushed the horse and its rider into the river.

Meanwhile the Emperor's family and ministers, and all the ladies of the Court, were gathered round the coffin in the Hall of the White Tiger, sadly performing the last rites of the Imperial mourning. Suddenly there came from within the coffin a stifled cry, 'He has drowned me, he has drowned me!' The mourners were so startled that no one dared approach the coffin and see what was amiss. At last the upright Hsü, the valiant Ch'in and the dauntless Ching-tê approached the coffin, and bending over it said, 'If your Majesty is in any sort of discomfort, we beg that you will tell us about it frankly. But we must ask you not to indulge in any spookeries or ghost-tricks, or you will unnerve your family.' 'It isn't a question of spookeries or anything of the kind,' insisted the minister Wei Chêng. 'The simple fact of the matter is that his Majesty has come back to life. Bring tools at once.' They accordingly prised open the coffin, and there was the Emperor sitting inside, still shouting, 'He's drowned me. Will no one fish me out?' 'Your Majesty will soon come to your senses,' they said, supporting him on each side. 'Your ministers are all here in attendance upon you.' 'I was in a very awkward fix just now,' said the Emperor, opening his eyes. 'I had hardly escaped from the Courts of

Death, when I was pushed into the water and almost drowned.' 'Pray calm yourself,' said his ministers, 'and tell us what water it was that you were drowning in.' 'I was on horseback,' he said, 'and had just reached the Wei river, when I noticed a pair of fishes playing in the stream. While I was watching them, Captain Chu pushed my horse, and I fell headlong into the river.' 'Your Majesty is not yet quite in possession of your living senses,' said Wei Chêng. The Court physician was hastily summoned, and prescribed restorative medicines, and gruel was prepared. After a few doses the Emperor was completely restored and capable of transacting affairs.

At next day's Court, after pronouncing a general amnesty, the Emperor issued an appeal for a volunteer who would undertake to bring melons to the Judges of the Dead. At the same time he ordered the Treasurer to go with gold and silver to K'ai-fêng, and repay Hsiang Liang. After a few days a certain Liu Ch'üan, a man of considerable wealth, answered the appeal with regard to the melons. It appeared that one day his wife, Blue Lotus, was standing at the door of the house, when a priest passed by, and she took out her golden hair-pin and gave it to him as alms. Liu spoke roughly to her, saying that a woman had no right to be in the front part of the house at all. Blue Lotus, stung to the quick by his reproaches, immediately hanged herself, leaving behind her two little girls who wept piteously night and day. Liu now began to feel such remorse that he decided to end his life, and he was quite ready to take the melons with him. When he reported to the Emperor, he was asked to go to the storerooms, where he was given a pair of southern melons, yellow cash was put into his sleeve, and a dose of poison into his mouth.

He arrived at the frontier-gates of Death carrying the melons on his head. When the guardian ghost asked him his business, he explained that he was bringing the melons as a present to the Judges of the Dead from his majesty, the King of China. The guardian hesitated to show him in. 'He's a truthful, reliable fellow, that Emperor!' said Yama, King of

Death. 'That's fine!' He took the melons, and asked Liu who he was. 'I am called Liu Ch'üan,' said Liu. 'My wife hanged herself, leaving me with two small girls. I decided to do away with myself, and wishing at the same time to do a service to my country, I undertook to bring with me this present of melons which the Emperor of China wishes to give your Majesty as a thank-offering.' When Yama and the Judges heard this they sent for the ghost of Blue Lotus, whom the ghostly messengers at once discovered and brought to Liu. Reference to the Registers of Death showed that both of them were destined to live to a ripe old age. But when Yama ordered them to be taken back to life, the messenger objected that Blue Lotus's spirit had been in the underworld for a considerable time, and he doubted whether the body which she had left behind would still be serviceable. 'The Emperor's sister Jade Bud is due to die,' said Yama. 'You had better borrow her body.'

So the messenger took the souls of Liu and his wife to the frontiers of the World of Death; and if you do not know the manner of their return to life, you must listen to what is told in the next chapter.

Chapter 12

The gale of dark wind that blew through the gates of Death when they were opened, carried Liu, his wife and the demon that escorted them, all the way to the city of Ch'ang-an. Liu's soul was blown straight to the Imperial Stores; but Blue Lotus's soul was carried to the inner gardens. It happened that at this time the princess Jade Bud was walking slowly on the green moss under the blossoming trees. The demon-escort gave her a shove, and she fell on to the ground. Whereupon he filched her soul and inserted Blue Lotus's in its place. Then he vanished to the Realms of Death.

The princess's attendants, seeing her lying as though dead, rushed into the Palace of Golden Bells, crying 'Our lady the princess has fallen down dead!' The Empress in turn rushed in consternation to the Emperor, who nodded and sighed, saying 'This does not surprise me. When I asked the Judges of Death about the prospects of my family, they told me that my sister had not long to live.' When they all went to the spot where the princess had fallen, they found that she was still breathing faintly. 'Raise no cry!' commanded the Emperor. 'We must not disturb her.' He then supported the princess's head with his hand and after a moment announced, 'She is coming to.' The princess now suddenly rolled over and cried, 'Wait for me, husband! I can't keep pace with you.' 'Sister,' said the Emperor, 'we are all here.' She raised her head and stared at him. 'Who are you,' she cried, 'and how dare you lay hands upon me?' 'I am your royal brother, royal sister,' he said. 'I haven't got any royal brother,' she cried, 'and I am not any one's royal sister, either. I am Blue Lotus, and my husband is Liu Ch'üan. We are both from the city of Chün-chou. Three months ago I had words with my husband and hanged myself from the house-beam with my sash. My husband followed me to death, bringing some melons as a present to the Judges of the Dead. Yama took pity on us and sent us back to life. He went on ahead, and hurrying after him I tripped and fell. But that's no reason why you should mishandle me. Here you are, mauling me about, and you didn't even know my name!' 'I can't make head or tail of this,' said the Emperor. 'Evidently she has hurt herself and is delirious.' He ordered the Court physician to bring medicines, and help the princess back to her apartments.

Presently it was announced that the melon-bearer had returned, and Liu Ch'üan was shown in, and gave a full report on his mission. 'But what has become of my wife,' he wound up, 'I have no idea.' 'Did Yama say anything in particular to her?' asked the Emperor. 'He said nothing,' replied Liu, 'but I heard a demon officer say that her body would be no good, as she had been dead too long, and Yama said, "The princess Jade Bud is due to die; you had better take her body and put Blue Lotus's soul into it." I don't know where this princess is to be found. If I did, I should go and call upon her.'

'Why, that explains everything!' said the Emperor. 'You remember how the princess said, "Husband, wait for me," and so on. All is now clear.' 'Let us send for the princess herself,' suggested Wei Chêng, 'and see what she has to say.' The ladies who went to fetch the princess found her in her rooms, shouting, 'What are you trying to dose me for? This isn't my home. I live in a decent tiled house, not in a sickly yellow place like this, that looks as if it had got the jaundice. Let me out, let me out!'

A number of ladies-in-waiting and eunuchs caught hold of her and carried her, still shouting and protesting, into the Emperor's presence. 'Would you recognise your husband?' he asked. 'What a question!' she exclaimed. 'We were pledged to one another when we were children, and I have had children by him. How could I fail to know him?' Liu Ch'üan was then sent for, and she rushed at him saying, 'Why ever did you go on ahead like that, and not wait for me? I stumbled and fell down. When I came to, I found all these people gathered round me. I'd like to know what it all means.' Liu did not know what to do. The voice was certainly that of his wife; but her appearance was entirely different. The kindly Emperor stepped in, ordering that all the princess's toilet boxes, dresses, combs and what-not should be handed over to Liu Ch'üan, exactly as though he had been giving him his sister in marriage. He also granted Liu permanent exemption from forced labour, and sent the pair back to Chün-chou.

Meanwhile the minister Wei-ch'ih went to Kai-fêng with a store of silver and gold, to pay back the money lent by Hsiang Liang. Now Hsiang Liang was a water-carrier, and his wife made a living by selling pottery. They only spent on themselves what was necessary to keep them alive; all the rest they gave to priests, or spent on paper cash which they dedicated and burned. Consequently, though in this world they ranked as pious people, but very poor, in the world below they gradually accumulated a very considerable fortune. When Wei-ch'ih came to their door, laden with silver and gold, their astonishment knew no bounds, accompanied as he was by a numerous following of horsemen and coaches. They were reduced to speechless consternation, and throwing themselves on to their knees they bowed low and long. 'Rise!' cried Wei-ch'ih, 'I have merely come to repay the money that you were good enough to lend to his Majesty the Emperor.' 'We have never lent money to anyone,' they stammered, 'and cannot possibly accept what does not belong to us.' 'I am aware,' said he, 'that you are poor people. But owing to your constant alms and dedication of paper cash to the spirits of the world below, you have great sums to your credit in that world. Recently when the Emperor spent three days in the realms of Death, he had occasion to borrow heavily from your account there, and now I have come to repay the debt.' 'It is true,' they said, 'that we have something to our account in that world. But what proof have we that his Majesty borrowed from us there? We could not dream of accepting.' 'The loan,' said Wei-ch'ih, 'was authorised by Ts'ui Chio, one of the assessors there, and he could bear testimony.' 'That's as may be,' they said, 'but nothing will induce us to accept.' Finding that they were obdurate, Wei-ch'ih sent a report to the Emperor, who remarked on reading it, 'Such virtue is indeed rare among the rich!' And he issued a rescript, that with the money a temple was to be built, and a shrine at the side of it, dedicated to the Hsiangs. A site was found on ground not required either by the people or the military authorities, to the extent of fifty acres, and when the building was finished it was called the Hsiang Kuo National Temple, and a great inscription gave an account of its inauguration and the fact that the building of it had been superintended by Wei-ch'ih. This is the Great Hsaing Kuo Temple that still stands today.

The next thing to think about was the General Mass for the Dead that the Emperor had promised to celebrate. Priests of particular learning and piety were collected from all over China, and asked to sit in solemn congregation, and select from among their number one whose outstanding holiness fitted him to take charge of the ceremonies. The choice fell upon the priest Hsüan Tsang, who was brought before the Emperor and presented by the minister Hsiao Yü and the rest, who said, 'We have carried out the august commands, and this is the holy man on whom the choice has fallen. He is called Hsüan Tsang.' After reflecting for a while, the Emperor said, 'The choice is a good one. I have heard of this priest, and it is certain that he is a man of high virtue and great powers of concentration.' And turning to Hsüan Tsang he said, 'I bestow upon you the rank of Supreme Controller of all priests and all matters of religion throughout the land,' And in addition he gave him a cassock of brocade and a golden skull-cap, bidding him use his best endeavours. Then he sent him back to his own temple to choose a lucky day for the great ceremony. Hsüan Tsang, when the necessary seats and benches had been made and the music provided, selected one thousand two hundred worthy priests to take part in the ceremony. The third day of the ninth month was found by the astrologers to be favourable, and on that day began the Great Mass that was to last for forty-nine days, and was attended by the Emperor and his family, the Court and all the ministers civil and military.

Meanwhile the Bodhisattva Kuan-yin had been looking everywhere in Ch'ang-an for a priest to fetch the scriptures from India. Hearing that the Emperor T'ai Tsung was celebrating a great Mass, and that the ceremony was being directed by that River Float with whose birth she had herself been connected, 'Who,' she asked herself, 'could be better fitted for that mission than he?' And she set out into the streets, taking with her Moksha, and the treasures that Buddha had given to her. 'What were these treasures?' you ask. They were a magic brocaded cassock, and a priest's staff with nine rings. Apart from these, there were the three magic fillets which she left in safe keeping for future use, only taking with her the cassock and staff. Wandering about the streets of Ch'ang-an was a stupid priest who had failed to be chosen to take part in the Mass. Seeing the Bodhisattva, disguised as a shabby priest, barefoot and in rags, holding up this shining cassock as though for sale, he remembered that he still had a few strings of cash upon him, and coming forward he said, 'What would you take for the cassock?' 'The cassock,' said Kuan-yin, 'is worth five thousand pounds; the staff, two thousand.' 'Seven thousand pounds for a couple of coarse, low-class articles like that! You must be mad,' he said. 'Why, if it were guaranteed that the user of them would be immortal, or that he would become a living Buddha, they wouldn't fetch that price. Be off with you! I don't want them.'

The Bodhisattva said not a word more, but signing to Moksha went on her way. They had not gone far before they reached the Eastern Flower Gate, where whom should they meet but the minister Hsiao Yü, just returning from Court. His outriders were clearing the streets, but Kuan-yin, so far from removing herself, stood right in the minister's path, holding up the cassock. He reined in his horse, and seeing this dazzling object held up in front of him, he told a servant to ask the price. 'Five thousand pounds for the cassock and two thousand for the staff,' said Kuan-yin. 'What makes them so expensive?' asked Hsiao. 'The cassock,' said Kuan-yin, 'would be valuable to some people and quite the reverse to others; it would cost some people a lot of money, and others none at all.' 'What does that mean?' asked Hsiao. 'The wearer of my cassock,' said Kuan-yin, 'will not be drowned or poisoned or meet wild beasts upon his way. But that is only if he is a good man; if it gets on to the back of a gluttonous, lustful priest, or one who does not keep his vows, or of a layman who destroys scriptures and speaks evil of Buddha, he will rue the day that he saw this cassock.' 'And what do you mean,' asked Hsiao, 'by saying that it would cost some people a lot of money and others none at all?'

'To a purchaser who does not reverence Buddha's Law and Three Treasures, the price of the cassock and staff together would be seven thousand pounds,' said Kuan-yin. 'But a pious and reverent man, devoted to our Buddha, could have them both for the asking.' Hearing this, Hsiao dismounted, and bowing respectfully, 'Reverend Sir,' he said, 'the Emperor of this great land is himself a most devout man, and all his ministers vie with one another in carrying out his behests. At present he is celebrating a Great Mass, and this cassock might well be worn by the high priest Hsüan Tsang, who is in charge of the whole ceremony. Let us go to the palace and speak to the Emperor about this.'

The Emperor was delighted at this proposal, and at once told Hsüan Tsang to put on the cassock and hold the staff in his hand. Then he appointed a retinue to accompany him, and had him led through the city in triumph, for all the world like a successful candidate at the examinations. In the great city of Ch'ang-an travelling merchants and tradesmen, princes and nobles, writers and scholars, grown men and young girls all fought with one another for good places from which to view the procession. 'A noble priest! A Lohan come to earth, a living Bodhisattva!' they cried in admiration when they saw Hsüan Tsang pass. And the priests in his temple when he returned, seeing him thus accoutred, could scarcely believe that it was not the Bodhisattva Kshitigarbha himself who had come to visit them.

Time passed, and now at last came the final ceremonies of the forty-ninth day, at which Hsüan Tsang was to deliver the closing sermon. 'The Great Mass closes today,' said Kuan-yin to Moksha. 'Let us mingle in the throng, so that we may see how the ceremonies are conducted and what blessing there is in our gift, and hear what school of Buddhism he preaches.' The great Hsüan Tsang, mounted on a high dais, first read the Sūtra on the Salvation of the Dead, then discussed the Collect upon the Security of kingdoms, and finally expounded the Exhortation to Pious Works. At this point Kuan-yin approached the dais, and cried in a loud voice, 'Why can't you give us some Big Vehicle Scriptures?' So far from being put out by this interruption, Hsüan Tsang was delighted to hear of other scriptures, and scrambling down from the dais he saluted his interrupter and said, 'Reverend Sir, forgive me for not knowing that I had one so learned as you in my audience. It is true that we have none of us any knowledge of the Big Vehicle, and have only expounded the Little Vehicle.' 'Your Little Vehicle,' said Kuan-yin, 'cannot save the souls of the dead, and only leads to general misapprehension and confusion. I have three sections of Great Vehicle teaching, called the Tripitaka or Three Baskets. These can carry the souls of the dead to Heaven, can save all those that are in trouble, can add immeasurably to life's span, and can deliver those that trust in it from the comings and goings of Incarnation.'

At this point one of the ushers rushed to the Emperor and announced that two shabby priests had interrupted the Master, pulled him down from the dais and started some nonsensical argument with him. The Emperor ordered them to be seized and brought to him. On appearing before the Emperor they did not prostrate themselves or even salute him, but merely asked what he wanted of them. 'Are you not the priest who gave me the cassock the other day?' said the Emperor. 'I am,' said Kuan-yin. 'You had a perfect right,' said the Emperor, 'to come here and listen to the preaching, eat with the other priests, and go away quietly. But you have no business to interrupt the preaching and disturb the whole proceedings.' 'Your preacher,' Kuan-yin said, 'knows only about the Little Vehicle, which cannot save souls. We possess the Tripitaka of the Big Vehicle, which saves the souls of the dead and succours those that are in peril.' The Emperor was delighted at this news, and asked at once where it was. 'It is in India,' said Kuan-yin, 'at the temple of the Great Thunder Clap, where the Buddha Tathāgata dwells.' 'Do you know these teachings by heart?' asked the Emperor. 'I do,' said the Bodhisattva. 'Then Hsüan Tsang shall retire,' said the Emperor, 'and you shall mount the dais and expound them to us.' But instead of doing so Kuan-yin floated up into the sky and revealed herself in all the glory of her true form, holding the willow-spray and the sacred vase, while Moksha stood at her left side, holding his staff.

The Emperor hastened to prostrate himself, and all his ministers knelt down and burned incense, while the audience, priests, nuns, officers, craftsmen and merchants, bowed down, crying, 'The Bodhisattva, the Bodhisattva!'

The Emperor's joy was so great that he forgot his rivers and hills, his ministers in their excitement broke every rule of etiquette, and all the multitude murmured again and again 'Glory be to the Great Bodhisattva Kuan-yin.' His Majesty decided to have a picture of the Bodhisattva painted by a skilful artist, in full colours. His choice fell upon Wu Tao-tzu, that genius of the brush, that prodigy of portraiture, that fabulous embodiment of vision and inspiration. It was this painter who afterwards made the portraits of the heroes of the dynasty in the Tower of Rising Smoke. He now wielded his magic brush and rendered every detail of these sacred forms. Presently the figures began to recede further and further into the sky, and finally their golden effulgence could be seen no more.

At this point the Emperor dismissed the assembly, and declared that the next thing to do was to find a traveller who would go to India and fetch the Scriptures. An enquiry was made in the temple, and Hsüan Tsang immediately came forward and bowing low said, 'I am a humble cleric, devoid of any capacity; but I am ready to undertake the quest of these Scriptures, be the fatigues and difficulties what they may, if by doing so I may promote the security of your

Majesty's streams and hills.' The Emperor was delighted, and raising him from his knees with his royal hand, 'Reverend Sir,' he said, 'if indeed you are willing to do me this loyal service, undeterred by the length of the journey and all the mountains and rivers that you will have to cross, I will make you my bond-brother.' And true to his word, in front of the Buddha image in that temple, he bowed four times to Hsüan Tsang and addressed him as 'Holy Priest, my brother.' Hsüan Tsang on his side, burning incense before the Buddha, swore to do all that lay in his power to reach India. 'And if I do not reach India and do not bring back the Scriptures, may I fall into the nethermost pit of Hell, rather than return empty-handed to China.'

When Hsüan Tsang rejoined the other priests, they pressed round him, asking whether it was indeed true that he had sworn to go to India. 'For I have heard,' one of them said, 'that it is a very long way and that on the road there are many tigers, panthers and evil spirits. I fear you will not come back to us alive.' 'I have taken my oath,' said Hsüan Tsang, 'and I must faithfully fulfil it. I know well enough that the hazards of such a journey are great.' And presently he said, 'My disciples, I may be away for two or three years, or five, or seven. If you see the branches of the pine tree at the gate turning eastward, you will know I am coming back. If not, it will mean that I shall never return.'

Early next day, in the presence of all his ministers, the Emperor signed a rescript authorizing Hsüan Tsang's quest, and stamped it with the seal of free passage. The astrologers announced that the posture of the heavens made the day particularly favourable for the start of a long journey. At this point, Hsüan Tsang himself was announced. 'Brother,' said the Emperor, 'I am told that this would be a lucky day for you to start. Here are your travelling papers, and here is a golden bowl for you to collect alms in during your journey. I have chosen two followers to go with you, and a horse for you to ride. It only remains for you to start.' Hsüan Tsang was ready enough, and taking the Emperor's present set out towards the gates of the city, accompanied by the Emperor

127

and a host of officials. When they reached the gates, they found that the priests of the Hung-fu temple were waiting there with a provision of winter and summer clothing. When it had been added to the luggage, the Emperor told a servant to bring wine, and raising the cup he asked Hsüan Tsang if he had a by-name. 'Being a priest,' said Hsüan Tsang, 'I have not thought it proper to assume a by-name.' 'The Bodhisattva mentioned,' said the Emperor, 'that the Scriptures in India are called the Tripitaka. How would it be if you took "Tripitaka" as your by-name?' Hsüan Tsang accepted with thanks, but when he was offered the wine-cup, he declined, saying that abstinence from wine was the first rule of priesthood, and that he never took it. This is an exceptional occasion,' said the Emperor, 'and the wine is not at all strong; just drink one cup to speed you on your journey.' Tripitaka dared not refuse; but just as he was going to drink, the Emperor stooped down and with his royal fingers scooped up a handful of dust and threw it into the cup. At first Tripitaka could not make out why he had done this, but the Emperor said laughing, 'Tell me, brother, how long do you expect to be away?' 'I hope,' said Tripitaka, 'to be back in three years.' 'That's a long time,' said the Emperor, 'and you have a long way to go. You would do well to drink this cup, for are we not told that a handful of one's country's soil is worth more than ten thousand pounds of foreign gold?' Then Tripitaka understood why the Emperor had thrown the dust into the cup, drank it down to the last dregs, and set out upon his way. And if you do not know how he fared upon that way, listen to what is told in the next chapter.

Chapter 13

It was three days before the full moon, in the ninth month of the thirteenth year of Chêng Kuan, when Tripitaka, seen off by the Emperor and all his ministers, left the gates of Ch'ang-an. After a day or two of hard riding, he reached the Temple of the Law Cloud. The abbot and some five hundred priests, drawn up in two files, ushered him into the temple. After supper, sitting by lamplight, they discussed questions of religion and the purpose of Tripitaka's quest. Some spoke of how wide the rivers were that he must cross and how high the mountains that he must climb. Some spoke of the roads being infested by panthers and tigers, some of precipices hard to circumvent and demons impossible to overcome. Tripitaka said nothing, but only pointed again and again at his own heart. The priests did not understand what he meant, and when at last they asked him to explain, he said, 'It is the heart alone that can destroy them. I made a solemn vow, standing before the Buddha's image, to carry through this task, come what may. Now that I have started I cannot go back till I have reached India, seen Buddha, got the Scriptures, and turned the wheel of the Law, that our holy sovereign's great dynasty may forever be secure.' 'A loyal, a valiant cleric,' they all cried in chorus, as they escorted Hsüan Tsang to his bed.

Next morning Tripitaka rose early, eager to be on his way again. It was now far on into the autumn, and if he had waited till cockcrow, it would have been the fourth watch before he started. A bright moon glistened on the frosty ground as he and his two followers set out. They had not gone ten leagues when they came to a mountain range. The path they had been following vanished and the going became excessively difficult. It seemed only too probable that they had missed their way. They were discussing the position, when suddenly the ground gave way under their feet and they fell into a deep pit, the horse floundering along with them. They had hardly recovered from their first astonishment when they heard voices calling 'Seize them! Seize them!' and looking up they saw fifty or sixty ogres crowding round the hole. The three travellers were hauled to the surface, and Tripitaka, when he could summon enough courage to look round, saw a demon king, of the most terrifying aspect, who was obviously the leader of the gang. He gave orders that the captives should be bound, and a band of lesser ogres had already trussed them up, and were about to prepare them for eating, when there was a bustle outside and someone announced that My Lord of the Bear-Mount and the Steer Hermit had arrived. Looking up, Tripitaka saw a swarthy fellow followed by a great hulking fellow. The demon king hastened to welcome them, as they came lurching and swaggering along. 'General Yin,' said the one, 'you are looking very pleased with yourself. I congratulate you.' 'General Yin,' said the other, 'you're looking in very fine form. You may congratulate yourself!' 'How have you two been getting on?' asked the demon king. 'Just managing to exist,' said the one. 'Just jogging on somehow,' said the other. While they were talking one of Tripitaka's followers, who had been trussed very tight, screamed with pain. 'Where did you find these three?' asked the swarthy fellow. 'I didn't find them,' said the demon, 'they just came here of their own accord.' The Hermit laughed. 'May we venture to impose on your hospitality?' he asked. 'If you will do me the favour,' said the demon. 'There is more than we should get through at one meal,' said the lord of the Bear Mountain. 'How about eating two, and keeping one?' The demon accordingly gave orders that the two followers should be carved up at once; the heads, hearts and livers were to be offered to the guests. He himself bespoke the arms and legs. The other odds and ends were to go to the sundry lesser ogres. A frightful scrunching ensued, for all the world like a tiger devouring its prey. By the time the meal was over, Tripitaka was almost dead with horror and fright.

It was now beginning to grow light, and the two guests retired. Tripitaka was in the depths of despair, and had lost all hope of escaping with his life, when suddenly an old man appeared, carrying a heavy staff. Coming forward, he pulled at Tripitaka's ropes, which fell away at the first touch. Then he blew into his face, with the result that Tripitaka suddenly revived and, falling upon his knees, profusely thanked his rescuer. 'That's all right,' said the old man. 'Pray get up. And tell me, have you lost anything?' 'My two followers,' said Tripitaka, 'have been devoured by ogres. What has become of my luggage and horses I have no idea.' 'I see a horse over there,' said the old man, 'and two saddle-packs. I don't know whether by any chance they belong to you.' Tripitaka looked in the direction in which the old man was pointing with his staff, and there, sure enough, was the horse, saddle-packs and all, quite unharmed. 'What place is this,' asked Tripitaka, brightening a little, 'and what are the three ogres that haunt it?' 'It is called the Two Forked Ridge,' said the old man, 'and is a place much infested by tigers and wolves; you would have done well to keep clear of it. As for the ogres, the Hermit is a buffalo-spirit, the lord of the Bear Mountain is a bear-spirit, and General Yin is a tiger-spirit. The other lesser ogres are all animal-spirits of one kind and another. The purity of your inner nature made it impossible for them to eat you. Follow me and I will put you on to the proper path.' Full of gratitude, Tripitaka adjusted the saddle-packs, and pulling the horse by its halter, succeeded in getting it out of the hole. When they were back on the right track, Tripitaka tied up the horse at the path-side and turned to thank the old man, only to discover that he was already rapidly disappearing into the sky, on the back of a white crane. Presently there came fluttering down from the sky a paper-strip on which was written, 'I am the spirit of the Planet Venus, I came to earth on purpose to rescue you. During the course of your journey you will at all times enjoy the assistance of spiritual beings, who will see to it that you do not succumb to the perils that will beset you on your path.'

Tripitaka bowed in the direction whence the strip had come, and then set off alone. He travelled over difficult country for half a day, without seeing any sign of human habitation. He was now very hungry, and the road was extremely precipitous. He was at the height of his difficulties when he heard two tigers roaring just ahead of him and saw behind him several huge serpents twisting and twining. To make matters worse, on his left was some species of deadly scorpion, and on his right a wild beast of unknown species. To cope single-handed with such a situation was clearly impossible, and there was nothing for it but to resign himself to his fate. Soon his horse sank quivering on to its knees and refused to budge. Suddenly a medley of tigers and wolves, with other wild and fearful creatures, set upon him all together. He would have been utterly lost, had there not at this very moment appeared a man with a three-pronged spear in his hand and bow and arrows at his waist. 'Save me, save me!' cried Tripitaka. The man rushed forward and throwing aside his spear, raised Tripitaka from his knees. 'Do not be afraid,' he said. 'I am a hunter, and I came out to find a couple of mountain creatures to eat for my supper. You must forgive me for intruding upon you so unceremoniously.' Tripitaka thanked the hunter, and explained what brought him to this place. 'I live near here,' said the hunter, 'and spend all my time in dealing with tigers and serpents and the like, so that such creatures are afraid at the sight of me and run away. If you indeed come from the Court of T'ang we are fellow-countrymen, for the frontier of the empire is a little way beyond here. Do not be afraid, but follow me back to my house, where you and your horse can rest. Tomorrow I will put you on your way.'

Tripitaka was glad to accept, and set out in company with the hunter. When they had crossed the neighbouring ridge, there came once more the sound of fierce growling. 'That's a "mountain-cat" coming,' said the hunter. 'You sit here, and I will catch it for supper.' Tripitaka was again transfixed by fright. The hunter seized his spear and striding forward began to stalk the tiger. Suddenly a great striped tiger sprang right in his face. Tripitaka, who was entirely unused to watching such dangerous encounters, was once more on the verge of collapse. Man and tiger contended at the foot of the slope for about an hour. At last the creature began to tire, and the hunter was able to dispatch it by a thrust right through the chest. Dragging it away by the ear from the pool of blood in which it lay, the hunter without showing the slightest sign of concern hauled it to the road, remarking casually, 'This is a bit of luck. Here is meat enough to last you for several days.' Tripitaka was lost in admiration. 'Sir,' he said, 'you are a veritable god of the mountains!' 'I think that is going too far,' said the hunter. 'It was a very simple matter!' Then with a spear in one hand, and dragging the dead tiger with the other, he set out upon the road, followed by Tripitaka leading the horse.

They soon came to a mountain farm. At the gate, the hunter let go of the tiger and called to the farm-hands to come and carry it inside, skin it and get it prepared for cooking. 'For I have a guest,' he said. Then he brought Tripitaka in and presented him to his mother, explaining that he was a priest of great piety, who was on a mission to fetch Scriptures from India. 'Tomorrow,' she said, 'is the anniversary of your father's death. Let us ask his reverence to say a Mass, recite a scripture or two, and then start off again the next day.' The Hunter, though a rough, burly tiger-slayer, was very attentive to his mother, and as soon as she made this suggestion he ordered incense-paper to be prepared, and prevailed upon Tripitaka to spend the next day at the farm. It was now getting late, and the farm-hands set out tables and brought in several dishes of cooked tiger-flesh which they laid all sizzling in front of their master and his guest. 'I must tell you,' said Tripitaka, 'that I was admitted to the Order almost as soon as I left my mother's womb, and have never in my life indulged in meats of this kind.' The hunter thought for a while. 'My family,' he said at last, 'has on the contrary for generations past been accustomed to eat meat. So what are we to do? I am sorry to have asked you to do what your conscience forbids.' 'There is no need to worry,' broke in the hunter's mother, 'we can easily make him a vegetarian dish.' And she told her daughter-in-law to boil

133

some rice and make a salad. The hunter, removing himself to some distance, sat down to a meal of tiger's flesh, unseasoned and unsalted, with serpent's flesh, fox-flesh, rabbit and strips of dried venison, served in high-piled dishes. He was just beginning, and had hardly raised his chop-sticks, when he saw that Tripitaka, his palms pressed together, was reciting what he took to be some passage from a holy book. Very much taken aback, the hunter dropped his chop-sticks and rose to his feet. But after reciting only a few sentences, Tripitaka announced that he was ready to be served. 'That was a very short scripture,' said the hunter. 'It wasn't a scripture,' said Tripitaka. 'I was saying grace.' 'You priests certainly have some queer ways,' said the hunter. 'One would think you could at least take a meal without saying your prayers.'

After dinner the hunter took him to a thatched building at the back of the house. The walls were hung with bows, arrows, slings and the like, and over a beam hung two fetid, bloody tiger-skins. The hunter invited him to take a seat, but Tripitaka was very ill at ease in the presence of these gruesome and forbidding objects and hurried out of the building. They soon came to a large paddock, where great masses of chrysanthemums piled their gold and maples blazed their crimson. The hunter called, and ten fat deer sprang out of the bushes and not at all disconcerted by the arrival of human beings, came up nozzling and gambolling. 'These no doubt are creatures that you have tamed,' said Tripitaka. 'Yes,' said the hunter. 'Just as in Ch'ang-an people lay up stores of money, and farmers lay up stores of grain, so we hunters must always keep a few tame beasts, as a provision against dark days.'

Immediately after breakfast next day, the whole household assembled and Tripitaka was asked to begin his recitation. He washed his hands, and assisted by the hunter burnt incense in front of the house-shrine, then bowing to the house-shrine he beat on his wooden fish, and after reciting spells for the purification of the mouth and the body, he read a text on the salvation of souls. After this the hunter asked him to write a prayer-slip for the salvation of the dead, and he recited parts of the Diamond Cutter Scripture and the Scripture of Kuan-yin, each in a clear and loud voice. After the midday meal he recited chapters from the Lotus Scripture and the Scripture of Amitābha, and then told the story of the monks washing away their evil karma. As the day drew on, he burned further incense, along with paper horses and prayer-slips. When all was over, they went to bed.

That night the soul of the hunter's father appeared in dream to every member of the household, saying that he had for long been striving in vain to escape from the torments of the lower world. Now, thanks to the prayers and recitations of this pious priest, the evil karma that restrained him was wiped away, and Yama had ordered that he should be re-born as the child of a rich landowner. He asked them to tender his warmest thanks to his benefactor.

When the hunter's wife told him of her dream, it turned out that he too had a similar dream. Presently his mother came along, saying that she had something to tell him. They both burst out laughing when she told them her dream, which was the same as their own. The whole household was then roused and all in chorus thronged round him, saying, 'Reverend Sir, we cannot sufficiently express to you our gratitude. You have saved the soul of our late master.' 'I cannot think that anything I have done can deserve such thanks,' said Tripitaka. They told him of the dreams, and he was indeed delighted. They asked him to accept silver, but he absolutely refused. 'If you will have the goodness to escort me on the first stage of my journey,' he said, 'that will be ample recompense.'

The women hurriedly made ready some dried provisions, and the hunter, taking with him a few servants, all armed with their hunting gear, set out with Tripitaka upon the highway. Mountain scenery of indescribable beauty stretched out before them. Towards noon they came to a gigantic mountain, up which Tripitaka began to clamber with great pains, while the hunter sprang up it as though he had been walking on flat ground. Halfway up the hunter halted, and turning to Tripitaka, he said, 'I fear at this point we must part.' 'I entreat you to take me just one stage further,' begged Tripitaka. 'Sir,' said the hunter, 'you do not know. This mountain is called the Mountain of the Two Frontiers. It's east side belongs to our land of T'ang; on the west side lies the land of the Tartars. The wolves and tigers on the far side I have not subjected, moreover I have not the right to cross the frontier. You must go on alone.'

Tripitaka wrung his hands in despair, clutched at the hunter's sleeve and wept copiously. At this point there came from under the mountain a stentorian voice, crying repeatedly, 'The Master has come.' Both Tripitaka and the hunter started, in great surprise. If you do not know whose voice it was they heard, listen to what is told in the next chapter.

Chapter 14

The hunter and Tripitaka were still wondering who had spoken, when again they heard the voice saying, 'The Master has come.' The hunter's servants said, 'That is the voice of the old monkey who is shut up in the stone casket of the mountain side.' 'Why, to be sure it is!' said the hunter. 'What old monkey is that?' asked Tripitaka. 'This mountain,' said the hunter, 'was once called the Mountain of the Five Elements. But after our great T'ang Dynasty had carried out its campaigns to the West, its name was changed to Mountain of the Two Frontiers. Years ago a very old man told me that at the time when Wang Mang overthrew the First Han Dynasty, Heaven dropped this mountain in order to imprison a magic monkey under it. He has local spirits as his gaolers, who, when he is hungry give him iron pills to eat, and when he is thirsty give him copper-juice to drink, so that despite cold and short commons he is still alive. That cry certainly comes from him. You need not be uneasy. We'll go down and have a look.'

After going downhill for some way they came to the stone box, in which there was really a monkey. Only his head was visible, and one paw, which he waved violently through the opening, saying, 'Welcome, Master! Welcome! Get me out of here, and I will protect you on your journey to the West.' The hunter stepped boldly up, and removing the grasses from Monkey's hair and brushing away the grit from under his chin, 'What have you got to say for yourself?' he asked. 'To you, nothing,' said Monkey. 'But I have something to ask of that priest. Tell him to come here.' 'What do you want to ask me?' said Tripitaka. 'Were you sent by the Emperor of T'ang to look for Scriptures in India?' asked Monkey. 'I was,' said Tripitaka. 'And what of that?' 'I am the Great Sage Equal to Heaven,' said Monkey. 'Five hundred years ago I made trouble in the Halls of Heaven, and Buddha clamped me down in this place. Not long ago the

Bodhisattva Kuan-yin, whom Buddha had ordered to look around for someone to fetch Scriptures from India, came here and promised me that if I would amend my ways and faithfully protect the pilgrim on his way, I was to be released, and afterwards would find salvation. Ever since then I have been waiting impatiently night and day for you to come and let me out. I will protect you while you are going to get Scriptures and follow you as your disciple.'

Tripitaka was delighted. 'The only trouble is,' he said, 'that I have no axe or chisel, so how am I to get you out?' 'There is no need for axe or chisel,' said Monkey. 'You have only to want me to be out, and I shall be out.' 'How can that be?' asked Tripitaka. 'On the top of the mountain,' said Monkey, 'is a seal stamped with golden letters by Buddha himself. Take it away, and I shall be out.' Tripitaka was for doing so at once, but the hunter took him aside and said there was no telling whether one could believe the monkey or not. 'It's true, it's true!' screamed Monkey from inside the casket. At last the hunter was prevailed upon to come with him and, scrambling back again to the very top, they did indeed see innumerable beams of golden light streaming from a great square slab of rock, on which was imprinted in golden letters the inscription OM MANI PADME HUM.

Tripitaka knelt down and did reverence to the inscription, saying, 'If this monkey is indeed worthy to be a disciple, may this imprint be removed and may the monkey be released and accompany me to the seat of Buddha. But if he is not fit to be a disciple, but an unruly monster who would discredit my undertaking, may the imprint of this seal remain where it is.' At once there came a gust of fragrant wind that carried the six letters of the inscription up into the air, and a voice was heard saying, 'I am the Great Sage's gaoler. Today the time of his penance is ended and I am going to ask Buddha to let him loose.' Having bowed reverently in the direction from which the voice came, Tripitaka and the hunter went back to the stone casket and said to Monkey, 'The inscription is removed. You can come out.'

'You must go to a little distance,' said Monkey. 'I don't want to frighten you.' They withdrew a little way, but heard Monkey calling to them 'Further, further!' They did as they were bid, and presently heard a tremendous crushing and rending. They were all in great consternation, expecting the mountain to come hurtling on top of them, when suddenly the noise subsided, and Monkey appeared, kneeling in front of Tripitaka's horse, crying, 'Master, I am out!' Then he sprang up and called to the hunter, 'Brother, I'll trouble you to dust the grass-wisps from my cheek.' Then he put together the packs and hoisted them on to the horse, which on seeing him became at once completely obedient. For Monkey had been a groom in Heaven, and it was natural that an ordinary horse should hold him in great awe.

Tripitaka, seeing that he knew how to make himself useful and looked as though he would make a pretty tolerable śramana, said to him, 'Disciple, we must give you a name in religion.' 'No need for that,' said Monkey, 'I have one already. My name in religion is "Awe-of-Vacuity."' 'Excellent!' said Tripitaka. 'That fits in very well with the names of my other disciples. You shall be Monkey Aware-of-Vacuity.'

The hunter, seeing that Monkey had got everything ready, said to Tripitaka, 'I am very glad you have been fortunate enough to pick up this excellent disciple. As you are so well provided for, I will bid you good-bye and turn back.' 'I have brought you a long way from home,' said Tripitaka, 'and cannot thank you enough. Please also apologise to your mother and wife for all the trouble I gave, and tell them I will thank them in person on my return.'

Tripitaka had not been long on the road with Monkey and had only just got clear of the Mountain of the Two Frontiers, when a tiger suddenly appeared, roaring savagely and lashing its tail. Tripitaka was terrified, but Monkey seemed delighted. 'Don't be frightened, Master,' he said. 'He has only come to supply me with an apron.' So saying, he took a needle from behind his ear and, turning his face to the wind, made a few magic passes, and instantly it became a huge iron cudgel. 'It is five hundred years since I last used this precious thing,' he said, 'and today it is going to furnish me with a little much-needed clothing.'

Look at him! He strides forward, crying, 'Cursed creature, stand your ground!' The tiger crouched in the dust and dared not budge. Down came the cudgel on its head. The earth was spattered with its blood. Tripitaka rolled off his horse as best he could, crying with an awe-struck voice, 'Heavens! When the hunter killed that stripy tiger yesterday, he struggled with it for hours on end. But this disciple of mine walked straight up to the tiger and struck it dead. True indeed is the saying "Strong though he be, there is always a stronger." ' 'Sit down a while,' said Monkey, 'and wait while I undress him; then when I am dressed, we'll go on.' 'How can you undress him?' said Tripitaka. 'He hasn't got any clothes.' 'Don't worry about me,' said Monkey. 'I know what I am about.' Dear Monkey! He took a hair from his tail, blew on it with magic breath, and it became a sharp little knife, with which he slit the tiger's skin straight down and ripped it off in one piece. Then he cut off the paws and head, and trimmed the skin into one big square. Holding it out, he measured it with his eye, and said, 'A bit too wide. I must divide it in two.' He cut it in half, put one half aside and the other round his waist, making it fast with some rattan that he pulled up from the roadside. 'Now we can go,' he said, 'and when we get to the next house, I'll borrow a needle and thread and sew it up properly.'

'What has become of your cudgel?' asked Tripitaka, when they were on their way again. 'I must explain to you,' said Monkey. 'This cudgel is a piece of magic iron that I got in the Dragon King's palace, and it was with it that I made havoc in Heaven. I can make it as large or as small as I please. Just now I made it the size of an embroidery needle and put it away behind my ear, where it is always at hand in case I need it.' 'And why,' asked Tripitaka, 'did that tiger, as soon as it saw you, crouch down motionless and allow you to strike it just as you chose?' 'The fact is,' said Monkey, 'that not only tigers but dragons too dare not do anything against me. But that is not all. I have such arts as can make rivers turn back in their course, and can raise tempests on the sea. Small wonder, then, that I can filch a tiger's skin. When we get into real difficulties you will see what I am really capable of.'

'Master,' said Monkey presently, 'it is getting late. Over there is a clump of trees, and I think there must be a house. We had better see if we can spend the night there.' Tripitaka whipped his horse, and soon they did indeed come to a farm, outside the gates of which he dismounted. Monkey cried 'Open the door!' and presently there appeared a very old man, leaning on a staff. Muttering to himself, he began to push open the door, but when he saw Monkey, looking (with the tiger skin at his waist) for all the world like a thunder demon, he was terrified out of his wits and could only murmur 'There's a devil at the door, sure enough there's a devil!' Tripitaka came up to him just in time to prevent him hobbling away. 'Old patron,' he said, 'you need not be afraid. This is not a devil; it is my disciple.' Seeing that Tripitaka at any rate was a clean-built, comely man, he took comfort a little and said, 'I don't know what temple you come from, but you have no right to bring such an evil-looking fellow to my house.' 'I come from the Court of T'ang,' said Tripitaka, 'and I am going to India to get Scriptures. As my way brought me near your house, I have come here in the hope that you would consent to give me a night's lodging. I shall be starting off again tomorrow before daybreak.' 'You may be a man of T'ang,' said the old man, 'but I'll warrant that villainous fellow is no man of T'ang!' 'Have you no eyes in your head,' shouted Monkey. 'The man of T'ang is my master. I am his disciple, and no man of T'ang or sugar-man[1] or honey-man either. I am the Great Sage Equal to Heaven. You people here know me well enough, and I have seen you before.' 'Where have you seen me?' he asked. 'Didn't you when you were small cut the brushwood from in front of my face and gather the herbs that grew on my cheek?' 'The stone monkey in the stone casket!' gasped the old man. 'I see that you are a little like him. But how did you get out?'

[1] Sugar in Chinese is *T'ang*.

141

Monkey told the whole story, and the old man at once bowed before him, and asked them both to step inside. 'Great Sage, how old are you?' the old man asked, when they were seated. 'Let us first hear your age,' said Monkey. 'A hundred and thirty,' said the old man. 'Then you are young enough to be my great-great-grandson at least,' said Monkey. 'I have no idea when I was born. But I was under that mountain for five hundred years.' 'True enough,' said the old man. 'I remember my grandfather telling me that this mountain was dropped from Heaven in order to trap a monkey divinity, and you say that you have only just got out. When I used to see you in my childhood, there was grass growing out of your head and mud on your cheeks. I was not at all afraid of you then. Now there is no mud on your cheeks and no grass on your head. You look thinner, and with that tiger-skin at your waist, who would know that you weren't a devil?' 'I don't want to give you all a lot of trouble,' said Monkey presently, 'but it is five hundred years since I last washed. Could you let us have a little hot water? I am sure my Master would be glad to wash too.'

When they had both washed, they sat down in front of the lamp. 'One more request,' said Monkey. 'Could you lend me a needle and thread?' 'By all means, by all means,' said the old man, and he told his old wife to bring them. Just then Monkey caught sight of a white shirt that Tripitaka had taken off when he washed and not put on again. He snatched it up and put it on. Then he wriggled out of the tiger-skin, sewed it up in one piece, made a 'horse-face fold'[1] and put it round his waist again, fastening the rattan belt. Presenting himself to Tripitaka he said, 'How do you like me in this garb? Is it an improvement?' 'Splendid!' said Tripitaka. 'Now you really do look like a pilgrim.' 'Disciple,' added Tripitaka, 'if you don't mind accepting an off-cast, you can have that shirt for your own.'

They rose early next day, and the old man brought them washing-water and breakfast. Then they set out again on

[1] Meaning uncertain. The modern edition substitutes 'sewed it into a skirt'.

142

their way, lodging late and starting early for many days. One morning they suddenly heard a cry and six men rushed out at them from the roadside, all armed with pikes and swords. 'Halt, priest!' they cried. 'We want your horse and your packs, and quickly too, or you will not escape with your life.'

Tripitaka, in great alarm, slid down from his horse and stood there speechless. 'Don't worry,' said Monkey. 'This only means more clothes and travelling-money for us. 'Monkey, are you deaf?' said Tripitaka. 'They ordered us to surrender the horse and luggage, and you talk of getting clothes and money from them!' 'You keep an eye on the packs and the horse,' said Monkey, 'while I settle matters with them! You'll soon see what I mean.' 'They are very strong men and there are six of them,' said Tripitaka. 'How can a little fellow like you hope to stand up against them single-handed?'

Monkey did not stop to argue, but strode forward and, folding his arms across his chest, bowed to the robbers and said, 'Sirs, for what reason do you stop poor priests from going on their way?' 'We are robber kings,' they said, 'mountain lords among the Benevolent.[1] Everyone knows us. How comes it that you are so ignorant? Hand over your things at once, and we will let you pass. But if half the word "no" leaves your lips, we shall hack you to pieces and grind your bones to powder.' 'I, too,' said Monkey, 'am a great hereditary king, and lord of a mountain for hundreds of years; yet I have never heard your name.' 'In that case, let us tell you,' they said. 'The first of us is called Eye that Sees and Delights; the second, Ear that Hears and is Angry; the third, Nose that Smells and Covets; the fourth, Tongue that Tastes and Desires; the fifth, Mind that Conceives and Lusts; the sixth, Body that Supports and Suffers.' 'You're nothing but six hairy ruffians,' said Monkey, laughing. 'We priests, I would have you know, are your lords and masters, yet you dare block our path. Bring out all the stolen goods you have about you and divide them into seven parts. Then, if you leave me one part, I will spare your lives.'

[1] 'Benevolent' was thieves' slang for 'bandit'.

The robbers were so taken aback that they did not know whether to be angry or amused. 'You must be mad,' they said. 'You've just lost all you possess, and you talk of sharing our booty with us!' Brandishing their spears and flourishing their swords they all rushed forward and began to rain blows upon Monkey's head. But he stood stock still and betrayed not the slightest concern. 'Priest, your head must be very hard!' they cried. 'That's all right,' said Monkey, 'I'm not in a hurry. But when your arms are tired, I'll take out my needle and do my turn.' 'What does he mean?' they said. 'Perhaps he's a doctor turned priest. But we are none of us ill, so why should he talk about using the needle?'

Monkey took his needle from behind his ear, recited a spell which changed it into a huge cudgel, and cried, 'Hold your ground and let old Monkey try his hand upon you!' The robbers fled in confusion, but in an instant he was among them and striking right and left he slew them all, stripped off their clothing and seized their baggage. Then he came back to Tripitaka and said laughing, 'Master, we can start now; I have killed them all.' 'I am very sorry to hear it,' said Tripitaka. 'One has no right to kill robbers, however violent and wicked they may be. The most one may do is to bring them before a magistrate. It would have been quite enough in this case if you had driven them away. Why kill them? You have behaved with a cruelty that ill becomes one of your sacred calling.' 'If I had not killed them,' said Monkey, 'they would have killed you.' 'A priest,' said Tripitaka, 'should be ready to die rather than commit acts of violence.' 'I don't mind telling you,' said Monkey, 'that five hundred years ago, when I was a king, I killed a pretty fair number of people, and if I had held your view I should certainly never have become the Great Sage Equal to Heaven.' 'It was because of your unfortunate performances in Heaven,' said Tripitaka, 'that you had to do penance for five hundred years. If now that you have repented and become a priest you go on behaving as in old days, you can't come with me to India. You've made a very bad start.' The one thing Monkey had never been able to bear was to be scolded, and when Tripitaka began to

144

lecture him like this, he flared up at once and cried, 'All right! I'll give up being a priest, and won't go with you to India. You needn't go on at me any more. I'm off!' Tripitaka did not answer. His silence enraged Monkey even further. He shook himself and with a last 'I'm off!' he bounded away. When Tripitaka looked up, he had completely disappeared. 'It's no use trying to teach people like that,' said Tripitaka to himself gloomily. 'I only said a word or two, and off he goes. Very well then. Evidently it is not my fate to have a disciple; so I must get on as best I can without one.'

He collected the luggage, hoisted it on to the horse's back and set out on foot, leading the horse with one hand and carrying his priest's staff with the other, in very low spirits. He had not gone far, when he saw an old woman carrying a brocaded coat and embroidered cap. As she came near, Tripitaka drew his horse to the side of the road to let her pass. 'Where are you off to all alone?' she asked. 'The Emperor of China has sent me to India to fetch Scriptures,' said Tripitaka. 'The Temple of the Great Thunder Clap where Buddha lives,' said she, 'is a hundred and one thousand leagues away. You surely don't expect to get there with only one horse and no disciple to wait upon you?' 'I picked up a disciple a few days ago,' said Tripitaka, 'but he behaved badly and I was obliged to speak rather severely to him; whereupon he went off in a huff, and I have not seen him since.' 'I've got a brocade coat and a cap with a metal band,' said the old woman. 'They belonged to my son. He entered a monastery, but when he had been a monk for three days, he died. I went and fetched them from the monastery to keep in memory of him. If you had a disciple, I should be very glad to let you have them.' 'That is very kind of you,' said Tripitaka, 'but my disciple has run away, so I cannot accept them.' 'Which way did he go?' asked the old woman. 'The last time I heard his voice, it came from the east,' said Tripitaka. 'That's the way that my house lies,' said the old woman. 'I expect he'll turn up there. I've got a spell here which I'll let you learn, if you promise not to teach it to anybody. I'll go and look for him and send him back to you. Make him wear this cap and coat. If he disobeys you, say the spell, and he'll give no more trouble and never dare to leave you.' Suddenly the old woman changed into a shaft of golden light, which disappeared towards the east. Tripitaka at once guessed that she was the Bodhisattva Kuan-yin in disguise. He bowed and burned incense towards the east. Then having stored away the cap and the coat he sat at the roadside, practising the spell.

After Monkey left the Master, he somersaulted through the clouds and landed right in the palace of the Dragon King of the Eastern Ocean. 'I heard recently that your penance was over,' said the dragon, 'and made sure you would have gone back to be king in your fairy cave.' 'That's what I am doing,' said Monkey. 'But to start with I became a priest.' 'A priest?' said the dragon. 'How did that happen?' Kuan-yin persuaded me to accompany a priest of T'ang,' said Monkey, 'who is going to India to get Scriptures; so I was admitted to the Order.' 'That's certainly a step in the right direction, said the dragon. 'I am sure I congratulate you. But in that case, what are you doing here in the east?' 'It comes of my master being so unpractical,' said Monkey. We met some brigands, and naturally I killed them. Then he started scolding me. You may imagine I wasn't going to stand that. So I left him at once, and am going back to my kingdom. But I thought I would look you up on the way, and see if you could give me a cup of tea.'

When he had been given his cup of tea, he looked round the room, and saw on the wall a picture of Chang Liang offering the slipper. Monkey asked what it was about. 'You were in Heaven at the time,' said the dragon, 'and naturally would not know about it. The immortal in the picture is Huang Shih Kung, and the other figure is Chang Liang. Once when Shih Kung was sitting on a bridge, his shoe came off and fell under the bridge. He called to Chang Liang to pick it up and bring it to him. Chang Liang did so, where-upon the Immortal at once let it fall again, and Chang Liang again fetched it. This happened three times, without Chang Liang showing the slightest sign of impatience. Huang Shih

Kung then gave him a magic treatise, by means of which he defeated all the enemies of the House of Han, and became the greatest hero of the Han dynasty. In his old age he became a disciple of the Immortal Red Pine Seed and achieved Tao. Great Sage, you must learn to have a little more patience, if you hope to accompany the pilgrim to India and gain the Fruits of Illumination.' Monkey looked thoughtful. 'Great Sage,' said the dragon, 'you must learn to control yourself and submit to the will of others, if you are not to spoil all your chances.' 'Not another word!' said Monkey, 'I'll go back at once.'

On the way he met the Bodhisattva Kuan-yin. 'What are you doing here?' she asked. 'The seal was removed and I got out,' said Monkey, 'and became Tripitaka's disciple. But he said I didn't know how to behave, and I gave him the slip. But now I am going back to look after him.' 'Go as fast as you can,' said the Bodhisattva, 'and try to do better this time.' 'Master,' said Monkey, when he came back and found Tripitaka sitting dejectedly by the roadside, 'what are you doing still sitting here?' 'And where have you been?' asked Tripitaka. 'I hadn't the heart to go on, and was just sitting here waiting for you.' 'I only went to the dragon of the eastern ocean,' said Monkey, 'to drink a cup of tea.' 'Now Monkey,' said Tripitaka, 'priests must always be careful to tell the truth. You know quite well that the dragon king lives far away in the east, and you have only been gone an hour.' 'That's easily explained,' said Monkey. 'I have the art of somersaulting through the clouds. One bound takes me a hundred and eight thousand leagues.' 'It seemed to me that you went off in a huff,' said Tripitaka, 'because I had to speak rather sharply to you. It's all very well for you to go off and get tea like that, if you are able to. But I think you might remember that I can't go with you. Doesn't it occur to you that I may be thirsty and hungry too?' 'If you are,' said Monkey, 'I'll take a bowl and go and beg for you.' 'There isn't any need to do that,' said Tripitaka. 'There are some dried provisions in the pack.' When Monkey opened the pack, his eye was caught by something bright. 'Did you bring this coat and cap with you from the east?' he asked. 'I used to wear them when I was young,' replied Tripitaka, saying the first thing that came into his head. 'Anyone who wears this cap can recite scriptures without having to learn them. Anyone who wears this coat can perform ceremonies without having practised them.' 'Dear Master,' said Monkey, 'let me put them on.' 'By all means,' said Tripitaka. Monkey put on the coat and cap, and Tripitaka, pretending to be eating the dried provisions, silently mumbled the spell. 'My head is hurting!' screamed Monkey. Tripitaka went on reciting, and Monkey rolled over on the ground, frantically trying to break the metal fillet of the cap. Fearing that he would succeed, Tripitaka stopped for a moment. Instantly the pain stopped. Monkey felt his head. The cap seemed to have taken root upon it. He took out his needle and tried to lever it up; but all in vain. Fearing once more that he would break the band, Tripitaka began to recite again. Monkey was soon writhing and turning somersaults. He grew purple in the face and his eyes bulged out of his head. Tripitaka, unable to bear the sight of such agony, stopped reciting, and at once Monkey's head stopped hurting.

'You've been putting a spell upon me,' he said. 'Nothing of the kind,' said Tripitaka. 'I've only been reciting the Scripture of the Tight Fillet.' 'Start reciting again,' said Monkey. When he did so, the pain began at once. 'Stop, stop!' screamed Monkey. 'Directly you begin, the pain starts; you can't pretend it's not you that are causing it.' 'In future, will you attend to what I say?' asked Tripitaka. 'Indeed I will,' said Monkey. 'And never be troublesome again?' said Tripitaka. 'I shouldn't dare,' said Monkey. So he said, but in his heart there was still lurking a very evil intent. He took out his cudgel and rushed at Tripitaka, fully intending to strike. Much alarmed, the Master began to recite again, and Monkey fell writhing upon the ground; the cudgel dropped from his hand. 'I give in, I give in!' he cried. 'Is it possible,' said Tripitaka, 'that you were going to be so wicked as to strike me?' 'I shouldn't dare, I shouldn't dare,' groaned Monkey. 'Master, how did you come by this spell?' 'It was taught me by an old woman whom I met just now,' said Tripitaka. 'Not another word!' said Monkey. 'I know well enough who she was. It was the Bodhisattva Kuan-yin. How dare she plot against me like that? Just wait a minute while I go to the Southern Ocean and give her a taste of my stick.' 'As it was she who taught me the spell,' said Tripitaka, 'she can presumably use it herself. What will become of you then?' Monkey saw the logic of this, and kneeling down he said contritely, 'Master, this spell is too much for me. Let me go with you to India. You won't need to be always saying this spell. I will protect you faithfully to the end.' 'Very well then,' said Tripitaka. 'Help me on to my horse.' Very crestfallen, Monkey put the luggage together, and they started off again towards the west.

If you do not know how the story goes on, you must listen to what is told in the next chapter.

Chapter 15

It was mid-winter, a fierce north wind was blowing and icicles hung everywhere. Their way took them up precipitous cliffs and across ridge after ridge of jagged mountain. Presently Tripitaka heard the roaring of a torrent and asked Monkey what this river might be. 'I remember,' said Monkey, 'that there is a river near here called the Eagle Grief Stream.' A moment later they came suddenly to the river side, and Tripitaka reined in his horse. They were looking down at the river, when suddenly there was a swirling sound and a dragon appeared in mid-stream. Churning the waters, it made straight for the shore, clambered up the bank and had almost reached them, when Monkey dragged Tripitaka down from the horse and turning his back to the river, hastily threw down the luggage and carried the Master up the bank. The dragon did not pursue them, but swallowed the horse, harness and all, and then plunged once more into the stream. Meanwhile Monkey had set down Tripitaka upon a high mound, and gone back to recover the horse and luggage. The luggage was there, but the horse had disappeared. He brought up the luggage to where Tripitaka was sitting. 'The dragon has made off,' he said. 'The only trouble is that the horse has taken fright and bolted.' 'How are we to find it?' asked Tripitaka. 'Just wait while I go and have a look,' said Monkey. He sprang straight up into the sky, and shading his fiery eyes with his hand he peered down in every direction. But nowhere was the least sign of the horse. He lowered his cloud-trapeze. 'I can't see it anywhere,' he said. 'There is only one thing that can have happened to it. It has been eaten by the dragon.' 'Now Monkey, what can you be thinking of?' said Tripitaka, 'It would have to have a big mouth indeed to swallow a large horse, harness and all. It is much more likely that it bolted and is hidden by a fold of the hill. You had better have another look.' Master, you underrate my powers,' said Monkey. 'My sight is so good that in daylight I can see everything that happens a thousand leagues around. Within a thousand leagues a gnat cannot move its wings without my seeing it. How could I fail to see a horse?' 'Well, suppose it has been eaten,' said Tripitaka, 'how am I to travel? It's a great deal too far to walk.' And as he spoke his tears began to fall like rain. 'Don't make such an object of yourself,' shouted Monkey, infuriated by this exhibition of despair. 'Just sit here, while I go and look for the wretch and make him give us back the horse.' 'You can't do anything unless he comes out of the water,' said Tripitaka, 'and if he does it will be me that he will eat this time,' 'You're impossible, impossible,' thundered Monkey, angrier than ever. 'You say you need the horse to ride, and yet you won't let me go and recover it. At this rate, you'll sit here staring at the luggage for ever.'

He was still storming, when a voice spoke out of the sky, saying, 'Monkey, do not be angry. Priest of T'ang, do not weep. We divinities have been sent by Kuan-yin to protect you in your quest.' Tripitaka at once did obeisance. 'Which divinities are you?' cried Monkey. 'Tell me your names, and I'll tick you off on the roll.' 'Here present are Lu Ting and Lu Chia,' they said, 'the Guardians of the Five Points, the Four Sentinels and the Eighteen Protectors of Monasteries. We attend upon you in rotation.' 'And which of you are on duty this morning?' asked Monkey. 'Lu Chia, one Sentinel and the Protectors are on duty,' they said, 'and the Golden-headed Guardian is always somewhere about, night and day.' 'Those who aren't on duty can retire,' said Monkey. 'But Lu Ting, the Sentinel of the day, and all the Guardians had better stay and look after the Master, while I go to the river and look for that dragon, and see if I can get him to return the horse.' Tripitaka, feeling somewhat reassured, sat down on the bank, begging Monkey to be careful. 'Don't you worry about me!' said Monkey.

Dear Monkey! He tightened the belt of his brocade jacket, hitched up his tiger-skin, grasped his iron cudgel, and going straight down to the water's edge called in a loud voice, 'Cursed fish, give me back my horse!' The dragon was lying quietly at the bottom of the river, digesting the white horse. But hearing some one cursing him and demanding his prey, he fell into a great rage, and leapt up through the waves crying, 'Who is it that dares make such a hullabaloo outside my premises?' 'Stand your ground,' hissed Monkey, 'and give me back my horse.' He brandished his cudgel and struck at the dragon's head. The dragon advanced upon him with open jaws and threatening claws. It was a valiant fight that those two had on the banks of the river. To and fro they went, fighting for a long while, hither and thither, round and round. At last the dragon's strength began to fail, he could hold out no longer, and with a rapid twist of the tail he fled from the encounter and disappeared in the river. Monkey, standing on the bank, cursed and taunted him unceasingly, but he turned a deaf ear. Monkey saw nothing for it but to go back and report to Tripitaka. 'Master,' he said, 'I taunted him till he came out and fought many bouts, and in the end he took fright and ran away. He is now at the bottom of the river and won't come out.' 'We are still not sure whether he did swallow the horse,' said Tripitaka. 'How can you say such a thing?' said Monkey. 'If he hadn't eaten it, why should he have come out and answered my challenge?' 'The other day when you dealt with that tiger,' said Tripitaka, 'you mentioned that you could also subdue dragons. I don't understand why you are having such difficulties with this dragon today.' To such a taunt as this no one could be more sensitive than Monkey. 'Not another word!' he cried, stung to the quick. 'I'll soon show you which is master!'

He strode to the stream-side, and used a magic which stirred up the clear waters of the river till they became as turbulent as the waves of the Yellow River. The dragon soon became very uncomfortable as he lay at the bottom of the stream. 'Misfortunes never come singly,' he thought to himself. 'Hardly a year has passed since I barely escaped with my life from the Tribunal of Heaven and was condemned to this exile; and now I have fallen foul of this cursed monster, who seems determined to do me injury.' The more he thought, the angrier he became. At last, determined not to

152

give in, he leapt up through the waves and gnashing his teeth he snarled, 'What monster are you, and where do you come from, that you dare affront me in this fashion?' 'Never mind where I come from or don't come from,' said Monkey. 'Just give me back my horse, or you shall pay for it with your life.' 'Your horse,' said the dragon, 'is inside me. How am I to give it back to you? And anyhow, if I don't, what can you do to me?' 'Have a look at this cudgel,' said Monkey. 'If you don't give me back the horse you shall pay for it with your life.' Again they fought upon the bank, and after several rounds the dragon could hold out no longer, made one great wriggle and, changing itself into a water-snake, disappeared into the long grass. Beating the grass with his cudgel, Monkey pranced wildly about, trying to track it down, but all in vain. At last, fuming with impatience he uttered a loud OM, as a secret summons to the spirits of the locality. In a moment they were kneeling before him. 'Hold out your shanks,' said Monkey, 'and I'll give you each five strokes with the cudgel just to relieve my feelings.' 'Great Sage,' they besought him, 'pray give us a chance to put our case to you. We had no idea that you had been released from your penance, or we should have come to meet you before. We humbly beg you to forgive us.' 'Very well then,' said Monkey. 'You shan't be beaten. But answer me this. Where does this dragon come from, who lives in the Eagle Grief River? Why did he swallow my Master's white horse?' 'Great Sage,' they said, 'in old days you had no Master, and indeed refused obedience to any power in Heaven or Earth. What do you mean by your Master's horse?' 'After I got into trouble about that affair in Heaven,' said Monkey, 'I had to do penance for five hundred years. But now I have been taken in hand by the Bodhisattva Kuan-yin and put in charge of a priest who is going to India to fetch Scriptures. I was travelling with him as his disciple, when we lost my Master's horse.' 'If you want to catch this dragon, surely your best plan would be to get the Bodhisattva to come and deal with it,' they said. 'There used not to be any dragon here, and it is she who sent it.' They all went and told Tripitaka of this plan. 'How long shall you be?' he asked. 'Shan't I be dead of cold or starvation before you come back?' While he spoke, the voice of the Golden-headed Guardian was heard saying from the sky, 'None of you need move a step. *I* will go and ask the Bodhisattva.' 'Much obliged,' said Monkey. 'Pray go at once.' The Guardian soared up through the clouds and made straight for the Southern Ocean. Monkey told the local deities to look after the Master, and the Sentinels to supply food. Then he went back to the banks of the river. 'What have you come for?' asked the Bodhisattva, when the Golden-headed Guardian was brought to her where she sat in her bamboo-grove. 'The priest of T'ang,' said he, 'has lost his horse at the Eagle Grief River. It was swallowed by a dragon, and the Great Sage sent me for your help,' 'That dragon,' said Kuan-yin, 'is a son of the dragon-king of the Western Ocean. By his carelessness he set fire to the magic pearls in the palace and they were destroyed. His father accused him of subversive intents, and the Tribunal of Heaven condemned him to death. I saw the Jade Emperor about it, and asked that the sentence might be commuted if the dragon consented to carry the priest of T'ang on his journey to India. I cannot understand how he came to swallow the horse. I'll come and look into it.' She got down from her lotus seat, left her fairy cave, and riding on a beam of magic light crossed the Southern Sea. When she came near the River of Eagle Grief, she looked down and saw Monkey on the bank uttering ferocious curses. She sent the Guardian to announce her arrival. Monkey at once sprang into the air and shouted at her, 'A fine "Teacher of the Seven Buddhas", a fine "Founder of the Faith of Mercy" you are, to plot in this way against us!' 'You impudent stableman, you half-witted red-bottom,' said the Bodhisattva. 'After all the trouble I have taken to find someone to fetch scriptures, and tell him to redeem you, instead of thanking me you make a scene like this!' 'You've played a fine trick on me,' said Monkey. 'You might in decency, when you let me out, have allowed me to go round and amuse myself as I pleased. But you gave me a dressing down and told me I was to spend all my time and energy in looking after this T'ang priest. Very well! But why did you give him a cap that he coaxed me into putting on, and now I can't get it off, and whenever he says some spell or other I have frightful pains in the head?' 'Oh Monkey,' laughed Kuan-yin, 'if you were not controlled in some such way as this, there would be no doing anything with you. Before long we should have you at all your old tricks again.' 'It's no good trying to put the blame on me,' said Monkey. 'How comes it that you put this dragon here, after he had been condemned by the Courts, and let him eat my Master's horse? It was you who put it in his way to continue his villainies here below. You ought to be ashamed of yourself!' 'I specially asked the Jade Emperor,' said Kuan-yin, 'to let this dragon be stationed here, so that he might be used to carry the master on his way to India. No ordinary Chinese horse would be able to carry him all that way.' 'Well, now he is frightened of me and is hiding,' said Monkey, 'so what is to be done?' Kuan-yin called the Golden-haired Guardian and said to him, 'Go to the edge of the river and cry "Third son of the Dragon King, come out! The Bodhisattva is here." He'll come out all right.' The dragon leapt up through the waves and immediately assumed human form. 'Don't you know that this is the Scripture-seeker's disciple?' Kuan-yin said, pointing at Monkey. 'Bodhisattva,' said the young dragon, 'I've been having a fight with him. I was hungry yesterday and ate his horse. He never once mentioned anything about "Scripture-seeking." ' 'You never asked my name,' said Monkey, 'so why should I tell you?' 'Didn't I ask you what monster you were and where you came from?' asked the dragon. 'And didn't you shout at me "Never mind where I came from or didn't come from, but just give me back my horse"? You never so much as mentioned the word T'ang.' 'Monkey is fonder of showing off his own powers than mentioning his connection with other people,' said Kuan-yin. 'But in future if anyone questions him, he must be sure to say that he is seeking Scriptures. Then there will be no more trouble.'

The Bodhisattva then went to the dragon and removed the

jewel of wisdom from under his chin. Then she took her willow-spray and sprinkled him all over with sweet dew, and blowing upon him with magic breath cried 'Change!' Whereupon the dragon immediately changed into the exact image of the lost horse. She then solemnly called upon the once-dragon to turn from his evil ways, and promised that when his task was ended he should be given a golden body and gain illumination. The young dragon humbled himself and promised faithfully to do as he was bid. Then she turned to go, but Monkey grabbed at her, crying 'This is not good enough! The way to the West is very bad going, and it would be difficult enough in any case to get an earthly priest over all those precipices and crags. But if we are going to have encounters like this all the time, I shall have hard work keeping alive at all, let alone any thought of achieving salvation. I'm not going on!' 'That's odd,' said the Bodhisattva, 'because in the old days you used to be very keen on obtaining illumination. I am surprised that, having escaped from the punishment imposed upon you by Heaven, you should be so unwilling to take a little trouble. When you get into difficulties you have only to call upon Earth, and Earth will perform its miracles. If need be, I will come myself to succour you. And, by the way, come here! I am going to endow you with one more power.' She took the willow leaves from her willow-spray, and dropping them down Monkey's back cried 'Change.' At once they changed into three magic hairs. 'These,' she said, 'will get you out of any trouble, however menacing.' Monkey thanked the Bodhisattva, who now set out for the Southern Heaven, and taking the horse by the forelock he led it to Tripitaka, saying, 'Master, here's a horse any way!' 'It's in much better condition than the old one,' said Tripitaka. 'However did you manage to find it?' 'What have you been doing all the while? Dreaming?' said Monkey. 'The Golden-haired Guardian sent for Kuan-yin, who changed the dragon into the exact image of our white horse. The only thing it lacks is harness.' 'Where is the Bodhisattva?' asked Tripitaka, very much surprised. 'I should like to thank her.' 'You're too late,' said

Monkey. 'By this time she is already crossing the Southern Ocean.' However Tripitaka burned incense and bowed towards the south. Then he helped Monkey to put together the luggage, and they set out. 'It's not going to be easy to ride a horse without saddle and reins,' said Tripitaka. 'I'd better find a boat to get across the river, and see if I can't get some harness on the other side.' 'That's not a very practical suggestion,' said Monkey. 'What chance is there of finding a boat in this wild, desolate place? The horse has lived here for some time and must know his way through the waters. Just sit tight on his back and let him carry you across.' They had got to the river bank, Tripitaka astride the horse and Monkey carrying the luggage, when an old fisherman appeared upstream, punting a crazy old raft. Monkey waved to him, crying, 'We have come from the east to fetch scriptures. My Master does not know how to get across, and would like you to ferry him.' The old man punted rapidly towards them, and Monkey told Tripitaka to dismount. He then helped him on board, and embarked the horse and luggage. The old man punted them swiftly across to the far side, where Tripitaka told Monkey to look in the pack for some Chinese money to give to the old fisherman. But the old man pushed off again at once, saying he did not want money. Tripitaka felt very uncomfortable and could only press together his palms in token of gratitude. 'Don't you worry about him,' said Monkey. 'Didn't you see who he really is? This is the river divinity who failed to come and meet us. I was on the point of giving him a good hiding, which he richly deserved. The fact that I let him off is payment enough. No wonder he hadn't the face to take your cash.' Tripitaka was not at all sure whether to believe this story or not. He got astride the horse once more, and followed Monkey along the road to the west. And if you do not know where they got to, you must listen to what is told in the next chapter.

Chapter 16

They had been travelling for several days through very wild country when at last, very late in the evening, they saw a group of houses in the far distance. 'Monkey,' said Tripitaka, 'I think that is a farm over there. Wouldn't it be a good plan to see if we can't sleep there tonight?' 'Let me go and have a look at it,' said Monkey, 'to see whether it looks lucky or unlucky, and we can then act accordingly.' 'You can proceed,' Monkey reported presently. 'I am certain that good people live there.' Tripitaka urged on the white horse and soon came to a gate leading into a lane down which came a lad with a cotton wrap round his head, wearing a blue jacket, umbrella in hand and a bundle on his back. He was striding along, with a defiant air. 'Where are you off to?' said Monkey stopping him. 'There's something I want to ask you. What place is this?' The man tried to brush him aside, muttering, 'Is there no one else on the farm, that you must needs pester me with questions?' 'Now don't be cross,' said Monkey laughing. 'What harm can it do you to tell me the name of a place? If you're obliging to us, maybe we can do something to oblige you.' Finding he could not get past, for Monkey was holding on to him tightly, he began to dance about in a great rage. 'It's enough to put anyone out,' he cried. 'I've just been insulted by the master of the house, and then I run straight into this wretched bald-pate, and have to swallow his impudence!' 'Unless you're clever enough to shake me off, which I very much doubt,' said Monkey, 'here you'll stay.' The man wriggled this way and that, but all to no purpose. He was caught as though by iron pincers. In the struggle he dropped his bundle, dropped his umbrella, and began to rain blows on Monkey with both fists. Monkey kept one hand free to catch on to the luggage, and with the other held the lad fast. 'Monkey,' said Tripitaka, 'I think there's someone coming over there. Wouldn't it do just as well if you asked him, and let this lad go?' 'Master,' said Monkey, 'you don't know what you're talking about. There's no point in asking anyone else. This is the only fellow out of whom we can get what we want.'

At last, seeing that he would never get free, the lad said, 'This is called old Mr Kao's farm. Most of the people that live and work here have the surname Kao, so the whole place is called Kao Farm. Now let me go!' 'You look as if you were going on a journey,' said Monkey. 'Tell me where you are going, and on what business, and I will let you go.'

'My name,' he said, 'is Kao Ts'ai. Old Mr Kao has a daughter about twenty years old and unmarried. Three years ago she was carried off by a monster, who since has kept her as his wife, and lived with her here on the farm. Old Mr Kao was not pleased. "To have a monster as a son-in-law in the house," he says, "doesn't work very well. It's definitely discreditable to the house, and unpleasant not to be able to look forward to comings and goings between the two families." He did everything in his power to drive away the monster, but it was no good; and in the end the creature took the girl and locked her away in that back building, where she has been for six months and no one in the family has seen her.

'Old Mr Kao gave me two or three pieces of silver and told me to go and find an exorcist, and I spent a long time chasing round all over the countryside. I succeeded at last in getting the names of three or four practitioners, but they all turned out to be unfrocked priests or mouldy Taoists, quite incapable of dealing with such a monster. Mr Kao only just now gave me a great scolding and accused me of bungling the business. Then he gave me five pieces of silver to pay for my travelling expenses and told me to go on looking till I found a really good exorcist, and I should be looking for one now if I hadn't run into this little scamp who won't let me pass. There! You have forced me to tell you how things are, and now you can let me go.' 'You've thrown a lucky number,' said Monkey. 'This is just my job. You needn't go a step further or spend an ounce of your silver. I'm no unfrocked priest or mouldy Taoist, I really do know how to catch monsters. You've "got your stye cured on the way to the

159

doctor's." I'll trouble you to go to the master of the house, and tell him that a priest and his disciple have come, who are on their way to get scriptures in India, and that they can deal with any monster.' 'I hope you're telling me the truth,' said the lad. 'You'll get me into great trouble if you fail.' 'I'll positively guarantee,' said Monkey, 'that I'm not deceiving you. Make haste and lead us in.'

The lad saw nothing for it but to pick up his bundle and go back to the house. 'You half-wit,' roared old Mr Kao, 'what have you come back for?' But as soon as he had heard the lad's story, he quickly changed into his best clothes and came out to greet the guests, smiling affably. Tripitaka returned his greeting, but Monkey did not bow or say a word. The old man looked him up and down, and not knowing quite what to make of him did not ask him how he did. 'And how about me? Don't you want to know how I am?' said Monkey. 'Isn't it enough to have a monster in the house as son-in-law,' grumbled the old man, 'without your bringing in this frightful creature to molest me?' 'In all the years you've lived,' said Monkey, 'you've evidently learnt very little wisdom. If you judge people by their appearances, you'll always be going wrong. I'm not much to look at, I grant; but I have great powers, and if you are having any trouble with bogeys or monsters in the house, that's just where I come in. I'm going to get you back your daughter, so you had better stop grumbling about my appearance.' Mr Kao, trembling with fear, managed at last to pull himself together sufficiently to invite them both in. Monkey, without so much as by-your-leave, led the horse into the courtyard and tied it to a pillar. Then he drew up an old weather-beaten stool, asked Tripitaka to be seated, and taking another stool for himself calmly sat down at Tripitaka's side. 'The little priest knows how to make himself at home,' said Mr Kao. 'This is nothing,' said Monkey. 'Keep me here a few months and you'll see me really making myself at home!' 'I don't quite understand,' said the old man, 'whether you've come for a night's lodging or to drive out the monster.' 'We've come for a night's lodging,' said Monkey, 'but if there are any monsters about I

160

don't mind dealing with them, just to pass the time. But first, I should like to know how many of them there are?' 'Heavens!' cried the old man, 'isn't one monster enough to afflict the household, living here as my son-in-law?' 'Just tell me about it from the beginning,' said Monkey. 'If I know what he's good for, I can deal with him.' 'We'd never had any trouble with ghosts or goblins or monsters on this farm before,' said the old man. 'Unfortunately I have no son, but only three daughters. The eldest is called Fragrant Orchid, the second Jade Orchid, and the third Blue Orchid. The first two were betrothed from childhood into neighbouring families. Our plan for the youngest was to marry her to someone who would come and live with her here and help look after us in our old age. About three years ago a very nice-looking young fellow turned up, saying that he came from Fu-ling, and that his surname was Hog. He said he had no parents or brothers and sisters, and was looking for a family where he would be taken as son-in-law, in return for the work that he did about the place. He sounded just the sort we wanted, and I accepted him. I must say he worked very hard. He pushed the plough himself and never asked to use a bull; he managed to do all his reaping without knife or staff. For some time we were perfectly satisfied, except for one thing – his appearance began to change in a very odd way.' 'In what way!' asked Monkey. 'When he first came,' said the old man, 'he was just a dark, stoutish fellow. But afterwards his nose began to turn into a regular snout, his ears became larger and larger, and great bristles began to grow at the back of his neck. In fact, he began to look more and more like a hog. His appetite is enormous. He eats four or five pounds of rice at each meal, and as a light collation in the morning I've known him get through over a hundred pasties. He's not at all averse to fruit and vegetables either, and what with this and all the wine he drinks, in the course of the last six months he's pretty well eaten and drunk us out of house and home.' 'No doubt,' said Tripitaka, 'anyone who works so hard as he does needs a lot of nourishment.' 'If it were only this business of food,' said the old man, 'it wouldn't be so bad. But he frightens everybody round by raising magic winds, suddenly vanishing and appearing again, making stones fly through the air and such like tricks. Worst of all, he has locked up Blue Orchid in the back outhouse, and it is six months since wet set eyes on her. We don't even know if she's dead or alive. It is evident that he's an ogre of some kind, and that is why we were trying to get hold of an exorcist.' 'Don't you worry,' said Monkey. 'This very night I'll catch him and make him sign a Deed of Relinquishment and give you back your daughter.' 'The main thing is to catch him,' said Mr Kao. 'It doesn't so much matter about documents.' 'Perfectly easy,' said Monkey. 'Tonight as soon as it is dark, you'll see the whole thing settled.' 'What weapons do you need, and how many men to help you?' asked Mr Kao. 'We must get on with the preparations.' 'I'm armed already,' said Monkey. 'So far as I can see, all you've got between you is a priest's staff,' said the old man. 'That wouldn't be much use against such a fiend as this.' Monkey took his embroidery needle from behind his ear and once more changed it into a great iron cudgel. 'Does this satisfy you?', he asked. 'I doubt if your house could provide anything tougher.' 'How about followers?' said the old man. 'I need no followers,' said Monkey. 'All I ask for is some decent elderly person to sit with my master and keep him company.' Several respectable friends and relatives were fetched, and having looked them up and down Monkey said to Tripitaka, 'Sit here quietly and don't worry. I'm off to do this job.' 'Take me to the back building,' he said to Mr Kao, grasping his cudgel. 'I'd like to have a look at the monster's lodging-place.' 'Give me the key,' he said, when they came to the door. 'Think what you're saying,' said the old man. 'Do you suppose that if a key was all that was wanted, we should be troubling you?' 'What's the use of living so long in the world if you haven't learnt even to recognise a joke when you hear one?' said Monkey laughing. Then he went up to the door and with a terrific blow of his cudgel smashed it down. Within, it was pitch dark. 'Call to your daughter and see if she is there,' said Monkey. The old man summoned up his courage and cried, 'Miss Three!'

Recognising her father's voice, she answered with a faint 'Papa, I am here.' Monkey peered into the darkness with his steely eyes, and it was a pitiable sight that he saw. Unwashed cheeks, matted hair, bloodless lips, weak and trembling. She tottered towards her father, flung her arms round him and burst into tears. 'Don't make that noise,' said Monkey, 'but tell us where your monster is.' 'I don't know,' she said. 'Nowadays he goes out at dawn and comes back at dusk, I can't keep track of him at all. He knows that you're trying to find someone to exorcise him; that's why he keeps away all day.' 'Not a word more!' said Monkey. 'Old man, take your darling back to the house and calm her down. I'll wait here for the monster. If he doesn't come, it is not my fault, and if he comes I'll pluck up your trouble by the roots.'

Left alone, Monkey used his magic arts to change himself into the exact image of Blue Orchid, and sat waiting for the monster to return. Presently there was a great gust of wind; stones and gravel hurtled through the air. When the wind sudsided there appeared a monster of truly terrible appearance. He had short bristles on his swarthy cheeks, a long snout and huge ears. He wore a cotton jacket that was green but not green, blue but not blue, and had a spotted handkerchief tied round his head. 'That's the article,' laughed Monkey to himself.

Dear Monkey! He did not go to meet the monster or ask him how he did, but lay on the bed groaning, as though he were ill. The monster, quite taken in, came up to the bed and grabbing at Monkey tried to kiss him. 'None of your lewd tricks on old Monkey!' laughed Monkey to himself, and giving the monster a great clout on the nose sent him reeling. 'Dear sister,' said the monster, picking himself up, 'why are you cross with me today? Is it because I am so late?' 'I'm not cross,' said Monkey. 'If you're not cross,' said the monster, 'why do you push me away?' 'You've got such a clumsy way of kissing,' said Monkey. 'You might have known that I'm not feeling well today, when you saw I did not come to the door to meet you. Take off your clothes and get into bed.' Still suspecting nothing the monster began to

163

undress. Monkey meanwhile jumped up and sat on the commode. When the monster got into bed he felt everywhere but could not find his bride. 'Sister,' he called, 'what has become of you? Take off your clothes and get into bed.' 'You go to sleep first,' said Monkey. 'I'll follow when I've done my duties.' Monkey suddenly began to sigh, murmuring 'Was there ever such an unhappy girl as I?' 'What are you grumbling about?' said the monster. 'Since I came here, I've cost you something in food and drink, that I own. But I've more than earned what I have got. Haven't I cleaned the ground and drained ditches, carried bricks and tiles, built walls, ploughed fields, planted grain, and improved the farm out of all knowing? You've good clothes to wear and all the food you need. What's all this childish nonsense about being unhappy?' 'That's not it at all,' said Monkey. 'Today my parents came and made a fearful scene through the partition wall.' 'What did they make a scene about?' said the monster. 'They don't like having you here as their son-in-law,' said Monkey. 'They say you've got an ugly face, and they don't know who your father is and haven't seen any of your relations. They say you come and go no one knows when or where, and it's bad for the credit of the house that we don't know your name or anything at all about you.' That's what they said, and it has made me miserable.' 'What do looks matter?' said the monster. 'It's a strong man they need about the place, and they can't say anything against me on that score. And if they think so ill of me, why did they accept me here at all? As for who I am, there's no mystery about it. I come from the Cloud-Ladder Cave at Fu-ling, and because I look a bit like a pig they call me Pigsy – Pigsy Bristles; next time they ask just tell them that.' 'Confiding monster!' thought Monkey. 'It needs no tortures to get a confession from him. Now we know where he comes from and who he is. It only remains to catch him.' 'They are looking for an exorcist to drive you away,' he said to the monster. 'Go to sleep,' said Pigsy, 'and don't worry about them any more. Am not I strong enough, with my nine-pronged muck-rake, to frighten off any exorcist or priest or what-not? Even if

164

your old man's prayers could bring down the master of all devils from the Ninth Heaven, as a matter of fact he's an old friend of mine and wouldn't do anything against me.' 'He's done more than that,' said Monkey. 'He has called in the Great Sage, who five hundred years ago made turmoil in Heaven.' 'If that's so,' said Pigsy, 'I'm off! There'll be no more kissing tonight!' 'Why are you going?' asked Monkey. 'You don't know,' said Pigsy. 'That chap is terribly powerful, and I don't know that I could deal with him. I'm frightened of losing my reputation.' He dressed hastily, opened the door and went out. But Monkey caught hold of him and making a magic pass changed himself back into his true form. 'Monster, look round,' he cried, 'and you will see that I am he.'

When Pigsy turned and saw Monkey with his sharp little teeth and grinning mouth, his fiery, steely eyes, his flat head and hairy cheeks, for all the world like a veritable thunder-demon, he was so startled that his hands fell limp beside him and his legs gave way. With a scream he tore himself free, leaving part of his coat in Monkey's hand, and was gone like a whirlwind. Monkey struck out with his cudgel; but Pigsy had already begun to make for the cave he came from. Soon Monkey was after him, crying, 'Where are you off to? If you go up to Heaven I will follow you to the summit of the Pole Star, and if you go down into the earth I will follow you to the deepest pit of hell.'

If you do not know how far he chased him or which of them won the fight, you must listen to what is told in the next chapter.

Chapter 17

The monster fled with Monkey at his heels, till they came at last to a high mountain, and here the monster disappeared into a cave, and a moment later came back brandishing a nine-pronged muck-rake. They set to at once and battled all night long, from the second watch till dawn began to whiten in the sky. At last the monster could hold his ground no longer, and retreating into the cave bolted the door behind him. Standing outside the cave-door, Monkey saw that on a slab of rock was the inscription 'Cloudladder Cave'. As the monster showed no sign of coming out again and it was now broad daylight, Monkey thought to himself, 'The Master will be wondering what has happened to me. I had better go and see him and then come back and catch the monster.' So tripping from cloud to cloud he made his way back to the farm.

Tripitaka was still sitting with the old man, talking of this and that. He had not slept all night. He was just wondering why Monkey did not return when Monkey alighted in the courtyard, and suddenly stood before them. 'Master, here I am,' he said. The old men all bowed down before him, and supposing that he had accomplished his task thanked him for all his trouble. 'You must have had a long way to go, to catch the creature,' said Tripitaka. 'Master,' said Monkey, 'the monster is not a common incubus or elf. I have recognised him as a former inhabitant of Heaven, where he was in command of all the watery hosts. He was expelled to earth after an escapade with the daughter of the Moon Goddess, and though he was here re-incarnated with a pig-like form, he retains all his magic powers. I chased him to his mountain-cave, where he fetched out a nine-pronged muck-rake, and we fought together all night. Just at dawn he gave up the fight, and locked himself up in his cave. I would have beaten down the door and forced him to fight to a decision, but I was afraid the Master might be getting anxious, so I thought I had better come back first and report.'

'Reverend Sir,' said old Mr Kao to Monkey, 'I am afraid this hasn't helped matters much. True, you have driven him away; but after you have gone he's certain to come back again, and where shall we be then? We shall have to trouble you to catch him for us. That is the only way to pluck out our trouble by the root. I'll see to it that you have no cause to regret the trouble you take. You shall have half of all that is ours, both land and goods. If you like, my friends and relations shall sign a document to this effect. It will be well worth their while, if only we can remove this shame from our home.'

'I think you make too much of the whole affair,' said Monkey. 'The monster himself admits that his appetite is large; but he has done quite a lot of useful work. All the recent improvements in the estate are his work. He claims to be well worth what he costs in keep, and does not see why you should be so anxious to get rid of him. He is a divinity from Heaven, although condemned to live on earth, he helps to keep things going, and so far as I can see he hasn't done any harm to your daughter.' 'It may be true,' said old Mr Kao, 'that he's had no influence upon her. But I stick to it that it's very bad for our reputation. Wherever I go I hear people saying "Mr Kao has taken a monster as his son-in-law." What is one to say to that?' 'Now, Monkey,' said Tripitaka, 'don't you think you had better go and have one more fight with him and see if you can't settle the business once and for all?' 'As a matter of fact,' said Monkey, 'I was only having a little game with him, to see how things would go. This time I shall certainly catch him and bring him back for you to see. Don't you worry!' 'Look after my master,' he cried to Mr Kao, 'I'm off!'

So saying, he disappeared into the clouds and soon arrived at the cave. With one blow of his cudgel he beat the doors to bits, and standing at the entrance he cried, 'You noisome lout, come out and fight with Old Monkey.' Pigsy lay fast asleep within, snoring heavily. But when he heard the door being beaten down and heard himself called a noisome lout, he was so much enraged that he snatched up his rake, pulled himself together and rushed out, crying, 'You wretched stableman, if ever there was a rogue, you're he! What have I to do with you, that you should come and knock down my door? Go and look at the Statute Book. You'll find that "obtaining entry to premises by forcing a main door" is a Miscellaneous Capital Offence.' 'You fool,' said Monkey. 'Haven't I a perfectly good justification at law for forcing your door? Remember that you laid violent hands on a respectable girl, and lived with her without matchmaker or testimony, tea, scarlet, wine or any other ceremony. Are you aware that heads are cut off for less than that?' 'Stop that nonsense, and look at Old Pig's rake,' cried Pigsy. He struck out, but Monkey warded off the blow, crying, 'I suppose that's the rake you used when you worked on the farm. Why should you expect me to be frightened of it?' 'You are very much mistaken,' said Pigsy. 'This rake was given to me by the Jade Emperor himself.' 'A lie!' cried Monkey. 'Here's my head. Hit as hard as you please, and we'll see!' Pigsy raised the rake and brought it down with such force on Monkey's head that the sparks flew. But there was not a bruise or scratch. Pigsy was so much taken aback, that his hands fell limp at his side. 'What a head!' he exclaimed. 'You've still something to learn about me,' said Monkey. 'After I made havoc in Heaven and was caught by Erh-lang, all the deities of Heaven hacked me with their axes, hammered me with their mallets, slashed me with their swords, set fire to me, hurled thunderbolts at me, but not a hair of my body was hurt. Lao Tzu put me in his alchemic stove and cooked me with holy fire. But all that happened was that my eyes became fiery, my head and shoulders hard as steel. If you don't believe it, try again, and see whether you can hurt me or not.' 'I remember,' said Pigsy, 'that before you made havoc in Heaven, you lived in the Cave of the Water Curtain. Lately nothing has been heard of you. How did you get here? Perhaps my father-in-law asked you to come and deal with me.' 'Not at all,' said Monkey, 'I have been converted and am now a priest, and am going with a Chinese pilgrim

168

called Tripitaka, who has been sent by the Emperor to fetch scriptures from India. On our way we happened to come past Mr Kao's farm, and we asked for a night's lodging. In the course of conversation Mr Kao asked for help about his daughter. That's why I'm after you, you noisome lout!'

No sooner did Pigsy hear these words than the rake fell from his hand. 'Where is that pilgrim?' he gasped. 'Take me to him.' 'What do you want to see him for?' asked Monkey. 'I've been converted,' said Pigsy. 'Didn't you know? The Bodhisattva Kuan-yin converted me and put me here to prepare myself by fasting and abstention for going to India with a pilgrim to fetch scriptures; after which, I am to receive illumination. That all happened some years ago, and since then I have had no news of this pilgrim. If you are his disciple, what on earth possessed you not to mention this scripture-seeking business? Why did you prefer to pick a quarrel and knock me about in front of my own door?' 'I suspect,' said Monkey, 'that you are just making all this up, in order to get away. If it's really true that you want to escort my Master to India, you must make a solemn vow to Heaven that you're telling the truth. Then I'll take you to him.' Pigsy flung himself upon his knees and, kowtowing at the void, up and down like a pestle in the mortar, he cried 'I swear before the Buddha Amitabha, praised be his name, that I am telling the truth; and if I am not, may I be condemned once more by the tribunals of Heaven and sliced into ten thousand pieces.'

When Monkey heard him make this solemn vow, 'Very well then,' he said. 'First take a torch and burn down your lair, and then I will take you with me.' Pigsy took some reeds and brambles, lit a fire and soon reduced the cave to the state of a burnt-out kiln. 'You've nothing against me now,' he said. 'Take me along with you.' 'You'd better give your rake to me,' said Monkey. When Pigsy had handed over the rake, Monkey took a hair, blew on it with magic breath, and changed it into a three-ply hemp cord. Pigsy put his hands behind his back and let himself be bound. Then Monkey caught hold of his ear and dragged him along, crying,

'Hurry up! Hurry up!' 'Don't be so rough,' begged Pigsy. 'You're hurting my ear.' 'Rough indeed!' said Monkey. 'I shouldn't get far by being gentle with you. The proverb says, "The better the pig, the harder to hold." Wait till you have seen the Master and shown that you are in earnest. Then we'll let you go.'

When they reached the farm, Monkey twitched Pigsy's ear, saying, 'You see that old fellow sitting so solemnly up there? That's my Master.' Mr Kao and the other old men, seeing Monkey leading the monster by the ear, were delighted beyond measure, and came out into the courtyard to meet him. 'Reverend Sir,' they cried, 'that's the creature, sure enough, that married our master's daughter.' Pigsy fell upon his knees and with his hands still tied behind his back, kowtowed to Tripitaka, crying, 'Master, forgive me for failing to give you a proper reception. If I had known that it was you who were staying with my father-in-law I would have come to pay my respects, and all these unpleasantnesses would never have happened.' 'Monkey,' said Tripitaka, 'how did you manage to bring him to this state of mind?' Monkey let go his ear, and giving him a knock with the handle of the rake, shouted, 'Speak, fool!' Pigsy then told how he had been commissioned by Kuan-yin. 'Mr Kao,' said Tripitaka, when he heard the story, 'this is the occasion for a little incense.' Mr Kao then brought out the incense tray, and Tripitaka washed his hands, and burning incense he turned towards the south and said, 'I am much beholden, Bodhi-sattva!' Then he went up into the hall and resumed his seat, bidding Monkey to release Pigsy from his bonds. Monkey shook himself; the rope became a hair again and returned to his body. Pigsy was free. He again did obeisance, and vowed that he would follow Tripitaka to the west. Then he bowed to Monkey, whom as the senior disciple he addressed as 'Elder Brother and Teacher'.

'Where's my wife?' said Pigsy to Mr Kao. 'I should like her to pay her respects to my Father and Brother in the Law.' 'Wife indeed!' laughed Monkey. 'You haven't got a wife now. There are some sorts of Taoists that are family men;

170

but who ever heard of a Buddhist priest calmly talking about his "wife"? Sit down and eat your supper, and early to-morrow we'll all start out for India.' After supper Kao brought out a red lacquer bowl full of broken pieces of silver and gold, and offered the contents to the three priests, as a contribution towards their travelling expenses. He also offered them three pieces of fine silk to make clothes. Tripi-taka said, 'Travelling priests must beg their way as they go. We cannot accept money or silk.' But Monkey came up and plunging his hand into the dish took out a handful of gold and silver, and called to the lad Kao Ts'ai, 'You were kind enough yesterday to introduce my Master into the house and we owe it to you that we have found a new disciple. I have no other way of showing my thanks but giving you these broken pieces of gold and silver, which I hope you will use to buy yourself a pair of shoes. If you come across any more monsters, please bespeak them for me, and I shall be even further obliged to you.' 'Reverend Sirs,' said Mr Kao, 'if I can't persuade you to accept silver or gold, I hope that you will at least let me show my gratitude by giving you these few pieces of course stuff, to make into cassocks.' 'A priest who accepts so much as a thread of silk,' said Tripitaka, 'must do penance for a thousand aeons to expiate his crime. All I ask is a few scraps left over from the household meal, to take with us as dry provisions.' 'Wait a minute,' cried Pigsy. 'If I get my due for all I've done on this estate since I married into the family, I should carry away several tons of provisions. That's by the way. But I think my father-in-law might in decency give me a new jacket. My old one was torn by Brother Monkey in the fight last night. And my shoes are all in pieces; I should be glad of a new pair.'

Mr Kao acceded to his request, and Pigsy, delighted by his new finery, strutted up and down in front of the com-pany, calling to Mr Kao, 'Be so kind as to inform my mother-in-law, my sisters-in-law and all my kinsmen by marriage that I have become a priest and must ask their pardon for going off without saying good-bye to them in person. And father-in-law, I'll trouble you to take good care of my bride.

For if we don't bring off this scripture business, I shall turn layman again and live with you as your son-in-law.' 'Lout!' cried Monkey. 'Don't talk rubbish.' 'It's not rubbish,' said Pigsy. 'Things may go wrong, and then I shall be in a pretty pass! No salvation, and no wife either.' 'Kindly stop this silly argument,' said Tripitaka. 'It is high time we started.' So they put together the luggage, which Pigsy was told to carry, and when the white horse was saddled Tripitaka was set astride. Monkey, with his cudgel over his shoulder, led the way. And so, parting from Mr Kao and all his relations, the three of them set out for the West. And if you do not know what befell them, you must listen to what is told in the next chapter.

Chapter 18

So the three of them travelled on towards the West, and came at last to a great plain. Summer had passed and autumn come. They heard 'the cicada singing in the rotten willow', saw 'the Fire-Star rolling to the west'. At last they came to a huge and turbulent river, racing along with gigantic waves. 'That's a very broad river,' cried Tripitaka from on horseback. 'There does not seem to be a ferry anywhere about. How are we to get across?' 'A boat wouldn't be much use in waters as rough as that,' said Pigsy. Monkey leapt up into the air, and shading his eyes with his hand gazed at the waters. 'Master,' he cried, 'this is going to be no easy matter. For me, yes. I should only have to shake my hips, and I should be across at one bound. But for you it's not going to be such easy work.' 'I can't even see the other side,' said Tripitaka. 'How far is it, do you suppose?' 'About eight hundred leagues,' said Monkey. 'How do you come to that reckoning?' asked Pigsy. 'I'll tell you frankly,' said Monkey. 'My sight is so good that I can see everything, lucky or unlucky, a thousand leagues away, and when I looked down on this river from above I could see well enough that it must be a good eight hundred leagues across.' Tripitaka was very much depressed, and was just turning his horse when he saw a slab of stone on which was the inscription 'River of Flowing Sands'. Underneath in small letters was the verse:

> In the Floating Sands, eight hundred wide,
> In the Dead Waters, three thousand deep,
> A goose-feather will not keep afloat,
> A rush-flower sinks straight to the bottom.

They were looking at this inscription when suddenly a monster of horrifying aspect came surging through the mountainous waves. His hair was flaming red, his eyes were like two lanterns; at his neck were strung nine skulls, and he carried a huge priest's-staff. Like a whirlwind he rushed straight at the pilgrims. Monkey seized Tripitaka and hurried him up the bank to a safe distance. Pigsy dropped his load and rushed at the monster with his rake. The monster fended off the blow with his priest's-staff. The fight that followed was a good one, each displaying his powers on the shores of the River of Flowing Sands. They fought twenty bouts without reaching a decision. Monkey, seeing the grand fight that was in progress, itched to go and join in it. At last he said to Tripitaka, 'You sit here and don't worry. I am going off to have a bit of fun with the creature.' Tripitaka did his best to dissuade him. But Monkey with a wild whoop leapt into the fray. At this moment the two of them were locked in combat, and it was hard to get between them. But Monkey managed to put in a tremendous blow of the cudgel right on the monster's head. At once the monster broke away, and rushing madly back to the water's edge leapt in and disappeared. Pigsy was furious. 'Heigh, brother,' he cried. 'Who asked you to interfere? The monster was just beginning to tire. After another three or four rounds he would not have been able to fend off my rake, and I should have had him at my mercy. But as soon as he saw your ugly face he took to his heels. You've spoilt everything!' 'I'll just tell you how it happened,' said Monkey. 'It's months since I had a chance to use my cudgel, and when I saw you having such a rare time with him my feet itched with longing not to miss the fun, and I couldn't hold myself back. How was I to know that the monster wouldn't play?' So hand in hand, laughing and talking, the two of them went back to Tripitaka. 'Have you caught the monster?' he asked. 'He gave up the fight,' said Monkey, 'and went back again into the water.' 'It wouldn't be a bad thing,' said Tripitaka, 'if we could persuade him to show us how to get across. He's lived here a long time, and must know this river inside out. Otherwise I don't see how we are to get across an enormous river like this without a boat.' 'There is something in that,' said Monkey. 'Does not the proverb say "You cannot live near cinnabar without becoming red, or near ink without becoming black." If we succeed in catching him we certainly ought not

174

to kill him, but make him take the Master across this river and then dispose of him.' 'You shall have your chance this time,' said Pigsy to Monkey. 'I'll stay here and look after the Master.'

'That's all very well,' said Monkey, 'but this job is not at all in my line. I'm not at my best in the water. To get along here, I have to change myself into some water creature, such as a fish or crab. If it were a matter of going up into the clouds, I have tricks enough to deal with the ugliest situation. But in the water I confess I am at a disadvantage.' 'I used, of course,' said Pigsy, 'to be Marshal of the River of Heaven, and had the command of eighty thousand watery fellows, so that I certainly ought to know something about that element. My only fear is that if whole broods of water-creatures were to come to the monster's help, I might get myself into a bit of a fix.' 'What you must do,' said Monkey, 'is to lure the monster out, and not get yourself involved in more of a scrap than you can help. Once he is out, I'll come to your assistance.' 'That's the best plan,' said Pigsy, 'I'll go at once.' So saying, he stripped off his blue embroidered jacket and shoes, and brandishing his rake plunged into the river. He found that he had forgotten none of his old water-magic, and lashing through the waves soon reached the bed of the stream and made his way straight ahead. After retiring from the fight, the monster lay down and had a nap. Soon however he was woken by the sound of someone coming through the water, and starting up he saw Pigsy pushing through the waves, rake in hand. Seizing his staff, he came towards him shouting, 'Now then, shaven pate, just look where you're going or you'll get a nasty knock with this staff!' Pigsy struck the staff aside with his rake, crying, 'What monster are you, that you dare to bar my path?' 'I'm surprised that you don't recognise me,' said the monster. 'I am not an ordinary spook, but a divinity with name and surname,' 'If that is so,' said Pigsy, 'what are you doing here, taking human lives? Tell me who you are, and I'll spare you!'

'So great was my skill in alchemic arts,' said the monster, 'that I was summoned to Heaven by the Jade Emperor and

175

became a Marshal of the Hosts of Heaven. One day, at a celestial banquet, my hand slipped and I broke a crystal cup. The Jade Emperor was furious, and I was hurried away to the execution ground. Fortunately for me the Red-legged Immortal begged for my release, and my sentence was changed to one of banishment to the River of Flowing Sands. When I am hungry I go ashore and eat whatever living thing comes my way. Many are the woodmen and fishermen who have fallen to me as my prey, and I don't mind telling you I am very hungry at this moment. Don't imagine that your flesh would be too coarse for me to eat. Chopped up fine and well sauced, you'll suit me nicely!' 'Coarse indeed!' said Pigsy. 'I'm a dainty enough morsel to make any mouth water. Mind your manners, and swallow your grandfather's rake!' The monster ducked and avoided the blow. Then both of them came up to the surface of the water, and treading the waves fought stubbornly for two hours without reaching a decision. It was a case of 'the copper bowl meeting the iron broom, the jade gong confronted by the metal bell.'

After some thirty rounds Pigsy pretended to give in, and dragging his rake after him made for the shore, with the monster hard on his heels. 'Come on!' cried Pigsy. 'With firm ground under our feet we'll have a better fight than before.' 'I know what you're up to,' cried the monster. 'You've lured me up here, so that your partner may come and help you. We'll go back into the water and finish the fight there.' The monster was too wily to come any further up the bank and they soon were fighting again, this time at the very edge of the water. This was too much for Monkey, who was watching them from a distance. 'Wait here,' he said to Tripitaka, 'while I try the trick called "The ravening eagle pouncing on its prey." ' So saying, he catapulted into the air and swooped down on the monster, who swiftly turning his head and seeing Monkey pouncing down upon him from the clouds, leapt straight into the water and was seen no more. 'He's given us the slip,' said Monkey. 'He's not likely to come out on the bank again. What are we going to do?'

'It's a tough job,' said Pigsy, 'I doubt if I can beat him. Even if I sweat till I burst I can't get beyond quits.' 'Let's go and see the Master,' said Monkey.

They climbed the bank, and finding Tripitaka they told him of their predicament. Tripitaka burst into tears. 'We shall never get across,' he sobbed. 'Don't you worry,' said Monkey. 'It is true that with that creature lying in wait for us, we can't get across. But Pigsy, you stay here by the Master and don't attempt to do any more fighting. I am going off to the Southern Ocean.' 'And what are you going to do there?' asked Pigsy. 'This scripture-seeking business,' said Monkey, 'is an invention of the Bodhisattva, and it was she who converted us. It is surely for her to find some way of getting us over this river. I'll go and ask her. It's a better idea than fighting with the monster.' 'Brother,' said Pigsy, 'when you're there you might say a word to her for me; tell her I'm very much obliged indeed for having been put on the right way.' 'If you are going,' said Tripitaka, 'you had better start at once and get back as soon as you can.'

Monkey somersaulted into the clouds, and in less than half an hour he had reached the Southern Ocean and saw Mount Potalaka rise before him. After landing, he went straight to the Purple Bamboo Grove, where he was met by the Spirits of the Twenty-Four Ways. 'Great Sage, what brings you here?' they said. 'My Master is in difficulties,' said Monkey, 'and I wish to have an interview with the Bodhisattva.' 'Sit down,' they said, 'and we will announce you.' The Bodhisattva was leaning against the parapet of the Lotus Pool, looking at the flowers, with the Dragon King's daughter, bearer of the Magic Pearl, at her side. 'Why aren't you looking after your Master?' she said to Monkey, when he was brought in. 'When we came to the River of Flowing Sands,' said Monkey, 'we found it guarded by a monster formidable in the arts of war. My fellow-disciple Pigsy, whom we picked up on the way, did his best to subdue the creature, but was not successful. That is why I have ventured to come and ask you to take pity on us, and rescue my Master from this predicament.' 'You obstinate ape,' said the Bodhisattva, 'this is the same thing all over again. Why didn't you say that you were in charge of the priest of 'T'ang?' 'We were both far too busy trying to catch him and make him take the Master across,' said Monkey. 'I put him there on purpose to help scripture-seekers,' said Kuan-yin. 'If only you had mentioned the fact that you had come from China to look for scriptures, you would have found him very helpful.'

'At present,' said Monkey, 'he is skulking at the bottom of the river. How are we to get him to come out and make himself useful? And how is Tripitaka going to get across the river?' The Bodhisattva summoned her disciple Hui-yen, and taking a red gourd from her sleeve she said to him, 'Take this gourd, go with Monkey to the river and shout "Sandy!" He will come out at once, and you must then bring him to the Master to make his submission. Next string together the nine skulls that he wears at his neck according to the disposition of the Magic Square, with the gourd in the middle, and you will find you have a holy ship that will carry Tripitaka across the River of Flowing Sands.'

Soon Hui-yen and Monkey alighted on the river-bank. Seeing who Monkey had brought with him, Pigsy led forward the Master to meet them. After salutations had been exchanged, Hui-yen went to the edge of the water and called, 'Sandy, Sandy! The scripture-seekers have been here a long time. Why do you not come out and pay your respects to them?'

The monster Sandy, knowing that this must be a messenger from Kuan-yin, hastened to the surface, and as soon as his head was above water he saw Hui-yen and Monkey. He put on a polite smile and came towards them bowing and saying to Hui-yen, 'Forgive me for not coming to meet you. Where is the Bodhisattva?' 'She has not come,' said Hui-yen. 'She sent me to tell you to put yourself at Tripitaka's disposal and become his disciple. She also told me to take the skulls that you wear at your neck and this gourd that I have brought, and make a holy ship to carry the Master across.'

'Where are the pilgrims?' asked Sandy. 'Sitting there on

the eastern bank,' said Hui-yen. 'Well,' said Sandy, looking at Pigsy, 'that filthy creature never said a word about scriptures, though I fought with him for two days.' Then seeing Monkey, 'What, is that fellow there too?' he cried. 'He's the other's partner. I'm not going near them.' 'The first is Pigsy,' said Hui-yen, 'and the second is Monkey. They are both Tripitaka's disciples and both were converted by the Bodhisattva. You have nothing to fear from them. I myself will introduce you to the Master.' Sandy put away his staff, tidied himself and scrambled up the bank. When they reached Tripitaka, Sandy knelt before him, exclaiming, 'How can I have been so blind as not to recognise you? Forgive me for all my rudeness!' 'You brazen creature,' said Pigsy, 'why did you insist on having a row with us, instead of joining our party from the start?' 'Brother,' laughed Monkey, 'don't scold him. It is we who are to blame, for never having told him that we were going to get scriptures.' 'Is it indeed your earnest desire to dedicate yourself to our religion?' asked Tripitaka. Sandy bowed his assent, and Tripitaka told Monkey to take a knife and shave his head. He then once more did homage to Tripitaka, and in a less degree to Monkey and Pigsy. Tripitaka thought that Sandy shaped very well as a priest, and was thoroughly satisfied with him.

'You had better be quick and get on with your boat-building,' said Hui-yen.

Sandy obediently took the skulls from his neck, and tying them in the pattern of the Magic Square he put the Bodhisattva's gourd in the middle, and called to Tripitaka to come down to the water. Tripitaka then ascended the holy ship, which he found as secure as any light craft. Pigsy supported him on the left, Sandy on the right, while Monkey in the stern held the halter of the white horse, which followed as best it could. Hui-yen floated just above them. They soon arrived in perfect safety at the other side.

And if you do not know how long it was before they got Illumination you must listen to what is told in the next chapter.

Chapter 19

Tripitaka sat in the Zen Hall of the Treasure Wood Temple, under the lamp; he recited the Water Litany of the Liang Emperor and read through the True Scripture of the Peacock. It was now the third watch (12 p.m.), and he put his books back into their bag, and was just going to get up and go to bed when he heard a great banging outside the gate and felt a dank blast of ghostly wind. Fearing the lamp would be blown out, he hastened to screen it with his sleeve. But the lamp continued to flicker in the strangest way, and Tripitaka began to tremble. He was, however, very tired, and presently he lay down across the reading-desk and dozed. Although his eyes were closed, he still knew what was going on about him, and in his ears still sounded the dark wind that moaned outside the window. And when the wind had passed by, he heard a voice outside the Zen Hall whispering: 'Master!'

Tripitaka raised his head, and in his dream he saw a man standing there, dripping from head to foot, with tears in his eyes, and continually murmuring, 'Master, Master.' Tripitaka sat up and said, 'What can you be but a hobgoblin, evil spirit, monster or foul bogey, that you should come to this place and molest me in the middle of the night? But I must tell you that I am no common scrambler in the greedy world of man. I am a great and illustrious priest who at the bidding of the Emperor of T'ang am going to the West to worship the Buddha and seek scriptures. And I have three disciples, each of whom is adept in quelling dragons and subduing tigers, removing monsters and making away with bogeys. If these disciples were to see you, they would grind you to powder. I tell you this for your own good, in kindness and compassion. You had best hide at once, and not set foot in this place of Meditation.' But the man drew nearer to the room and said, 'Master, I am no hobgoblin, evil spirit, monster, nor foul bogey either.' 'If you are none of these things,' said Tripitaka, 'what are you doing here at depth of night?' 'Master,' said the man, 'rest your eyes upon me and look at me well.' Then Tripitaka looked at him with a fixed gaze and saw that there was a crown upon his head and a sceptre at his waist, and that he was dressed and shod as only a king can be.

When Tripitaka saw this he was much startled and amazed. At once he bowed down and cried out with a loud voice: 'Of what court is your majesty the king? I beg of you, be seated.' But the hand he stretched to help the king to his seat plunged through empty space. Yet when he was back in his seat and looked up, the man was still there. 'Tell me, your majesty,' he cried, 'of what are you emperor, of where are you king? Doubtless there were troubles in your land, wicked ministers rebelled against you and at midnight you fled for your life. What is your tale? Tell it for me to hear.' 'Master,' he said, 'my home is due west of here, only forty leagues away. At that place, there is a city moated and walled, and this city is where my kingdom was founded.' 'And what is its name?' asked Tripitaka. 'I will not deceive you,' he said. 'When my dynasty was set up there, a new name was given to it, and it was called Crow-cock.' 'But tell me,' said Tripitaka, 'what brings you here in such consternation?' 'Master,' he said, 'five years ago there was a great drought. The grass did not grow and my people were all dying of hunger. It was pitiful indeed!' Tripitaka nodded. 'Your majesty,' he said, 'there is an ancient saying, "Heaven favours, where virtue rules." I fear you have no compassion for your people; for now that they are in trouble, you leave your city. Go back and open your storehouses, sustain your people, repent your misdeeds, and do present good twofold to make recompense. Release from captivity any whom you have unjustly condemned, and Heaven will see to it that rain comes and the winds are tempered.' 'All the granaries in my kingdom were empty,' he said, 'I had neither cash nor grain. My officers civil and military were unpaid, and even at my own board no relish could be served. I have shared sweet and bitter with my people no less than Yü the Great when he quelled the floods; I have bathed and done penance; morn-

181

ing and night I have burnt incense and prayed. For three years it was like this, till the rivers were all empty, the wells dry.

'Suddenly, when things were at their worst, there came a magician from the Chung-nan mountains who could call the winds and summon the rain, and make stones into gold. First he obtained audience with my many officers, civil and military, and then with me. At once I begged him to mount the altar and pray for rain. He did so, and was answered; no sooner did his magic tablet resound than floods of rain fell. I told him three feet would be ample. But he said after so long a drought, it took a lot to soak the ground, and he brought down another two inches. And I, seeing him to be of such great powers, prostrated myself before him and treated him henceforth as my elder brother.' 'This was a great piece of luck,' said Tripitaka. 'Whence should my luck come?' asked he. 'Why,' said Tripitaka, 'if your magician could make rain when you wanted it, and gold whenever you needed it, what did you lack that you must needs leave your kingdom and come to me here?'

'For two years,' he said, 'he was my fellow at board and bed. Then at spring time when all the fruit trees were in blossom and young men and girls from every house, gallants from every quarter, went out to enjoy the sights of spring, there came a time when my officers had all returned to their desks and the ladies of the court to their bowers. I with that magician went slowly stepping hand in hand, till we came to the flower-garden and to the eight-cornered crystal well. Here he threw down something, I do not know what, and at once there was a great golden light. He led me to the well-side, wondering what treasure was in the well. Then he conceived an evil intent, and with a great shove pushed me into the well; then took a paving-stone and covered the well-top and sealed it with clay, and planted a banana-plant on top of it . . . Pity me! I have been dead three years; I am the phantom unavenged of one that perished at the bottom of a well.'

When the man said that he was a ghost, Tripitaka was

terrified; his legs grew flabby beneath him, and his hair stood on end. Controlling himself at last, he asked him saying, 'Your Majesty's story is hard to reconcile with reason. You say you have been dead for three years. How is it that in all this time none of your officers civil and military, nor of your queens and concubines and chamberlains ever came to look for you?' 'I have told you already,' the man said, 'of the magician's powers. There can be few others like him in all the world. He had but to give himself a shake, and there and then, in the flower-garden, he changed himself into the exact image of me. And now he holds my rivers and hills, and has stolen away my kingdom. All my officers, the four hundred gentlemen of my court, my queens and concubines – all, all are his.'

'Your Majesty is easily daunted,' said Tripitaka. 'Easily daunted?' he asked. 'Yes,' said Tripitaka, 'that magician may have strange powers, turn himself into your image, steal your lands, your officers knowing nothing, and your ladies unaware. But you that were dead at least knew that you were dead. Why did you not go to Yama, King of Death, and put in a complaint?'

'The magician's power,' he said, 'is very great, and he is on close terms with the clerks and officers of Death. The Spirit of Wall and Moat is forever drinking with him; all the Dragon-kings of the Sea are his kinsmen. The God of the Eastern Peak is his good friend; the ten kings of Judgement are his cousins. I should be barred in every effort to lay my plaint before the King of Death.'

'If your Majesty,' said Tripitaka, 'is unable to lay your case before the Courts of the Dead, what makes you come to the world of the living with any hope of redress?' 'Master,' he said, 'how should a wronged ghost dare approach your door? The Spirit that Wanders at Night caught me in a gust of magic wind and blew me along. He said my three years' water-misery was ended and that I was to present myself before you; for at your service, he said, there was a great disciple, the Monkey Sage, most able to conquer demons and subdue impostors. I beg of you to come to my kingdom, lay hands on the magician and make clear the false from the true. Then, Master, I would repay you with all that will be mine to give.'

'So then,' said Tripitaka, 'you have come to ask that my disciple should drive out the false magician?' 'Indeed, indeed,' he said. 'My disciple,' said Tripitaka, 'in other ways is not all that he should be. But subduing monsters and evil spirits just suits his powers. I fear however that the circumstances make it hard for him to deal with this evil power.' 'Why so?' asked the king. 'Because,' said Tripitaka, 'the magician has used his magic powers to change himself into the image of you. All the officers of your court have gone over to him, and all your ladies have accepted him. My disciple could no doubt deal with them; but he would hesitate to do violence to them. For should he do so, would not he and I be held guilty of conspiring to destroy your kingdom? And what would this be but to paint the tiger and carve the swan?'[1]

'There is still someone of mine at Court,' he said. 'Excellent, excellent,' said Tripitaka. 'No doubt it is some personal attendant, who is guarding some fastness for you.' 'Not at all,' he said. 'It is my own heir apparent.' 'But surely,' said Tripitaka, 'the false magician has driven him away.' 'Not at all,' he said. 'He is in the Palace of Golden Bells, in the Tower of the Five Phoenixes, studying with his tutor, or on the steps of the magician's throne. But all these three years he has forbidden the prince to go into the inner chambers of the Palace, and he can never see his mother.' 'Why is that?' asked Tripitaka. 'It is the magician's scheme,' he said. 'He fears that if they were to meet, the queen might in the course of conversation let drop some word that would arouse the prince's suspicions. So these two never met, and he all this long time has lived secure.'

'The disaster that has befallen you, no doubt at Heaven's behest, is much like my own misfortune. My own father was killed by brigands, who seized my mother, and after three

[1] *i.e.*, an enterprise which, if successful, does more harm than inaction.

months she gave birth to me. I at length escaped from their hands and by good chance met with kindness from a priest of the Golden Mountain Temple, who brought me up. Remembering my own unhappy state, without father or mother, I can sympathise with your prince, who has lost both his parents. But tell me, granted that this prince is still at Court, how can I manage to see him?' 'What difficulty in that?' he said. 'Because he is kept under strict control,' said Tripitaka, 'and is not even allowed to see the mother who bore him. How will a stray monk get to him?' 'Tomorrow,' the king said, 'he leaves the Court at daybreak.' 'For what purpose?' 'Tomorrow, early in the morning, with three thousand followers and falcons and dogs, he will go hunting outside the city, and it will certainly be easy for you to see him. You must then tell him what I have told you, and he cannot fail to believe you.' 'He is only a common mortal,' said Tripitaka, 'utterly deceived by the false magician in the palace, and at every turn calling him father and king. Why should he believe what I tell him?' 'If that is what worries you,' the king said, 'I will give you a token to show to him.' 'And what can you give me?'

In his hand the king carried a tablet of white jade, bordered with gold. This he laid before Tripitaka saying, 'Here is my token.' 'What thing is this?' asked Tripitaka. 'When the magician disguised himself as me,' said the king, 'this treasure was the one thing he forgot about. When the queen asked what had become of it, he said that the wonder-worker who came to make rain took it away with him. If my prince sees it, his heart will be stirred towards me and he will avenge me.' 'That will do,' said Tripitaka. 'Wait for me a little, while I tell my disciple to arrange this matter for you. Where shall I find you?' 'I dare not wait,' he said. 'I must ask the Spirit that wanders at Night to blow me to the inner chambers of the palace, where I will appear to the queen in a dream and tell her how to work with her son, and to conspire with you and your disciple.' Tripitaka nodded and agreed, saying, 'Go, if you will.' Then the wronged ghost beat its head on the floor and turned as though to depart.

Somehow it stumbled, and went sprawling with a loud noise that woke Tripitaka up. He knew that it had all been a dream, and finding himself sitting with the dying lamp in front of him, he hurriedly cried: 'Disciple, disciple!' 'Hey, what's that?' cried Pigsy, waking up and coming across to him. 'In the old days when I was a decent chap and had my whack of human flesh whenever I wanted, and all the stinking victuals I needed, that was a happy life indeed. A very different matter from coddling an old cleric on his journey! I thought I was to be an acolyte, but this is more like being a slave. By day I hoist the luggage and lead the horse; by night I run my legs off bringing you your pot. No sleep early or late! What's the matter this time?' 'Disciple,' said Tripitaka, 'I was dozing just now at my desk, and had a strange dream.'

At this point Monkey sat up, and coming across to Tripitaka said, 'Master, dreams come from waking thoughts. Each time we come to a hill before we have even begun to climb it, you are in a panic about ogres and demons. And you are always brooding about what a long way it is to India, and wondering if we shall ever get there; and thinking about Ch'ang-an, and wondering if you will ever see it again. All this brooding makes dreams. You should be like me. I think only about seeing Buddha in the West, and not a dream comes near me.' 'Disciple,' said Tripitaka, 'this was not a dream of home-sickness. No sooner had I closed my eyes than there came a wild gust of wind, and there at the door stood an Emperor, who said he was the King of Crow-cock. He was dripping from head to foot, and his eyes were full of tears.' Then he told Monkey the whole story. 'You need say no more,' said Monkey. 'It is clear enough that this dream came to you in order to bring a little business my way. No doubt at all that this magician is an ogre who has usurped the throne. Just let me put him to the test. I don't doubt my stick will make short work of him.' 'Disciple,' said Tripitaka, 'he said the magician was terribly powerful.' 'What do I care how powerful he is?' said Monkey. 'If he had any inkling that Monkey might arrive on the scene, he would have cleared out long ago.' 'Now I come to think of it,' said

186

Tripitaka, 'he left a token.' Pigsy laughed. 'Now, Master,' he said, 'you must pull yourself together. A dream's a dream. Now it is time to talk sense again.' But Sandy broke in, ' "He who does not believe that straight is straight must guard against the wickedness of good." Let us light torches, open the gate, and see for ourselves whether the token has been left or not.'

Monkey did indeed open the gate, and there, in the light of the stars and moon, with no need for torches, they saw lying on the ramp of the steps a tablet of white jade with gold edges. Pigsy stepped forward and picked it up, saying, 'Brother, what's this thing?' 'This,' said Monkey, 'is the treasure that the king carried in his hand. It is called a jade tablet. Master, now that we have found this thing, there is no more doubt about the matter. Tomorrow it will be my job to catch this fiend.'

Dear Monkey! He plucked a hair from his tail, blew on it with magic breath, cried out 'Change!' and it became a casket lacquered in red and gold; he laid the tablet in it, and said, 'Master, take this in your hand, and when day comes put on your embroidered cassock, and sit reading the scriptures in the great hall. Meanwhile I will inspect that walled city. If I find that an ogre is indeed ruling there, I will slay him, and do a deed by which I shall be remembered here. But if it is not an ogre, we must beware of meddling in the business at all.' 'You are right,' said Tripitaka. 'If,' said Monkey, 'the prince does not go out hunting, then there is nothing to be done. But if the dream comes true, I will bring him here to see you.' 'And if he comes here, how am I to receive him?' 'When I let you know that he is coming, open the casket and wait while I change myself into a little priest two inches long, and put me in the casket. When the prince comes here, he will go and bow to the Buddha. Don't you take any notice of the prince or kneel down before him. When he sees that you, a commoner, do not bow down to him, he will order his followers to seize you. You will, of course, let yourself be seized, and beaten too, if they choose to beat you, and bound if they choose to bind you. Let them

187

kill you, indeed, if they want to.' 'They will be well armed,' said Tripitaka. 'They might very well kill me. That is not a good idea at all.' 'It would not matter,' said Monkey. 'I could deal with that. I will see to it that nothing really serious happens. If he questions you, say that you were sent by the Emperor of China to worship Buddha and get scriptures, and that you have brought treasures with you. When he asks what treasures, show him your cassock and say it is the least of the three treasures, and that there are two others. Then show him the casket and tell him that there is a treasure within that knows what happened five hundred years ago, and what will happen in five hundred years long hence, and five hundred years between. One thousand five hundred years in all, of things past and present. Then let me out of the casket and I will tell the prince what was revealed in the dream. If he believes, I will go and seize the magician and the prince will be avenged upon his father's murderer and we shall win renown. But if he does not believe, I will show him the jade tablet. Only I fear he is too young, and will not recognise it.' Tripitaka was delighted. 'An excellent plan,' he said. 'But what shall we call the third treasure? The first is the embroidered cassock, the second the white jade tablet. What is your transformation to be called?' 'Call it,' said Monkey, 'the Baggage that makes Kings.' Tripitaka agreed, and committed the name to memory.

Neither disciple nor teacher could sleep. How gladly would they have been able, by a nod, to call up the sun from the Mulberry Tree where it rests, and by a puff of breath blow away the stars that filled the sky!

However, at last it began to grow white in the East, and Monkey got up and gave his orders to Pigsy and Sandy. 'Do not,' he said, 'upset the other priests in the temple by coming out of your cell and rollicking about. Wait till I have done my work, and then we will go on again together.'

As soon as he had left them he turned a somersault and leapt into the air. Looking due west with his fiery eyes he soon saw a walled and moated city. You may ask how it was that he could see it. Well, it was only forty leagues away from

188

the temple, and being so high in the air he could see as far as that.

Going on a little way and looking closely, he saw that baleful clouds hung round the city and fumes of discontent surrounded it, and suspended in mid-air Monkey recited:

Were he a true king seated on the throne,
Then there would be a lucky gleam and fire-coloured clouds.
But as it is, a false fiend has seized the Dragon Seat,
And coiling wreaths of black fume tarnish the Golden Gate.

While he was gazing at this sad sight, Monkey suddenly heard a great clanging, and looking down he saw the eastern gate of the city open, and from it a great throng of men and horses come out; truly a host of huntsmen. Indeed, a brave show; look at them:

At dawn they left the east of the Forbidden City;
They parted and rounded up in the fields of low grass,
Their bright banners opened and caught the sun,
Their white palfreys charged abreast the wind.
Their skin drums clatter with a loud roll;
The hurled spears fly each to its mark.

The hunters left the city and proceeded eastwards for twenty leagues towards a high plain. Now Monkey could see that in the midst of them was a little, little general in helmet and breastplate, in his hand a jewelled sword, riding a bay charger, his bow at his waist. 'Don't tell me!' said Monkey in the air, 'that is the prince. Let me go and play a trick on him.'

Dear Monkey! He lowered himself on his cloud, made his way through the ranks of the huntsmen and, when he came to the prince, changed himself into a white hare and ran in front of the prince's horse. The prince was delighted, took an arrow from his quiver, strung it and shot at the hare, which he hit. But Monkey had willed the arrow to find its aim, and with a swift grab, just as it was about to touch him, he caught hold of it and ran on.

The prince, seeing that he had hit his mark, broke away from his companions and set out in pursuit. When the horse galloped fast, Monkey ran like the wind; when it slowed down, Monkey slowed down. The distance between them remained always the same, and so bit by bit enticed the prince to the gates of the Treasure Wood Temple. The hare had vanished, for Monkey went back to his own form. But in the door-post an arrow was stuck.

'Here we are, Master,' said Monkey, and at once changed again into a two-inch priest and hid in the casket.

Now when the prince came to the temple-gate and found no hare, but only his own arrow sticking in the gate-post, 'Very strange!' said the prince, 'I am certain I hit the hare. How is it that the hare has disappeared, but the arrow is here? I think it was not a common hare, but one that had lived too long and changed at last into a sprite.'

He pulled out the arrow, and looking up saw that above the gate of the temple was an inscription which said 'Treasure Wood Temple, erected by Royal Command.' 'Why, of course!' said the prince. 'I remember years ago my father the king ordered an officer to take gold and precious stuffs to the priests of this temple, so that they might repair the chapel and images. I little thought that I would come here one day like this! A couplet says:

> Chance brought me to a priest's cell
> and I listened to his holy talk;
> From the life of the troubled world I got
> Half a day's rest.

I will go in.'

The prince leapt from his horse's back and was just going in when three thousand officers who were in attendance upon him came galloping up in a great throng, and were soon pouring into the courtyard. The priests of the temple, much astonished, came out to do homage to the prince, and escort him into the Buddha Hall, to worship the Buddha. The prince was admiring the cloisters, when suddenly he came upon a priest who sat there and did not budge when he came

190

past. 'Has this priest no manners?' the prince cried in a rage. 'As no warning was given that I was visiting this place, I could not expect to be met at a distance. But so soon as you saw men-at-arms approaching the gate, you ought to have stood up. How comes it that you are still sitting here without budging? Seize him!'

No sooner had he uttered the command than soldiers rushed from the sides, dragged Tripitaka off with them and made ready to bind him hand and foot. But Monkey in the casket soundlessly invoked the guardian spirits, Devas that protect the Law, and Lu Ting and Lu Chia: 'I am now on an errand to subdue an evil spirit. But this prince, in his ignorance, has bade his servants bind my master, and you must come at once to his aid. If he is indeed bound, you will be held responsible!'

Thus secretly addressed by Monkey, how could they venture to disobey? They set a magic ring about Tripitaka, so that each time any one tried to lay hands on him, he could not be reached, any more than if he had been hedged in with a stout wall. 'Where do you come from,' the prince asked at last, 'that you can cheat us like this, making yourself unapproachable?' Tripitaka now came forward and bowed. 'I have no such art,' he said. 'I am only a priest from China, going to the West to worship Buddha and get scriptures.'

'China?' said the prince. 'Although it is called The Middle Land, it is a most destitute place. Tell me, for example, if you have anything of value upon you.' 'There is the cassock on my back,' said Tripitaka. 'It is only a third-class treasure. But I have treasures of the first and second class, which are far superior.'

'A coat like yours,' said the prince, 'that leaves half the body bare! It seems a queer thing to call that a treasure.' 'This cassock,' said Tripitaka, 'although it covers only half my body, is described in a poem:

Buddha's coat left one side bare,
But it hid the Absolute from the world's dust.
Its ten thousand threads and thousand stitches fulfilled the
    fruits of Meditation.

Is it a wonder that when I saw you come
        I did not rise to greet you?
You who call yourself a man, yet have failed to avenge a
  father's death!'

'What wild nonsense this priest is talking!' said the prince
in a great rage. 'That half-coat, if it has done nothing else
for you, has given you the courage to babble ridiculous
fustian. How can my father's death be unavenged, since he is
not dead? Just tell me that!'

Tripitaka came one step forward, pressed the palms of his
hands together and said: 'Your Majesty, to how many things
does man, born into the world, owe gratitude?' 'To four
things,' said the prince. 'To what four things?' 'He is grateful,' said the prince, 'to Heaven and Earth for covering and
supporting him, to the sun and moon for shining upon him,
to the king for lending him water and earth, and to his father
and mother for rearing him.'

Tripitaka laughed. 'To the other three he owes gratitude
indeed,' he said. 'But what need has he of a father and
mother to rear him?' 'That's all very well for you,' said the
prince, 'who are a shaven-headed, disloyal, food-cadging
wanderer. But if a man had no father or mother, how could
he come into the world?' 'Your Majesty,' said Tripitaka, 'I
do not know. But in this casket there is a treasure called
"The baggage that makes kings." It knows everything that
happened during the five hundred years long ago, the five
hundred years between, and the five hundred years to come,
one thousand five hundred years in all. If he can quote a case
where there was no gratitude to father and mother, then let
me be detained captive here.'

'Show him to me,' said the prince. Tripitaka took off the
cover and out jumped monkey, and began to skip about this
way and that. 'A little fellow like that can't know much,'
said the prince. Hearing himself described as too small,
Monkey used his magic power and stretched himself till he
was three feet four inches high. The huntsmen were
astonished, and said, 'If he goes on growing like this, in a few
days he will be bumping his head against the sky.' But when

he reached his usual height, Monkey stopped growing. At this point the prince said to him, 'Baggage who Makes Kings, the old priest says you know all things good and ill, in past and present. Do you divine by the tortoise or by the milfoil? Or do you decide men's fates by sentences from books?' 'Not a bit of it,' said Monkey; 'all I rely on is my three inches of tongue, that tells about everything.'

'This fellow talks great nonsense,' said the prince. 'It has always been by the *Book of Changes* that mysteries have been elucidated and the prospects of the world decided, so that people might know what to pursue and what to avoid. Is it not said: "The tortoise for divination, the milfoil for prognostication?" But so far as I can make out you go on no principle at all. You talk at random about fate and the future, exciting and misleading people to no purpose.' 'Now don't be in a hurry, Your Highness,' said Monkey, 'but listen to me. You are the Crown Prince of Crow-cock. Five years ago there was a famine in your land. The king and his ministers prayed and fasted, but they could not get a speck of rain. Then there came a wizard from the Chung-nan mountains who could call the winds, fetch rain, and turn stone into gold. The king was deceived by his wiles and hailed him as elder brother. Is this true?'

'Yes, yes, yes,' said the prince. 'Go on!' 'For the last three years the magician has not been seen,' said Monkey. 'Who is it that has been on the throne?' 'It is true about the wizard,' said the prince. 'My father did make this wizard his brother, and ate with him and slept with him. But three years ago, when they were walking in the flower garden and admiring the view, a gust of magic wind that the magician sent, blew the jade tablet that the king carried, out of his hand, and the magician went off with it straight to the Chung-nan mountains. My father still misses him and has no heart to walk in the flower garden without him. Indeed, for three years it has been locked up and no one has set foot in it. If the king is not my father, who is he?'

At this Monkey began to laugh, and did not stop laughing when the prince asked him what was the matter, till the prince lost his temper. 'Why don't you say something?' he said, 'instead of standing there laughing.' 'I have quite a lot to say,' said Monkey, 'but I cannot say it in front of all these people.' The prince thought this reasonable, and motioned to the huntsmen to retire. The leader gave his orders, and soon the three thousand men and horses were all stationed outside the gates. None of the priests of the temple were about. Monkey stopped laughing and said, 'Your Highness, he who vanished was the father that begot you; he who sits on the throne is the magician that brought rain.'

'Nonsense,' cried the prince. 'Since the magician left us, the winds have been favouring, the people have been at peace. But according to you it is not my father who is on the throne. It is all very well to say such things to me who am young and let it pass; but if my father were to hear you uttering this subversive talk, he would have you seized and torn into ten thousand pieces.' He began railing at Monkey, who turned to Tripitaka and said, 'What is to be done? I have told him and he does not believe me. Let's get to work. Show him your treasure, and then get your papers seen to, and go off to India.' Tripitaka handed the lacquer-box to Monkey, and Monkey taking it gave himself a shake, and the box became invisible. For it was in reality one of Monkey's hairs, which he had changed into a box, but now put back again as a hair on his body. But the white jade tablet he presented to the prince.

'A fine sort of priest,' the prince exclaimed. 'You it was who came five years ago disguised as a magician, and stole the family treasure, and now, disguised as a priest, are offering it back again! Seize him!' This command startled Tripitaka out of his wits and pointing at Monkey, 'It's you,' he cried, 'you wretched horse-groom, who have brought this trouble on us for no reason at all.' Monkey rushed forward and checked him. 'Hold your tongue,' he said, 'and don't let out my secrets. I am not called "the Baggage that Makes Kings." My real name is quite different.' 'I shall be glad to know your real name,' said the prince, 'that I may send you to the magistrate to be dealt with as you deserve.'

'My name then,' said Monkey, 'is the Great Monkey Sage, and I am this old man's chief disciple. I was going with my Master to India to get scriptures, and last night we came to this temple and asked for shelter. My Master was reading scriptures by night, and at the third watch he had a dream. He dreamt that your father came to him and said he had been attacked by that magician, who in the flower garden pushed him into the eight-cornered crystal well. Then the wizard changed himself into your father's likeness. The court and all the officers were completely deceived; you yourself were too young to know. You were forbidden to enter the inner apartments of the Palace and the flower garden was shut up, lest the secret should get out. Tonight your father came and asked me to subdue the false magician. I was not sure that he was an evil spirit, but when I looked down from the sky I was quite certain of it. I was just going to seize him, when I met you and your huntsmen. The white hare you shot was me. It was I who led you here and brought you to my Master. This is the truth, every word of it. You have recognised the white tablet, and all that remains is for you to repay your father's care and revenge yourself on his enemy.'

This upset the prince very much. 'If I do not believe this story,' he said to himself, 'it must in any case have an unpleasant amount of truth in it. But if I believe it, how can I any longer look upon the present king as my father?' He was in great perplexity. 'If you are in doubt,' said Monkey, 'ride home and ask your mother a question that will decide it. Ask whether she and the king, as man and wife, are on changed terms, these last three years.'

'That is a good idea,' said the prince. 'Just wait while I go and ask my mother.' He snatched up the jade tablet and was about to make off, when Monkey stopped him, saying, 'If all your gentlemen follow you back to the palace, suspicions will be aroused, and how can I succeed in my task? You must go back all alone and attract no attention. Do not go in at the main gate but by the back gate. And when you get to the inner apartments and see your mother, do not speak loudly or clearly, but in a low whisper; for if the magician should hear you, so great is his power that your life and your mother's would be in danger.'

The prince did as he was told, and as he left the temple he told his followers to remain there on guard and not to move. 'I have some business,' he said. 'Wait till I have got to the city and then come on yourselves!' Look at him!

> He gives his orders to the men-at-arms,
> Flies on horseback home to the citadel.

If you do not know whether on this occasion he succeeded in seeing his mother, and if so what passed between them, you must listen to the next chapter.

196

Chapter 20

The prince was soon back at the city of Crow-cock, and as instructed he made no attempt to go in by the main gate, but without announcing himself went to the back gate, where several eunuchs were on guard. They did not dare to stop him, and (dear prince!) he rode in all alone, and soon reached the Arbour of Brocade Perfume, where he found his mother surrounded by her women, who were fanning her, while she leant weeping over a carven balustrade. Why, you will ask, was she weeping? At the fourth watch she had had a dream, half of which she could remember and half of which had faded; and she was thinking hard. Leaping from his horse, the prince knelt down before her and cried 'Mother!' She forced herself to put on a happier countenance, and exclaimed, 'Child, this is a joy indeed! For years past you have been so busy in the men's quarters at the Palace, studying with your father, that I have never seen you, which has been a great sorrow to me. How have you managed to find time today? It is an unspeakable pleasure! My child, why is your voice so mournful? Your father is growing old. Soon the time will come when the "dragon returns to the pearl-grey sea, the phoenix to the pink mists"; you will then become king. Why should you be dispirited?'

The prince struck the floor with his forehead. 'Mother, I ask you,' he said, 'who is it that sits upon the throne?' 'He has gone mad,' said the queen. 'The ruler is your father and the king. Why should you ask?' 'Mother,' the prince said, 'if you will promise me forgiveness I will speak. But if not, I dare not speak.' 'How can there be questions of guilt and pardon between mother and son? Of course, you are free to speak. Be quick and begin.' 'Mother,' said the prince, 'if you compare your life with my father these last three years with your life with him before, should you say that his affection was as great?' Hearing this question the queen altogether lost her presence of mind, and leaping to her feet

197

ran down from the arbour and flung herself into his arms, saying, 'Child, why, when I have not seen you for so long, should you suddenly come and ask me such a question?' 'Mother,' said the prince hotly, 'do not evade this question. For much hangs upon the answer to it.'

Then the queen sent away all the Court ladies, and with tears in her eyes said in a low voice, 'Had you not asked me, I would have gone down to the Nine Springs of Death without ever breathing a word about this matter. But since you have asked, hear what I have to say:

> What three years ago was warm and bland,
> These last three years has been cold as ice.
> When at the pillow's side I questioned him,
> He told me age had impaired his strength
> and that things did not work.'

When he heard this, the prince shook himself free, gripped the saddle and mounted his horse. His mother tried to hold him back, saying, 'Child, what is it that makes you rush off before our talk is done?' The prince returned and knelt in front of her. 'Mother,' he said, 'I dare not speak. Today at dawn I received a command to go hunting outside the city with falcon and dog. By chance I met a priest sent by the Emperor of China to fetch scriptures. He has a chief disciple named Monkey, who is very good at subduing evil spirits. According to him my father the king was drowned in the crystal well in the flower garden, and a wizard impersonated him and seized his throne. Last night at the third watch my father appeared in a dream to this priest and asked him to come to the city and seize the impostor. I did not believe all this, and so came to question you. But what you have just told me makes me certain that it is an evil spirit.'

'My child,' said the queen, 'why should you believe strangers, of whom you have no knowledge?' 'I should not, said the prince, 'have dared to accept the story as true, had not the king my father left behind a token in the hands of these people.' The queen asked what it was, and the prince took out from his sleeve the white jade tablet bordered with gold, and handed it to his mother. When she saw that it was indeed a treasure that had been the king's in old days, she could not stop her tears gushing out like a water-spring. 'My lord and master,' she cried, 'why have you been dead three years and never come to me, but went first to a priest and afterwards to the prince?' 'Mother,' said the prince, 'what do these words mean?' 'My child,' she said, 'at the fourth watch I too had a dream. I dreamt I saw your father stand in front of me, all dripping wet, saying that he was dead, and that his soul had visited a priest of T'ang and asked him to defeat the false king and rescue his own body from where it had been thrown. That is all I can remember, and it is only half. The other half I cannot get clear, and I was puzzling about it when you came. It is strange that you should just at this moment come with this tale, and bring this tablet with you. I will put it away, and you must go and ask that priest to come at once and do what he promises. If he can drive away the impostor and distinguish the false from the true, you will have repaid the king your father for the pains he bestowed upon your upbringing.'

The prince was soon back at the gates of the Treasure Wood Temple, where he was joined by his followers. The sun's red disc was now falling. He told his followers to stay quietly where they were, went into the temple alone, arranged his hat and clothes, and paid his respects to Monkey, who came hopping and skipping from the main hall. The prince knelt down, saying, 'Here I am again, Father.' Monkey raised him from his knees. 'Did you ask anyone anything when you were in the city?' he said. 'I questioned my mother,' said the prince; and he told the whole story. Monkey smiled. 'If it is as cold as that,' he said, 'he is probably a transformation of some chilly creature. No matter! Just wait while I mop him up for you. But today it is growing late, and I cannot very well start doing anything. You go back now, and I will come early tomorrow.'

'Master,' said the prince, kneeling before him, 'let me wait here till the morning, and then go along with you.' 'That will not do,' said Monkey. 'If I were to come into the city at the same time as you, the suspicions of the impostor would be aroused. He would not believe that I forced myself upon you, but would be sure you had invited me. And in this way the blame would fall on you.'

'I shall get into trouble anyhow,' said the prince, 'if I go into the city now.' 'What about?' asked Monkey. 'I was sent out hunting,' said the prince, 'and I have not got a single piece of game. How dare I face the king? If he accuses me of incompetence and casts me into prison, who will you have to look after you when you arrive tomorrow? There is not one of the officers who knows you.' 'What matter?' said Monkey. 'You have only to mention that you need some game, and I will procure it for you.' Dear Monkey! Watch him while he displays his arts before the prince. He gives himself a shake, jumps up on to the fringe of a cloud, performs a magic pass and murmurs a spell which compels the spirits of the mountain and the local deities to come before him and do obeisance. 'Great Sage' they said, 'what orders have you for us little divinities?' 'I guarded a priest of T'ang on his way here,' said Monkey. 'I want to seize an evil spirit, but this prince here has nothing to show for his hunting, and does not dare return to Court. I have sent for you divinities to ask you to do me a favour. Find some musk deer, wild boar, hares and so on – any wild beasts or birds you can discover, and bring them here.' The divinities dared not disobey. 'How many do you require of each?' they asked. 'It does not matter exactly how many,' said Monkey. 'Just bring some along; that is all.'

Then these divinities, using the secret instruments that appertained to them, made a magic wind that drew together wild beasts. Soon there were hundreds and thousands of wild fowl, deer, foxes, hares, tigers, panthers and wolves collected in front of Monkey. 'It is not I who want them!' he cried. 'You must get them on the move again, and string them out on each side of the road for forty leagues. The hunters will be able to take them home without use of falcon or dog. That is all that is required of you.'

The divinities obeyed, and spread out the game on each side of the road. Monkey then lowered his cloud and said to the prince, 'Your Highness may now go back. There is game all along the road; you have only to collect it.'

When the prince saw him floating about in the air and exercising magic powers, he was deeply impressed, and bent his head on the ground in prostration before Monkey, from whom he humbly took his leave. He then went out in front of the temple and gave orders to the huntsmen to return to Court. They were astonished to find endless wild game on each side of the road, which they took without use of falcon or dog, merely by laying hands upon it. They all believed that this blessing had been vouchsafed to the prince, and had no idea that it was Monkey's doing. Listen to the songs of triumph that they sing as they throng back to the city!

When the priests of the temple saw on what terms Tripitaka and the rest were with the prince, they began to treat them with a new deference. They invited them to refreshments, and again put the Zen Hall at Tripitaka's disposal. It was near the first watch; but Monkey had something on his mind and could not get to sleep at once. Presently he crept across to Tripitaka's bed and called, 'Master!' Tripitaka was not asleep either; but knowing that Monkey liked giving people a start, he pretended to be asleep. Monkey rubbed his tonsure and shaking him violently, he said, 'Master, why are you sleeping?' 'The rogue!' cried Tripitaka crossly. 'Why can't you go to sleep, instead of pestering me like this?' 'Master,' said Monkey, 'there is something you must give me your advice about.' 'What is that?' said Tripitaka. 'I talked very big to the prince,' said Monkey, 'giving him to understand that my powers were high as the hills and deep as the sea, and that I could catch the false wizard as easily as one takes things out of a bag – I had only to stretch out my hand and carry him off. But I cannot get to sleep, for it has occurred to me that it may not be so easy.' 'If you think it's too difficult, why do it?' said Tripitaka. 'It's not that there's any difficulty about catching him,' said Monkey. 'The only question is whether it is legal.' 'What nonsense this monkey talks,' said Tripitaka. 'How can it be illegal to arrest a monster that has seized a monarch's throne?' 'You only know how to read scriptures, worship Buddha and practise Zen, and have never studied the Code of Hsiao Ho. But you must at least know the proverb "Take robber, take loot." The magician has been king for three years and not the slightest suspicion has been felt by anyone. All the late king's ladies sleep with him, and the ministers civil and military disport themselves with him. Even if I succeed in catching him, how am I to convince anyone of his guilt?' 'What is the difficulty?' asked Tripitaka. 'Even if he were as dumb as a calabash, he would be able to talk one down. He would say boldly, "I am the king of Crow-cock. What crime have I committed against Heaven that you should arrest me?" How would one argue with him then?' 'And you,' said Tripitaka, 'what plan have you got?' 'My plan is already made,' said Monkey smiling. 'The only obstacle is that you have a partiality.' 'A partiality for whom?' said Tripitaka. 'Pigsy,' said Monkey; 'you have a preference for him because he is so strong.' 'What makes you think that?' said Tripitaka. 'If it were not so,' said Monkey, 'you would pull yourself together and have the courage to stay here with Sandy to look after you, while I and Pigsy go off to the city of Crow-cock, find the flower garden, uncover the well, and bring up the Emperor's body, which we will wrap in our wrapper, and next day bring to Court. There we will get our papers put in order, confront the Magician, and I will fell him with my cudgel. If he tries to exonerate himself, I will show him the body and say, "Here is the man you drowned." And I will make the prince come forward and wail over his father, the queen come out and recognise her husband, the officers civil and military look upon their lord, and then I and my brother will get to work. In this way the whole thing will be on a proper footing.'

Tripitaka thought this was a splendid plan, but he was not sure that Pigsy would consent. 'Why not?' said Monkey. 'Didn't I say you were partial to him and did not want him to go? You think he would refuse to go because you know that when I call you it is often half an hour before you take any notice. You'll see when I start, that I shall only need a turn or two of my three-inch tongue, and no matter if he is Pigsy or Wigsy I am quite capable of making him follow me.' 'Very well,' said Tripitaka, 'call him when you go.'

'Pigsy, Pigsy,' cried Monkey at Pigsy's bedside. That fool did most of the hard work when they were on the road, and no sooner did his head touch the pillow than he was snoring, and it took a great deal more than a shout to wake him.

Monkey pulled his ears, tweaked his bristles and dragged him from the pillow, shouting 'Pigsy!' That fool pushed him away. Monkey shouted again. 'Go to sleep and don't be so stupid,' Pigsy said. 'Tomorrow we have got to be on the road again.' 'I am not being stupid,' said Monkey, 'there is a bit of business I want your help in.' 'What business?' asked Pigsy. 'You heard what the prince said?' said Monkey. 'No,' said Pigsy, 'I did not set eyes on him, or hear anything he said.' 'He told me,' said Monkey, 'that the magician has a treasure worth more than an army of ten thousand men. When we go to the city tomorrow, we are sure to fall foul of him, he will use it to overthrow us. Wouldn't it be much better if we got in first and stole the treasure?'

'Brother,' said Pigsy, 'are you asking me to commit robbery? If so, that's a business I have experience of and can really be of some help. But there is one thing we must get clear. If I steal a treasure or subdue a magician I expect more than a petty, skunking share. The treasure must be mine.' 'What do you want it for?' asked Monkey. 'I am not so clever as you are at talking people into giving me alms. I am strong, but I have a very common way of talking, and I don't know how to recite the scriptures. When we get into a tight place, wouldn't this treasure be good to exchange for something to eat and drink?' 'I only care for fame,' said Monkey. 'I don't want any treasures. You may have it all to yourself.'

That fool, when he heard that it was all to be his, was in

203

high glee. He rolled out of bed, hustled into his clothes and set out with Monkey.

> Clear wine brings a blush to the cheeks;
> Yellow gold moves even a philosophic heart.

The two of them opened the temple gate very quietly and, leaving Tripitaka, mounted a wreath of cloud and soon reached the city, where they lowered their cloud, just as the second watch was being sounded on the tower. 'Brother! it's the second watch,' said Monkey. 'Couldn't be better,' said Pigsy. 'Everyone will just be deep in their first sleep.'

They did not go to the main gate, but to the back gate, where they heard the sound of the watchman's clappers and bells. 'Brother,' said Monkey, 'they are on the alert at all the gates. How shall we get in?' 'When did thieves ever go in by a gate?' said Pigsy. 'We must scramble over the wall.' Monkey did so, and at a bound was over the rampart and wall. Pigsy followed, and the two stealthily made their way in, soon rejoining the road from the gate. They followed this till they came to the flower garden.

In front of them was a gate-tower with three thatched white gables, and high up was an inscription in shining letters, catching the light of the moon and stars. It said 'Imperial Flower Garden.' When Monkey came close, he saw that the locks were sealed up several layers deep, and he told Pigsy to get to work. That fool wielded his iron rake, which he brought crashing down upon the gate and smashed it to bits. Monkey stepped over the fragments, and once inside could not stop himself jumping and shouting for joy. 'Brother,' said Pigsy, 'you'll be the ruin of us. Who ever heard of a thief making all that noise? You'll wake everyone up we shall be arrested and taken before the judge, and if we are not condemned to death we shall certainly be sent back to where we came from and drafted into the army.' 'Why try to make me nervous?' said Monkey. 'Look!

> The painted and carven balustrades are scattered and
>   strewn;

The jewel-studded arbours and trees are toppling down.
The sedgy islands and knot-weed banks are buried in
    dust;
The white peonies and yellow glove-flowers, all dust-
    destroyed.
Jasmine and rose perfume the night;
The red peony and tiger-lily bloom in vain,
The hibiscus and Syrian mallow are choked with weeds;
Strange plant and rare flower are crushed and die.'

'And what does it matter if they do,' said Pigsy. 'Let's get on with our business.' Monkey, although deeply affected by the scene, called to mind Tripitaka's dream, in which he was told that the well was underneath a banana-plant, and when they had gone a little further they did indeed discover a most singular banana-plant, which grew very thick and high.

'Now Pigsy,' said Monkey. 'Are you ready? The treasure is buried under this tree.' That fool lifted his rake in both hands, beat down the banana-tree and began to nuzzle with his snout till he had made a hole three or four feet deep. At last he came to a slab of stone. 'Brother,' he cried, 'here's luck. We've found the treasure. It's bound to be under this slab. If it's not in a coffer it will be in a jar.' 'Hoist it up and see,' said Monkey. Pigsy went to work again with his snout and raised the slab till they could see underneath. Something sparkled and flashed. 'Didn't I say we were in luck,' said Pigsy. 'That is the treasure glittering.' But when they looked closer, it was the light of the stars and moon reflected in a well. 'Brother,' said Pigsy, 'you should not think so much of the trunk that you forget the root.' 'Now, what does that mean?' asked Monkey. 'This is a well,' said Pigsy 'If you had told me before we started that the treasure was in a well, I should have brought with me the two ropes we tie up our bundles with, and you could have contrived to let me down. As it is, how are we to get at anything down there and bring it up again?' 'You intend to go down?' said Monkey. 'That's what I should do,' said Pigsy, 'if I had any rope.' 'Take off your clothes,' said Monkey, 'and I'll manage it for you.'

'I don't go in for much in the way of clothes,' said Pigsy. 'But I'll take off my jerkin, if that's any good.'

Dear Monkey! He took out his metal-clasped cudgel, called to it 'Stretch!' and when it was some thirty feet long he said to Pigsy, 'You catch hold of one end, and I'll let you down.' 'Brother,' said Pigsy, 'let me down as far as you like, so long as you stop when I come to the water.' 'Just so,' said Monkey. Pigsy caught hold of one end of the staff, and was very gently raised and let down into the well by Monkey. He soon reached the water. 'I'm at the water,' he called up. Monkey, hearing this, let him down just a little further. That fool Pigsy, when he felt the water touch him, began to beat out with his trotters, let go of the staff and flopped right into the water. 'The rascal!' he cried, spluttering and blowing. 'I told him to stop when I came to the water, and instead he let me down further.'

Monkey only laughed, and withdrew the staff. 'Brother,' he said, 'have you found the treasure?' 'Treasure indeed!' said Pigsy. 'There's nothing but well-water.' 'The treasure is under the water,' said Monkey. 'Just have a look.'

Pigsy, it so happened, was thoroughly at home in the water. He took a great plunge straight down into the well. But, oh what a long way it was to the bottom! He dived again with all his might, and suddenly opening his eyes saw in front of him an entrance, above which was written 'The Crystal Palace.' This astonished him very much. 'That finishes it,' he cried. 'I've come the wrong way and got into the sea! There is a Crystal Palace in the sea; but I never heard of one down a well.' For he did not know that the Dragon King of the Well also had a Crystal Palace.

Pigsy was thus debating with himself when a yaksha, on patrol-duty in the waters, opened the door, saw the intruder, and immediately withdrew to the interior, announcing: 'Great King, a calamity! A long-snouted, long-eared priest has dropped down into our well, all naked and dripping. He is still alive, and speaks to himself rationally.'

The Dragon King of the Well was, however, not at all surprised. 'If I am not mistaken,' he said, 'this is General

Pigsy. Last night the Spirit that Wanders by Night received orders to come here and fetch the soul of the king of Crowcock and bring it to the priest of T'ang to ask the Monkey Sage to subdue the wicked magician. I imagine that Monkey has come, as well as General Pigsy. They must be treated with great consideration. Go at once and ask the General to come in.' The Dragon King then tidied his clothes, adjusted his hat, and bringing with him all his watery kinsmen he came to the gate and cried in a loud voice: 'General Pigsy, pray come inside and be seated!' Pigsy was delighted. 'Fancy meeting with an old friend!' he said. And without thinking what he was in for, that fool went into the Crystal Palace. Caring nothing for good manners, all dripping as he was, he sat down in the seat of honour. 'General,' said the Dragon King, 'I heard lately that your life was spared to you on condition you should embrace the faith of Sākyamuni and protect Tripitaka on his journey to India. What then are you doing down here?' 'It's just in that connection that I come,' said Pigsy. 'My brother Monkey presents his best compliments and sends me to fetch some treasure or other.' 'I am sorry,' said the Dragon King, 'but what should I be doing with any treasure? You're mixing me up with the dragons of the Yangtze, the Yellow River, the Huai and the Chi, who soar about the sky and assume many shapes. They no doubt have treasures. But I stay down here all the time in this wretched hole never catching a glimpse of the sky above. Where should I get a treasure from?' 'Don't make excuses,' said Pigsy. 'I know you have got it; so bring it out at once.' 'The one treasure I have,' said the Dragon King, 'can't be brought out. I suggest you should go and look at it for yourself.' 'Excellent,' said Pigsy. 'I'll come and have a look.' The Dragon King led him through the Crystal Palace till they came to a cloister in which lay a body six feet long. Pointing at it the Dragon King said, 'General, there is your treasure.' Pigsy went up to it, and oh! what did he see before him? It was a dead Emperor, on his head a tall crown, dressed in a red gown, on his feet upturned shoes, girded with a belt of jades, who lay stretched full length upon the

207

floor. Pigsy laughed. 'You won't kid me like that,' he said. 'Since when did this count as a treasure? Why, when I was an ogre in the mountains I made my supper on them every day. When one has not only seen a thing time after time, but also eaten it again and again, can one be expected to regard it as a treasure.'

'General,' said the Dragon King, 'you do not understand. This is the body of the King of Crow-cock. When he fell into the well I preserved him with a magic pearl, and he suffered no decay. If you care to take him up with you, show him to Monkey and succeed in bringing him back to his senses, you need worry no more about "treasures," you'll be able to get anything out of him that you choose to ask for.' 'Very well then,' said Pigsy, 'I'll remove him for you, if you'll let me know how much I shall get as my undertaker's fee.' 'I haven't got any money,' said the Dragon King. 'So you expect to get jobs done for nothing?' said Pigsy. 'If you haven't got any money I won't remove him.' 'If you won't,' said the Dragon King, 'I must ask you to go away.' Pigsy at once retired. The Dragon King ordered two powerful yakshas to carry the body to the gate of the Crystal Palace and leave it just outside. They removed from the gate its water-fending pearls, and at once there was a sound of rushing waters! Pigsy looked round. The gate had vanished, and while he was poking about for it, his hand touched the dead king's body, which gave him such a start that his legs gave way under him. He scrambled to the surface of the water, and squeezing against the well-wall, he cried, 'Brother, let down your staff and get me out of this.' 'Did you find the treasure?' asked Monkey. 'How should I?' said Pigsy. 'All I found was a Dragon King at the bottom of the water, who wanted me to remove a corpse. I refused, and he had me put out at the door. Then his palace vanished, and I found myself touching the corpse. It gave me such a turn that I feel quite weak. Brother, you must get me out of this.' 'That was your treasure,' said Monkey. 'Why didn't you bring it up with you?' 'I knew he had been dead a long time,' said Pigsy. 'What was the sense of bringing him?' 'You'd better,' said

Monkey, 'or I shall go away.' 'Go?' said Pigsy. 'Where to?' 'I shall go back to the temple,' said Monkey, 'and go to sleep like Tripitaka.' 'And I shall be left down here?' said Pigsy. 'If you can climb out,' said Monkey, 'there is no reason why you should stay here; but if you can't there's an end of it.' Pigsy was thoroughly frightened; he knew he could not possibly climb out. 'Just think,' he said, 'even a city wall is difficult to get up. But this well-shaft has a big belly and a small mouth. Its walls slope in, and as no water has been drawn from it for several years they have become all covered with slime. It's far too slippery to climb. Brother, just to keep up a nice spirit between friends, I'll carry it up.'

'That's right,' said Monkey. 'And be quick about it, so that we can both of us go home to bed.'

That fool Pigsy dived down again, found the corpse, hoisted it on to his back, clambered up to the surface of the water, and propped himself and the body against the wall. 'Brother,' he called. 'I've brought it.' Monkey peered down, and seeing that Pigsy had indeed a burden on his back, he lowered his staff into the well.

That fool was a creature of much determination. He opened his mouth wide, bit hard on the staff, and Monkey pulled him gently up. Putting down the corpse, Pigsy pulled himself into his clothes. The Emperor, Monkey found on examining him, was indeed in the most perfect preservation. 'Brother,' he asked, 'how comes it that a man who has been dead for three years can look so fresh?' 'According to the Dragon King of the Well,' said Pigsy, 'he used a magic pearl which prevented the body from decaying.' 'That was a bit of luck,' said Monkey. 'But it still remains to take vengeance upon his enemy and win glory for ourselves. Make haste and carry him off.' 'Where to?' asked Pigsy. 'To the temple,' said Monkey, 'to show him to Tripitaka.' 'What an idea!' grumbled Pigsy to himself. 'A fellow was having a nice, sound sleep, and along comes this baboon with a wonderful yarn about a job that must be done, and in the end it turns out to be nothing but this silly game of carting about a corpse. Carry that stinking thing! It will dribble filthy water all over me and dirty my clothes; there's no one to wash them for me. There are patches in several places, and if the water gets through I have nothing to change into.' 'Don't worry about your clothes,' said Monkey. 'Get the body to the temple, and I will give you a change of clothes.' 'Impudence!' cried Pigsy. 'You've none of your own. How can you give me any to change into?' 'Does that twaddle mean that you won't carry it?' asked Monkey. 'I'm not going to carry it,' said Pigsy. 'Then hold out your paw and take twenty,' said Monkey. 'Brother,' said Pigsy, much alarmed, 'that cudgel is very heavy; after twenty strokes of it there would not be much to choose between me and this Emperor.' 'If you don't want to be beaten,' said Monkey, 'make haste and carry it off.'

Pigsy did indeed fear the cudgel, and sorely against his will he hoisted the corpse on to his back and began to drag himself along towards the garden gate. Dear Monkey! He performed a magic pass, recited a spell, traced a magic square on the ground, and going to it blew a breath that turned into a great gust of wind which blew Pigsy clean out of the palace grounds and clear of the city moat. The wind stopped, and alighting they set out slowly on their way. Pigsy was feeling very ill-used and thought of a plan to revenge himself. 'This monkey,' he said to himself 'has played a dirty trick on me, but I'll get even with him all right when we get back to the temple. I will tell Tripitaka that Monkey can bring the dead to life. If he says he can't, I shall persuade Tripitaka to recite the spell that makes this monkey's head ache, and I shan't be satisfied till his brains are bursting out of his head.' But thinking about it as he went along, he said to himself, 'That's no good! If he is asked to bring the king to life, he won't have any difficulty; he will go straight to Yama, King of Death, ask for the soul, and so bring the king to life. I must make it clear that he is not to go to the Dark Realm, but must do his cure here in the World of Light. That's the thing to do.'

They were now at the temple gate, went straight in, and put down the corpse at the door of the Zen Hall, saying,

'Master, get up and look!' Tripitaka was not asleep, but was discussing with Sandy why the others were away so long. Suddenly he heard them calling, and jumping up he said, 'Disciples, what is this I see?' 'Monkey's father-in-law,' said Pigsy; 'he made me carry him.' 'You rotten fool,' said Monkey, 'where have I any father-in-law?' 'Brother, if he isn't your father-in-law,' said Pigsy, 'why did you make me carry him? It has been tiring work for me, I can tell you that!'

When Tripitaka and Sandy examined the body, and saw that the Emperor looked just like a live man, Tripitaka suddenly burst into lamentation. 'Alas, poor Emperor,' he cried, 'in some forgotten existence you doubtless did great wrong to one that in this incarnation has now confounded you, and brought you to destruction. You were torn from wife and child; none of your generals or counsellors knew, none of your officers were aware. Alas, for the blindness of your queen and prince that offered no incense, no tea to your soul!' Here he broke down, and his tears fell like rain. 'Master,' said Pigsy, 'what does it matter to you that he is dead? He is not your father or grandfather, why should you wail over him?' 'Disciple,' said Tripitaka, 'for us who are followers of Buddha compassion is the root, indulgence the gate. Why is your heart so hard?' 'It isn't that my heart is hard,' said Pigsy. 'But Brother Monkey tells me he can bring him to life. If he fails I am certainly not going to cart him about any more.'

Now Tripitaka, being by nature pliable as water, was easily moved by that fool's story. 'Monkey,' he said, 'if you can indeed bring this Emperor back to life, you will be doing what matters more than that we should reach the Holy Mountain and worship the Buddha. They say "To save one life is better than to build a seven-storeyed pagoda." ' 'Master,' said Monkey, 'do you really believe this fool's wild talk? When a man is dead, in three times seven, five times seven, or at the end of seven hundred days, when he has done penance for his sins in the World of Light, his turn comes to be born again. This king has been dead for three years. How can he possibly be saved?' 'I expect we had better give up the idea,' said Tripitaka, when he heard this. But Pigsy was not to be cheated of his revenge. 'Don't let him put you off,' he said to Tripitaka. 'Remember, his head is very susceptible. You have only to recite that stuff of yours, and I guarantee that he'll turn the king into a live man.'

Tripitaka accordingly did recite the head-ache spell, and it gripped so tight that Monkey's eyes started out of his head, and he suffered frightful pain.

If you do not know whether in the end this king was brought to life, you must listen to what is unfolded in the next chapter.

212

Chapter 21

The pain in that great Monkey Sage's head was so severe that at last he could bear it no longer and cried piteously, 'Master, stop praying, stop praying! I'll doctor him.' 'How will you do it?' asked Tripitaka. 'The only way is to visit Yama, King of Death, in the Land of Darkness, and get him to let me have the king's soul,' said Monkey. 'Don't believe him, Master,' said Pigsy. 'He told me there was no need to go to the Land of Darkness. He said he knew how to cure him here and now, in the World of Light.' Tripitaka believed this wicked lie, and began praying again; and Monkey was so harassed that he soon gave in. 'All right, all right,' he cried. 'I'll cure him in the World of Light.' 'Don't stop,' said Pigsy. 'Go on praying as hard as you can.' 'You ill-begotten idiot,' cursed Monkey, 'I'll pay you out for making the Master put a spell upon me.' Pigsy laughed till he fell over. 'Ho, ho, brother,' he cried, 'you thought it was only on me that tricks could be played. You didn't think that I could play a trick on you.' 'Master, stop praying,' said Monkey, 'and let me cure him in the World of Light.' 'How can that be done?' asked Tripitaka. 'I will rise on my cloud-trapeze,' said Monkey, 'and force my way into the southern gate of Heaven. I shall not go to the Palace of the Pole and Ox, nor to the Hall of Holy Mists, but go straight up to the thirty-third heaven, and in the Trayaśimstra Courtyard of the heavenly palace of Quit Grief I shall visit Lao Tzu and ask for a grain of his Nine Times Sublimated Life Restoring Elixir, and with it I shall bring the king back to life.'

This suggestion pleased Tripitaka very much. 'Lose no time about it,' he said. 'It is only the third watch,' said Monkey. 'I shall be back before it is light. But it would look all wrong if the rest of you went quietly to sleep. It is only decent that someone should watch by the corpse and mourn.' 'You need say no more,' said Pigsy. 'I can see that you expect me to act as mourner.' 'I should like to see you refuse!' said Monkey. 'If you don't act as mourner, I certainly shan't bring him to life.' 'Be off, Brother,' said Pigsy, 'and I'll do the mourning.' 'There are more ways than one of mourning,' said Monkey. 'Mere bellowing with dry eyes is no good. Nor is it any better just to squeeze out a few tears. What counts is a good hearty howling, with tears as well. That's what is wanted for a real, miserable mourning.' 'I'll give you a specimen,' said Pigsy. He then from somewhere or other produced a piece of paper which he twisted into a paper-spill and thrust up his nostrils. This soon set him snivelling and his eyes running, and when he began to howl he kept up such a din that anyone would have thought he had indeed lost his dearest relative. The effect was so mournful that Tripitaka too soon began to weep bitterly. 'That's what you've got to keep up the whole time I'm away,' said Monkey laughing. 'What I am frightened of is that this fool, the moment my back is turned, will stop wailing. I shall creep back and listen, and if he shows any sign of leaving off he will get twenty on the paw.' 'Be off with you,' laughed Pigsy. 'I could easily keep this up for two days on end.'

Sandy, seeing that Pigsy had settled down to his job, went off to look for some sticks of incense to burn as an offering. 'Excellent!' laughed Monkey. 'The whole family is engaged in works of piety! Now's the time for Old Monkey to get to business.'

Dear Monkey! Just at midnight he left his teacher and fellow-disciples, mounted his cloud-trapeze and flew in at the southern gate of Heaven. He did not indeed call at the Precious Hall of Holy Mists or go to the Palace of the Pole and Ox, but only along a path of cloudy light went straight to the thirty-third heaven, to the Trayaśimstra Courtyard of the heavenly palace of Quit Grief. Just inside the gate he saw Lao Tzu in his alchemical studio, with a number of fairy boys holding banana-leaf fans, and fanning the fire in which the cinnabar was sublimating.

As soon as Lao Tzu saw him coming, he called to the boys, 'Be careful, all of you. Here's the thief who stole the elixir come back again.' Monkey bowed, and said laughing, 'Reverend Sir, there is no need to be in such a fret. You need take no precautions against me. I have come on quite different business.' 'Monkey,' said Lao Tzu, 'five hundred years ago you made great trouble in the Palace of Heaven, and stole a great quantity of my holy elixir; for which crime you were arrested and placed in my crucible, where you were smelted for forty-nine days, at the cost of I know not how much charcoal. Now you have been lucky enough to obtain forgiveness, enter the service of Buddha, and go with Tripitaka, the priest of T'ang, to get scriptures in India. Some while ago you quelled a demon in the Flat Topped Mountain and tricked disaster, but did not give me my share in the treasure. What brings you here today?' 'In those old days,' said Monkey, 'I lost no time in returning to you those five treasures of yours. You have no reason to be suspicious of me.' 'But what are you doing here?' asked Lao Tzu, 'creeping into my palace instead of getting on with your journey?' 'On our way to the West,' said Monkey, 'we came to a country called Crow-cock. The king of the country employed a wizard, who had disguised himself as a Taoist, to bring rain. This wizard secretly did away with the king, whose form he assumed, and now he is ensconced in the Hall of Golden Bells. My Master was reading the scriptures in the Treasure Wood Temple, when the soul of the king came to him and earnestly requested that I might be sent to subdue the wizard, and expose his imposture. I felt that I had no proof of the crime, and went with my fellow-disciple Pigsy. We broke into the flower garden by night and looked for the crystal well into which the king had been thrown. We fished him up, and found him still sound and fresh. When we got back to the temple and saw Tripitaka, his compassion was aroused and he ordered me to bring the king to life. But I was not to go to the World of Darkness to recover his soul; I must cure him here in the World of Light. I could think of no way but to ask for your help. Would you be so kind as to lend me a thousand of your nine times sublimated life-restoring pills? Then I shall be able to set him right.' 'A

215

thousand pills indeed!' exclaimed Lao Tzu. 'Why not two thousand? Is he to have them at every meal instead of rice? Do you think one has only to stoop and pick them up like dirt from the ground? Shoo! Be off with you! I've nothing for you.' 'I'd take a hundred,' said Monkey laughing. 'I dare say,' said Lao Tzu. 'But I haven't any.' 'I'd take ten,' said Monkey. 'A curse on this Monkey!' said Lao Tzu, very angry. 'Will he never stop haggling? Be off with you immediately.' 'If you really haven't got any,' said Monkey, 'I shall have to find some other way of bringing him to life.' 'Go, go, go!' screamed Lao Tzu. Very reluctantly Monkey turned away. But suddenly Lao Tzu thought to himself: 'This monkey is very crafty. If he really went away and stayed away, it would be all right. But I am afraid he will slip back again and steal some.' So he sent a fairy boy to bring Monkey back, and said to him, 'If you are really so anxious to have some, I'll spare you just one pill.' 'Sir,' said Monkey, 'if you had an inkling of what I can do if I choose, you would think yourself lucky to go shares in it with me. If you hadn't given in, I should have come with my dredge and fished up the whole lot.' Lao Tzu took a gourd-shaped pot and, tilting it up, emptied one grain of elixir and passed it across to Monkey, saying, 'That's all you'll get, so be off with it. And if with this one grain you can bring the king back to life, you are welcome to the credit of it.' 'Not so fast,' said Monkey. 'I must taste it first. I don't want to be put off with a sham.' So saying, he tossed it into his mouth. Lao Tzu rushed forward to stop him, and pressing his fists against his skull-cap he cried in despair, 'If you swallow it, I shall kill you on the spot!' 'Revolting meanness,' said Monkey. 'Keep calm; no one is eating anything of yours. And how much is it worth, anyhow? It's pretty wretched stuff, and come to that, I haven't swallowed it; it's here.'

For the fact is that monkeys have a pouch under the gullet, and Monkey had stored the grain of elixir in his pouch. Lao Tzu pinched him and said, 'Be off with you, be off with you, and don't let me find you hanging round here any more.' So Monkey took leave of him, and quitted the Trayaśimstra

Heaven. In a moment he had left by the Southern Gate, and turning eastward he saw the great globe of the sun just mounting. Lowering his cloud-seat, he soon reached the Treasure Wood Temple, where even before he entered the gate he could hear Pigsy still howling. He stepped briskly forward and cried 'Master.' 'Is that Monkey?' said Tripitaka delightedly. 'Have you got your elixir?' 'Certainly,' said Monkey. 'What's the use of asking?' said Pigsy. 'You can count on a sneak like that to bring back some trifle that doesn't belong to him.' 'Brother,' laughed Monkey, 'you can retire. We don't need you any more. Wipe your eyes, and if you want to do more howling do it elsewhere. And you, Sandy, bring me a little water.' Sandy hurried out to the well behind the temple, where there was a bucket of water ready drawn. He dipped his bowl into it and brought half a bowlful of water. Monkey filled his mouth with water, and then spat out the elixir into the Emperor's lips. Next he forced open his jaws, and pouring in some clean water, he floated the elixir down into his belly. In a few moments there was a gurgling sound inside; but the body still did not move. 'Master,' said Monkey, 'what will become of me if my elixir fails? Shall I be beaten to death?' 'I don't see how it can fail,' said Tripitaka. 'It's already a miracle that a corpse that has been dead so long can swallow water. After the elixir entered his belly, we heard the guts ring. When the guts ring, the veins move in harmony. It only remains to get the breath into circulation. But even a piece of iron gets a bit rusty when it has been under water for three years; it is only natural that something of the same kind should happen to a man. All that's wrong with him is that he needs a supply of breath. If someone puts a mouthful of good breath into him, he would be quite himself again.'

Pigsy at once offered himself for this service, but Tripitaka held him back. 'You're no use for that,' he cried. 'Let Monkey do it.' Tripitaka knew what he was talking about. For Pigsy had in his early days eaten living things, and even monstrously devoured human flesh, so that all his stock of breath was defiled. Whereas Monkey had always lived on pine-seeds, cypress cones, peaches and the like, and his breath was pure.

So Monkey stepped forward, and putting his wide mouth against the Emperor's lips he blew hard into his throat. The breath went down to the Two-Storeyed Tower, round the Hall of Light, on to the Cinnabar Field, and from the Jetting Spring went back again into the Mud Wall Palace. Whereupon there was a deep panting sound. The king's humours concentrated, his spirits returned. He rolled over, brandished his fist, and bent his legs. Then with a cry 'Master!' he knelt down in the dust and said, 'Little did I think, when my soul visited you last night, that today at dawn I should again belong to the World of Light!' Tripitaka quickly raised him from his knees and said, 'Your Majesty, this is no doing of mine. You must thank my disciple.' 'What talk is that?' said Monkey laughing. 'The proverb says "A household cannot have two masters." There is no harm in letting him pay his respects to you.'

Tripitaka, still feeling somewhat embarrassed, raised the Emperor to his feet and brought him to the Hall of Meditation, where he and his disciples again prostrated themselves, and set him on a seat. The priests of the temple had got ready their breakfast, and invited Tripitaka and his party to join them. Imagine their astonishment when they saw an Emperor, his clothes still dripping. 'Don't be surprised,' said Monkey, coming forward. 'This is the King of Crow-cock, your rightful lord. Three years ago he was robbed of his life by a fiend, and tonight I brought him back to life. Now we must take him to the city and expose the impostor. If you have anything for us to eat, serve it now, and we will start as soon as we have breakfasted.'

The priests brought the Emperor hot water to wash in, and helped him out of his clothes. The almoner brought him a cloth jacket, and instead of his jade belt tied a silk sash round his waist; took off his upturned shoes, and gave him a pair of old priest's sandals. Then they all had breakfast, and saddled the horse. 'Pigsy, is your luggage very heavy?' asked Monkey. 'Brother, I've carried it so many days on end

218

that I don't know whether it's heavy or not.' 'Divide the pack into two,' said Monkey, 'take one half yourself, and give the other to this Emperor to carry. In that way we shall get quicker to the city and dispose of our business.' 'That's a bit of luck,' said Pigsy. 'It was a nuisance getting him here. But now that he's been made alive, he is coming in useful as a partner.'

Pigsy then divided the luggage after his own methods. Borrowing a hod from the priests of the temple he put everything light into his own load, and everything heavy into the king's. 'I hope your Majesty has no objection,' said Monkey laughing, 'to being dressed up like this, and carrying the luggage, and following us on foot.' 'Master,' said the Emperor, instantly flinging himself upon his knees, 'I can only regard you as my second progenitor, and let alone carrying luggage for you, my heartfelt desire is to go with you all the way to India, even if I were only to serve you as the lowest menial, running beside you whip in hand as you ride.'

'There's no need for you to go to India,' said Monkey. 'That's our special concern. All you have to do is to carry the luggage forty leagues to the city and then let us seize the fiend. After which you can go on being Emperor again, and we can go on looking for scriptures.'

'That's all very well,' said Pigsy. 'But in that case he gets off with forty leagues, while I shall be on the job all the time.' 'Brother,' said Monkey, 'don't talk nonsense, but be quick and lead the way out.' Pigsy and the Emperor accordingly led the way, while Sandy supported Tripitaka on his horse and Monkey followed behind. They were accompanied to the gates by five hundred priests in gorgeous procession, blowing conches as they walked. 'Don't come with us any further,' said Monkey. 'If some official were to notice, our plans might get out, and everything would go wrong. Go back at once, and have the Emperor's clothes well cleaned, and send them to the city tonight or early tomorrow. I will see to it that you are well paid for your pains.'

They had not travelled for half a day when the walls and

219

most of the city of Crow-cock came into view. 'Monkey,' said Tripitaka, 'I think this place in front of us must be the city of Crow-cock.' 'It certainly is,' said Monkey. 'Let us hurry on and do our business.'

When they reached the city they found the streets and markets thronging with people, and everywhere a great stir and bustle. Soon they saw rising before them towers and gables of great magnificence. 'Disciples,' said Tripitaka, 'let us go at once to Court and get our papers put in order. Then we shall have no more trouble hanging about in government offices.' 'That is a good idea,' said Monkey. 'We will all come with you; the more the tellers, the better the story.' 'Well, if you all come,' said Tripitaka, 'you must behave nicely, and not say anything till you have done homage as humble subjects of the throne.' 'But that means bowing down,' said Monkey. 'To be sure,' said Tripitaka. 'You have to bow down five times and strike your forehead on the ground three times.' 'Master,' said Monkey, 'that's not a good idea. To pay homage to a thing like that is really too silly. Let me go in first, and I will decide what we are to do. If he addresses us, let me answer him. If you see me bow, then you must bow too; if I squat, then you must squat.'

Look at him, that Monkey King, maker of many troubles, how he goes straight up to the door and says to the high officer in charge: 'We were sent by the Emperor of China to worship Buddha in India, and fetch scriptures. We want to have our papers put in order here, and would trouble you to announce our arrival. By doing so, you will not fail to gain religious merit.' The eunuch went in and knelt on the steps of the throne, announcing the visitors and their request. 'I did not think it right to let them straight in,' he said. 'They await your orders outside the door.' The false king then summoned them in. Tripitaka entered, accompanied by the true king, who as he went could not stop the tears that coursed down his cheeks. 'Alas,' he sighed to himself, 'for my dragon-guarded rivers and hills, my iron-girt shrines! Who would have guessed that a creature of darkness would possess you all?' 'Emperor,' said Monkey, 'you must control your emotion, or we shall be discovered. I can feel the truncheon behind my ear twitching, and I am certain that I shall be successful. Leave it to me to slay the monster and when things are cleaned up, those rivers and hills will soon be yours again.'

The true king dared not demur. He wiped away his tears, and followed as best he could. At last they reached the Hall of Golden Bells, where they saw the two rows of officials civil and military, and the four hundred Court officers, all of imposing stature and magnificently apparelled. Monkey led forward Tripitaka to the white jade steps, where they both stood motionless and erect. The officials were in consternation. 'Are these priests so utterly bereft of decency and reason?' they exclaimed. 'How comes it that, seeing our king, they do not bow down or greet him with any word of blessing? Not even a cry of salutation escaped their lips. Never have we seen such impudent lack of manners!' 'Where do they come from?' interrupted the false king. 'We were sent from the eastern land of T'ang in Southern Jambudvīpa,' said Monkey haughtily, 'by royal command, to go to India that is in the Western Region, and there to worship the Living Buddha in the Temple of the Great Thunder Clap, and obtain true scriptures. Having arrived here we dare not proceed without coming first to you to have our passports put in order.' The false king was very angry. 'What is this eastern land of yours?' he said. 'Do I pay tribute to it, that you should appear before me in this rude fashion, without bowing down? I have never had any dealings with your country.' 'Our eastern land,' said Monkey, 'long ago set up ı Heavenly Court and became a Great Power. Whereas yours is a Minor Power, a mere frontier land. There is an old saying, "The King of a Great Country is father and lord; the king of a lesser country is vassal and son." You admit that you have had no dealings with our country. How dare you contend that we ought to bow down?' 'Remove that uncivil priest,' the king called to his officers of war. At this all the officers sprang forward. But Monkey made a magic pass and cried 'Halt!' The magic of the pass was such that these offi-

221

cers all suddenly remained rooted to the spot and could not stir. Well might it be said:

> The captains standing round the steps became like figures of wood,
> The generals on the Royal Dais were like figures of clay.

Seeing that Monkey had brought his officers and military to a standstill, the false king leapt from his Dragon Couch and made as though to seize him. 'Good,' said Monkey to himself. 'That is just what I wanted. Even if his hand is made of iron, this cudgel of mine will make some pretty dents in it!'

But just at this moment a star of rescue arrived. 'Who can this have been?' you ask. It was no other than the prince of Crow-cock, who hastened forward and clutched at the false king's sleeve, and kneeling before him cried, 'Father and king, stay your anger.' 'Little son,' asked the king, 'why should you say this?' 'I must inform my father and king,' said the prince. 'Three years ago I heard someone say that a priest had been sent from T'ang to get scriptures in India, and it is he who has now unexpectedly arrived in our country. If my father and king, yielding to the ferocity of his noble nature, now arrests and beheads this priest, I fear that the news will one day reach the Emperor of T'ang, who will be furiously angry. You must know that after Li Shih-min had established this great dynasty of T'ang and united the whole land, his heart was still not content, and he has now begun to conquer far-away lands. If he hears that you have done harm to his favourite priest, he will raise his hosts and come to make war upon you. Our troops are few and our generals feeble. You will, when it is too late, be sorry indeed that you provoked him. If you were to follow your small son's advice, you would question these four priests, and only punish such of them as are proved not to travel at the King of China's bidding.'

This was a stratagem of the prince's. For he feared that harm might come to Tripitaka, and therefore tried to check the king, not knowing that Monkey was ready to strike.

The false king believed him, and standing in front of the Dragon Couch, he cried in a loud voice: 'Priest, how long ago did you leave China, and why were you sent to get scriptures?'

'My Master,' said Monkey haughtily, 'is called Tripitaka, and is treated by the Emperor of China as his younger brother. The Emperor in a vision went to the Realms of Death, and on his return he ordered a great Mass for all souls in torment. On this occasion my Master recited so well and showed such compassionate piety that the Goddess Kuan-yin chose him to go on a mission to the West. My Master vowed that he would faithfully perform this task in return for his sovereign's bounties, and he was furnished by the Emperor with credentials for the journey. He started in the thirteenth year of the Emperor's reign, in the ninth month, three days before the full moon. After leaving China, he came first to the Land of the Two Frontiers, where he picked up me, and made me his chief disciple. In the hamlet of the Kao family, on the borders of the country of Wu-ssu, he picked up a second disciple, called Pigsy; and at the river of Flowing Sands he picked up a third, whom we call Sandy. Finally a few days ago, at the Temple of the Treasure Wood, he found another recruit – the servant who is carrying the luggage.'

The false king thought it unwise to ask any more questions about Tripitaka; but he turned savagely upon Monkey and addressed to him a crafty question. 'I can accept,' he said, 'that one priest set out from China, and picked up three priests on the way. But your story about the fourth member of your party I altogether disbelieve. This servant is certainly someone whom you have kidnapped. What is his name? Has he a passport, or has he none? Bring him before me to make his deposition!'

The true king shook with fright. 'Master,' he whispered, 'what am I to depose?' 'That's all right,' said Monkey. 'I'll make your deposition for you.'

Dear Monkey! He stepped boldly forward and cried to the magician in a loud, clear voice: 'Your Majesty, this old man

223

is dumb and rather hard of hearing. But it so happens that when he was young, he travelled in India, and knows the way there. I know all about his career and origins and with your Majesty's permission I will make a deposition on his behalf.' 'Make haste,' said the false king, 'and furnish a true deposition or you will get into trouble.'

Monkey then recited as follows:

The subject of this deposition is far advanced in years; he is deaf and dumb, and has fallen upon evil days. His family for generations has lived in these parts; but five years ago disaster overtook his house. Heaven sent no rain; the people perished of drought, the lord king and all his subjects fasted and did penance. They burned incense, purified themselves and called upon the Lord of Heaven; but in all the sky not a wisp of cloud appeared. The hungry peasants dropped by the roadside, when suddenly there came a Taoist magician from the Chung-nan Mountains, a monster in human form. He called to the winds and summoned the rain, displaying godlike power; but soon after secretly destroyed this wretched man's life. In the flower-garden he pushed him down into the crystal well; then set himself on the Dragon Throne, none knowing it was he. Luckily I came and achieved a great success; I raised him from the dead and restored him to life without hurt or harm. He earnestly begged to be admitted to our faith, and act as carrier on the road, to join with us in our quest and journey to the Western Land. The false king who sits on the throne is that foul magician; he that now carries our load is Crow-cock's rightful king!

When the false king in the Palace of Golden Bells heard these words, he was so startled that his heart fluttered like the heart of a small deer. Then clouds of shame suffused his face, and leaping to his feet he was about to flee, when he remembered that he was unarmed. Looking round he saw a captain of the Guard with a dagger at his waist, standing there dumb and foolish as a result of Monkey's spell. The false king rushed at him and snatched the dagger; then leapt upon a cloud and disappeared into space.

Sandy burst into an exclamation of rage, and Pigsy loudly

abused Monkey for his slowness. 'It's a pity you didn't look sharp and stop him,' he said. 'Now he has sailed off on a cloud, and we shall never be able to find him.' 'Don't shout at me, brothers!' said Monkey laughing. 'Let us call to the prince to come and do reverence to his true father, and the queen to her husband.' Then undoing by a magic pass the spell that he had put upon the officers, he told them to wake up and do homage to their lord, acknowledging him as their true king. 'Give me a few facts to go upon,' he said, 'and as soon as I have got things clear, I will go and look for him.'

Dear Monkey! He instructed Pigsy and Sandy to take good care of the prince, king, ministers, queen and Tripitaka; but while he was speaking he suddenly vanished from sight. He had already jumped up into the empyrean, and was peering round on every side, looking for the wizard. Presently he saw that monster flying for his life towards the north-east. Monkey caught him up and shouted, 'Monster, where are you off to? Monkey has come.' The wizard turned swiftly, drew his dagger and cried, 'Monkey, you scamp, what has it got to do with you whether I usurp someone else's throne? Why should you come calling me to account and letting out my secrets?' 'Ho, ho,' laughed Monkey. 'You impudent rascal! Do you think I am going to allow you to play the emperor? Knowing who I am you would have done well to keep out of my way. Why did you bully my master, demanding depositions and what not? You must admit now that the deposition was not far from the truth. Stand your ground and take old Monkey's cudgel like a man!'

The wizard dodged and parried with a thrust of his dagger at Monkey's face. It was a fine fight! After several bouts the magician could no longer stand up against Monkey, and suddenly turning he fled back the way he had come, leapt into the city and slipped in among the officers who were assembled before the steps of the throne. Then giving himself a shake, he changed into an absolute counterpart of Tripitaka and stood beside him in front of the steps. Monkey rushed up and was about to strike what he supposed to be the wizard, when this Tripitaka said, 'Disciple, do not strike!

It is I!' It was impossible to distinguish between them. 'If I kill Tripitaka, who is a transformation of the wizard, then I shall have achieved a glorious success; but supposing, on the other hand, it turns out that I have killed the real Tripitaka, that would not be so good . . . ' There was nothing for it but to stay his hand, and calling to Pigsy and Sandy he asked, 'Which really is the wizard, and which is our master? Just point for me, and I will strike the one you point at.' 'We were watching you going for one another up in the air,' said Pigsy, 'when suddenly we looked round and saw that there were two Tripitakas. We have no idea which is the real one.'

When Monkey heard this, he made a single pass and recited a spell to summon the *devas* that protect the Law, the local deities and the spirits of the neighbouring hills, and told them of his predicament. The wizard thought it time to mount the clouds again, and began to make towards the door. Thinking that Tripitaka was clearing the ground for him, Monkey raised his cudgel, and had it not been for the deities he had summoned he would have struck such a big blow at his master as would have made mince-meat of twenty Tripitakas. But in the nick of time the guardian deities stopped him, saying, 'Great Sage, the wizard is just going to mount the clouds again.' Monkey rushed after him, and was just about to cut off his retreat, when the wizard turned round, slipped back again into the crowd, and was once more indistinguishable from the real Tripitaka.

Much to Monkey's annoyance, Pigsy stood by, laughing at his discomfiture. 'You've nothing to laugh at, you hulking brute,' he said. 'This means you've got two masters to order you about. It's not going to do you much good.' 'Brother,' said Pigsy, 'you call me a fool, but you're a worse fool than I. You can't recognise your own Master, and it's a waste of effort to go on trying. But you would at least recognise your own headache, and if you ask our Master to recite his spell, Sandy and I will stand by and listen. The one who doesn't know the spell will certainly be the wizard. Then all will be easy.' 'Brother,' said Monkey, 'I am much obliged to you. There are only three people who know that spell. It sprouted from the heart of the Lord Buddha himself; it was handed down to the Bodhisattva Kuan-yin, and was then taught to our master by the Bodhisattva herself. No one else knows it. Good, then! Master, recite!'

The real Tripitaka at once began to recite the spell; while the wizard could do nothing but mumble senseless sounds. 'That's the wizard,' cried Pigsy. 'He's only mumbling.' And at the same time he raised his rake and was about to strike when the wizard sprang into the air and ran up along the clouds. Dear Pigsy! With a loud cry he set off in pursuit, and Sandy, leaving Tripitaka, hastened to the attack with his priest's staff. Tripitaka stopped reciting, and Monkey, released from his headache, seized his iron cudgel and sped through the air. Heigh, what a fight! Three wild priests beleagured one foul fiend. With rake and staff Pigsy and Sandy assailed him from the right and left. 'If I join in,' said Monkey, 'and attack him in front, I fear he is so frightened of me that he will run away again. Let me get into position above him and give him a real garlic-pounding blow that will finish him off for good and all.' He sprang up into the empyrean, and was about to deliver a tremendous blow when, from a many-coloured cloud in the north-east, there came a voice which said, 'Monkey, stay your hand!' Monkey looked round and saw it was the Bodhisattva Manjuśrī. He withdrew his cudgel, and coming forward did obeisance, saying 'Bodhisattva, where are you going to?' 'I came to take this monster off your hands,' said Manjuśrī. 'I am sorry you should have the trouble,' said Monkey. The Bodhisattva then drew from his sleeve a magic mirror that showed demons in their true form. Monkey called to the other two to come and look, and in the mirror they saw the wizard in his true shape. He was Manjuśrī's lion! 'Bodhisattva,' said Monkey, 'this is the blue-maned lion that you sit upon. How comes it that it ran away and turned into an evil spirit? Can't you keep it under control?' 'It did not run away,' said Manjuśrī. 'It acted under orders from Buddha himself.' 'You mean to tell me,' said Monkey, 'that it was Buddha who told

227

this creature to turn into an evil spirit and seize the Emperor's throne? In that case all the troubles I meet with while escorting Tripitaka are very likely ordered by His Holiness. A nice thought!'

'Monkey,' said Manjuśrī, 'you don't understand. In the beginning the king of Crow-cock was devoted to good works and the entertaining of priests. Buddha was so pleased that he sent me to fetch him away to the Western Paradise, where he was to assume a golden body and become an Arhat. As it was not proper for me to show myself in my true form I came disguised as a priest and begged for alms. Something I said gave him offence, and not knowing that I was anyone in particular he had me bound and cast into the river, where I remained under water for three nights and three days, till at last a guardian spirit rescued me and brought me back to Paradise. I complained to Buddha, who sent this creature to throw the king into the well, and let him remain there three years as a retaliation for the three days that I was in the river. You know the saying: "Not a sip, not a sup . . ."[1] But now you have arrived on the scene, the episode is successfully closed.' 'That is all very well,' said Monkey. 'All these "sips and sups" may have enabled you to get even with your enemy. But what about all the unfortunate people whom this fiend has ruined?' 'He hasn't ruined any one,' said Manjuśrī. 'During the three years that he was on the throne, rain has fallen, the crops have been good, and the people at perfect peace. How can you speak of his ruining people?' 'That may be,' said Monkey. 'But how about all the ladies of the Court who have been sleeping with him and unwittingly been led into a heinous and unnatural offence? They would hardly subscribe to the view that he had done no harm.' 'He isn't in a position to defile anyone,' said Manjuśrī. 'He's a gelded lion!' At this Pigsy came up to the wizard and felt him. 'Quite true,' he announced, laughing. 'This is a "blotchy nose that never sniffed wine"; "a bad name and nothing to show for it."'

[1] Everything that happens depends on *karma*.

'Very well then,' said Monkey. 'Take him away. If you had not come just in time, he'd have been dead by now.' Mañjuśrī then recited a spell and said, 'Creature, back to your true shape and look sharp about it!' The wizard at once changed into his real lion form, and Mañjuśrī, putting down the lotus that he carried in his hand, harnessed the lion, mounted him and rode away over the clouds.

If you do not know how Tripitaka and his disciples left the city you must listen while it is explained to you in the next chapter.

Chapter 22

Monkey and the other two disciples lowered the clouds on which they rode and returned to Court, where they received the humble thanks of the king, his ministers, heir and consort, and all the officers. Monkey told them how Mañjuśrī had reclaimed the fiend, at which they prostrated themselves with extreme awe and reverence. In the midst of these congratulations and rejoicings a eunuch suddenly arrived, saying, 'My lord and master, four more priests have arrived.' 'Brother,' said Pigsy, in consternation, 'what if it should turn out that the fiend, having disguised himself as Mañjuśrī and taken us all in, has now turned himself into a priest, in the hope of confounding us?' 'Impossible!' said Monkey, and he ordered them to be shown in. The officers of the Court sent word that they were to be admitted, and when they appeared Monkey saw at once that they were priests from the Treasure Wood Temple, bringing the crown, belt, cloak and upturned shoes of the king. 'Just at the right moment!' said Monkey, delighted. He then called to the 'porter' to come forward, took off his head-wrap and put on the crown, took off his cloth coat and put on the royal robe, undid the sash and girded him with the belt of jades, slipped off his priest's sandals and put on the upturned shoes. Then he told the prince to bring out the white jade tablet, and put it in the king's hand, bidding him mount the dais and proclaim his sovereignty, in accordance with the old saying 'A court must not, even for a day, be without a sovereign'.

But the king was very loth to sit upon the throne, and weeping bitterly he knelt on the centre of the steps, saying, 'I was dead for three years, and having now by your doing been brought back to life, how can I dare proclaim myself your sovereign? It would be better that one of you priests should be king, and that I should take my wife and child and live like a commoner outside the walls of the city.'

Tripitaka of course would not accept, as his heart was set

upon going to worship the Buddha and get scriptures. The king then asked Monkey. 'Gentlemen,' said Monkey laughing, 'I will not deceive you. If I had wanted to be an Emperor, I could have had the throne in any of the ten thousand lands and nine continents under heaven. But I have got used to being a priest and leading a lazy, comfortable existence. An Emperor has to wear his hair long; at nightfall he may not doze, at the fifth drum he must be awake. Each time there is news from the frontier his heart jumps; when there are calamities and disasters he is plunged in sorrow and despair; I should never get used to it. You go back to your job as Emperor, and let me go back to mine as priest, doing my deeds and going upon my way.'

Seeing that it was useless to refuse, the king at last mounted the dais, turned towards his subjects and proclaimed his sovereignty, announcing a great amnesty throughout his realm. He loaded the prists from the Treasure Wood Temple with presents and sent them home. Then he opened the eastern upper room and held a banquet for Tripitaka. He also sent for a painter to make portraits of the blessed countenances of Tripitaka and his disciples, which were to be hung in the Palace of Golden Bells, and reverenced as objects of worship.

Having put the king upon his throne, Tripitaka and his disciples were anxious to start out again as soon as possible. The king, his ladies, the prince and all the ministers pressed upon them all the heirlooms of the kingdom, and gold, silver, silks and satins, to show their deep gratitude. But Tripitaka would not accept so much as a split hair, and when their passports had been put in order, he urged Monkey and the rest to get the horse saddled, so that they might start at once. The king, very loth to part with them, ordered his State Coach to be got ready and made Tripitaka ride in it. He was drawn by officers civil and military, while the prince and ladies of the Court pushed at the sides, till they were beyond the walls of the town. Here Tripitaka alighted, and took leave of them all. 'Master,' said the king, 'on your way back from India, when you pass this way, you must certainly visit me.' 'I shall obey your command,' said Tripitaka. Then with his eyes full of tears the king, accompanied by all his ministers, returned to the Palace.

The Master and his three disciples travelled westward, going slowly the better to enjoy the scenery, when suddenly they heard what sounded like the hubbub of a hundred thousand voices. Tripitaka, much alarmed, reined in his horse, and turning to Monkey said, 'Where does that strange noise come from?' 'It sounds to me like a landslide,' broke in Pigsy. 'I should say it was a thunderstorm,' said Sandy. 'I'm certain it is men shouting and horses neighing,' said Tripitaka. 'You're all wrong,' laughed Monkey. 'Wait while I go and have a look.' Dear Monkey! He gave himself a shake, sprang straight up into the clouds and looked down. Below him he saw a moated city. The vapours that surrounded it were all of good omen; none were baleful. Monkey thought to himself, 'Where can all that noise come from? I see no banners or halberds, no artillery. Yet certainly there is a din of horses and men.'

While he was debating with himself, his eye fell upon a tall sandy cliff outside the city, near which were gathered together a great crowd of Buddhist priests dragging a cart; and to give themselves courage for their task, each time they hauled they cried out all together the name of the Bodhisattva of Power. This was the noise that had alarmed Tripitaka. Lowering his cloud Monkey saw that the cart was loaded with bricks, tiles, timber, earth-clods and the like. The cliff was almost perpendicular, but a narrow path ran up between steep walls. How they were going to get the cart up this path defied imagination. It was a hot day; but they were all still clad in full monastic robes. Seeing them in this plight, Monkey could think of no better explanation than that they were building a temple, and, unable to obtain labourers because the harvest was in process, they had found nothing for it but to take on the work themselves. While he was thus speculating, the gates of the city opened and two young Taoists came out. No sooner did the Buddhists see them than in an evident agony of apprehension they redoubled their

232

efforts, tugging madly at the cart. 'Aha!' said Monkey to himself. 'Now all is plain. The priests are afraid of those Taoists. I have heard it said that on the way to the west there is a place where Taoists are in power and Buddhism has been destroyed. This must be the place that was meant. However, if go back at once and tell the Master he will say this is all mere guess-work and scold me for not bringing back a trustworthy report. I will go down and find out all about it before I speak to the Master.' He gave himself a shake and changed into the guise of a wandering Taoist magician. On his left arm he carried a hamper and in his right hand a tambourine, and singing Taoist songs as he went he strolled towards the two Taoists. 'Masters, I salute you most humbly,' he said bowing. 'Where do you come from?' they asked. 'Your disciple,' said Monkey, 'wanders through the world like a cloud. The four corners of the earth are his home. His purpose in coming here is to collect subscriptions for works of piety. In what quarters of this city of yours is the Way loved, in what streets are the worthy esteemed? For I feel like going and begging a little supper.' 'Sir,' said the two Taoists, 'we are surprised to hear you speak so humbly.' 'What do you mean by "humbly"?' asked Monkey. 'You spoke of begging for your supper,' they said. 'Is not that a humble way of talking?' 'That is how those who have left the world must get their bread,' said Monkey, 'for they have no money to buy it with.' 'It is clear,' they said, smiling, 'that you have no knowledge of how things stand in these parts. In this city not only do all the officials and officers love the Way, and all rich merchants and tradesmen esteem its adepts, so that there is not a man or woman, young or old, who does not bow down before us and ask to be allowed to supply our needs – that would be a small thing, hardly worth mentioning. What is singular in this country is that the king himself is a devout supporter of Taoism.' 'I am young,' said Monkey, 'and come from far away. It is natural that I should know nothing of this. I must trouble you to tell me the name of this country, and how it comes about that the king is such a lover of the Way, that I may know just how things stand with my fellow-

233

Taoists in this country.' 'This country,' they said, 'is called Cart Slow, and the king is our kinsman.' 'He is, I suppose, a Taoist priest who became king,' said Monkey. 'No,' they said. 'Twenty years ago there was a famine here. The whole Court and all the people purified themselves and prayed fervently for rain. Their prayers were not answered; but just when all seemed lost, three Immortals suddenly came from the sky and saved us. Today they are our masters, and we are their disciples.' 'What are their names?' asked Monkey. 'Their leader,' said the Taoists, 'is called the Tiger Strength Immortal, and the two others are called Deer Strength Immortal and Ram Strength Immortal.' 'And what powers of magic have they?' asked Monkey. 'They can summon the wind or bring rain,' said the Taoists, 'by a mere turn of the hand. They can point at water, and it becomes oil; prick stones and they become gold, as easily as one turns in bed. Small wonder that the king and his ministers fell down before them and are eager to count us Taoists as their kin.' 'Your king is a lucky man,' said Monkey. 'And if your masters have such arts there must be few who would be sorry to claim kinship with them. Indeed, if it isn't making too bold, I should take it as a great kindness if I might be allowed to meet them for a moment myself.' 'There is no difficulty about that,' they said. 'We two are the most favoured and trusted of all their disciples. Moreover, such is their love of Taoism, that they have only to hear the word mentioned and they immediately come out, overflowing with welcome. If we were to introduce you, the thing would be as easy as blowing ashes from a tray.' 'Bravo!' cried Monkey. 'Let us go to them at once.' 'You must wait a few minutes,' they said. 'We have some business to attend to.' 'I don't quite understand,' said Monkey. 'Those who have left the world are bound by no ties. How can you speak of business to conduct?' 'Those people over there,' they said, pointing to the priests by the cliff, 'are working for us. We have to go and check them off by the list, in case some should be playing truant.' 'You must be mistaken,' said Monkey. 'Those are Buddhists, but they are priests just as we are.

234

What right have we to set them to work or check them off on a list?'

'You do not understand,' said the Taoists. 'At the time of the great drought the Buddhists prayed to Buddha and the Taoists to the Pole Star. The Buddhists had no success at all; in vain they prayed, in vain they recited their scriptures. But in the nick of time our Masters appeared, and at once rain fell and the suppliant crowds were saved. Our Masters then demanded that as the Buddhists had proved themselves to be impostors their temples and images should be destroyed and their passports taken away from them, so that they might not flee to their homes. They were then given to us to work for us as slaves. It is they who light our fires, they who sweep our floors, they who are the porters at our gate. At the back of our temple there is a building which is not yet finished; so we set them to bring tiles and bricks and logs up the cliff. It was feared they might be shirking their work or not pulling hard enough at the cart. So we two were sent to see what was happening.' 'This is all most unfortunate,' said Monkey, bursting into tears. 'It is quite impossible for me to meet your Masters.' 'How is that?' they asked. 'I must tell you,' said Monkey, 'that the purpose of my wanderings is in part to discover a lost relation.' 'What relation?' they asked. 'I have an uncle,' said Monkey, 'who when he was young became a Buddhist priest. During the famine he went to distant parts to beg alms and has not been seen since. It is very possible that he is detained here and cannot get home. I cannot go with you to the city till I have found out whether he is here.' 'That can easily be done,' they said. 'We'll sit here, and you can go to the cliff and do our business for us. There are five hundred names on the list. You have only to check the list and see that they are all there. If you find your uncle among them, in consideration of the fact that you are a Taoist yourself we should gladly release him. Then we would take you to the city.'

Monkey thanked them heartily and set out towards the cliff, beating his drum as he went. When he reached them, the priests flung themselves to their knees and beating their heads upon the ground cried out, 'Spare us, Father! There is not one among us that has been idle, nor of all the five hundred is there any that has absented himself, or failed to haul the cart.' 'Aha!' thought Monkey to himself, 'these priests are clearly used to being roughly handled. If they cringe like this to me, I think they must pretty well die of fright when their real masters go near them.' He motioned to them to rise, saying, 'You have nothing to be afraid of. I am not here to see that you do your work. I have come to look for a lost kinsman.' On hearing this they all pressed round, each stretching out his head with upturned face, hoping that he might be claimed as kin. 'Which of us is it?' they asked. After having looked attentively at each of them, Monkey burst out laughing. 'It seems you have not found your relative,' they said. 'Why then are you laughing?' 'I am laughing,' said Monkey, 'to think what a strange notion you have of the duties of your Order. Having been born under an unlucky star you quarrelled with your parents or some such thing, and were disowned by them and sent to be priests. One would have thought that you would then at least have devoted yourselves to reading the scriptures and other holy works. How is it that instead I find you hiring yourselves out to Taoists and working as their servants?' 'Why have you come to mock at us?' they cried. 'But you are evidently a stranger, and perhaps do not know of our plight.' 'That is the case,' said Monkey. 'The king of this country,' they said, 'has turned his heart away from the true Law, and gives his favour to these heretical Masters and their crew.' 'How came that about?' asked Monkey. 'The three Immortals,' they said, 'having obtained the king's confidence by bringing rain, persuaded him to destroy us; all our temples were pulled down, our passports taken away, so that we could not return to our homes. Nor were we allowed to labour for our own support, but were given over to the Immortals as their drudges and bondsmen. The moment any Taoist itinerant magic-maker sets foot in the town, he is sent for by the king and loaded with presents;

236

whereas if a Buddhist comes, whether from far or near, he is seized and given to the Immortals as a labourer.' 'Those Taoists,' said Monkey, 'must certainly possess more than the common arts, or they would never have found their way to the king's heart. After all, summoning the wind and bringing rain are common, trumpery practices, such as would not move a monarch's heart.' 'True enough,' they said. 'These Immortals can also make the philosopher's stone, go into trances, turn water into oil and stones into gold. And now they have built a temple dedicated to the Taoist Trinity where all day and all night they read scriptures and perform rites to preserve the king's youth; and this no doubt gratifies his Majesty.'

'Things being as they are,' said Monkey, 'I can't imagine why you do not simply run away.' 'Father,' they said. 'How can we run away? The Immortals have persuaded the king to have portraits of us painted, which are hung up in every part of the land. There is not a hamlet in the whole kingdom that has not got copies of these pictures, inscribed at the top in the king's own hand. Any official who catches a Buddhist priest is at once promoted three stages, and a private person is given a reward of fifty weights of silver. We should never succeed in escaping. Why, not to speak of priests, anyone with his hair cut a bit short or a little thin on top would as likely as not be grabbed! The whole land swarms with police and detectives. Judge for yourself what chance anyone would have of getting clear. We have no choice but to stay here and bear our sufferings.' 'I wonder you are alive to tell the tale,' said Monkey. 'Father,' they cried, 'many have died. The priests who belonged to this place, together with those who were arrested in various parts of the kingdom, were about two thousand in all. Of these some six or seven hundred died of exhaustion, of exposure to heat and cold, or through lack of food; and seven or eight hundred took their own lives. The five hundred whom you see here are those who failed to die.' 'What do you mean by "failed to die,"' asked Monkey. 'The rope broke,' they said, 'or the blade was blunt, or the poison did not work, or the backwash carried them to the surface of the water and they did not drown.' 'Lucky fellows!' said Monkey. 'Heaven has blessed you with long life.' 'Say rather "cursed us with eternal torment,"' they cried. 'What do you suppose they give us to feed on? Water that the cheapest rice has been cooked in, three times a day! And where do we sleep? Here in the open, at the foot of this cliff. But the moment we close our eyes, spirits come to keep watch over us.' 'Quite so,' said Monkey. 'You have nightmares as the result of all your sufferings.' 'That is not so at all,' they said. 'The Six Guardians and the Defenders of Religion come to watch over us, and if any of us is at the point of death they revive him.' 'More fools they!' said Monkey. 'They ought to let you die and go to Heaven as quickly as possible.' 'They tell us in our dreams,' the Buddhists said, 'that we must hold out a little longer, despite our torments. For soon, they said, a pilgrim will come, who is on his way to India to get scriptures. With him is a disciple named the Great Sage Equal to Heaven, who has great magic powers, which he uses to right the wrongs of the oppressed. He will destroy the Taoists and bring the followers of Zen once more into respect.' Monkey smiled to himself. 'That really makes me feel quite important,' he said to himself. 'Fancy having spirits announcing one's arrival beforehand!'

He turned his heel on them and beating his drum strode on towards the city gate. 'Did you find your kinsman,' the two Taoists asked. 'They are all my kinsmen,' said Monkey. 'What the whole five hundred?' they asked. 'Two hundred on my father's side, two hundred on my mother's; and the rest are my bond-brothers,' said Monkey. 'If you will release the whole lot of them, I'll go back with you.' 'You must be mad,' they said. 'These Buddhists were given to us by the king to be our slaves. We might, to oblige you, release one or two of them. But we should have to manage it by first sending in a report that they were ill, and then another, that they had died. We can't suddenly release the whole gang. These things are looked into. Why, the king himself might take it into his head to come and see how the work is going.' 'So you won't let them go?' cried Monkey. 'Very well then!' And taking his cudgel from behind his ear he rushed at them and gave each such a blow upon the head that their brains gushed out and they fell dead where they had stood. 'Oh, what have you done!' cried the Buddhists, leaving their carts and rushing up to Monkey in utter consternation. 'You have killed the king's favourites!' 'How so?' said Monkey. 'These Taoists,' they said, 'are always at the king's side, and in the presence of all the Court he humbles himself before them. The two whom you have slain were sent to supervise our work. It will at once be said that it was we who killed them. You must come with us to the city immediately and confess your crime.' 'Enough of all this noise,' said Monkey. 'I am not the mendicant that I appear. It is I who am your saviour.' 'You, a murderer!' they cried, 'who have added immeasurably to our burdens by your deed of violence. You our saviour!' 'I am the Great Sage of whom you spoke,' said Monkey, 'and have come to rescue you.' 'It is not true,' they said. 'We should recognise him.' 'You have never seen him,' said Monkey. 'How could you recognise him?' 'An old man,' they said, 'often came to us in our dreams, telling us that he was the Spirit of the Planet Venus. He gave us such a complete description of the Great Sage, that we could not fail to recognise him. "Flat forehead, bright steely eyes, a round head, hairy cheeks and no chin." ' 'The old scamp!' said Monkey, secretly flattered that spirits should have prepared the way for him. 'You are perfectly right,' he said suddenly, 'I am not the Monkey Sage I am only one of his disciples. There goes Monkey!' The Buddhists turned in the direction to which he pointed, and while their backs were turned Monkey resumed his true form. Turning round, they at once recognised him, and flinging themselves upon their knees, 'Father,' they cried, 'forgive us that we did not know you in your disguise. We beg of you to come with us at once to the city, put down the imposters and give the right its due.' 'Follow me!' cried Monkey; and they pressed about him on either side.

They came first to the cliff, where Monkey, using his

magic power, hauled the carts to the top and tilted them over the edge, so that they crashed at the bottom into a thousand pieces. 'Now go your ways!' he said to the Buddhists, 'and let not one of you show that he has any connection with me. Tomorrow I will go to the king and compass the Taoists' undoing.' 'Father,' they said, 'we dare not stir from here, or the magistrates will lay hands on us again and we shall have been ransomed only to fall into fresh trouble.' 'I will give you a magic that will keep you safe,' said Monkey.

Dear Monkey! He plucked out a handful of his hairs, chewed them into small pieces and gave a piece to each Buddhist, saying 'Put it under the nail of your thumb and clench your fist. Then you can go where you will, and no one will dare touch you. You have only to press your thumb into the palm of your hand and cry "Great Sage!" I will come at once to help you.' 'But father,' they said, 'suppose we were a long way off and you could not hear us, what then?' 'That is all right,' said Monkey. 'If I were ten thousand leagues away, it would make no difference; you would still come to no harm.'

Some of the bolder among them experimented, murmuring 'Great Sage!' while they pressed their thumbs. At once a thundergod armed with an iron cudgel hovered before the face of each, ready to protect him against a whole army of attackers. 'Father a marvellous manifestation!' they cried. 'When the danger is past,' said Monkey, 'you have only to cry "Quiet!" and the apparition will vanish.' And sure enough when they cried "Quiet!" the thunder-gods changed back into hairs and returned to their place under the thumbnail.

The Buddhists now began to disperse. 'Don't go too far away,' cried Monkey. 'Look out for news of me in the city, and as soon as a summons to Buddhists is sent out, come and give me back my hairs.'

Meanwhile Tripitaka, waiting at the roadside, was wondering what had become of Monkey. At last he ordered Pigsy to lead the horse and was just setting out towards the west, when they met a number of Buddhist priests scattering in every direction. Presently, near the city gates, they met Monkey himself, still accompanied by a few priests who had stayed behind. 'Monkey,' cried Tripitaka, 'I sent you to discover the cause of that strange noise. Why were you so long about it?' Monkey brought the priests to Tripitaka and made them do reverence to him. Then he told what had happened. 'And what am *I* to do?' asked Tripitaka. 'Our temple,' the priests said, 'has not been destroyed. That is because it contains an image of the king's ancestor, having been built by his order. We invite you to come and rest there, till the Great Sage has done his work.'

The sun was setting as they crossed the drawbridge and went through the triple gates. Seeing that Tripitaka was accompanied by Buddhist priests, the people in the street all drew away from him. When they reached the temple, Tripitaka took out his cassock and bowed before the golden body of Buddha. An old priest who looked after the building was called out and on seeing Monkey he cried, 'So you have come here, Father!' 'Whom do you take me for?' said Monkey. 'I know that you are the Great Sage Equal to Heaven,' he said. 'Again and again I have dreamed of you. The Spirit of the Planet Venus came to me in my sleep and described you to me, telling me you would soon come and save our lives. It is as well you have come now; for if you had waited another day we should have been ghosts, not living men!' 'Get up, get up!' said Monkey. 'Tomorrow all will be set right.'

They then had supper and went to bed. But the second watch came and still Monkey could not sleep, so full was his head of tomorrow's plans. Somewhere near by he heard the sound of conches, and dressing quietly he leapt into the air and looked down. To the south he saw a flare of lanterns and torches. Lowering his cloud he looked more closely and saw that the Taoists in their great temple were celebrating a service of supplication to the Pole-star. In front of the gate was an inscription made of letters embroidered in yellow silk: "Wind and rain in due season; for our lord, ten thousand years of happy reign!" Conspicuous were three venerable Taoists in full sacramental robes, whom Monkey took to be the Tiger Strength, Deer Strength and Ram Strength Immortals. Before them was ranged a crowd of some eight hundred worshippers, beating drums and gongs, offering incense and confessing their sins.

'I would go down and mingle with the crowd,' said Monkey to himself. 'But "a single strand does not make a thread nor can one hand clap." I will go and get Pigsy and Sandy to come and share the fun.' He found the two sleeping huddled together. 'Why aren't you asleep?' Sandy asked when Monkey woke him. 'Get up and come with me,' said Monkey. 'We're all going to have a treat.' 'Who wants a treat in the middle of the night,' said Sandy, 'when one's mouth is dry and one's eyes won't stay open?' 'The Taoists are celebrating a Mass in their great temple,' said Monkey, 'and the whole place is littered with offerings. There are dumplings that must weigh a quart, and cakes weighing fifty pounds, and all kinds of dainties and fruits. Come and enjoy yourself.' Pigsy, hearing in his sleep something about things to eat, at once woke with a start. 'Brother, you're not going to leave me out of it?' he cried. 'If you like the idea of something to eat,' said Monkey, 'don't make a fuss and wake up the Master, but both of you come quietly with me.'

They dressed quickly and followed Monkey. As soon as they came into the light of the torches, Pigsy wanted to rush in and get to work. 'There's no hurry,' said Monkey. 'Wait till the congregation disperses; then we'll go in and set to.' 'But they're praying for all they're worth,' said Pigsy. 'They have evidently no idea of dispersing.' 'I'll see to that,' said Monkey; and reciting a spell he drew a magic diagram on the ground. Then standing upon it he blew with all his might. At once a great wind rose, which blew down all the flower-vases and lamp-stands and smashed the ex-votos hanging on the walls. The whole place was suddenly in darkness. The Taoists were frightened out of their wits. 'I must ask the congregation to disperse,' said the Tiger Strength Immortal. 'The wind will no doubt subside, and tomorrow morning we will recite a few more scriptures, so that the prescribed number may be reached.'

As soon as the place was empty, the three of them slipped in, and that fool Pigsy began to stuff himself with victuals. Monkey gave him a sharp rap over the knuckles. Pigsy drew back his hand and retreated, saying, 'Wait a bit. I've hardly had time to get my tongue round the things, and he begins hitting me!' 'Mind your manners,' said Monkey. 'Let's sit down and enjoy ourselves decently.' 'I like that,' said Pigsy. 'If we're to sit down and behave ourselves decently when we are stealing a meal, what play should we do if we were invited?' 'What are those Bodhisattvas up there?' asked Monkey. 'If you don't recognise the Taoist Trinity,' said Pigsy, 'what deities would you recognise, I wonder?' 'What are they called?' asked Monkey. 'The one in the middle,' said Pigsy 'is the Great Primordial, the one on the left is the Lord of the Sacred Treasure, and the one on the right is Lao Tzu.'

'Let's take their places,' said Monkey. 'Then we can eat decently and comfortably.' The smell of the offerings made Pigsy in a great hurry to begin eating, and scrambling up on to the altar he knocked down the figure of Lao Tzu with a thrust of his snout, saying, 'You've sat there long enough, old fellow. Now it's Pig's turn.' Monkey meanwhile took the seat of the Great Primordial, and Sandy that of the Lord of the Sacred Treasure, pushing the images out of the way. As soon as he was seated, Pigsy snatched at his big dumpling and began to gobble it down. 'Not so fast!' cried Monkey. 'Surely, brother,' said Pigsy, 'now that we've taken our places, it's time to begin.' 'We mustn't give ourselves away just for the sake of a small thing like a bite of food. If we leave these images lying there on the floor, some Taoist monk may come along at any minute to clean the place up, and trip over them. Then he'll know at once that there is something wrong. We had better put them away somewhere.' 'I don't know my way about here,' said Pigsy. 'There may be a door somewhere, but I shouldn't find it in the dark. Where am I to put these images?' 'I noticed a small door on the

243

right as we came in,' said Monkey. 'Judging from the smell that came from it, I should think it must be a place of metabolic transmigration. You had better take them there.' That fool Pigsy was uncommonly strong. He hoisted the three images on to his back and carried them off. When he reached the door, he kicked it open, and sure enough it was a privy. 'That chap Monkey finds some wonderful expressions,' he said laughing. 'He contrives to find a grand Taoist title even for a closet!' Before depositing them, he addressed the images as follows: Blessed Ones, having come a long way, we were hungry and decided to help ourselves to some of your offerings. Finding nowhere comfortable to sit, we have ventured to borrow your altar. You have sat there for a very long time, and now for a change you are going to be put in the privy. You have always had more than your share of good things, and it won't do you any harm to put up with a little stink and muck.' So saying, he pitched them in. There was a splash, and, not retreating quickly enough, he found that his coat was in a filthy state. 'Have you disposed of them successfully?' asked Monkey. 'I've disposed of them all right,' said Pigsy, 'but I have splashed myself and my coat is all filthy. If you notice a queer smell you'll know what it is.' 'That's all right for the moment. Come and enjoy yourself,' said Monkey. 'But you'll have to clean yourself up a bit before you go out into the street.' That fool Pigsy then took Lao Tzu's seat and began to help himself to the offerings. Dumplings, pasties, rice-balls, cakes . . . one after another he gobbled them down. Monkey never cared much for cooked food, and only ate a few fruits, just to keep the others in countenance. The offerings vanished swiftly as a cloud swept away by a hurricane, and when there was nothing left to eat, instead of starting on their way, they fell to talking and joking, while they digested their food. Who would have thought of it? There was a little Taoist who suddenly woke up and remembered that he had left his handbell in the temple. 'If I lose it,' he said to himself, 'I shall get into trouble with the Master tomorrow.' So he said to his bedfellow, 'You go on sleeping. I must go and look for my bell.'

He did not put on his lower garments, but just threw on his coat over his shoulders and rushed to the temple. After fumbling about for some time, he succeeded in finding it, and was just turning to go when he heard a sound of breathing. Very much alarmed, he ran towards the door, and in his hurry slipped on a lychee seed and fell with a bang smashing his bell into a thousand pieces. Pigsy could not stop himself from breaking into loud guffaws of laughter, which frightened the little Taoist out of his wits. Stumbling at every step he dragged himself back to the sleeping-quarters and, banging on his Master's door, he cried, 'Something terrible has happened!' The Three Immortals were not asleep, and coming to the door they asked what was the matter. 'I forgot my bell,' he said, trembling from head to foot, 'and when I went to the temple to look for it, I suddenly heard someone laughing. I nearly died of fright.' The Immortals called for lights, and startled Taoists came scrambling out of all the cells, carrying lanterns and torches. They all went off to the temple to see what evil spirit had taken possession there.

If you are not sure what came of it, you must listen to what is told in the next chapter.

Chapter 23

Monkey pinched Sandy with one hand and Pigsy with the other. They understood what he meant and both sat stock still, while the three Taoists advanced, peering about in every direction. 'Some rascal must have been here,' said the Tiger Strength Immortal. 'All the offerings have been eaten up.' 'It looks as though ordinary human beings have been at work,' said the Deer Strength Immortal. 'They've spat out the fruit stones and skins. It's strange that there is no one to be seen.' 'It's my idea,' said the Ram Strength Immortal, 'that the Three Blessed Ones have been so deeply moved by our prayers and recitations that they have vouchsafed to come down and accept our offerings. They may easily be hovering about somewhere on their cranes, and it would be a good plan to take advantage of their presence. I suggest that we should beg for some holy water and a little Elixir. We should get a lot of credit at Court if we could use them to the king's advantage.' 'A good idea,' said the Tiger Strength Immortal. And sending for some of his disciples, he bade them recite the scriptures, while he himself in full robes danced the dance of the Dipper Star, calling upon the Trinity to vouchsafe to its devout worshippers a little Elixir and holy water, that the king might live for ever.

'Brother,' whispered Pigsy and Monkey, 'there was no need to let ourselves in for this. Directly we finished eating we ought to have bolted. How are we going to answer their prayers?' Monkey pinched him, and then called out in a loud, impressive voice, 'My children,' he said, 'I must ask you to defer this request. My colleagues and I have come on straight from a peach banquet in Heaven, and we haven't got any holy water or elixir with us.' Hearing the deity condescend to address them, the Taoists trembled with religious awe. 'Father,' they said, 'you surely realise that for us this is too good an opportunity to be lost. Do not, we beseech you, go back to Heaven without leaving us some sort of magical receipt.' Sandy pinched Monkey. 'Brother,' he whispered, 'they are praying again. We're not going to get out of this so easily.' 'Nonsense,' whispered Monkey. 'All we've got to do is to answer their prayers and give them something.' 'That would be easier if we had anything to give,' whispered Pigsy. 'Watch me,' whispered Monkey, 'and you'll see that you are just as capable of satisfying them as I am.' 'Little ones,' he said, addressing the Taoists, 'I am naturally not keen on letting my congregation die out; so I'll see if we can manage to let you have a little holy water, to promote your longevity.' 'We implore you to do so,' they said, prostrating themselves. 'All our days shall be devoted to the propagation of the Way and its Power, to the service of our king and the credit of the Secret School.' 'Very well then,' said Monkey. 'But we shall need something to put it into.' The Tiger Strength Immortal bustled off and soon reappeared carrying, single-handed, an enormous earthenware jar. The Deer Strength Immortal brought a garden-vase and put it on the altar. The Ram Strength Immortal took the flowers out of a flower-pot and put it between the other two. 'Now go outside the building, close the shutters and stay there,' said Monkey. 'For no one is permitted to witness our holy mysteries.' When all was ready, Monkey got up, lifted his tiger-skin and pissed into the flower-pot. 'Brother,' said Pigsy, highly delighted. 'We've had some rare games together since I joined you, but this beats all.' And that fool Pigsy, lifting his dress, let fall such a cascade as would have made the Lü Liang Falls seem a mere trickle. Left with the big jug, Sandy could do no more than half fill it. Then they adjusted their clothes, and sat down decorously as before. 'Little ones,' Monkey called out, 'you can come and fetch your holy water.' The Taoists returned, full of gratitude and awe. 'Bring a cup,' said the Tiger Strength Immortal to one of his disciples. 'I should like to taste it.' The moment he tasted the contents of the cup, the Immortal's lip curled wryly. 'Does it taste good?' asked the Deer Strength Immortal. 'It's rather too full-flavoured for my liking,' said the Tiger Strength Immortal. 'Let me taste it,' said the Ram

Strength Immortal. 'It smells rather like pig's urine,' he said doubtfully, when the cup touched his lips. Monkey saw that the game was up. 'We've played our trick,' he said to the others, 'and now we'd better take the credit for it.' 'How could you be such fools,' he called out to the Taoists, 'as to believe that the Deities had come down to earth? We're no Blessed Trinity, but priests, from China. And what you have been drinking is not the Water of Life, but just our piss!'

No sooner did the Taoists hear these words than they rushed out, seized pitchforks, brooms, tiles, stones and whatever else they could lay hands on, and with one accord rushed at the impostors. In the nick of time Monkey grabbed Sandy with one hand and Pigsy with the other, and rushed them to the door. Riding with him on his shining cloud they were soon back at the temple where Tripitaka was lodged. Here they slipped back into bed, taking care not to wake the Master. 'Now we are all going to Court to get our passports put in order,' Tripitaka announced when he woke.

The king of the country, on hearing that three Buddhist pilgrims sought admittance to the palace, was in a tearing rage. 'If they must needs court death,' he said, 'why should they do it here, of all places? And what were the police doing, I should like to know. They ought never to have been let through.' At this, a minister stepped forward. 'The country of T'ang,' he said, 'is ten thousand leagues away and the road is as good as impassable. If they do indeed come from there, they must be possessed of some mysterious power. I am in favour of verifying their papers and letting them proceed. It would be wiser not to get on to bad terms with them.'

The king agreed, and ordered the passports to be sent in. When he had examined them, he told a eunuch to show the Buddhists in, and coming down from his Dragon Throne, went out to meet them, having ordered attendants to put ready three embroidered cushions. Turning his head as he went in, Tripitaka saw three Taoist dignitaries strutting along, accompanied by a tousle-headed acolyte. The whole

Court, at the sight of them, waited with bowed back and eyes upon the ground, while the immortals strode up to the dais without so much as a nod to the king of the land. 'To what am I indebted for the honour of this visit?' the king said humbly. 'An incident has occurred which we feel bound to report,' they said. 'From what country do these four priests come?' 'From China,' said the king. 'They are on their way to India to fetch scriptures, and have come to present their passports.' The Taoists clapped their hands and laughed aloud: 'Well, of all the odd places for them to have escaped to!' they exclaimed. 'I don't follow you,' said the king. 'They have just arrived with their passports, and as they are only passing through this kingdom and it would be unwise to pick a quarrel with China, it seems best to check their papers and let them go. I hope they have not shown disrespect to my reverend Preceptors?' 'Disrespect!' cried the Taoists. 'Yesterday they killed two of our disciples, released five hundred priests who were working for us, and smashed up our carts. Then at night they slipped into our temple, threw down the three holy images and ate all the offerings. We naturally imagined that the Deities had descended from Heaven and deigned to accept the offerings. We thought it a good opportunity to ask for a little holy water, for your Majesty's use. The rogues then tried to trick us by giving us their urine. We were not taken in, and were just going to lay hands on them when they made off. And here they are! "Narrow is the way of the evil-doer!"'

The king flew into a great rage and was for executing the four of them on the spot. But Monkey cried out in a loud voice, 'Let your Majesty stay the thunderbolts of his wrath and hear what we priests have to say.' 'Do you dare claim,' said the king, 'that the Heads of Religion have misinformed me?' 'What proof can they bring,' said Monkey, 'that it was we who killed the two Taoists? And even if we were identified, you would have the right to seize two of us and to forfeit their lives; the others you would have to send on their way. As for breaking carts, that is not a crime deserving of the death penalty, and if it can be brought home to us, it would be enough for one of us to be brought to justice. As for the defilement of your temple – the charge is clearly a plant.' 'In what sense a plant?' asked the king. 'We are newcomers here,' said Monkey. 'How could we have found our way to the temple in the dark? And if we defiled it, why were we not arrested on the spot, instead of being suddenly accused here? You must be aware that cases of mistaken identity occur everywhere and every day. How do you know that we are the true culprits? I submit that your Majesty should make proper investigation.'

The king had not at the best of times a very clear head, and having heard Monkey's speech he felt thoroughly perplexed. He was trying to make up his mind what to do, when a eunuch announced that a number of village elders were asking to be admitted to the Throne.

'Your Majesty,' they said, when they were brought in, 'there has been no rain all the spring, and we hope you will ask the Immortals to bring us rain and save the people from drought.' 'You may retire,' said the king. 'You shall have your rain.' 'If you want to know,' said he, turning to Tripitaka, 'why I suppressed Buddhism here, it was because some years ago the Buddhists were unable to bring rain, not a drop of it. Fortunately these Immortals arrived and saved us in the nick of time. You have come from a distant land and attacked the Taoists and their institutions. I ought to deal severely with you, but I am willing to give you one more chance. You shall have a rain-making competition with the Immortals. If you can produce rain, I will pardon you, sign your passports and let you go. But if you lose, I shall execute you all on the spot.' Monkey laughed. 'I don't know about the others,' he said, 'but if it's a matter of praying I can claim to understand something about it, I assure you.'

An altar was built and the Emperor went to an upper window of his palace to watch the ceremony. Tripitaka and the other pilgrims waited below, while the Immortals accompanied the king. When all the preparations were complete, the Immortals were called upon to perform. The Deer Strength Immortal left the king's side and came downstairs.

'Where are you off to?' said Monkey. 'I am going to the altar to pray for rain,' said he. 'That's not very good manners, is it?' said Monkey. 'Strangers first is the rule. But "the dragon does not deign to crush the earthworm." You shall have first turn. But you must make your announcement.' 'What announcement?' the Immortal asked. 'You must say exactly what you are going to bring about,' said Monkey. 'Otherwise who's to know whether you have been successful?' 'It's really surprising how sensibly that little priest talks,' said the king. 'He'll have more surprises before he's finished with Monkey,' Sandy whispered. 'I see no need for a statement,' said the Immortal. 'The king knows what I am going to do.' 'That's not to the point,' said Monkey. 'We must each have our programme; otherwise there'll be a mix-up.' 'Very well then,' said the Immortal. 'I shall fix my eyes on this magic table and give a cry. At the first cry, wind will come. At the second cry, clouds will rise. At the third cry, thunder will sound, and at the fourth rain will begin. I shall cry out a last time, and the rain will cease.' 'Pray begin,' said Monkey. 'This will be most entertaining for us.'

The altar that had been built was about thirty feet high. On each side were ranged the banners of the twenty-eight lunar Mansions. On a long table stood incense-burners from which the smoke rose curling, and at each side torches flamed. At the side of each brazier was a metal plate inscribed with the name of a thunder-spirit, and at the foot of the table were five great basins full of clear water, in each of which a willow-spray floated, to which was attached an iron plaque inscribed with the magic diagram of one of the Lords of Thunder. Behind the altar were some Taoists writing out texts. There were also a number of statues representing the deities controlled by the magic diagrams, together with the figures of local deities and patron spirits.

The Immortal strode up to the altar, where an acolyte handed to him a yellow paper inscribed with diagrams and a sword. Sword in hand he recited some spells and burned a diagram. Then several Taoists came forward with images and a written text, which they burned. A stinging sound came

251

from the tablet which the Immortal was carrying, and at the same moment there was a rush of wind in the air above. 'That's bad,' whispered Pigsy. 'His tablet sounded and he has got as far as producing a gust of wind.' 'Be quiet, brother.' said Monkey. 'You'll have enough to do looking after the Master. You may leave the rest to me.'

Dear Monkey! He leapt into the air and cried, 'Who's supposed to be in charge of the wind?' At once the Old Woman of the Wind appeared, hugging her bag, while Sun Erh-lang held tight the rope at the mouth of the bag, and both bowed low. 'I am protecting Tripitaka on his way to India,' said Monkey, 'and we are having a competition in rain-making with the Immortals here. Why are you helping them instead of us? I'll let you off lightly if you call in the wind. But if there is breeze enough to stir those Taoists' whiskers, you will each get twenty with this iron cudgel.' 'We shouldn't dare,' said the Old Woman. And immediately the wind ceased. Pigsy could not refrain from bawling out, 'Those Taoists must step down. There is not a breath of wind. They must make way for us at once. Again the Immortal grasped his tablet, burnt magic slips and struck the altar with a resounding crash. At once the sky became full of clouds and mist. 'Who's supposed to be in charge of the clouds?' Monkey cried, looking up into the sky; and the Cloud Boy and Mist Lad appeared before him, bowing low. When Monkey had explained the situation to them, they immediately cleared the sky, and not a cloud or wreath of mist was left. 'You've been swindling your Emperor,' jeered Pigsy, 'and all your magic is bunkum. You stand there fiddling with your tablet, and there isn't a cloud in the sky.'

Now extremely perturbed, the Immortal leant on his long sword and loosed his hair. Then he burned more slips and recited more spells, banging once more with his tablet. All that happened was that in a moment or two the Thunder God and Mother of Lightnings appeared in the sky, bowing towards Monkey. 'What brings you here?' he said. 'The magic of this Immortal,' they said, 'is perfectly correct and valid. The spells that he burnt reached the Jade Emperor, and he ordered us to come and make a storm.' 'The storm is all right,' said Monkey, 'provided that it happens when I want it. But you must hold it up for a bit.' They bowed assent, and no thunder rolled, no lightning flashed.

The Immortal, in a perfect frenzy, was burning strips, reciting spells, and striking again and again with his tablet. Nothing happened. 'Now it's my turn,' said Monkey. 'I'm not going to burn any magic writings or bang with a tablet. I rely on you two divinities to help me out.' 'Tell us what you want done,' said the Thunder God, 'and we will do it. Otherwise rain and thunder and lightning will come all mixed up together, and you won't get proper credit.' 'I intend to direct the proceedings with my cudgel.' 'Father,' said the God of Thunder, 'you're surely not going to cudgel us?' 'Not at all,' said Monkey. 'I merely ask you to watch my cudgel. When I point it upwards, you're to send a blast of wind.' 'We're standing by, ready with our wind-bag,' said the Old Woman of the Wind. 'The second time I point it upwards,' said Monkey, 'there are to be clouds, and the third time, thunder and lightning. The fourth time, rain; and the fifth time, the whole storm must cease.'

Very crestfallen, the Immortal left the altar and went to join the king in his upper room. 'I've been watching the proceedings attentively,' said the king. 'You don't seem to have been able to produce either wind or rain. What's wrong?' 'The rain-dragons are not at home today,' said the Immortal. 'Don't you believe him,' cried Monkey. 'They are all at home. The trouble is that this Immortal has no real power over them. We Buddhists will soon set them to work. Just you see!' 'All right,' said the king. 'Go to the altar, and I'll wait here and see if there is any rain.' 'Come along now,' said Monkey to Tripitaka. 'You've got to help me.' 'My dear disciple,' said Tripitaka, 'don't you think that *I* know anything about making rain!' 'Don't let him drag you into it,' whispered Pigsy. 'He's only trying to have someone to put the blame on if no rain comes.' 'It's true you don't know how to make rain,' said Monkey to Tripitaka. 'But you know how to recite scriptures. I'll do the rest.' Tripitaka went up to the altar, sat down, and composing his mind began silently to recite the Heart Sutra. Suddenly an official rushed up and said, 'Where is your tablet? Why aren't you burning magic strips?' 'We do our work quietly,' said Monkey, 'without all that needless fuss.'

When Tripitaka had finished reciting, Monkey took out his cudgel and expanding it, pointed towards the sky. The Old Woman of the Wind at once brought out her bag, Erh-lang loosed the rope at its mouth, and with a great roar the wind rushed out. All through the city tiles were lifted through the air, bricks hurtled, sand and stones flew. When the wind was at its height, Monkey again pointed with his stick, and such a black cloud covered the sky that the whole town was dark and even the neighbouring palace utterly disappeared.

Presently Monkey pointed again, and deafening peals of thunder shook the earth. It was as though a hundred thousand chariots were rolling by. The inhabitants of the town were frightened out of their wits and one and all began burning incense and saying their prayers. 'Now Thunder God,' screamed Monkey, 'do your work! Strike down all greedy and corrupt officials, all disobedient and surly sons, as a warning to the people!' The din grew louder than ever. Monkey pointed again, and such a rain fell that it seemed as if the whole Yellow River had suddenly fallen out of the sky. This rain fell from early morning till noon. The town was already one vast swamp, when the king sent a message saying, 'That's enough rain. If there is much more it will ruin the crops and we shall be worse off than ever.'

Monkey at once pointed with his cudgel, and in an instant the storm completely ceased, and there was not a cloud in the sky. The king was delighted, and his officers cried out in admiration, 'Wonderful priests! It is true indeed that there is always a stronger than the strongest! In the past we have seen our Immortals bring rain successfully. But even they could not stop the rain all in a moment. It always went on drizzling for the rest of the day. Whereas when these priests signalled for the rain to stop, not a drop more rain fell and the whole sky cleared immediately.' The king announced that he would return to the Palace and deal with the passports at once. 'Pardon me, your Majesty,' said the Deer Strength Immortal, 'it was I, not the Buddhists, who produced this rain.' 'You said just now,' protested the king, 'that the dragons were not at home and that this made it impossible to get rain. But directly the Buddhists set to work, in their quiet way, rain fell. I do not see how you can claim any credit.' 'There was evidently some little difficulty about getting into touch with the executive officers in charge of wind, cloud, thunder and rain,' said the Immortal. 'The dragons would not in any case dare to neglect our instructions. By the time the Buddhists had approached the altar, contact had been made and our orders were being carried out.' The king felt thoroughly confused and was still turning over this claim in his mind, when Monkey came forward and cried, 'Your Majesty, this was after all a trifling and commonplace performance, and it is not worth while disputing who should get the credit for it. The four dragon kings, who came at our bidding, are however still waiting, invisible, not far off in the sky. If these Immortals can induce them to show themselves, I will admit that they should be given the credit.' 'I've been king for twenty-three years,' said the king. 'But no one has ever been able to show me a dragon, and I hardly know what one looks like. I am prepared to reward anyone who can do this, and I shall certainly punish anyone who claims to be able to do so, and fails.'

The Taoists knew quite well that such a thing was beyond their powers. All the same, they called; but no dragon dared answer the summons, with Monkey standing there. Now it was Monkey's turn. 'Dragon Ao-kuang,' he called, 'are you there? Let's have a look at you and your brothers.' The four dragons at once appeared, surging through the clouds towards the summit of the Hall of Golden Bells. The king immediately began to burn incense, and his ministers all knelt down in adoration on the steps of the throne. 'I feel ashamed of having troubled these honoured forms to appear,' said the king. 'By all means tell them that I would not dream

255

of detaining them further. I will shortly find an opportunity of repaying them by offerings.' 'Spirits,' cried Monkey, 'you can now retire. The king will repay you with offerings at the earliest opportunity.' The dragons at once retired to their respective oceans, and the various other spirits went back to the sky.

And if you do not know how the Immortals were eventually disposed of, you must listen to what is told in the next chapter.

Chapter 24

Seeing that Monkey had even dragons at his beck and call, the king was just at the point of stamping the passports with his jewelled seal and sending the pilgrims on their way, when the three Taoists rushed forward and put in a petition, kneeling as they did so, which was quite contrary to their usage. The king, helping them to rise, asked why they had suddenly become so ceremonious. 'For twenty years,' they said, 'we have done everything in our power to guard and succour your subjects and realms. Today these Buddhists have robbed us of all our credit. But we feel sure that you will not forgive murderers only on the strength of a single shower of rain. Can it be that you suddenly hold us so cheap?'

The king, in great perplexity, after havering for a long while, at last consented to withhold the passports if the Taoists would accept another trial of strength. 'How about a contest in meditation?' said the Tiger Strength Immortal. 'I think that would be a mistake,' said the king. 'Meditation is the special business of these Buddhists, and if they were not particularly distinguished in this line, they would not have been chosen to go on this pilgrimage.' 'We have our own form of meditation,' said the Tiger Strength Immortal. 'It is called the Cloud Ladder. We shall require a hundred small tables, fifty for each performer. They are piled one on top of the other, and one has then to levitate to the top without touching with one's hands, sit down and remain in motionless trance for several hours.' 'Could any of you manage that?' said the king to Monkey. Monkey hummed uneasily and did not answer. 'What's the matter, brother?' whispered Pigsy. 'Why don't you speak?' 'If it were just a matter of playing football with the firmament, stirring up the ocean, turning back rivers, carrying away mountains, seizing the moon, moving the Pole-star or shifting a planet, I could manage it easily enough. Even if it were a question of my head being cut off and the brain removed or my belly being ripped open and my heart cut out, or any kind of transference or transformation, I would take on the job at once,' said Monkey. 'But if it comes to sitting still and meditating, I am bound to come off badly. It's quite against my nature to sit still. Even if you chained me to the top of an iron pillar, I should start trying to swarm up and down and should never think of sitting still.' 'I can practise meditation,' Tripitaka interposed. 'Excellent, excellent!' said Monkey. 'How long on end can you stay still?' 'I had first-rate masters when I was young,' said Tripitaka, 'and can remain suspended at the frontier between life and death for two or three years.' 'Don't do that,' said Monkey, 'or we shall never get to India. Two or three hours would be quite enough. Then you can come down.' 'My trouble is,' said Tripitaka, 'I don't know how I shall ever succeed in getting up.' 'Take this job on,' said Monkey, 'and I'll see to it that you get up all right.' Tripitaka accordingly pressed the palms of his hands together, and addressing the king said, 'I beg to inform your Majesty that I can meditate.'

Strong men were sent for, and in half an hour or so the two towers were complete. The Tiger Strength Immortal came down from the palace, and making a magic pass produced a carpet of cloud on which he floated up to the top of one of the towers. Monkey then made a five coloured magic cloud on which he transported Tripitaka to the top of the other tower. When Tripitaka was safely seated, Monkey transformed himself into a gnat and flying close to Pigsy's ear he said to him, 'Brother, keep an eye on the Master, and leave all the talking to me.' That fool laughed and said, 'As you wish, as you wish!'

Seeing after a time that there was nothing to choose between the competitors, one of the other Immortals decided to give his colleague a little assistance. He plucked some short hairs from the back of his head, twisted them into a pellet and tossed them on to the top of Tripitaka's head. Here they changed into a louse which began to bite him. Tripitaka felt first an irritation and then a sharp pain. But when people are meditating they are not allowed to move their hands; if they do, it counts as a point against them. After a time, unable to bear it any longer, he wriggled his head against his collar. 'Look out!' cried Pigsy. 'He's going to throw a fit.' 'I don't think so,' said Sandy. 'It's just that he's giddy.' 'The Master is a gentleman,' said Monkey. 'If he says that he knows how to meditate he does know how to meditate, and if he said he didn't know how to, he wouldn't know how to. Gentlemen always tell the truth. You two keep quiet, while I go and have a look.' Still in the form of a gnat, Monkey flew with a buzz to Tripitaka's head and saw that on top of it was a louse the size of a small bean, which he hastily brushed off, and the Master, relieved of his pain, once more sat stiff and straight. 'On a shaven head like that,' thought Monkey, 'one might easily find a flea, but how did a louse get there? It's certainly the doing of one of those Immortals. Ha, ha! Now that I've spoilt his trick I'll try one of my own.' He flew off and settled on the Immortal's head where he changed into a centipede and crept into his nostril. The Immortal began to wobble and soon fell head-long from his seat. Had he not been lucky enough to be caught by some officials who were standing near, he would undoubtedly have lost his life. The king was horrified, and ordered the minister on duty to take the Immortal to the Hall of Ornate Flowers and clean him up.

Monkey then lowered his Master on a platform of cloud and Tripitaka was acclaimed as victor.

The king was just about to let them go, when the Deer Strength Immortal came forward and said, 'Your Majesty, my brother has been suffering from a suppressed chill, which the draught up there brought on again. That is the only reason that he lost the match. But keep them a little longer and I will have a match with him at "guessing what is behind the boards." '

'What do you call "guessing what is behind the boards?" ' asked the king. 'I am able to guess what is behind boards,' said the Immortal. 'Let us see whether this Buddhist can do the same. If he guesses better than I, let him go on his way. But if he cannot guess, let him be punished as you find fit, that our fraternity may be avenged and the services that we have done to your country for twenty years may not be dragged in the dirt.'

So besotted was the king that he listened to this cajolery and ordered a red-lacquered coffer to be brought. This was carried by eunuchs to the women's quarters and the queen was asked secretly to deposit a treasure of some kind in it. Soon it was brought out again and laid on the white jade steps of the throne. 'Both sides must now guess what treasure lies in this coffer,' said the king. 'Disciple,' murmured Tripitaka, 'how can one possibly know what is inside a box?' 'Don't you worry,' said Monkey, turning once more into a gnat and settling on Tripitaka's head. 'I'll go and have a look.' He flew lightly to the box, crept under it and noticed that there was a slight chink between two boards at the bottom. He made his way through and found a court robe, laid upon a red lacquered dish. He bit his tongue and spat upon it, crying 'Change!' At once it became a cracked old kitchen dish, with nothing but dust on it. Then he crept out and flying to Tripitaka's ear, he whispered, 'Guess that it is an old cracked dish.' 'I was to guess what treasure it was,' said Tripitaka. 'An old cracked dish is not a treasure.' 'Don't worry about that,' said Monkey, 'but just guess as I told you to.' Tripitaka stepped forward and was just going to guess, when the Deer Strength Immortal asked to be allowed to have the first turn. 'I guess that in the box there is a royal garment covered with symbols of Earth and Sky,' he said. 'No, no!' cried Tripitaka. 'It is an old cracked dish.' 'That's not very polite,' said the king. 'You seem to be making fun of my kingdom by suggesting that an old cracked dish is the best I can do in the way of treasure.' And turning to his officers, he said 'Seize the fellow!' They were just about to lay hands on Tripitaka when he cried, 'Your Majesty, wait at least till the box has been opened. If it is indeed found that there is a treasure in it, then I am grievously to blame. But should it prove that no treasure is there, you will have done me a great wrong by laying hands on me.' The king ordered the box to be opened, and sure enough there was nothing but an old cracked dish. 'Who put this in the box?' roared the king. 'My Master,' said the queen, slipping from behind the Dragon Throne, 'I put in a royal garment covered with the symbols of Earth and Sky. This I did with my own hands, and I cannot conceive how it has changed into what is there now.' 'Wife, get out of my sight!' cried the king. 'Such a tale as that you cannot expect me to believe. Everything used in your apartments is of the finest. Such a cast-off as this old dish could not exist there.' And turning to his officers, he said, 'Follow me with the box. I'm going to put something in myself and try again.' The king went to the flower-garden behind the palace and picking a large peach he put it in the box, which was then carried out to the front of the palace and the guessing began again. 'Disciple,' whispered Tripitaka, 'you must help me again.' 'That's all right,' said Monkey, 'I'll go and have a look.' He flew to the box and crept in as before. What he found there was thoroughly to his liking. He resumed his proper form, squatted in the box and ate up the peach with great relish, licking even the pouches in his cheeks quite clean. Then leaving the peach-stone, he changed back into a gnat and flying to Tripitaka, whispered in his ear, 'Guess it is a peach-stone.' 'Disciple,' said Tripitaka, 'don't tease me. Last time, if I hadn't spoken up quickly, I should in another minute have been seized and executed. This time I had certainly better guess that it is a treasure. You can't call a peach-stone a treasure.' 'Don't be afraid,' said Monkey, 'Just guess and win.'

This time the Ram Strength Immortal insisted on guessing first, and at once said it was a peach. 'It's not a peach,' said Tripitaka, 'it's only a peach-stone.' 'How can it only be the stone?' roared the king, 'I put in a peach myself only a moment ago. The Immortal guessed rightly.' 'Perhaps your Majesty would not mind having the box opened before reaching a final decision,' said Tripitaka. The box was accordingly opened, and all that it contained was the stone, without a trace of skin or fruit. The king was astounded. 'You'd better give up trying to compete with these people,'

261

he said, 'and let them go. I put in a peach, and now there is only a stone. Someone must have eaten it. The truth is, I suspect, that spirits of some kind are secretly aiding them.' 'They little know what a long record of peach-eating lies behind him,' tittered Pigsy to Sandy.

At this moment the Tiger Strength Immortal reappeared, washed and combed. 'Your Majesty,' said he, 'these Buddhists have the art of transforming lifeless objects. But if the box is brought again, you will see that they cannot transform human beings. If we put this acolyte of ours into the box, I guarantee that they will not be able to transform him.' The acolyte was accordingly put into the box and the lid fastened down. 'Now priest,' said the king. 'Here is a third test for you. Tell me what is inside the box. 'More guessing!' groaned Tripitaka, 'That's all right,' said Monkey, 'I'll go and have a look.' On creeping into the box again, he shook himself and changed into the semblance of an old Taoist. 'Master what lesson have you to teach me?' asked the boy. 'Those Buddhists saw you put into the box,' said Monkey. 'They will guess that a little Taoist is in the box, and we shall not win. Here's an idea: I'll shave your head and tell the Immortals to say there is a little Buddhist inside.' 'I'll do anything you like,' said the boy, 'provided it brings us victory. We can't afford to go on being beaten again and again like this. We are rapidly losing our credit at Court.' 'Quite true,' said Monkey. 'Come here, and when we've won, you shall have a handsome present.' He took his cudgel, shook it and changed it into a razor. Then flinging his arms round the boy's neck, he said, 'Now mind you don't scream if it hurts, ducky!'

In a twinkling he had shaved the boy's head and stuffed the hair behind the lining of the box. Then patting his shaven pate, he said, 'Now child, you have got a priest's head; but your clothes are all wrong. Take them off and I'll put that right.' The boy was wearing a 'cranedown' of onion-white colour, embroidered with the cloud-pattern and bordered with brocade. When he had taken it off, Monkey breathed upon it with magic breath and it became a brown straight-

262

coat, which he made him put on. Then he plucked some of his hairs, which he changed into a wooden fish such as is carried by priests, and put it into the boy's hand, saying 'Listen here, my disciple. If you hear them say "Taoist acolyte," stay where you are. But if you hear anyone say "Buddhist," raise the lid, beat with your wooden fish and come out, reciting a Buddhist scripture.' 'I can only say the Book of the Three Primordials, the Book of the Pole-star and so on,' said the boy. 'Don't you know any prayers to Buddha?' asked Monkey. 'Anyone can say O-mi-to Fo,'[1] said the boy. 'That's good enough,' said Monkey. 'It will save me the trouble of teaching you. Don't forget what you're to do. I'm off.' And changing once more into a gnat and flying to Tripitaka's ear, he said, 'Guess that it's a Buddhist.' 'This time I feel confident of success,' said Tripitaka. 'Why are you so sure?' asked Monkey. 'Because,' said Tripitaka, 'in the scriptures Buddha, the Law and the Congregation are called the Three Treasures. So certainly a Buddhist is a treasure.' At this moment the Tiger Strength Immortal stepped forward and said, 'Your Majesty, this time it is a Taoist acolyte.' Hearing these words the boy did not stir. But when Tripitaka said, 'It is a Buddhist,' echoed loudly by Pigsy, the boy pushed up the lid, beat with his wooden fish, and calling upon the name of Buddha, scrambled out of the chest. All the spectators burst into loud applause, while the three Immortals maintained a gloomy silence.

'There is no doubt about it,' said the king, 'that these Buddhists are being helped by unseen influences. A Taoist entered the box, and here is a Buddhist! An accomplice might have crept in and shaved the boy's head. But he is dressed to match and is calling upon Buddha's name. You had better let these people go!'

'Your Majesty,' said the Tiger Strength Immortal, 'the proverb says: "The chess-player needs a worthy adversary, just as the carpenter needs good wood." I own we should very much like to challenge these people to a competition in some tricks we learnt when we were young.' 'What arts are

[1] Equivalent to 'God bless me!'

these?' asked the king. 'My head can be cut off and I can put it back in its place,' said he. 'The Second Immortal's heart can be removed and he can make himself whole again. The Third Immortal can take a bath in a cauldron of boiling oil.' The king was much astonished. 'That all sounds to me like taking frightful risks,' he said. 'We can manage these things all right,' said the Immortal, 'and insist upon this final trial being made.' 'Priests from China, the Immortals are unwilling to let you go until they have had a final competition with you in head-cutting, belly-ripping and bathing in boiling oil,' said the king.

On hearing this Monkey at once changed into his true form and laughed aloud. 'That's luck,' he cried. 'More business coming my way!' 'I don't know why you should talk of business coming your way,' said Pigsy. 'I can't think of three quicker ways to perdition.' 'You don't know all my tricks,' said Monkey. 'Brother,' said Pigsy, 'I am willing to credit you with all sorts of transferences and transformations, but this sort of thing is beyond you.' 'Not at all,' said Monkey. 'Cut off my head, and I can still talk. Cut off my arms, and I can still strike. Cut off my legs, and I can still walk. Rip out my heart, and I can mysteriously recover. I can bathe in boiling oil with no other result than that I come out cleaner than I went in.' Sandy and Pigsy roared with laughter. Monkey then stepped forward and said, 'Your Majesty, I am quite willing to have my head cut off.' 'What gives you such confidence?' asked the king. 'Well,' said Monkey, 'years ago a first-class Zen adept taught me the art of having one's head cut off, I don't know whether I can remember it or not; but I am quite willing to experiment.' 'My dear little fellow,' said the king, 'you don't know what you are talking about. Headcutting is no matter for experiment. The head is the chief of the six repositories of the element *yang*, and if it is cut off death ensues.' 'Your Majesty,' said the Tiger Strength Immortal, 'don't discourage him. This is just the very way for us to get our revenge.'

A place of execution was accordingly laid out, and three thousand soldiers of the guard were drawn up in file. 'My turn first!' cried Monkey blithely, and was rushing off to the place of execution, when Tripitaka caught hold of him, saying, 'Disciple, take care what you are doing. It looks over there as if they meant business.' 'I'm not afraid,' said Monkey. 'Take your hand away and let me go.' On arriving at the place of execution he was seized by the executioner, bound with ropes and led to the top of a small mound. At the word 'Strike,' there was a swishing sound and Monkey's head fell upon the ground, where the executioner gave it a kick that sent it rolling, just like a melon, thirty or forty paces away. No blood came from the trunk, but a voice, coming from deep down inside cried 'Head, come back!' The Deer Strength Immortal, seeing that Monkey had some trick, recited a spell to summon the local deities, to whom he said: 'Keep that head where it is, and your shrine shall be rebuilt as a great temple, while your clay images shall be replaced by statues of gold.' The deities were compelled by the Immortal's magic and did indeed stay Monkey's head, and though he cried again, 'Come here, head!' the head remained rooted to the spot. But suddenly from Monkey's trunk came the cry 'Grow!' and a new head shot up from inside him and replaced the old one. The executioner and the soldiers were thunderstruck, and the officer in charge of the proceedings rushed off to the king and announced that Monkey had grown a new head. 'He's cleverer than we thought,' whispered Pigsy. 'Well,' said Sandy, 'he's known to have seventy-two transformations, so I suppose he has got seventy-two heads.' At this point Monkey came running up to Tripitaka. 'Dear disciple,' said Tripitaka, 'it must have hurt terribly.' 'It didn't hurt at all,' said Monkey, 'and I found it rather fun.' 'Brother,' said Pigsy, 'I suppose you've put something on the scar.' 'Feel my neck,' said Monkey, 'and see whether there's a scar.' That fool Pigsy put out his hand and felt. To his astonishment he found that there was not the faintest scar or mark. The new head had simply taken the place of the old. 'Here are your passports,' said the king, 'and I advise you to start immediately.' 'Thanks for the passports,' said Monkey. 'But before we start, the Immortal must try the same experiment.' 'This was to be a competition,' said the king to the Immortals, 'and you must not let me down by allowing these priests to go away victorious.'

Exactly the same proceeding was accordingly gone through with the Tiger Strength Immortal; but when he cried 'Head, come back!' Monkey at once plucked a hair, blew on it with magic breath and cried 'Change!' It changed into a brown dog which ran at the head, took it up in its mouth, and carrying it away to the royal moat dropped it in. Three times the Immortal cried 'Head, come back!'; but the head did not appear. He had not Monkey's art of growing a new head. Alas! blood spouted from the trunk, the Immortal tottered, and presently fell prostrate in the dust. The officer in charge rushed to the spot, and on returning to the king reported, 'Your Majesty, where the Immortal fell, all that is now to be seen is a headless brown-coated tiger.' The king turned deadly pale, while he fixed his gaze upon the two remaining Immortals. 'My brother is undoubtedly no more,' said the Deer Strength Immortal. 'But I cannot admit that this brown tiger has any connection with him. That is merely an illusion created by these ruffians. They must not be allowed to depart, till I have competed with them in the ordeal of belly-ripping.' 'That would suit me very well,' said Monkey. 'Generally speaking I do not eat cooked food; but a few days ago a kind patron induced me to try some pastries, and since then I have had a pain inside. I think the pastries have gone bad, and I was just on the point of asking if I might borrow your Majesty's knife, so that I might rip open my belly, take out my guts and give them a good cleaning. I don't want to have any trouble on the journey.' 'Take him along!' cried the king.

'You need not drag me,' said Monkey, when the executioner's men seized him. 'I am perfectly ready to go. All I ask is that my hands shall be left free. I shall need them for cleaning my entrails.' 'Don't bind his hands,' ordered the king.

When they had tied him to a stake and ripped open his belly, Monkey calmly took out his guts and after manipulating them for some time put them back inside him, coil for coil exactly in the right place. Then he blew on his belly with magic breath and the hole closed up.

'Here are your passports,' said the king. 'I won't delay your journey any further.' 'It does not matter so much about the passports,' said Monkey. 'The next thing is for the Second Immortal to have his belly ripped open.' 'This has nothing to do with me,' said the king to the Deer Strength Immortal. 'But it was you who challenged them to this contest, and I must ask you to go and submit yourself to the ordeal.' 'That's quite all right,' said the Immortal. 'I am quite confident of success.'

The Immortal was just beginning to manipulate his guts as he had seen Monkey do, when Monkey plucked a hair, blew on it with magic breath, cried 'Change!' and it changed into a ravening hawk which spread its claws and snatching the Immortal's guts flew off with them to devour them at leisure far away out of sight. After a short while the Immortal collapsed against the stake. The executioners rushed up, and what should they find but the body of a lifeless white deer!

'It seems that my poor brother has succumbed,' said the Third Immortal. 'But that this should be his corpse is impossible. A foul trick has been played upon us by these ruffians, and I must have my revenge.' 'In what ordeal do you hope to get the better of them?' asked the king. 'I wager that he cannot bathe in boiling oil,' said the Immortal. A large cauldron was accordingly filled with oil. 'Thank you for this kind attention,' said Monkey. 'It's a long time since I had a bath, and my skin was beginning to feel rather irritable. This will do me good.' Faggots were laid under the cauldron and when the oil was well boiling, Monkey was invited to get in. 'Is it to be a civil bath or a military bath?' he asked. 'I don't know the difference,' said the king. 'For a civil bath one does not undress,' said Monkey, 'but simply folds one's hands like this and bobs in rapidly. One must not dirty one's clothes. If there is a single speck of oil on them, it counts as a defeat. For a military bath, a clothes-stand is necessary, and a towel. One must completely undress, jump right in and

267

play about in the bath, turning somersaults and splash-about at one's ease!' 'Which do you prefer?' said the king to the Ram Strength Immortal. 'If I choose a civil bath,' said he, 'I know this wretch would put some stuff on his clothes to keep off the oil. Let it be a military bath.'

'Forgive my forwardness if I again claim the first turn,' said Monkey. Look at him! He leaps straight into the cauldron, plunging about in the burning oil for all the world like a dolphin in the seawaves. Pigsy seeing him bit his finger-tip and whispered to Sandy, 'We have really never taken this ape seriously enough. We should have taken a very different tone about him if we had known he was capable of such a performance as this!' Seeing them whispering together, Monkey thought they were making fun of him. 'After all,' he said to himself, 'it's I who have all the work to do, while the incompetents sit round and enjoy results. It wouldn't be a bad plan to give them a bit of a fright.' He made a tremendous splash and then suddenly sank to the bottom and changed himself into a tin-tack. In this form he lay at the bottom of the cauldron, and the officer in charge presently reported, 'Your Majesty, the boiling oil has done its work. The little priest is dead.' Much relieved, the king ordered the executioner to fish up the corpse. He began to fish about in the cauldron with an iron skimmer, but the holes in the skimmer were large, and Monkey in his present form was very small. Each time he was scooped up he slipped back again through a hole. 'He was very delicately built,' reported the executioner, 'and seems to have evaporated, bone and all.' 'Seize the other Buddhists!' said the king. Officers of the Guard rushed upon Pigsy from each side, threw him down and bound him. 'Your Majesty,' cried Tripitaka in great perturbation, 'grant me a few moments grace. This discipline of mine, since he embraced the Faith, has performed many deeds of prowess. Now that he has met his match in this Third Immortal and perished in the cauldron of burning oil, I do not care what becomes of us. You are a king, and all who come under your sway must bow to your will. Command that I am to die, and I will gladly die. But this much I ask – give me half a bowl of cold rice gruel and three paper horses, and let me offer them to the soul of the departed. Then I will accept my fate.'

'It is just as I have always heard,' said the king. 'These Chinese are great sticklers for ceremony. Let him have what he asks.' Beckoning to Sandy to come with him, Tripitaka went to the side of the cauldron, and some officers of the Guard caught hold of Pigsy by the ear and dragged him along too. 'Disciple,' said Tripitaka, addressing Monkey's soul, 'ever since you joined our Order you have faithfully protected me on my journey to the West. Little did I think that today you would go down to Darkness. Alive, you set your heart on the quest of scriptures; dead, you still carry the name of Buddha in your heart, and who knows but that I shall find your ghost waiting for me in the Temple of the Thunder-Clap?'

'Master,' said Pigsy, 'that's not the way to talk to him. Sandy, give me a little of that rice-broth, and let me address his soul.' Then lying bound with ropes upon the ground, that fool grunted out the following invocation: 'Cursed ape, senseless groom, you looked for trouble and have found it. That cauldron has settled your account for good and all. We're well rid of you, Monkey! We've seen the last of you, insensate groom!'

Hearing the fool's jibes, Monkey could not restrain himself, and resuming his proper form, he stood up in the cauldron. 'You worthless lout,' he screamed, 'whom are you insulting!'

'Dear disciple,' said Tripitaka, 'you nearly frightened me to death.' 'Was anything cleverer ever seen,' said Sandy, 'than the way our brother pretended to be dead?' In consternation all the officials, military and civil, rushed to the king and reported, 'The priest is not dead after all. He is standing up in the cauldron of boiling oil.' 'Not at all,' said the officer in charge, 'he is dead right enough. But it happens to be an unlucky day and this is his ghost appearing.' At this Monkey jumped right out of the cauldron, wiped off the oil, dressed, and seizing his cudgel rushed at the officer and pounding his head with it cried, 'So I'm a ghost, am I!'

Terrified out of their wits the other officers let go of Pigsy, and kneeling before Monkey cried, 'Forgive us, forgive us!' The king sprang from his throne and was rushing away, when Monkey stopped him, saying, 'Your Majesty, don't leave us. The Third Immortal has still to take his bath.' 'Immortal,' said the king, trembling from head to foot, 'I must trouble you to get into the cauldron at once, or this priest will cudgel me to death.' The Ram Strength Immortal went to the cauldron and undressing just as Monkey had done got into it and began to bathe himself. Seeing him looking quite comfortable Monkey called to the stokers to put on more fuel. Presently he went up to the cauldron and put his finger in. To his astonishment he found that the oil was quite cold. 'It was hot enough when I was in,' thought Monkey to himself. 'What can have happened? I have it! There must be some chilly dragon hiding there.' And jumping into the air he uttered a sonorous OM, by which he summoned the Dragon King of the Northern Ocean. 'Now then, you horrid earthworm, you scaly loach, how dare you help this Taoist by allowing a chilly dragon to hide in the cauldron? Do you want to make a hero of him and see me defeated?' 'Great Sage, you do not understand,' said the Dragon King. 'This creature by practising considerable austerities was able to escape from his original shape; but the only magic powers that he acquired were the Five Thunder Methods. Apart from that he only learnt a few paltry tricks that have nothing to do with true Taoism. By acquiring this chilly dragon as a familiar spirit he has been able to play all kinds of tricks upon the world at large. But you, Great Sage, should not have been deceived. I will at once call back this chilly dragon, and I will guarantee that the Immortal will be boiled, bones, skin and all.' 'Call it in quickly,' said Monkey, 'or you'll get a good hiding.' The Dragon King, in the form of a magic whirlwind, rushed to the cauldron and seizing the chilly dragon carried it away to the Northern Ocean.

Returning from the air, Monkey joined Tripitaka, Pigsy and Sandy, and they soon saw the Immortal struggling and squirming. He made frantic efforts to get out, but all in vain, and in a little while it was all over with him. 'Your Majesty,' announced the officer in charge, 'the Third Immortal has succumbed.' The king, in utter despair, wept copiously and beat upon the table with his fists.

If you do not know how Tripitaka and the others set things right, listen to what is told in the next chapter.

Chapter 25

The king's tears gushed like a fountain all the time till darkness fell. 'How can you be so deluded?' said Monkey, coming up to him. 'Have you not seen that the first Immortal's corpse showed him to have been merely a tiger? The second has turned out to be a common deer. And if you have the bones of the third fished out of the cauldron, you will find that he was nothing but a ram, the bones of which could never be mistaken for those of any human being. All of them were bewitched wild animals who came here plotting your destruction; but seeing that your ascendancy was still strong, they did not dare lay hands upon you. In a year or two, when your ascendancy will be on the wane, they would have taken your life and stolen all your streams and hills. Luckily for you we came in time to save you from these monsters. Why then should you weep? Make haste to give us our passports and send us on our way.'

The king, on hearing this, began to come to his senses, and soon afterwards his officers approached him. 'Your Majesty,' they said. 'It is indeed the fact that a ram's bones have been found at the bottom of the cauldron. This holy Buddhist's words must be accepted as truth.' 'I must confess,' said the king, 'that I am grateful to him. But it is late. You, my chief Minister, must invite these priests to spend the night in the Temple of the Pool of Knowledge. Early tomorrow, make ready the eastern tower of the palace and tell my stewards to prepare a meatless banquet, that may repay them for their great achievement.'

Next day at his morning Court the king ordered a decree to be promulgated, summoning all Buddhists to the city, and it was displayed at all four gates and in every street. Then Tripitaka and the rest were summoned to the eastern tower and were entertained at a great feast.

When the fugitive Buddhists heard that a decree had been displayed, summoning them back to their homes, they came in high delight, looking everywhere for Monkey. For they wished to thank him, and hand back the hairs that he had given them for their protection. When the feast was over and the passports had been put in order, the king and queen, with all the ladies of the Court and officials military and civil, escorted Tripitaka and the rest to the gates of the palace. What should they find there but a crowd of priests kneeling at the side of the street crying, 'Great Sage, our Father, we are the priests who were in durance at the sandy cliff. Hearing that you had destroyed the fiends and worked our deliverance, also that our king had issued a mandate calling back all Buddhists, we have come to give you back your hairs and express our thanks.' 'How many are you?' asked Monkey. 'Father,' they said, 'of the five hundred not half a one is missing.' Monkey, with a twist of his body, resumed the hairs, and addressing himself to all present, he said, 'It was I who released these priests. It was I who destroyed the carts and it was I who slew the two task-masters. Now the whole pest has been extirpated and you see with your own eyes that Buddhism is the true way. Never again follow false doctrines nor follow foolish courses, but know that the Three Religions are one. Reverence priests, reverence Taoists too, and cultivate the faculties of man. I will see to it that these hills and streams are safe forever.'

The king bowed his assent, confessing the deepest gratitude, and then escorted Tripitaka well beyond the city walls.

They travelled on for many days and autumn had already come when late one evening Tripitaka reined in his horse and said, 'Disciple, where are we going to halt tonight?' 'Master,' said Monkey, 'that is a question for ordinary men to ask, not for such pilgrims as we.' 'Wherein lies the difference?' asked Tripitaka. 'Ordinary people at this hour,' said Monkey, 'are hugging their children or cuddling their wives in soft beds under warm coverlets, lying snug and comfortable as you please. But how can we pilgrims expect any such thing? By moonlight or starlight on we must go, supping on the air and braving the wet, so long as the road lasts.' 'Brother,' said Pigsy, 'you know your side of the question, but not mine.

These roads are very hilly and with such a load as I am carrying it's difficult going. I must find somewhere to get a bit of sleep and refresh myself, or I shan't be able to manage this load tomorrow.' 'We'll go on a bit further, while the moon is still up,' said Monkey, 'and if we come to a house, we'll stop.' They had not gone far before they heard a noise of water. 'Here we are!' said Pigsy. 'This is as far as the road goes.' 'There's a great river right in front of us,' said Sandy. 'We don't know whether it's deep or shallow,' said Pigsy. 'I'll find out.' 'Think what you're saying, Pigsy,' said Tripitaka. 'How can you find out whether water is deep?' 'By throwing a stone the size of a duck's egg into the middle,' said Pigsy. 'If there is a splash and foam comes up, that means it's shallow. If it goes down, down, down, with a gurgling sound, that means it is deep.' Pigsy found a stone and threw it in. As it went down to the bottom, there was a gurgling sound and bubbles rose. 'It's very deep indeed,' cried Pigsy. 'We can't go on.' 'You've found out that it's deep,' said Tripitaka. 'But we still don't know how wide it is.' 'True enough,' said Pigsy. 'Wait here,' said Monkey, 'while I go and have a look.' He sprang into the air and peered with steady eyes. A vast expanse of water spread out in the moonlight. It seemed to go on forever. There was no trace of a further shore. 'Master,' he said, lowering his cloud, 'it's very wide. You know that I have fiery, steely eyes, and even by night can see five hundred leagues. But now I cannot see the further shore. How can I measure how wide it is?' 'Dear disciple, what then are we to do?' said Tripitaka, sobs choking his words. 'Master,' said Sandy, 'don't break down. Isn't that a man that I see standing over there by the water?' 'It looks to me like a fisherman dragging his nets. I'll go and talk to him,' said Monkey. He had not gone far when there loomed up in front of him not a man, but a stone monument. On it was written 'The River that leads to Heaven,' and in smaller writing below, 'The way across is eight hundred leagues. Few are those that have reached the far side.'

'Come over here and look,' said Monkey. When Tripitaka read the inscription, he burst again into tears. 'Disciple,' he sobbed, 'when I left the Capital, I thought it an easy matter to go to India. Little I knew that at every turn demons would bar my path, and endless rivers and mountains have to be crossed.' 'Listen,' said Pigsy, 'isn't that the sound of cymbals? Somewhere priests are being feasted. If we get there in time we shall be able to join in the feast. Perhaps they will be able to tell us if there is a ford anywhere or a ferry, so that tomorrow we can get across.' Tripitaka could now hear the sound distinctly. 'That is certainly not Taoist music,' he said. 'I am sure that Buddhists are performing.' They set off in the direction of the sound, and presently saw a village of several hundred well-built houses. At the top of the street they saw a house with a flag hoisted outside the gate. The courtyard blazed with torches and a heavy smell of incense came towards them. 'Well,' said Tripitaka, 'that looks better than the hollow of a hill-side or a river bank. Under such substantial eaves we can at least count on being warm and getting a little quiet sleep. You'd better not come with me. I'll go in and explain. If they say I may stay, I'll call you in. If we can't stay you're not to rage and swear. I don't want the people to see you to start with, because you are not very good to look at, and if they take fright we shall have nowhere to stay.'

Tripitaka took off his broad-brimmed hat, and bareheaded, with staff in hand, he went up to the door. He found it ajar but did not dare go straight in. When he had waited for a moment, an old man came out, with a rosary hanging at his breast, mumbling his prayers as he came. 'Aged benefactor,' said Tripitaka politely, 'I should like to ask you a few questions.' 'You've arrived rather late,' said the old man. 'How do you mean?' said Tripitaka. 'Well, you've come too late to get anything much,' said he. 'The priests whom we are entertaining have each been given as much rice as they could eat, three hundred measures to take away, a strip of white cloth and ten pieces of copper cash. It's a pity you've come when you have.' 'Aged benefactor,' said Tripitaka, 'I did not come because of the feast.' 'Then why did you come?' asked the old man. 'I am from China and am going

275

to fetch scriptures from India,' said Tripitaka. 'Night overtook me when I was near your exalted abode, and hearing a
sound of Buddhist music I have come to ask you whether I
may lodge here tonight.' 'Sir,' said the old man, 'it is in-
cumbent upon those who have left the world to adhere
strictly to truth. Are you aware that China is 54,000 leagues
away? You cannot pretend that you have come that distance,
travelling all alone.' 'Aged benefactor, you are right,' said
Tripitaka. 'But I have three disciples who have helped me
over mountains and across rivers, and constantly mounted
guard over me. Otherwise I should never have got here.'
'Where are they?' said the old man. 'Please ask them to
come in and rest.' Tripitaka turned and called to his disciples.

Monkey was by nature too restless, Pigsy too coarse and
Sandy too simple to need a second bidding. Leading the
horse and shouldering the luggage they came tumbling in,
without a thought for what might come of it. The old man
was so frightened that he fell flat upon the ground, mumbling: 'There are demons in the yard, demons!' 'Aged benefactor,' said Tripitaka, dragging him to his feet, 'you need not
be afraid. These are not demons; they are my disciples.'
'How comes it,' he asked trembling, 'that a nice-looking
gentleman like yourself has managed to get such monsters
for his disciples?' 'I know they are ugly,' said Tripitaka, 'but
they are very good at subduing dragons and tigers and cap-
turing ogres.' The old man, only half-reassured, walked on
slowly, supported by Tripitaka. In the courtyard were some
priests reciting the scriptures. 'What's that you are reading?'
cried Pigsy, raising his long snout. Suddenly catching sight of
these three terrifying apparitions the priests leapt up and fled
in utter panic, upsetting the Buddhist images, stumbling,
crawling and banging into one another. Highly diverted by
this spectacle the three disciples clapped their hands and
roared with laughter. More frightened than ever, the priests
now ran for their lives. 'You wretches,' cried Tripitaka,
'you've spoilt everything. No one would think that I have
been teaching you and preaching to you in season and out for
all these months. The ancients said, "To be virtuous without

instruction is superhuman. To be virtuous after instruction is reasonable. To be instructed and remain incorrigible is to be a fool." You three have just shown yourselves to be fools of the very lowest description. Fancy charging in at the gate like that, without any regard for what was going on inside, frightening our benefactor, scaring away the priests who were reading the scriptures, and spoiling the whole ceremony! Don't you see that it is I who will bear the blame for all this?' Thus addressed, they did not dare reply, which fortunately convinced the old man that they were indeed his disciples. 'It's of no consequence,' he said, bowing to Tripitaka. 'We were just going to remove the lamps, scatter the flowers and terminate the proceedings.' 'Well, if you have finished the service,' said Pigsy, 'bring out the end-of-service wine and victuals, and we'll sup before we go to bed.' Just then the inner door opened and another old man came out, leaning on a staff. 'What devils are these,' he asked, 'who have come to our pious doors in the black of night?' The first old man rose quickly, and going to meet him said, 'Brother, calm yourself! They are not devils, but saints going to India to fetch Scriptures. The three disciples might well be better to look at; but they are good fellows.' The second old man laid down his staff and bowed to the pilgrims. Then he sat down and called for tea. He had to call several times. At last, in great trepidation, several servants came in, peering anxiously at the visitors. 'What are those fellows up to?' asked Pigsy. 'I've told them to fetch refreshments for your Reverence,' said the old man. 'How many men will serve us?' asked Pigsy, 'Eight,' said the old man. 'Who are they going to serve?' asked Pigsy. 'All of you,' said the old man. 'That pasty-faced Master of ours does not need more than one,' said Pigsy. 'That hairy-faced fellow can get on with two. That swarthy one needs eight to himself, and I can't do with less than twenty.' 'You must have a very big appetite,' said the old man. 'You'll soon see for yourself,' said Pigsy. 'I'm not short of men,' said he; and big and little, thirty or forty men were found to serve. When the pilgrims had conversed amiably with the two old men for some time everyone began to feel somewhat reassured. Tripitaka was put in the seat of honour, and before using his chopsticks began to recite the Fast-Breaking Scripture. Pigsy was in a hurry to begin, and without waiting for the end of grace, he snatched up a red lacquer wooden bowl, filled it with white rice and tilted it straight down his throat. Not a grain was left. A servant standing near him was much astonished. 'This reverend gentleman's doing things in the wrong order,' he said. 'Why does he help himself to rice before helping himself to dough nut? Won't he mess his clothes?' 'I didn't help myself to it,' said Pigsy, laughing. 'I ate it.' 'You didn't use your jaws,' said the servant. 'How can you have eaten it?' 'What nonsense you fellows talk,' said Pigsy. 'Of course I ate it, and if you are in any doubt, watch me while I do it again.' They filled his bowl again and that fool Pigsy in a flash had gulped it all down. 'Father,' they cried, 'you must have a grindstone in your throat. How else can all that go down so quickly and smoothly?' By the time Tripitaka had finished reading grace, he had got through six bowls. When the others started their meal, he continued to stuff himself with rice, bread, fruit, sweets, everything he could lay hands on. 'More, more!' he was soon calling to the servants. 'What has become of you all?' 'Don't be so greedy, brother,' said Monkey. 'If you only eat half your fill, it will still be better than you have fared lately in a hollow of the hills.' 'Mind your own business,' said Pigsy. 'The proverb says "Better bury a priest alive than stop him getting his fill." ' 'Clear the things away,' cried Monkey, 'and don't take any notice of him.' 'I am very sorry,' said their host, 'but it's getting late and we had only steamed a ton of flour, five bushels of rice and a load or two of vegetables. We had meant to invite some neighbours and the priests who read the service. The priests, as you know, ran away and we did not venture to invite our neighbours, so that we were able to offer you a humble meal. If you have not had enough, I'll order more rice to be steamed.' 'That's right,' said Pigsy, 'get it steamed.'

Meanwhile the old men turned to Tripitaka and asked, 'What made you turn aside from the main road?' 'We came

278

to a river,' said Monkey, 'and there seemed to be no way of getting across. So hearing a sound of cymbals coming from your house, we decided to come here and ask for a night's lodging.' 'Did you notice anything on the river bank?' 'All we saw was a monument,' said Monkey. 'Well, if you went and looked again, not much more than a league from there, you would come to the temple of the Great King of Miracles. Did you happen to see it?' 'We did not,' said Monkey. 'Pray, what are the miracles in question?' 'Father,' said the old man, 'it is this Great King who year by year sends us rain in due season and blesses us with fertility.' As he spoke he wept bitterly. 'If he sends you rain,' said Monkey, 'he is your good friend. How comes it that you show such distress when you speak of him?' 'Because,' said the old man, beating his breast, 'though his favours are many, he is a wrathful deity, and as the price of his blessings he demands each year the sacrifice of a boy or girl.' 'And he devours them?' asked Monkey. 'Alas, he does,' said the old man. 'I suppose your family too has had to take its turn,' said Monkey. 'Alas,' said the old man beating his breast, 'I and my brother here are both badly off for children. At the age of fifty I still had no child. My friends urged me to take a concubine, and at last, very unwillingly, I consented and a girl was born. She is now in her eighth year and is called Load of Gold.' 'A fine name,' said Pigsy. 'How came she by it?' 'Finding myself childless,' said he, 'I repaired bridges and roads, built temples and towers, gave alms and entertained priests. I kept an account of all I spent, and what with one thing and another, by the time my daughter was born, I had spent more than thirty catties of gold. Thirty catties make a load, and that is why she was called Load of Gold.' 'And your brother?' said Monkey. 'He too has only one child,' said the old man, 'a boy called War Boy.' 'How did he get such a name?' asked Monkey. 'There is a statue of the God of War in his house,' said the old man, 'and because he had prayed to this god before this child was born it is called War Boy. The joint age of us two brothers is over a hundred and twenty. Yet we only have these two children between us. But now it is our

279

family's turn to provide the victims, and we dare not demur. It was for the welfare of these children's souls that we held this ceremony.' On hearing this unhappy tale Tripitaka could not refrain from tears. 'Let me ask him a question,' said Monkey. 'Old man, have you a considerable amount of property?' 'I have forty or fifty acres of paddy,' said he, 'sixty or seventy acres of dry field and eighty or ninety pasture fields. Then I have two or three hundred water buffaloes, some thirty horses and mules, and any number of pigs, sheep, chickens and geese. I have more grain in my barns than we can get through and more silk in my stores than we can wear, and about the house we have everything we could possibly need.' 'If you are as well off as that,' said Monkey, 'it's a pity you are so economical.' 'Why do you call me economical?' said the old man. 'If you are as well off as this,' said Monkey, 'I cannot understand why you allow your daughter and nephew to be sacrificed. By spending fifty pieces of silver you could buy a girl, and for a hundred pieces you could buy a boy. Would not this be better than losing your own posterity?' 'You do not understand,' said the old man. 'The God is not so easy to deceive. He often comes to the village and goes about among us.' 'Then you must know what he looks like,' said Monkey. 'We don't see him,' said he. 'We only smell a strangely scented wind. That is how we know that he has come. We hasten to burn great quantities of incense, and all of us, young and old, bow down towards this wind. The God knows everything that goes on here, even the exact date at which each of us was born. He would not accept any child that was not ours. Let alone two hundred pieces of silver, not even a thousand or ten thousand pieces could buy two children of exactly the same appearance and age.' 'That is true,' said Monkey. 'But all the same I should very much like to have a look at this boy of yours.' Ch'ên Ch'ing, the old man's brother, hurried in, and bringing out the child War Boy in his arms, set him down in the lamp light. Knowing nothing of the terrible fate that was in store for it, the child capered about, munching at some fruit that it had brought tucked into its wide sleeves. Monkey, after having a look at it, murmured a spell, shook himself and changed into an exact counterpart of War Boy. The two children joined hands and capered together in the lamp light. The father in his astonishment at the miracle flung himself upon his knees. 'We are not worthy,' said Tripitaka. 'Pray, rise!' 'A moment ago I was talking to him,' said the old man, 'and now he has suddenly become the exact image of my child. When I call, both come running up. This is more than I can bear. Pray go back to your usual form.'

Monkey rubbed his cheek and in a moment had resumed his proper shape. 'Father,' said the old man, 'never would I have believed that such a miracle was possible.' 'Was I like your child?' asked Monkey. 'Like?' said the old man, 'I should think you were! Face, voice, height – everything was right.' 'And weight too,' said Monkey, 'as you would have found if you had tested us with the scales.' 'No doubt, no doubt,' cried the old man. 'In weight too!' 'Do you think I should have been accepted for sacrifice?' asked Monkey. 'I don't doubt it,' said the old man. 'Of course you would be accepted.' 'I am going to save this child's life, that you may have posterity to burn incense to your soul in time to come. I am ready to be sacrificed to the Great King.' 'Father,' said the old man, 'if you indeed perform this act of compassion, I will give your master a thousand pieces of silver to provide for his further journey to the West.' 'And won't you give anything to me?' asked Monkey. 'But you'll have been sacrificed,' said he, 'you won't be there to receive it.' 'How do you mean – I shan't be there?' said Monkey. 'The God will have eaten you,' said the old man. 'Do you think he'd dare?' said Monkey. 'If he doesn't eat you,' said the old man, 'it will only be because you smell worse than I believe.' 'Heaven's will be done,' said Monkey. 'If he eats me, that proves I was meant to die young. If he doesn't eat me, that's my luck. Anyway you may sacrifice me.'

Ch'ên Ch'ing poured out suitable thanks and added another five hundred pieces of silver to the sum he promised. Meanwhile his brother did not utter a word, but leant against the door, weeping bitterly. 'I fear you are worrying about your daughter,' said Monkey, coming up to him. 'Father,' said the old man, kneeling in front of him, 'I cannot part with her. It is something that my nephew is to be saved. But I have no other child, and if she is taken from me, who will there be to howl at my funeral? How can I give her up?' 'Go at once and steam another five pecks of rice and prepare some good vegetables. That's the way to win that long-snouted priest's heart. He will be only too glad to change himself into your girl, or anything else you ask of him. Then we'll both go and be sacrificed together.' 'Brother,' said Pigsy, horrified at this suggestion, 'you can play with your own life as you please, but you have no right to drag me into the adventure.' 'Brother,' said Monkey, 'the proverb says "Even a chicken must work for its food." We have both had a sumptuous feast. Instead of complaining that you haven't been given enough, you ought to be ready to do what you can for these people in their little trouble.' 'I'm no good at transformations,' said Pigsy. 'Nonsense,' said Monkey, 'you have thirty-six transformations.' 'Pigsy,' said Tripitaka, 'he's perfectly right. "To save one life is better than building a seven-storeyed pagoda." You ought to show your gratitude; and you would be accumulating secret merit into the bargain. You have nothing better to do tonight, and have no excuse for not going with your brother.' 'You don't know what you're saying, Master,' said Pigsy. 'I can change into a mountain, a tree, a scabby elephant, a water-buffalo or a pot-bellied rogue. But changing into a small girl is a much more difficult matter.' 'Don't believe him,' said Monkey, 'but bring out your child.' Ch'ên hurried into the house and came out carrying the child Load of Gold. With him came his wife and concubine and all the household, banging their heads on the floor and imploring Pigsy to save the child.

The little girl was wearing an emerald fillet with pearl pendants, a red hemp-thread bodice shot with yellow, a green satin coat with a chess-board patterned collar, a plum-blossom red silk skirt, toad's-head patterned pink hemp-thread shoes, and gold-kneed raw silk drawers. She, like her cousin, was nibbling at a piece of fruit. 'Here's the girl,

Pigsy,' said Monkey. 'Change quickly into a replica of her, and we'll go off and be sacrificed.' 'How am I to look as smart as that?' said Pigsy. 'Make haste,' said Monkey, 'or you'll feel my cudgel.' The fool wagged his head, muttered a spell and said 'Change!' His head began to change and soon became indistinguishable from that of the child. But his big belly remained just the same and quite spoilt the resemblance. 'Go on!' cried Monkey, laughing. 'You may beat me blue,' said Pigsy, 'but I swear I can't change any further. What's to be done?' 'You can't stay like that, with a girl's head and a priest's belly,' said Monkey. 'You're neither a man nor a woman; it's a bad mess. I must see what I can do with you.' He blew upon Pigsy with magic breath and immediately the change was completed, and he became exactly like the child from head to foot. 'To avoid any mistake, you had better take the real children away,' said Monkey. 'Then we shall know where we are. Give them some more fruit, for fear they should start crying. If the Great King heard them, he might come and look into it. Well, now we're both ready. But how are we served, trussed or tied? And shall we be hashed or boiled?' 'Look here, brother,' said Pigsy, 'it's no good trying these tricks on me. All this isn't in my line at all.' 'I assure you,' said Mr Ch'ên, 'there is no question of trussing or anything of the sort. We use two large red lacquer dishes. We shall ask you to sit in them and they will then be put upon two table tops, and a couple of strong young fellows will carry each of you to the temple.' 'Excellent,' said Monkey. 'Bring the dishes and we'll take a trial trip, just to see how it goes.' The old man brought out the dishes, Monkey and Pigsy sat in them and four young fellows lifted them on to the table-tops, and having taken the victims for a ride round the courtyard, set them down again in the front room. 'If it was just a question of being carried about like that,' said Pigsy, 'I'd be quite content to do it all night. But the idea of being carried to a temple and eaten is not so funny!' 'All you have got to do is to watch me,' said Monkey. 'While he is slicing me up and eating me, you can jump up and run away.' 'That's all right if he begins with the boy,' said Pigsy. 'But how do we know he isn't going to begin with the girl?' 'They always begin with the boy,' said Mr Ch'ên. 'Once or twice some plucky fellow has hidden at the back of the temple or under a table, and it was always the boy that he saw eaten first.' 'That's luck,' said Pigsy.

While they were talking, there was a great din of gongs and drums outside, and the glow of many lanterns. Someone opened the gate and cried, 'Bring out the boy and girl!' The old men burst into loud weeping, while the four strong men carried the two victims away. And if you do not know whether in the end they escaped with their lives, you must listen to what is told in the next chapter.

Chapter 26

'Great King, our Father,' said the worshippers, when all was ready, 'following our yearly custom, we now offer up to you a male child, War Boy, and a female child, Load of Gold, together with a pig, a sheep and a due portion of liquor. Grant that the winds may be temperate, that rain may fall in due season and all our crops thrive.' They then burned paper horses, and returned to their homes.

'I think I'll go home too,' said Pigsy. 'You haven't got a home,' said Monkey. 'I'll go to Mr Ch'ên's farm and have a nap,' said Pigsy. 'What nonsense the fool talks,' said Monkey. 'We have promised to take on this job, and we have got to see it through.' 'It's you who are the fool,' said Pigsy. 'I thought you were just having a game with him. You don't mean to say we are really going to be sacrificed?' 'We've got to do the thing properly,' said Monkey. 'In any case, we must wait till the King comes to eat us, or we shall spoil a good start by a poor finish. And if the king finds no victims, he will send plagues and calamities to the village. You surely don't want that?'

While they were talking, there suddenly came a great gust of wind. 'That's done it!' said Pigsy. 'Talk of the devil!' 'Let me do the talking,' said Monkey, and in another minute a most horrible apparition appeared at the doors of the temple, with eyes like blazing comets, tusks like the teeth of a huge saw. 'Well, which family is making the sacrifice this year?' he asked, halting at the entrance. 'The family of the two Ch'ên,' said Monkey, 'if I may make bold to reply.' The king was puzzled. 'This boy speaks up uncommonly boldly,' he said to himself. 'Usually at the first asking one gets no reply at all. At the second the victim faints with terror, and by the time I have laid hands on him, he is already dead with fright. It is odd that this child should speak up so boldly.' 'What are your names?' he presently asked. 'I am War Boy,' said Monkey, 'and the girl is called Load of Gold.' 'Well,

285

War Boy and Load of Gold,' said the monster, 'I must tell you that this sacrifice is a very old institution. You have been offered to me by your parents according to custom, and I am now going to eat you.' 'Help yourself!' said Monkey. 'We shan't put any obstacle in your way.' On hearing this the monster again hesitated. 'Now, none of your sauce!' he said. 'You're too forward. I usually begin with the boy, but this time I think I'll begin with the girl instead.' 'Stick to your rule, Great King,' gasped Pigsy. 'It's always a pity when old customs disappear.' But the monster was not in the mood to start a discussion, and striding forward he grabbed at Pigsy. That fool leapt off the dish, changed into his proper form and seized his rake. The monster fled, but Pigsy was in time to get in a tremendous blow. Something fell to the ground with a clang. 'I've smashed his helmet!' cried Pigsy. And Monkey, resuming his proper shape, picked up a great fish scale, about the size of an ice-dish. 'Up we go!' he shouted, and both of them sprang into the air. It so happened that the monster was on his way to a dinner-party and was therefore unarmed. 'Who are you?' he shouted up at them, 'that you should come here interfering with my rights and damaging my reputation?' 'It is time you should know,' said Monkey. 'We are disciples of Tripitaka, who is going to India to get scriptures. We heard last night of the filthy orgies in which you indulge, and determined to save the lives of the victims and put you under arrest. Come now, confess the truth. How long has this been going on? How many boys and girls have you devoured? If you render me a full account, perhaps I will spare your life.' At this, the monster fled, and before Pigsy could get in another blow he had changed into a gust of wind and disappeared into the river.

'We won't waste time in chasing him,' said Monkey. 'To-morrow we'll arrange a plan for disposing of him finally, and getting our Master across the river.' They went back to the temple, and collecting the beasts and other things brought for the sacrifice, they returned to the farm. Tripitaka, Sandy and the two brothers were anxiously waiting for news, when Monkey and Pigsy suddenly appeared in the courtyard, driving the sacrificial animals and dumping down the holy gear. 'How did the sacrifice go?' asked Tripitaka. Monkey told them what had happened. The two old men were delighted, and at once ordered the best room to be got ready for the pilgrims. Soon all were soundly asleep.

When the monster got back to his palace under the river, he threw himself on to his throne and sat in complete silence. His watery kinsfolk were astonished to see him looking so glum. 'You are usually in such high spirits after the sacrifice,' they said. 'Yes,' he said, 'and I have always been able to bring back some tit-bits for all of you. But today I didn't even get anything to eat myself. I met my match, and came near to losing my life.' And he told them his story. 'Tripitaka,' he added, 'is of such sanctity that anyone who ate the least scrap of his flesh would live forever. But now that he has got such disciples as this, I very much doubt if I can catch him.' Then from among his watery kinsmen there stepped out a stripy-coated perch-mother, wriggling and bowing. 'If you want to catch Tripitaka,' she said, 'nothing could be easier. But if I tell you how, what reward will you give me?' 'If you have a good plan and enable me to catch him,' said the monster, 'I will adopt you as my sister and you shall eat him sitting with me on the same mat.' 'Well then,' she said, 'I know that you can call the wind and make rain. But can you bring down snow?' 'Certainly,' he said. 'And can you make it so cold that everything freezes?' 'I can,' he said. 'In that case,' she said, 'all is easy.' 'Let's hear about it,' said the monster.

'It is already the third night watch,' said the perch-mother. 'You must get to work at once. First you must raise a cold wind then send down a great fall of snow, and make it so cold that the river freezes right across. Some of us who are good at transformations must take on human form and must go about on the ice, where the road runs down to the river, shouldering packs, umbrella in hand. Tripitaka is in a great hurry to get to India, and when he sees people walking on the ice he will insist on going across. You will be sitting quietly here at the heart of the river, and as soon as you hear his footfall above you, will cause the ice to crack. He and his disciples will all fall into the hole, and at one stroke you will have them all in your power.' 'Splendid!' cried the monster, and leaving his watery home he went up into the sky, set the wind in motion, made a snow-storm and caused the great river to freeze all over.

Just before dawn, Tripitaka and his disciples suddenly began to shiver. Pigsy kept on sneezing and coughing, and could not sleep. 'Brother, it's very cold!' he called out at last. 'Fool,' said Monkey. 'Where's your spirit? Pilgrims don't feel either heat or cold. What does it matter to us how much it freezes?' 'Disciple,' said Tripitaka, 'there is something in what he says; it is remarkably cold.' None of them could sleep, and soon they all tumbled out of bed, dressed, opened the door and looked out. Everything was white; it had evidently been snowing hard for some time. 'It's no wonder you were cold,' said Monkey, 'in such a snow-storm as this.' They all gazed at the lovely snow. Down it fluttered, in pale silken threads and flying splinters of jade. When they had admired its beauty for some time, two servants of the house came along and began to brush the paths. Others brought them hot water to wash in; and hot tea and milk-cakes soon followed. Braziers were brought and they all sat down in the parlour. By the time they had finished breakfast, it was snowing harder than ever, and soon there was more than two feet of snow on the ground. Tripitaka became very uneasy about the prospects of the journey, and burst into tears. 'Calm yourself, Father,' said Mr Ch'ên. 'The sight of so much snow need not distress you. The house is well stocked with provisions, and we can provide for you as long as you choose to stay.' 'You do not understand the cause of my anxiety,' said Tripitaka. 'When I received the Emperor's bidding to go upon this pilgrimage, his Majesty accompanied me to the frontier, and when presenting the cup of parting he asked me how long I should be away. I had no idea how difficult the journey would prove and promptly replied, "It will take me three years to fetch the scriptures and bring them back." But seven years have passed, and still I have not seen Buddha's

288

face. The thought that I have exceeded the appointed time weighs heavily upon me. Fortunately my disciples were able last night to render you a small service, and I was thinking of making bold to ask you if you could give us a boat in which to cross the river. But now this great snow-storm threatens to postpone our journey for I know not how many months, and my return is again delayed.' 'Surely a few days one way or the other cannot make all that difference,' said Mr Ch'ên. 'Wait till the weather clears, and I will undertake to get you across the river, even if it costs my whole patrimony.'

So elaborate was the luncheon that was served, that Tripitaka became quite uneasy. 'We can only consent to a further stay,' he said, 'if you are willing to treat us informally, as members of the family.' 'There is no number of banquets, however many days running,' said the old man, 'that could ever repay you for saving our children from their doom.' Soon afterwards the snow stopped, and people began to go about again. Seeing that Tripitaka was looking depressed, Mr Ch'ên had the paths of the flower garden swept. A big brazier was brought, and they all were invited to come and sit in a snow-cave, by way of distraction. 'What's this old fellow thinking of?' cried Pigsy. 'A flower garden is a place to go to in spring time. In this cold, with everything buried under the snow, what pleasure can it be?' 'Fool!' said Monkey. 'You do not know what you are talking about. Snow-bound scenes have a mysterious calm which is delightful to enjoy, and will soothe our Master's feelings.' When they had admired the scene for some while, they sat in the snow-cave, and some neighbours who had joined them were told about the pilgrimage. When they had all drunk perfumed tea Mr Ch'ên asked, 'Do you reverend gentlemen drink wine?' 'I do not,' said Tripitaka, 'but my disciples will drink a cup or two of weak wine.' It was now getting late, and it was announced that supper was ready in the house. At this moment someone in the street was heard saying, 'This is something like cold! The river has frozen.' 'Monkey, that sounds bad for us,' groaned Tripitaka. 'The cold came on very suddenly,' said Mr Ch'ên. 'Probably it only means that the shallow water near the bank has frozen.' But the man who had given the news replied, 'It is frozen the whole way across, smooth as the face of a mirror, and people are walking about on the ice, where the road goes down to the river.' When Tripitaka heard that people were walking on the ice, he wanted to go at once and look. 'Don't be in a hurry,' said Mr Ch'ên. 'It's late now. Tomorrow we will go and look.' They then parted with the neighbours, and when supper was over retired to rest. Pigsy, when he woke, announced that it was colder than ever. Tripitaka went to the door and prostrating himself uttered the following prayer: 'Deities that guard the Faith, in our journey to the West we have braved the perils of hill and stream, that we might at last see Buddha face to face. Never have we grumbled or repined. Now we see before us strong evidence of Heaven's help, in that this river has frozen so that it can be crossed. We swear that on our return we will inform our Emperor of this favour, and he will repay you with manifold offerings.'

Then he ordered Pigsy to saddle the horse, and get ready to cross the river while it was still frozen. 'Don't be in a hurry,' said Mr Ch'ên. 'In a few days the ice will have melted and I will do my poor best to provide you with a boat.' 'I'm not either for going at once or for staying on,' said Sandy. 'We have only heard about the river being frozen and have not seen for ourselves. While we are saddling the horses, I suggest that the Master should go and have a look.' 'There is some sense in that,' said Mr Ch'ên. And he told his servants to saddle six horses, but not to let Tripitaka's horse be saddled for the present. Then they all rode down to the river to look. It was true enough that people were walking across the ice. 'Where are they going?' asked Tripitaka. 'They are traders,' said Mr Ch'ên, 'from the country on the other side of the river. Things that here are worth a hundred strings of cash are worth ten thousand on the other side. And things that are worth only a hundred are here worth two thousand. So great are the profits to be made that they are willing to undertake the journey even at the risk of their lives. In ordinary times six or seven or even ten will pack into one boat and cross even in the heaviest storms. And directly they saw that the river was frozen they have naturally come pouring across on foot.' 'The men of the world,' said Tripitaka, 'stake all on profit and fame. But it must not be forgotten that we pilgrims too, in carrying out the Imperial behest, are also seeking fame, and we must not allow ourselves to feel too superior. Monkey, go back at once to our benefactor's house, put together the luggage, saddle the horse, and let us cross while the ice is thick.'

'Master,' said Sandy, 'the proverb says, "In a thousand days one eats up a thousand measures of rice." As we are offered the use of Mr Ch'ên's house, would it not be wiser to wait a few days till the weather changes and the ice melts, and then cross in a boat? It is a mistake to be in too much of a hurry.' 'I am surprised that you should take such a view,' said Tripitaka. 'If it were the end of winter and getting warmer every day, it might be good to wait till the ice melts. But it is the eighth month, when the weather grows colder every day. If we wait, we shall lose half a year of travelling.' 'Stop your chattering,' said Pigsy, dismounting from his horse, 'and let me go and see how thick the ice really is.' 'Fool,' said Monkey, 'do you think you can find that out by throwing a stone, as you found out how deep the water was before?' 'You don't understand,' said Pigsy. 'I'll strike the ice with my rake. If the ice breaks, that means it's thin and we won't trust it. If it doesn't give, that means it's thick, and we can walk on it.' 'That sounds sensible,' said Tripitaka. The fool hitched up his coat, went to the edge of the river, and lifting the rake in both hands struck with all his might. There was a tremendous bang and nine white marks appeared on the ice. 'Let's be off!' he cried. 'I'll guarantee that it's firm right to the bottom.' Tripitaka was delighted. They all went back to Mr Ch'ên's, and prepared for the journey. Unable to prevail upon them to stay, Mr Ch'ên insisted upon their accepting some dried provisions and pastries to take with them, and all the household gathered round bowing and kowtowing. A dish of broken pieces of gold was also brought, and Mr Ch'ên asked them to accept a small contribution to the expenses of their journey, as a return for the service that they had rendered to the family. Tripitaka shook his head. 'I have left the world,' he said. 'Of what use is money to me? It is our duty to live entirely on such alms as are offered to us upon the road. It is enough that we should accept the provisions you have kindly offered.' When the old man had renewed the offer several times, Monkey plunged his hand into the dish and brought out some pieces worth about five strings of cash in all. Giving them to Tripitaka he said, 'Here's some pocket money for you. Take it, or Mr Ch'ên will be disappointed.' Then they parted and made for the river bank. When they got on to the ice, the horse began to slip about and Tripitaka was nearly thrown. 'Master,' said Sandy, 'it's bad going.' 'We had better go back and ask them for some straw,' said Pigsy. 'Straw!' said Monkey. 'What for?' 'You wouldn't know,' said Pigsy. 'If we bind straw to the horse's hoofs, it wouldn't slip and the Master wouldn't fall off.' So they got some straw, and when Pigsy had tied it to the horse's hoofs, they set out once more.

They had gone three or four leagues, when Pigsy took Tripitaka's staff and made him carry it crosswise. 'Now what is this fool up to?' cried Monkey. 'It's his business to carry the staff. Why has he made the Master carry it?' 'You've never been on ice, so you don't know,' said Pigsy. 'Ice always has holes in it. If one put one's foot in a hole, down one goes, and unless one is holding a stick, crosswise like this, one can't stop oneself. The ice closes above like the lid of a kettle, and one never gets out again. The thing to do is to hold a stick crosswise like this.' 'One would think he had spent all his time going on the ice,' said Monkey, laughing. They all did as he said. Tripitaka held the staff across his knees, Monkey held his cudgel, Sandy his priest's staff, and Pigsy, who had the luggage on his back, tied the rake sideways at his waist. They went on, all feeling perfectly secure.

When darkness fell they ate some of their provisions, but did not dare halt, and, with the moonlight glittering in dazzling whiteness over the ice, they rode on, never closing their eyes all night. When it grew light, they ate some more of their provisions, and then went on towards the west. After some time a rending sound suddenly came from under the ice. The white horse plunged, and almost lost its footing. 'Disciple,' what is that noise?' asked Tripitaka. 'It is freezing so hard,' said Pigsy, 'that the earth at the bottom of the river is hardening. Soon we shall have one solid block under our feet.' Tripitaka was astonished and delighted. He whipped on his horse and away they went.

Meanwhile the Great King and his kinsfolk were waiting below. Hearing at last the sound of hoofs, he so deployed his magic power as to open a long cleft in the ice. Monkey immediately leapt into the air; but the white horse went straight in, and so did the other disciples. The monster grabbed at Tripitaka, and he and his kinsfolk swiftly carried him down to the Water Palace. 'Where's my perch sister?' shouted the Great King. 'At your service,' she said, approaching the gate and curtseying. 'But as for "sister" – no really, I can't allow it.' 'Be careful,' he said, 'or I shall take you at your word. "A team of horses cannot overtake a word that has left the mouth." I promised to call you my sister if your plan put Tripitaka into my hands, and sister you must be.' Then he called to his servants to set the tables, grind the knives, rip out Tripitaka's heart and then flay and carve him, and to see to it that there was music. 'For I and my sister are going to eat him,' he said, 'that we may live forever.'

'Great King,' she said, 'if we eat him now, his disciples may come in the middle and spoil the fun. We had better lie low for a couple of days, and if these wretches don't come to look for him, we'll split open his breast and hold our feast. You Majesty will preside, and all our tribe shall be there to entertain you with flute, string, song and dance. In that way we shall be able to enjoy the treat quite at our ease. Isn't that a better plan?' The king agreed, and Tripitaka was taken and laid in a long stone chest that stood at the back of the palace. The lid was put on, and there we leave him.

Meanwhile Pigsy and Sandy fished the luggage out of the water and packed it on the horse's back. Then they all began swimming towards the shore. 'What has become of Tripitaka?' asked Monkey, looking down from aloft. 'There's no such person,' said Pigsy. '"Down among the dead men"[1] is his ticket now. It's no use worrying any more about him. We're making for shore. When we get there, we'll decide what's to be done next.'

Now Pigsy had once been a marshal of the hosts of Heaven and had commanded eighty thousand water-warriors of the River of Heaven; Sandy came from the Flowing Sands, and the white horse was a grandchild of the Dragon King of the Western Ocean. So all three of them were quite at home in the water. Led by Monkey from above, they made the journey much quicker than they had come, and scrambling up the bank, they scrubbed down the horse, wrung out their clothes and, joined by Monkey, all went back to Mr Ch'ên's house. 'They have come back again,' someone announced to Mr Ch'ên, 'but there are only three of them.' As soon as they arrived at the door, Mr Ch'ên saw that their clothes were wet. 'I told you so!' he said. 'I begged you to stay, but you would not listen to me. If you had, you would not now be in this sad state. And what has become of Tripitaka?' 'That's not his name now,' said Pigsy. 'He's known as Old Down at the Bottom.' Both the old men burst into tears. If only he had waited till the ice melted, and taken a boat!' they wailed. 'His obstinacy has cost him his life.' 'Don't distress yourselves unduly,' said Monkey. 'I've a notion that the Master will live a long time yet. This is just a trick of that monster's. Meanwhile don't worry, but get our clothes put through the mangle, dry our passports, have the white horse well fed, and then we'll go and find this creature, rescue the Master, and get this business settled once and for all. Then I hope you'll all have a quiet time for a long while to come.' The old men were satisfied by this, and ordered a good supper to be brought in. When the pilgrims had eaten their fill, they asked the people of the place to look after the

[1] There is probably a pun here; but I cannot see it.

horse, and weapon in hand went off to the river to look for the monster.

And if you do not know how they saved Tripitaka, you must listen to what is told in the next chapter.

Chapter 27

'Now we have got to decide which of us is to go down under the water first,' said Monkey, when he reached the bank. 'Brother,' said Pigsy, 'neither Sandy nor I can match half your tricks. It's clear that you should go first.' 'The trouble is,' said Monkey, 'that I am not at my best in the water. I have to be making magic passes all the time to protect myself from it. You are both of you water-experts and had better go in together.' 'I can manage the water all right,' said Sandy, 'but I don't know what it's going to be like when we get to the bottom. Let's all go together.' 'Shall you transform yourself into something,' went on Sandy, 'or shall we carry you? In any case, when we get to the creature's lair, you must go on ahead and see how things stand. If the Master is really there and alive, we'll all charge to the assault. But it may turn out that it wasn't the Great King who carried him off at all; he may just have been drowned. On the other hand, the king may already have eaten him. In that case, there's no more we can do, and we had better make off in some other direction as fast as we can.' 'Good,' said Monkey. 'Which of you will carry me?' Pigsy saw his opportunity. 'This Monkey,' he said to himself, 'has had I don't know how many games at my expense. But he is not at home in the water, and if I offer to carry him, I shall have a chance of getting my own back.' 'I'll carry you, brother,' he said. Monkey saw at once that there was something in the wind, and made his plans accordingly. 'All right,' he said. 'You are stronger in the back than Sandy.' So Pigsy took him on his back and Sandy led the way. When they had almost reached the bottom, he began his game. Monkey felt that it was coming, and plucking a hair he changed it into the semblance of himself, which remained on Pigsy's back, while the real Monkey changed into a hog-louse and clung tight to Pigsy's ear. Pigsy as he went suddenly made a great jolt, intended to send Monkey flying over his head. But the sham

Monkey, being nothing but a transformed hair, merely fluttered away and disappeared. 'Brother,' said Sandy, 'do you know what you have done? It's not very good going, and anyone might slip about a bit. But you've jolted our brother right off your back, and how is anyone to know where he has fallen to?' 'That Monkey,' said Pigsy, 'ought surely to be able to stand a little jolting. What's the good of a fellow who just vanishes at the first jolt? Don't let us worry about what has become of him. You and I will go and look for the Master.' 'I'm not going without him,' said Sandy. 'You and I may be good at going in the water, but we are not up to half his tricks.' Monkey, firmly lodged in Pigsy's ear, could not refrain from crying out, 'I'm here.' 'That's done it!' said Sandy. 'Ghosts are heard but not seen. He is certainly dead. What possessed you to try that game with him?' Pigsy, in great perturbation, knelt down and said, kowtowing. 'Brother,' I ought not to have done it. When we have rescued Tripitaka and are on land again, I will apologise properly. Where are you talking from? You frightened me to death. Show yourself in your true form, and I will carry you properly and give you no more jolts.' 'You are carrying me now,' said Monkey, 'Gee up, and I won't tease you.'

Mumbling to himself about his apology, Pigsy scrambled to his feet and went on. Suddenly they saw a notice with 'Turtle House' written on it. 'This must be where the monster is living,' said Sandy. 'Let's go and taunt him to battle.' 'Do you suppose there is water at the gate?' said Monkey. 'There clearly isn't,' said Sandy. 'Well then,' said Monkey, 'you two go and hide at each side of the door, and I'll prospect.' So saying, he crawled out of Pigsy's ear, shook himself, changed into a long-legged crab mother and sidled in at the door. There was the monster, with his kinsfolk round him and the perch mother at his side. They were discussing how they should eat Tripitaka. But looking about on all sides Monkey could not anywhere see the Master. Presently he saw a crab mother sidling along the corridor. 'Granny,' he said, going up to her, 'they are deciding about the eating of this Chinese priest. What have they done with him in the meanwhile?' 'They've put him in the stone chest behind the palace,' said she. 'They are not going to eat him till tomorrow, for fear his disciples come along and kick up a fuss. If everything is all right then, there'll be music and great goings-on.' Monkey chatted with her for a little, and then went behind the palace, where sure enough he found a stone chest, rather like some pig-styes that people make of stone, or a sepulchral sarcophagus.

He bent over the chest, and soon heard Tripitaka blubbering piteously. 'Master,' he called, 'do not grieve. The Flood Scripture says, "Earth is the mother of the five elements, Water is the source of the five elements. Without earth we could not be born, but without water we could not grow." Take comfort in this and in the fact that I have come.' 'Save me, disciple!' groaned Tripitaka. 'Don't worry!' said Monkey. 'Wait till we have caught the monster; then we'll soon get you out.' 'I hope you'll be quick about it,' said Tripitaka. 'If I stay another day, I shall succumb.' 'That's all right,' said Monkey. 'Off I go!' 'Well, brother, how do things stand?' asked Sandy, when Monkey re-appeared in his true form. 'The Master has indeed been captured,' Monkey said. 'But so far no harm has been done to him. The Monster has put him in a stone chest. You two had better go and give battle, and I'll return to the surface. If you can catch the monster, do so. If you can't, pretend to give in and retreat to the surface, enticing him to follow you. Then you can leave him to me.'

Look at Pigsy! He goes blustering to the door. 'Monster, he cries, 'give us back our Master!' Some little imps at the door rushed in and announced, 'Great King, there is someone outside asking for his Master.' 'I know what that means,' said the monster. 'That cursed priest has come. Quick, bring me my whole outfit,' he cried. Armed to the teeth he called his imps to open the door and came striding out, followed by a hundred and ten satellites, all swinging halberds or brandishing swords. 'What temple do you come from, and why are you making this scene at my door?' he thundered.

'Insensate creature!' cried Pigsy. 'I had a chat with you only a few nights ago. How can you pretend that you do not know me? I am a disciple of Tripitaka who is going to India to fetch scriptures. You have the effrontery to call yourself Great King and think yourself entitled to eat girls and boys from the village. I am your victim, the girl Load of Gold. Don't you recognise me?' 'Are you aware that you could be sued for impersonation?' said the monster. 'As things turned out, I didn't eat you, and in fact did you no harm. But you gave me a nasty knock. I should have thought you would have been glad enough to escape alive instead of coming pestering me at home.' 'No harm indeed!' cried Pigsy. 'Isn't it enough that you trapped my Master under the ice? Give him back to us at once, and we will say no more about it. But if so much as half the word "No" leaves your lips – just have a look at this rake, and know what to expect!' 'Well, if you must needs know,' said the monster smiling sourly, 'I confess it was I who made the frost and seized upon your Master. But I must warn you that if you want to pick a quarrel with me, things won't go quite like last time. Then I was going to a dinner party, and had no weapons with me. This time I have got my battle-mallet. I challenge you to three bouts. If you can get the better of me, you shall have back your Master. But if you can't, I shall eat you as well as him.' 'Pretty fellow,' said Pigsy, 'all I ask for is a fight. Have a good look at this rake!' 'I can see that you were not a priest to start with,' said the monster. 'What makes you think that?' said Pigsy. 'I can tell by your rake,' said the monster. 'You must have worked in a vegetable garden, and run off with the owner's muck-rake.' 'My boy,' said Pigsy, 'you are much mistaken if you think that this is an ordinary garden rake. It could comb the ocean and scare the dragons out of their beds.' The monster paid no heed to these boastings, but raised his brazen mallet and struck at Pigsy's head. Pigsy warded off the blow with his rake, saying, 'Cursed creature, I can see that you were not an ogre to start with.' 'Can you indeed?' said the monster. 'How do you make that out?' 'I can tell by the way you use your mallet,' said Pigsy. 'You

299

must have worked in a silversmith's forge and run off with your master's mallet.' 'You're much mistaken,' said the monster, 'if you imagine that this is an ordinary silver-worker's mallet. It comes from the Garden of the Immortals, where it was tempered in magic fountains, so that no axe, spear, halberd nor sword can withstand it.' Sandy, seeing them engaged in dispute, could not refrain from stepping up and shouting, 'Monster, waste no more random talk! The men of old said, "What the mouth speaks proves nothing; only by deeds can men be judged." Stand your ground and eat my staff.' 'I can see that you weren't a priest to start with,' said the monster, fending off the blow. 'How do you know?' said Sandy. 'You look to me as though you had worked in a pastry-cook's shop at one time or another,' said he. 'What makes you think that?' said Sandy. 'Well, if not,' said the monster, 'where did you learn to use that rolling-pin of yours?' 'Monster,' cried Sandy, 'learn to use your eyes. This is no common article, but a weapon so unique in the world that few have ever heard of it. This staff came from the most secret recesses of the Palace of the Moon, and is guaranteed to shatter all the majesty of Heaven at a single blow.'

For two hours the three of them battled at the bottom of the water, without victory on either side. At last seeing that the monster could not be overcome, Pigsy winked at Sandy and both of them pretended to give up the fight, and made away at top speed. 'Little ones,' said the monster, 'stay on guard here while I chase these fellows. When I have caught them, you shall all have your share to eat!' Look at him! Like a leaf driven by the autumn wind or a fallen petal struck down by the rain, he fled after them up to the outer air.

Monkey was watching the water intently. Suddenly he saw a great heaving of the waves and heard a noise of grunting and panting. 'Here we are!' cried Pigsy, jumping out on to the bank. He was soon followed by Sandy, and a moment later the monster's head appeared above the water. 'Look out for my cudgel!' cried Monkey. The monster ducked, and
300

fended the blow with his mallet. They had not finished three bouts when the monster, unable any longer to fend Monkey's blows, and worn out, slipped down into the stream, and all was quiet again. 'Brother,' said Sandy, 'you were a match for him up here; but now that he's down below again, things are as bad as ever. How are we to rescue the Master?' 'It's no use going on like this,' said Monkey. 'You two stay here and see that he doesn't slip off somewhere, and I'll go away.' 'Away! Where to?' cried Pigsy. 'I'm going to the Bodhisattva in the Southern Ocean,' said Monkey, 'to find out who this monster really is. When I know, I shall go to his ancestral home, seize all his friends and relations, and then come back here, deal with the creature himself and rescue the Master.' 'Brother,' said Pigsy, 'that all sounds very roundabout and will waste a lot of time.' 'Not a bit of it,' said Monkey. 'I shan't waste a minute, I'll be back almost before I start.'

Dear Monkey! He shot up on a shaft of magic light and was soon at the Southern Ocean. In less than half an hour, Mt Potalaka rose up before him. He lowered his cloud, and was met by the twenty-four devas, the guardian spirits of the mountain, Moksha and the dragon king's daughter, carrying the Pearl. 'Great Sage, what brings you here?' they asked. 'I have business with the Bodhisattva,' he said. 'She left her cave early this morning,' said they, 'allowing no one to follow her, and went into the bamboo grove. But she evidently expected you; for she told us to receive you here, if you came, and not to bring you to her at once. Just sit down here for a while and wait till she comes out of the grove.' Monkey soon grew tired of waiting. 'You might tell her,' said he, 'that if she doesn't come soon, it may be too late to save Tripitaka's life.' 'We dare not do that,' said the divinities. 'The Bodhisattva said you were to wait till she came.' Monkey was by nature extremely impatient, and presently he strode off towards the grove. 'Hallo, Bodhisattva!' he cried when he reached it, 'your servant Monkey pays his humble compliments.' 'Kindly wait outside,' said Kuan-yin. 'Bodhisattva,' he cried, kowtowing, 'my Master is in difficulties, and I have come to you to get particulars about this monster who haunts the River that Flows to Heaven.' 'Go away and wait till I come out,' she repeated. Monkey dared not disobey and going back to the divinities he said, 'I got a glimpse of the Bodhisattva. I don't know what she's up to today. Instead of sitting on her lotus terrace, she is poked away all by herself in the bamboo grove, paring bamboo strips. She has not even bothered to make up, or put on her jewels.' 'We know no more than you do,' they said. 'But as she is expecting you, she is probably busy doing something on your behalf.' There was nothing for it but to wait again. After a while, the Bodhisattva came out of the grove, carrying a bamboo basket. 'Come along,' she said. 'We'll go and rescue Tripitaka.' 'I shouldn't like to hurry you,' said Monkey, kneeling. 'Wouldn't you like to finish dressing first?' 'I can't be bothered,' she said. 'I'm going just as I am.' She sailed away on her cloud roll, followed by Monkey. 'That's quick work,' said Pigsy, when they appeared above the river bank. 'It takes a lot of hustling to make a Bodhisattva come straight along, without even doing her hair or putting on her jewels.'

The Bodhisattva floated low over the river, and untying her sash tied the basket to it and trailed it through the water, upstream. 'The dead go, the living stay.' When she had repeated this charm seven times she drew up the basket. In it flashed the tail of a golden fish; its eyes blinked and its tail twitched. 'Go at once into the water and fetch up your Master,' cried the Bodhisattva. 'But I haven't dealt yet with the monster,' protested Monkey. 'The monster is in this basket,' said the Bodhisattva. 'What?' cried Pigsy and Sandy. 'A fish do all that harm?' 'It is a goldfish that I reared in my lotus pond. Every day it used to put its head out and listen to the scriptures, thus acquiring great magical powers. Its mallet was a lotus stalk, topped by an unopened bud, that this creature by its magic turned into a weapon. One day there was a flood and it got washed out of the pool and floated out to sea, finally reaching the place where you found him. Leaning on the balustrade and looking at the flowers, I was surprised not to see this fellow coming out to salute me. A close inspection of the ripples convinced me that he had gone this way, and might be molesting your Master. So without even stopping to comb my hair or put on my jewels. I plaited this magic basket to capture him in.' 'In that case,' said Monkey, 'wait a minute, and I'll call all the faithful of the village to come and gaze upon your golden visage. They will be glad to show their gratitude, and we can tell them just how the monster was recovered. That will increase the faith of these mortals, and promote their piety.'

'Very well then,' said the Bodhisattva. 'Go and fetch them quickly.' Pigsy and Sandy ran back to the farm and shouted, 'All of you come and see the living Bodhisattva!' Men and women, young and old, all trooped to the river bank, and regardless of puddles and mud flung themselves to their knees. Among them there happened to be a skilful painter, who made a portrait of the Bodhisattva; and this was the beginning of the form of Kuan-yin known as 'Kuan-yin with the Fish-basket.' Soon she withdrew to the Southern Ocean, and Pigsy and Sandy made their way down through the water to Turtle House. Here they found all the monster's fish followers lying dead and rotting. Going behind the palace they soon hoisted Tripitaka out of the stone chest and carried him back through the waves. 'We are afraid, reverend Sir, that you let yourself in for a very bad time by declining our invitation to stay on,' said the brothers Ch'ên, when Tripitaka arrived.' 'There is no need to harp on that now,' said Monkey. 'The main thing is that next year the village will not have to supply victims for the sacrifice. You are rid of your Great King forever, and need fear no more. We must now trouble you to find us a boat to take us across the river.' 'You shall have it!' cried Mr Ch'ên, and he ordered planks to be sawn and a boat made. The people of the village vied with one another in helping with the equipment. One promised to make himself responsible for the masts and sails, another for paddles and poles. One offered to supply ropes, another to pay the sailors. In the midst of all the commotion that was going on by the riverside, a voice was suddenly heard saying, 'Great Sage, you need not trouble to build a boat. It is a waste of good material. I will take you across.' So startled were they all that the more timid bolted back to the village, and even the bolder among them only dared peep cautiously in the direction from which the voice came. In a moment a square, white head appeared above the waves, and there presently emerged a huge white turtle. 'Great Sage,' the turtle said again, 'don't trouble to build a boat. I will take you across.' 'Cursed creature!' cried Monkey. 'Move an inch further and I'll club you to death with this cudgel.' 'I am deeply beholden to you,' said the turtle, 'and want to show my gratitude by taking you all across. Why do you threaten me with your cudgel?' 'For what are you beholden to me?' asked Monkey. 'Great Sage,' said the turtle, 'you do not realise that this Turtle House under the river was my home, and belonged to my ancestors for generations past. Owing to the magic powers that I won by my austerities I was able to improve the place considerably and make it into the handsome water palace that you saw. But one day this monster came churning through the waves and made a wanton attack upon me. In the fight that ensued many of my children were hurt and many of my kinsmen taken. I could not stand up against him and my home with all that was in it fell into his hands. But now, owing to your having persuaded the Bodhisattva to call in this monster, I have been able to recover possession of my house. I am happily installed there with the remaining kinsmen whom I have been able to gather about me. We are not left out in the mud, but can live comfortably in our old home. My gratitude for this is high as the hills and deep as the sea. But we are not the only ones to benefit. The people of the village will no longer have to supply children for the yearly sacrifice. It is indeed a case of two gains at one move! Surely it is natural that I should wish to show my gratitude.' 'Are we really to believe that you are speaking the truth?' said Monkey, withdrawing his cudgel. 'But Great Sage,' said the Turtle, 'how would I dare to deceive you, after all you have done for me?' 'Swear to Heaven that this is the truth,' said Monkey. The turtle opened its red mouth wide and swore as follows: 'If I do not bring Tripitaka safely across the river as I have promised to do, may my bones turn into water!' 'That's good enough,' said Monkey. 'You can come out.' The turtle then pushed close in to shore and lumbered up on to the bank. Pressing round him, the people saw that he had a great white carapace, full forty feet in diameter. 'Get on board,' said Monkey, 'and we'll all go across.' 'Disciple,' said Tripitaka, 'the ice was slippery; but at any rate it stayed still. I am afraid that this turtle's back will be very unsteady.' 'Don't worry,' said Monkey, 'when creatures can speak human language, they generally tell the truth. Come, brothers, make haste and bring our horse.'

The white horse was led on to the middle of the turtle's back; Tripitaka stood on the left, and Sandy on the right, while Pigsy stood behind its tail. Monkey placed himself in front of the horse's head, and fearing trouble undid the sash of his tiger-skin apron and tied it to the turtle's nose, holding the other end in one hand, while in the other hand he grasped his iron cudgel. Then with one foot on the creature's head and the other firmly on its carapace, 'Now turtle, go gently!' he cried. 'And remember, at the least sign of a wobble, you'll get a crack on the head.' 'I shouldn't dare,' said the turtle, 'I shouldn't dare.' Then while the turtle set off smoothly over the waters, the villagers on the bank burnt incense and kowtowed, murmuring 'Glory be to Buddha, glory be to Buddha'.

In less than a day they had safely traversed the whole eight hundred leagues and arrived with dry hand and dry foot at the further shore. Tripitaka disembarked, and with palms pressed together thanked the turtle, saying, 'It afflicts me deeply that I have nothing to give you in return for all your trouble. I hope that when I come back with the scriptures I shall be able to show you my gratitude.' 'Master,' said the turtle, 'I should not dream of accepting a reward; but there is one thing you can do for me. I have heard that the Buddha of the Western Heaven knows both the past and the future. I have been perfecting myself here for about one thousand years. This is a pretty long span, and I have already been fortunate enough to learn human speech; but I still remain a turtle. I should indeed be very much obliged if you would ask the Buddha how long it will be before I achieve human form.' 'I promise to ask,' said Tripitaka. The turtle then disappeared into the depths of the river. Monkey helped Tripitaka on to his horse, Pigsy shouldered the luggage and Sandy brought up the rear. They soon found their way back to the main road and set out for the West.

If you do not know how far they still had to travel and whether disasters still awaited them, you must listen to what is told in the next chapter.

Chapter 28

They travelled westward for many months, and at last began to be aware that the country through which they were now passing was different from any that they had seen. Everywhere they came across gem-like flowers and magical grasses, with many ancient cypresses and hoary pines. In the villages through which they passed every family seemed to devote itself to the entertainment of priests and other pious works. On every hill were hermits practising austerities, in every wood pilgrims chanting holy writ. Finding hospitality each night and starting again at dawn, they journeyed for many days, till they came at last within sudden sight of a cluster of high eaves and towers. 'Monkey, that's a fine place,' said Tripitaka, pointing to it with his whip. 'Considering,' said Monkey, 'how often you have insisted upon prostrating yourself at the sight of false magicians' palaces and arch impostors' lairs, it is strange that when at last you see before you Buddha's true citadel, you should not even dismount from your horse.' At this Tripitaka in great excitement sprang from his saddle, and walking beside the horse was soon at the gates of the high building. A young Taoist came out to meet them. 'Aren't you the people who have come from the east to fetch scriptures?' he asked. Tripitaka hastily tidied his clothes and looking up saw that the boy was clad in gorgeous brocades and carried a bowl of jade dust in his hand. Monkey knew him at once. 'This,' he said to Tripitaka, 'is the Golden Crested Great Immortal of the Jade Truth Temple at the foot of the Holy Mountain.' Tripitaka at once advanced bowing. 'Well, here you are at last!' said the Immortal. 'The Bodhisattva misinformed me. Ten years ago she was told by Buddha to go to China and find someone who would fetch scriptures from India. She told me she had found someone who would arrive here in two or three years. Year after year I waited, but never a sign! This meeting is indeed a surprise.' 'I cannot thank you enough, Great

Immortal, for your patience,' said Tripitaka.

Then they all went into the temple and were shown round by the Immortal; tea and refreshments were served, and perfumed hot water was brought for Tripitaka to wash in. Soon they all turned in for the night. Early next day Tripitaka changed into his brocaded cassock and jewelled cap, and staff in hand presented himself to the Immortal in the hall of the temple, to take his leave. 'That's better!' said the Immortal. 'Yesterday you were looking a bit shabby; but now you look a true child of Buddha!' Tripitaka was just going when the Immortal stopped him, saying, 'You must let me see you off.' 'It's really not necessary,' said Tripitaka. 'Monkey knows the way.' 'He only knows the way by air,' said the Immortal. 'You have got to go on the ground.' 'That's true enough,' said Monkey. 'We will trouble you just to set us on the right way. My Master is pining to get into the presence of the Buddha, and it would be a pity if there were any delay.' Taking Tripitaka by the hand he led him right through the temple and out at the back. For the road did not go from the front gate, but traversed the courtyards and led on to the hill behind. 'You see that highest point, wreathed in magic rainbow mists,' said the Immortal, pointing to the mountain. 'That is the Vulture Peak, the sacred precinct of the Buddha.' Tripitaka at once began kowtowing. 'Master,' said Monkey, 'you had better keep that for later on. If you are going to kowtow all the way up to the top, there won't be much left of your head by the time we get there. It's still a long way off.' 'You stand already on Blessed Ground,' said the Immortal. 'The Holy Mountain is before you. I shall now turn back.'

Monkey led them up the hill at a leisurely pace. They had not gone more than five or six leagues when they came to a great water about eight leagues wide. It was exceedingly swift and rough. No one was to be seen in any direction. 'I don't think this can be the right way,' said Tripitaka. 'Do you think the Immortal can possibly have been mistaken. This water is so wide and so rough that we cannot possibly get across.' 'This is the way all right,' said Monkey. 'Look!

Just over there is a bridge. That's the right way to Salvation.'
Presently Tripitaka came to a notice-board on which was
written Cloud Reach Bridge. But it proved, when they came
up to it, that the bridge consisted simply of slim tree trunks
laid end on end, and was hardly wider than the palm of a
mans' hand. 'Monkey,' protested Tripitaka in great alarm,
'it's not humanly possible to balance on such a bridge as that.
We must find some other way to get across.' 'This is the right
way,' said Monkey, grinning. 'It may be the right way,' said
Pigsy, 'but it's so narrow and slippery that no one would
ever dare set foot on it. And think how far there is to go, and
what it's like underneath.' 'All wait where you are, and
watch while I show you how,' cried Monkey. Dear Monkey!
He strode up to the bridge, leapt lightly on to it and had soon
slipped across. 'I'm over!' he shouted, waving from the other
side. Tripitaka showed no sign of following him, and Pigsy
and Sandy bit their fingers murmuring, 'Can't be done!
Can't be done!' Monkey sprang back again and pulled at
Pigsy, saying, 'Fool, follow me across.' But Pigsy lay on the
ground and would not budge. 'It's much too slippery,' he
said. 'Let me off. Why can't I have a wind to carry me?'
'What would be the good of that?' said Monkey. 'Unless you
go by the bridge you won't turn into a Buddha.' 'Buddha or
no Buddha,' said Pigsy, 'I'm not going on to that bridge.'
The quarrel was at its height, when Sandy ran between them
and at last succeeded in making peace. Suddenly Tripitaka
saw someone punting a boat towards the shore and crying,
'Ferry, ferry!' 'Stop your quarrelling, disciples,' said Tripitaka. 'A boat is coming.' They all gazed with one accord at
the spot to which he pointed. A boat was coming indeed; but
when it was a little nearer they saw to their consternation
that it had no bottom. Monkey with his sharp eyes had
already recognised the ferryman as the Conductor of Souls,
also called Light of the Banner. But he did not tell the
others, merely crying 'Ahoy, ferry, ahoy!' When the boat
was alongshore, the ferryman again cried 'Ferry, ferry!'
'Your boat is broken and bottomless,' said Tripitaka, much
perturbed. 'How can you take people across?' 'You may

well think,' said the ferryman, 'that in a bottomless boat such a river as this could never be crossed. But since the beginning of time I have carried countless souls to their Salvation.' 'Get on board, Master,' said Monkey. 'You will find that this boat, although it has no bottom, is remarkably steady, however rough the waters may be.' Seeing Tripitaka still hesitate, Monkey took him by the scruff of the neck and pushed him on board. There was nothing for Tripitaka's feet to rest on, and he went straight into the water. The ferryman caught at him and dragged him up to the side of the boat. Sitting miserably here, he wrung out his clothes, shook out his shoes, and grumbled at Monkey for having got him into this scrape. But Monkey, taking no notice, put Pigsy and Sandy, horse and baggage, all on board, ensconcing them as best he could in the gunwale. The ferryman punted them dexterously out from shore. Suddenly they saw a body in the water, drifting rapidly down stream. Tripitaka stared at it in consternation. Monkey laughed. 'Don't be frightened, Master,' he said. 'That's you.' And Pigsy said, 'It's you, it's you.' Sandy clapped his hands. 'It's you, it's you,' he cried. The ferryman too joined in the chorus. 'There *you* go!' he cried. 'My best congratulations.' He went on punting, and in a very short while they were all safe and sound at the other side. Tripitaka stepped lightly ashore. He had discarded his earthly body; he was cleansed from the corruption of the senses, from the fleshly inheritance of those bygone years. His was now the transcendent wisdom that leads to the Further Shore, the mastery that knows no bounds.

When they were at the top of the bank, they turned round and found to their astonishment that boat and ferryman had both vanished. Only then did Monkey tell them who the ferryman was. Tripitaka began thanking his disciples for all they had done for him. 'Every one of us,' said Monkey, 'is equally indebted to the other. If the Master had not received our vows and accepted us as his disciples we should not have had the chance to do good works and win salvation. If we had not protected the Master and mounted guard over him, he would never have got rid of his mortal body. Look,

310

Master, at this realm of flowers and happy creatures – of phoenixes, cranes and deer. Is it not a better place indeed than the haunted deserts through which you and I have passed?' Tripitaka still murmured his thanks, and with a strange feeling of lightness and exhilaration they all set off up the Holy Mountain and were soon in sight of the Temple of the Thunder Clap, with its mighty towers brushing the firmament, its giant foundations rooted in the seams of the Hill of Life.

Near the top of the hill they came upon a party of Upa-sakas filing through the green pinewoods, and under a clump of emerald cedars they saw bands of the Blessed. Tripitaka hastened to bow down to them. Worshippers male and female, monks and nuns pressed together the palms of their hands, crying, 'Holy priest, it is not to us that your homage should be addressed. Wait till you have seen Śākyamuni, and afterwards come and greet us each according to his rank.' 'He's always in too much of a hurry,' laughed Monkey. 'Come along at once and let us pay our respects to the people at the top.' Twitching with excitement Tripitaka followed Monkey to the gates of the Temple. Here they were met by the Vajrapani of the Four Elements. 'So your Reverence has at last arrived!' he exclaimed. 'Your disciple Hsüan Tsang has indeed arrived,' said Tripitaka, bowing. 'I must trouble you to wait here a moment, till your arrival has been announced,' said the Vajrapani. He then gave instructions to the porter at the outer gate to tell the porter at the second gate that the Vajrapani wished to report that the priest from China had arrived. The porter at the second gate sent word to the porter at the third gate. At this gate were holy priests with direct access to the Powers Above. They hurried to the Great Hall and informed the Tathāgata, the Most Honoured One, even Śākyamuni Buddha himself that the priest from the Court of China had arrived at the Mountain to fetch scriptures.

Father Buddha was delighted. He ordered the Bodhi-sattva, Vajrapanis, Arhats, Protectors, Planets and Temple Guardians to form up in two lines. Then he gave orders that the priest of T'ang was to be shown in. Again the word was passed along from gate to gate: 'The priest of T'ang is to be shown in.' Tripitaka, Monkey, Pigsy and Sandy, carefully following the rules of etiquette prescribed to them, all went forward, horse and baggage following. When they reached the Great Hall they first prostrated themselves before the Tathāgata and then bowed to right and left. This they repeated three times, and then knelt before the Buddha and presented their passports. He looked through them one by one and handed them back to Tripitaka, who bent his head in acknowledgment, saying, 'The disciple Hsüan Tsang has come by order of the Emperor of the great land of T'ang, all the way to this Holy Mountain, to fetch the true scriptures which are to be the salvation of all mankind. May the Lord Buddha accord this favour and grant me a quick return to my native land.'

Hereupon the Tathāgata opened the mouth of compassion and gave vent to the mercy of his heart: 'In all the vast and populous bounds of your Eastern Land, greed, slaughter, lust and lying have long prevailed. There is no respect for Buddha's teaching, no striving towards good works. So full and abundant is the measure of the people's sins that they go down forever into the darkness of Hell, where some are pounded in mortars, some take on animal form, furry and horned. In which guise they are done by as they did on earth, their flesh becoming men's food. Confucius stood by their side teaching them all the virtues, king after king in vain corrected them with fresh penalties and pains. No law could curb their reckless debauches, no ray of wisdom penetrate their blindness.

'But I have three Baskets of Scripture that can save mankind from its torments and afflictions. One contains the Law, which tells of Heaven, one contains the Discourses, which speak of Earth, one contains the Scriptures, which save the dead. They are divided into thirty-five sections and are written upon fifteen thousand one hundred and forty-four scrolls. They are the path to Perfection, the gate that leads to True Good. In them may be learnt all the motions of the stars and divisions of earth, all that appertains to man, bird, beast, flower, tree and implement of use; in short, all that concerns mankind is found therein. In consideration of the fact that you have come so far, I would give you them all to take back. But the people of China are foolish and boisterous; they would mock at my mysteries and would not understand the hidden meaning of our Order . . . Ānanda, Kāśyapa', he cried, 'take these four to the room under the tower, and when they have refreshed themselves, open the doors of the Treasury, and select from each of the thirty-five sections a few scrolls for these priests to take back to the East, to be a boon there forever.'

In the lower room they saw countless rarities and treasures, and were still gazing upon them in wonder when spirits ministrant began to spread the feast. The foods were all fairy fruits and dainties unknown in the common world. Master and disciples bowed acknowledgment of Buddha's favour and set to with a good will. This time it was Pigsy who was in luck and Sandy who scored; for Buddha had provided for their fare such viands as confer long life and health and magically transform the substance of common flesh and bone. When Ānanda and Kāśyapa had seen to it that the four had all they wanted, they went into the Treasury. The moment the door was opened, beams of magic light shot forth, filling the whole air far around. On chests and jewelled boxes were stuck red labels, on which were written the names of the holy books. The two disciples of Buddha led Tripitaka up to the place where the scriptures lay, and inviting him to study the titles said, 'Having come here from China you have no doubt brought a few little gifts for us. If you will kindly hand them over, you shall have your scriptures at once.' 'During all my long journey,' said Tripitaka, 'I have never once found it necessary to lay in anything of the kind.' 'Splendid,' said the disciples. 'So we're to spend our days handing over scriptures gratis! Not a very bright outlook for our heirs!' Thinking by their sarcastic tone that they had no intention of parting with the scriptures, Monkey could not refrain from shouting angrily, 'Come

313

along, Master! We'll tell Buddha about this and make him come and give us the scriptures himself.' 'Don't shout,' said Ananda. 'There's nothing in the situation that demands all this bullying and blustering. Come here and fetch your scriptures.' Pigsy and Sandy, mastering their rage and managing to restrain Monkey, came across to take the books. Scroll by scroll was packed away into the bundle, which was hoisted on to the horse's back. Then the two luggage packs were tied up and given to Pigsy and Sandy to carry. They first went and kowtowed their thanks to Buddha and then made for the gates. To every lesser Buddha that they met they bowed twice; to every Bodhisattva once. Then leaving the great outer gates they paid their respects to the groups of monks and nuns, and saying farewell, went back down the mountain as fast as they could.

Now in an upper room that looked on to the Treasury there happened to be sitting Dīpankara, the Buddha of the Past. He overheard the whole conversation about the handing over of the scriptures, and had a notion that if they were given no gratuity, Ānanda and Kāśyapa would revenge themselves by substituting scriptures with nothing in them. 'The poor fools,' he said to himself, 'certainly have no idea of the trick that is being played on them, and will discover too late that their whole journey has been wasted.' 'Is there anyone here that could take a message for me?' he asked. The White Heroic Bodhisattva stepped forward, 'I want you to put forth all your magic powers,' said Dīpankara, 'catch up Tripitaka, get those scriptures away from him and bring him back to get proper ones.'

The White Heroic Bodhisattva sat astride a whirlwind and made off as fast as his magic powers would carry him. The wind he rode on had a strange perfume, which Tripitaka, when he first perceived it, thought merely to be one of the portents of Paradise. But a moment later, a great rushing sound was heard, and a hand suddenly stretched out from space, seized the scriptures and bore them away. Tripitaka beat his breast and groaned, Pigsy rolled off in pursuit, while Sandy clutched at the empty pannier. Monkey leapt into the

314

air; but the White Heroic Bodhisattva, seeing him draw near, feared that he might strike out blindly with his cudgel before any explanation could be given. So he tore open the scripture-parcel and threw it to the ground.

Monkey, when he saw the parcel fall and its contents scattered by the scented gale, lowered his cloud and went to see in what condition the scrolls were. He was soon joined by Pigsy, who had given up the pursuit, and they both began collecting the scrolls and bringing them to where Tripitaka was waiting. He was weeping bitterly. 'Little did I think,' he sobbed, 'that even in Paradise we should be thus molested by savage demons!' Sandy now opened one of the scrolls that he had brought. It was snowy white; there was not a trace of so much as half a letter upon it. 'Master,' he said, handing it to Tripitaka, 'This scroll has got no writing in it.' Monkey then opened a scroll; it too was blank. Pigsy did the same; only to make the same discovery. 'We had better look at them all,' said Tripitaka. They did so, and found that all were blank. 'I must say it's hard luck on the people of China,' sobbed Tripitaka. 'What is the use of taking to them these blank books? How shall I dare face the Emperor of T'ang? He will say I am playing a joke on him and have me executed on the spot.'

Monkey had by now guessed what had happened. 'Master,' he said, 'I know what's at the bottom of this. It is all because we refused to give Ānanda and Kāśyapa their commission. This is how they have revenged themselves on us. The only thing to do is to go straight to Buddha and charge them with fraudulent withholding of delivery.' They all agreed, and were soon back at the temple gates. 'They've come back to change their scriptures,' said the bands of the blessed, laughing. This time they were allowed to go straight in. 'Listen to this!' shouted Monkey. 'After all the trouble we had getting here from China, and after you specially ordered that we were to be given the scriptures, Ānanda and Kāśyapa made a fraudulent delivery of goods. They gave us blank copies to take away; I ask you, what is the good of that to us?' 'You needn't shout,' said Buddha smiling. 'I quite expected that those two would ask for their commission. As a matter of fact, scriptures ought not to be given on too easy terms or received gratis. On one occasion some of my monks went down the mountain to Śrāvastī with some scriptures and let Chao, the Man of Substance, read them out loud. The result was that all the live members of his household were protected from all calamity and the dead were saved from perdition. For this they only charged gold to the weight of three pecks and three pints of rice. I told them they had sold far too cheap. No wonder they gave you blank copies when they saw you did not intend to make any payment at all. As a matter of fact, it is such blank scrolls as these that are the true scriptures. But I quite see that the people of China are too foolish and ignorant to believe this, so there is nothing for it but to give them copies with some writing on.' Then he called for Ānanda and Kaśyapa, and told them to choose a few scrolls with writing, out of each of the thirty-five divisions of the scriptures, hand them over to the pilgrims, and then inform him of the exact titles and numbers.

The two disciples accordingly took the pilgrims once more to the Treasury, where they again asked Tripitaka for a little present. He could think of nothing to give them except his golden begging bowl. He told Sandy to find it, and holding it up before him in both hands, he said to the two disciples, 'I am a poor man and have been travelling for a long time. I fear I have nothing with me that is suitable as a present; but perhaps you would accept this bowl which the Emperor of China gave me with his own hand, that I might use it to beg with on the road. If you will put up with so small a trifle, I am sure that when I return to China and report upon my mission, you may count upon being suitably rewarded. I hope on these terms you will this time give me scriptures with writing on them, or I fear his Majesty will be disappointed and think that all my efforts have been wasted. Ānanda took the bowl with a faint smile. But all the divinities in attendance – down to the last kitchen-boy god – clapped one another on the back and roared with laughter,

316

saying, 'Well, of all the shameless . . . ! They've made the scripture seekers pay them a commission!' The two disciples looked somewhat embarrassed, but Ānanda continued to clutch tightly at the bowl. Kāśyapa meanwhile began looking out the scriptures and handing them over to Tripitaka. 'Disciples,' said he, 'keep a sharp look out, to see that the same thing doesn't happen again.' Five thousand and forty-eight scrolls were duly handed over. All of them had writing. Then they were properly arranged and loaded on the horse's back, and a few that were over were made into a packet and given to Pigsy to carry. The other luggage was carried by Sandy, while Monkey led the horse. Tripitaka carried his priest's staff and wore his jewelled cap and brocaded cassock. In this guise they all once more presented themselves before Buddha.

Seated on his Lotus Throne, the Blessed One ordered the two Great Arhats to beat on their cloud gongs and summon to the Throne the three thousand Buddhas, the eight Vajrapanis, the four Bodhisattvas, the five hundred Arhats, the eight hundred monks and all the congregation of the faithful. Those that were entitled to be seated were ordered to sit upon their jewelled thrones, and those that were to stand were ranged in two files on either hand. Soon heavenly music was heard from afar, a magic radiance filled the air. When the whole company was duly assembled, Buddha asked his two disciples for an exact account of the scriptures that they had handed over. Ānanda and Kāśyapa then read over the list, beginning with the Book of the Great Decease, and ending with the Kośa Sāstra. 'These books,' said Ānanda, 'written on five thousand and forty-eight scrolls, have all been given to the priests of China to keep forever in their land. They are all now securely packed on their horse's back or in parcels to be carried by hand, and the pilgrims are here to thank you.'

Tripitaka and the disciples tethered the horse, put down the burdens and bowed with the palms of their hands pressed together. 'The efficacy of these scriptures is boundless,' said Buddha. 'They are not only the mirror of our Faith, but also

317

the source and origin of all three religions. When you return to the world and show them to common mortals, they must not be lightly handled. No scroll must be opened save by one who has fasted and bathed. Treasure them, value them! For in them is secreted the mystic lore of Immortality, in them is revealed the wondrous receipt for ten thousand transformations.'

Tripitaka kowtowed his thanks, doing leal homage, and prostrating himself three times, as he had done before. When they reached the outer gates, they paid their respects to the bands of the faithful, and went on their way.

After dismissing the pilgrims, Buddha broke up the assembly. Presently the Bodhisattva Kuan-yin appeared before the throne, saying, 'Long ago I was instructed by you to find someone in China who would come here to fetch scriptures. He has now achieved this task, which has taken him five thousand and forty days. The number of the scrolls delivered to him is five thousand and forty-eight. I suggest that it would be appropriate if he were given eight days in which to complete his mission, so that the two figures may concord.' 'A very good idea,' said Buddha. 'You may have that put into effect.' He then sent for the eight Vajrapanis and said to them, 'You are to exert your magic powers and carry back Tripitaka to the East. When he has deposited the scriptures, you are to bring him back here. All this must be done in eight days, that the number of days taken by the journey may concord with the number of scrolls allotted to him.' The Vajrapanis at once went after Tripitaka, caught him up and said to him, 'Scripture-taker, follow us.' A sudden lightness and agility possessed the pilgrims and they were borne aloft upon a magic cloud.

And if you do not know how they returned to the East and handed over the scriptures, you must listen to what is told in the next chapter.

Chapter 29

So the eight Vajrapanis escorted Tripitaka back to the East. Of this no more shall now be said. But it must be told that the Guardians of the Five Points, the Sentinels of the Four Watches and all the divinities who had protected Tripitaka during his journey now appeared before Kuan-yin and said, 'Your disciples have faithfully carried out your holy instructions and have, all unseen, guarded the Priest of T'ang in his journey to the West. You have reported to the Lord Buddha on the execution of your task, and we beg to report on our endeavours.' 'The presentation of a report is hereby authorised,' said the Bodhisattva. 'I should like first to know what disposition the pilgrims displayed during their journey.' 'They manifested the greatest determination and devotion,' said the divinities, 'a fact that has doubtless not escaped your inspired perspicacity. The tribulations endured by the pilgrims were indeed too many to be fully enumerated. But I have here a record of the major calamities.' The Bodhisattva took the record and examined it with care: 'Tripitaka falls into a pit, is attacked by tigers, but saved by his disciple Monkey; he is attacked by the Six Robbers . . . ' and so on, right down to his adventure in the boat with no bottom. 'In our Faith,' said the Bodhisattva, 'nine times nine is the crucial number. I see that the number of calamities listed here is eighty, thus falling short by one of the holy number.' Then turning to a Guardian she said, 'Catch up the Vajrapanis and tell them there has got to be one more calamity.' He flew through the clouds to the East, and in a single day and night he caught up the Vajrapanis and whispered something in their ears. 'By order of the Bodhisattva herself,' he said. 'Let there be no mistake!' The Vajrapanis at once withdrew the magic gale that was carrying the pilgrims through space. Horse, scriptures and all, they fell to earth with a bang.

Tripitaka was sorely taken aback to discover himself

319

standing upon solid ground. Pigsy roared with laughter. 'If ever there was a case of "more haste, less speed!" ' he said. 'I call it very considerate,' said Sandy. 'No doubt they thought that we weren't used to travelling so fast, and would like a rest.' 'Well,' said Monkey, 'the proverb says "sit tight for ten days, and in one day you'll shoot nine rapids." ' 'Will you stop talking nonsense,' said Tripitaka, 'and devote your ingenuity to discovering where we are.' 'I know, I know,' said Sandy, looking about him. 'Just listen to that sound of water!' 'It makes Sandy feel at home,' said Monkey. 'If it makes him feel at home,' said Pigsy, 'it must be the River of Flowing Sands. That's where he belongs.' 'Not at all,' said Sandy, 'it's the river that flows to Heaven.' 'Disciple,' said Tripitaka, 'go up on to the bank and have a look.' Monkey sprang up and shading his eyes with his hands, closely inspected the river. 'Master,' he reported, 'this is the western shore of the River that Flows to Heaven.' 'I remember now,' cried Tripitaka, 'on the other side is Mr Ch'ên's farm. When we passed this way, you saved the boy and girl. They were very grateful to us and wanted to make you a boat. In the end, a white turtle took us across. I remember that on this side there are no houses at all. How are we to manage this time?' 'A dirty trick like this would not surprise one if one were dealing with ordinary people,' said Pigsy, 'but it's a bit too much, coming from Buddha's own particular henchmen. He told them to take us straight back to the East. What do they mean by dropping us in the middle of the journey? They've left us in a bit of a fix!' 'I don't know what you two are grumbling about,' said Sandy. 'The Master is now no longer a common mortal. We saw his earthly body float by us down the Cloud River. There's no fear of his sinking this time. With all three of us to assist him, it would be strange if he couldn't get across,' Monkey smiled to himself. 'It's not going to be so easy as all that,' he said. Why did he say it was not going to be so easy? If it had been merely a question of possessing sufficient magic powers, all four of them could easily enough have floated across a thousand such rivers. But Monkey knew that the number 'nine times nine' was not yet fulfilled and that Buddha's inexorable will decreed for them yet another calamity. They were all walking slowly along the shore, discussing the situation as they went, when suddenly they heard a voice cry, 'Priest of T'ang, Priest of T'ang, come over here.' As no one was to be seen in the vicinity and there was no boat on the river, they were much astonished. But in a moment they caught sight of a large white head. The White Turtle was nearing the shore. 'I've been waiting for you all this time,' he said craning his neck. 'We are very glad to meet you,' said Monkey, 'come a little closer in.' The turtle then sidled up to the bank and Monkey led the horse on to its broad back. Pigsy squatted behind its tail, Tripitaka stood on one side of its head, Sandy on the other. Monkey stood with one foot on its neck and the other on its head. 'Now then, old turtle,' he cried, 'go steadily,' and the turtle set off smoothly and easily across the waters, carrying the whole company uneventfully till evening fell and they had almost reached the far side. Suddenly the turtle said, 'When I took you across last time I asked you to find out from Buddha how long it will be before I attain to human form. Did you remember to ask?' Unfortunately Tripitaka had been so much taken up with his own affairs – losing his mortal body, going up the Holy Mountain, meeting Buddha and all the Bodhisattvas and bands of the faithful, taking over the scriptures and so on, that he had no time to think of anything else, and had quite forgotten to ask about the turtle's prospects. Not daring to tell a downright lie, he hemmed and hawed, without giving any definite answer. The turtle saw at once that he had not asked and, much annoyed, dived straight into the water, leaving the four pilgrims, the horse and the scriptures floundering in the stream. It was lucky for Tripitaka that he had discarded his mortal frame and achieved the Way; otherwise he would have gone straight to the bottom. Fortunately, too, the white horse was really a dragon, and Pigsy and Sandy were both at home in the water. Monkey sprang up, and by a great display of his transcendent powers bore the Master safely to the shore. But the scriptures and all their other belongings got wet through.

They had climbed the bank and were getting things straight when a great wind began to blow, the sky became black, lightning flashed, and sand and grit whirled up in their faces. Tripitaka clutched the scripture-pack, Sandy clung to his packet, while Pigsy hung on to the white horse. Monkey meanwhile brandished his cudgel in both hands, now to one side now to the other. The storm was the outward sign of the invisible demons who were attempting to snatch away the Scriptures. Their attacks continued all night; but towards daybreak at last subsided. Tripitaka, soaked to the skin, was trembling from head to foot. 'Monkey, what does all this mean?' he asked. 'You do not seem to realise the immensity of our task,' said Monkey, 'in enabling you to secure these scriptures. We have incurred the envy of every spirit in heaven and earth; for our undying feat trespasses on the domain of their sovereign powers. They have been making every endeavour to snatch from us what we have gained. Had not the scriptures been wet through, and had you not held them with hands no longer mortal, and had not I kept our hidden foes at bay with this short cudgel, the magic gale would have blown them away before dawn came and the forces of light again prevailed.' Tripitaka and the rest then realised what had been afoot, and thanked Monkey for his protection.

When the sun was well up, they carried the scriptures on to a flat place above the bank and spread them out to dry. Till now the place is called 'The Rock Where Scriptures Were Dried.' They also dried their shoes and clothes. They were looking through the scriptures to see if they were all dry, when they saw some fishermen coming along the shore, among whom were some who seemed to recognise them. Are not you the reverend gentlemen who went across the river to fetch scriptures from India?' they said. 'That's right,' said Pigsy. 'Where do you come from, and how is it that you recognised us?' 'We are from Mr Ch'ên's farm,' said the fishermen. 'How far off is it?' asked Pigsy. 'If you went about twenty leagues straight south from here, you would come to it,' they said. 'Let's take the scriptures and dry them properly at the farm,' said Pigsy. 'There is much to be gained by going there. We can sit down comfortably for a bit, get something to eat, and ask the people there to wring out our clothes.' 'I'm not going,' said Tripitaka. 'We can dry the scriptures very well here, and then we'll collect them and start off again.' Meanwhile the fishermen who had started for home, happened to meet the younger Mr Ch'ên. 'Master,' they cried out, 'the priests who did away with the child-sacrifice here have come back.' 'Where did you see them?' he asked. 'They are drying some scrolls on that rock there,' said the fishermen. Mr Ch'ên, accompanied by some of his farm labourers, hurried towards the spot, and when he reached them he fell down upon his knees, crying, 'I see that you have got your scriptures and are returning in triumph. I feel rather hurt that instead of coming and visiting us you should be loitering about here. Pray come home with me at once.' 'Wait till our scriptures are dry, and we'll come home with you,' said Monkey. 'I see that all your clothes, as well as your scriptures, are wet,' said Mr Ch'ên. 'What has been happening to you?' Tripitaka told him of his unfortunate failure to remember the White Turtle's commission, and how this had led to their all being flung into the water. Mr Ch'ên pressed them very hard to come home with him, and in the end Tripitaka gave in. When they were collecting the scriptures, several scrolls of the Lalitavistara stuck to the rock, and a piece got torn from the end of the last scroll. That is why the Lalitavistara as we have it today is incomplete, and why there are still traces of writing on the Rock Where the Scriptures Were Dried. Tripitaka was much upset. 'I am afraid this was very careless of us,' he said. 'We ought to have gone slower and taken more trouble.' 'You have no reason to get into such a state about it,' said Monkey. 'These scriptures are now just as intact as they were intended to be. Heaven and Earth themselves are not more complete. The part now broken off contained a secret refinement of doctrine that was not meant for transmission, and no care on your part could have prevented this accident.'

When the scriptures had been collected, they all set out for the farm. The news of their arrival spread with astonishing rapidity and they were met by everyone in the place, young and old. As soon as he heard of the pilgrims' arrival, the elder Mr Ch'ên ordered an incense-stand to be set up, and awaited them at the gate. He also ordered music to be made, and to the accompaniment of flutes and drums led them in. He then told the whole household to come one by one and pay their respects to the benefactors who had saved the children from destruction. After this, tea and refreshments were brought in.

Tripitaka, since he had discarded his mortal body and become a Buddha and received magic viands from the Tathāgata's table, had evinced little taste for earthly food. It was only at the urgent instance of the two old men that he was persuaded to make some show of tasting what was put before him. Monkey, who in any case never ate cooked food, soon pushed his plate from him. Sandy too ate very little. Even Pigsy did not eat with anything like the zest that he had shown the last time they were here. 'Fool,' said Monkey, 'you are not doing yourself justice.' 'I don't know why it is,' said Pigsy. 'I've been a bit off my feed lately.' The tables were cleared, and Tripitaka told the whole story of their adventures, from the time they reached Paradise down to the attempts of unseen demons to seize the scriptures. Then he made to go; but the old men would not hear of it. 'We could think of no better way of showing our gratitude,' they said, 'than by setting up a shrine, which we call the Temple of Deliverance, where we continually burn incense in your honour.' After War Boy and the girl Load of Gold had been sent for and had kowtowed their gratitude, the pilgrims were invited to come and look at the shrine. On the upper floor were four statues, representing Tripitaka, Monkey, Pigsy and Sandy. 'Yours is very like,' said Pigsy, nudging Monkey. 'I think yours is a wonderful likeness too,' said Sandy to Pigsy, 'but the Master's really makes him out a little too handsome.' 'I think it's very good,' said Tripitaka.

On going down, they found more refreshments waiting for

them in one of the cloisters. 'By the way, what has become of the Great King's shrine?' asked Monkey. 'We pulled it down,' they said. 'But so great is your blessed power and protection that since we built this shrine in your honour we have had a bumper harvest every year.' 'Such blessings come from Heaven,' said Monkey. 'We don't claim to have any hand in it. But we will try henceforth to give you all such protection as we can. Your children and children's children shall be many, your herds shall give easy birth, the winds and rains shall come in due season.' The people thanked him again, and once more offerings of fruit and cake of every kind came pouring in from all sides. 'It's bad luck on me,' said Pigsy. 'In the old days when I really had some appetite, no one thought of pressing victuals on me. But today when I eat next to nothing, they swarm round me, pressing on one another's heels, and beg me to stuff myself. I suppose I mustn't be rude . . . ' And to spare their feelings he managed, without undue violence to his inside, to get through eight or nine dishes of vegetables and twenty or thirty pasties. They were still egging him on, when Tripitaka said, 'I don't know how you have managed to make yourself so popular. I think it would be better to call a halt for the present. Your friends can continue their attentions tomorrow morning.' It was now late in the night. Tripitaka did not dare leave the scriptures for a minute, and mounted watch over them in the lower part of the shrine. Just before the third watch he whispered, 'Monkey, the people here know that we have mastered the secrets of the Way. It is said "The Adept does not reveal himself; if he reveals himself, he is not an Adept." I am afraid that if we stay here too long, our secrets may be wormed out of us.' 'I agree with you,' said Monkey. 'We had better creep away quickly, while it is still night and everyone is asleep.' Pigsy was no longer a fool, Sandy had attained to perfect discretion, and the white horse was well able to see the point of an argument. So they all got up and prepared to start. When they got to the main gate of the shrine, they found it locked. But Monkey used a lock-breaking magic and they were soon through the double

325

gates, and seeking the road to the East. Suddenly came the voices of the eight Vajrapanis, crying from up above in the air, 'Now then! Where are you off to? Follow us!' Tripitaka smelt a great gust of perfumed wind, which caught him and bore him up into the air.

And if you want to know how he met the king of T'ang, you must listen to what is told in the next chapter.

Chapter 30

When day came, the people again began to pour in with offerings of fruit and other dainties. To their astonishment the pilgrims had vanished. After hunting high and low till they could think of nowhere else to look they gave up all hope, and cried to the Joiner of Days, 'Fie upon you, Limpid One! Why have you taken our Living Buddha away?' There was nothing for it but to lay the viands they had brought upon the altar of the shrine, where they burned paper slips and prayed for the acceptance of the offerings. Ever afterwards, four times a year, they performed a grand ceremony and twice a month a lesser ceremony at this shrine. And apart from this, at every hour of every day there would always be worshippers there, praying for recovery from illness or protection on a journey, praying for chattels or children.

Meanwhile it took less than a day for this second gale of magic wind to blow the pilgrims back to China, and soon they began to see the towers of Ch'ang-an. It was three days before the full moon of the ninth month in the thirteenth year of the period Chêng Kuan, that the Emperor escorted Tripitaka to the outskirts of the city. In the sixteenth year he ordered a pagoda to be built outside the western gates, called the Scripture Look-out Tower, and every year he visited it in person. It so happened that he was visiting the pagoda on the day when the pilgrims arrived. Looking out, he suddenly saw the whole western sky fill with a magic radiance; a moment later he noticed a strange perfume in the breeze.

'Well, here we are at Ch'ang-an,' cried the eight Vajrapanis, coming to a halt in mid-air. 'We would rather not alight, as the people in these parts are very tricky, and if they caught sight of us might make our presence known in undesirable quarters. There is also no reason for the three disciples to go down. But you, Master, had better go at once and hand over the scriptures, and then come back here.

327

We'll wait for you in mid-air, and then we will all go back and report in Paradise.' 'That's all very well,' said Monkey. 'But how is the Master to carry the scriptures, and who is to lead his horse? We had much better go with him, while you wait here. You may be sure we shan't get in his way.' 'The Bodhisattva promised Buddha that the whole business should only take eight days,' said the Vajrapanis. 'If you all go, we shall have Pigsy touting round for offerings, and get behind time.' 'You lousy old ruffians,' cried Pigsy, 'why should you think that I shall waste time touting round here? I am as anxious as anyone to get back to Paradise. The Master has become a Buddha, and I intend to become a Buddha too. You wait here, and the minute we have handed in the scriptures I'll come back with you and be canonised.' So Pigsy carrying the pack, Sandy leading the horse and Monkey accompanying Tripitaka, they alighted at the side of the pagoda. The Emperor and his ministers at once came down to meet them. 'So my dear brother has come at last!' he cried. Tripitaka bowed low. 'And who are these?' asked the Emperor. 'They are disciples I picked up on the road,' said Tripitaka. 'Saddle one of my chariot-horses,' said the Emperor to his servants, 'and my brother shall ride back with me to the Court.'

By the time they reached Ch'ang-an there was not a soul in the city who had not heard that the scripture-seekers had arrived. It was noticed by the priests in Tripitaka's old temple that a pine tree in the courtyard was bent towards the east. 'This is very strange,' they said. 'There was no wind to speak of in the night. How comes it that the top of this tree is bent down?' Among them was one of Tripitaka's old disciples. 'Go and get your cloaks at once,' he cried. 'The Master has come home with the scriptures.' 'How do you know?' they asked. 'He told us when he went away,' said he, 'that he might be absent for three, five, even seven years. But that if we saw the top of this pine tree bent towards the east, it would mean that he was coming back. Sooner would Buddha himself speak falsely than a lie escape my Master's lips. I know that he is here.' The priests hurriedly put on their cloaks and went out. They had not gone far before someone called to them, 'Have you heard the news? The scripture-seekers have just arrived and the Emperor himself met them and brought them back into the city.' Hearing this they hurried faster than ever and were just in time to meet the procession. They dared not approach too close, but followed the Imperial party till it reached the gates of the palace. When the pilgrims reached the Audience Hall the Emperor seated Tripitaka by his side, and ordered the scriptures to be brought in. Monkey and the rest delivered them to the chamberlains, who in turn laid them before the Emperor. 'How many scrolls are there,' he asked, 'and how were they given to you?'

Tripitaka described his arrival at the Holy Mountain, the trick played by Ānanda and Kāśyapa, and how he had in the end obtained written copies by parting with the begging-bowl given to him by his Majesty. 'As to the number of scrolls,' he said, 'there are five thousand and forty-eight, some chosen from each of the thirty-five sections.'

The Emperor was delighted, and ordered the Entertainment Board to prepare a banquet of welcome in the eastern tower. Suddenly his eye fell on the three disciples who were waiting at the far end of the Hall. Their appearance struck him as very unusual. 'I suppose these gentlemen are foreigners?' he said. 'My eldest disciple, named Monkey,' said Tripitaka, 'comes from the Water Curtain Cave, on the Mountain of Flowers and Fruit. Five hundred years ago he made trouble in Heaven and Buddha imprisoned him in a stone chest under the Mountain of the Two Frontiers. But he was converted by the Bodhisattva Kuan-yin, and on my way to India I was able to release him and take him with me as my disciple. His protection stood me in good stead, and had it not been for him I could never have fulfilled my mission. My second disciple, Pigsy, came from the Cloud Ladder Cave on Mount Fu-ling. He was haunting Mr Kao's farm when I came that way and picked him up. He has carried the luggage throughout our journey and also proved very useful when rivers had to be crossed. My third disciple, Sandy,

329

comes from the River of Flowing Sands. He too was converted by Kuan-yin and was received into the Order. The horse is not the one that you bestowed upon me.' 'Indeed?' said the Emperor. 'Its coat looks very similar. How came you to change horses?' When we were crossing the Falcon Grief Torrent,' said Tripitaka, 'the original horse was swallowed by this one. But Monkey went to Kuan-yin and enquired about the origins of this horse. It appears that it was a son of the Dragon King of the Western Ocean, but got into trouble and would have been executed, had not the Bodhisattva intervened and appointed it to be my steed. It was then that it changed into a horse with a coat exactly like that of my original mount. It has carried me faithfully over the most difficult crags and passes. On the way there, I rode on its back; on the way home it carried the scriptures. So that in one way and another we are much beholden to it.'

'You have been very well served,' said the Emperor. 'It would interest me to know exactly how far it is to India.' 'I remember,' said Tripitaka, 'that the Boddhisattva spoke of the distance as being a hundred and eight thousand leagues. We kept no exact count. But I know that summer turned to winter fourteen times, and that there was no day upon which we did not cross some range of hills. Often we had to make our way through vast forests or across huge rivers. As for the kingdoms through which we passed, you will find the seals of each one of them stamped upon our passports.' Then he called to his disciples to bring the passports for the Emperor's inspection. Seeing that they were marked as having been issued three days before the full moon of the ninth month of the thirteenth year of Chêng Kuan, the Emperor smiled. 'It has been a long job,' he said. 'It is now the twenty-seventh year!' Then he looked at the seals. There was the seal of the country of Crow-cock, the seal of the Cart Slow country, and many others. And finally, the seal of the Golden Treasury of Paradise. Having examined the passports, he handed them back. Just then an official announced that the banquet was ready, and taking Tripitaka by the hand, the Emperor led him down the Hall. 'Are your disciples familiar with Court Etiquette?' he asked. 'I am afraid not,' said Tripitaka. 'They have spent their time in uncouth and deeply rural surroundings. I fear they have no inkling of what the etiquette of the Chinese Court demands. I must ask your Majesty to be lenient towards them.' 'Don't worry,' said the Emperor. 'I shan't blame them. Tell them all to come along to the banquet.'

The pilgrims found themselves, along with all the officials civil and military, grouped on either side of the Imperial Seat. There was dancing and singing, and the music of flutes and drums. The whole entertainment was on the most magnificent scale, and it was indeed a happy day.

When evening came the guests expressed their thanks and withdrew. The Emperor betook himself to the women's apartments, and the officials to their residences. The pilgrims went to Tripitaka's old temple, where they were welcomed by kowtowing priests. 'Master,' they said, 'this tree this morning suddenly bent towards the East. We remembered what you told us, and went out to meet you.' Inside the temple, Pigsy did not shout for more food or create any disturbance. Monkey and Sandy behaved with perfect decorum. For all three were now Illumined, and it cost them no pains to stay quiet. When night came, they all went to sleep.

Early next morning, the Emperor said to his ministers at Court, 'All night long I could not sleep, so full were my thoughts of the magnitude of my brother's achievements, and the impossibility of making any adequate recompense. I ended by composing in my head a few clumsy sentences, which I hope may make him aware of my gratitude. I have not yet written them down.' Then he called for one of the Imperial Secretaries and said, 'I want to dictate something to you. Please take it down very accurately.' What the Emperor dictated is known to all, for it was the 'Introduction to Buddha's Holy Teachings,' [1] which still figures in the 'Canon.'[2]

[1] A translation will be found in Helen Hayes, *The Buddhist Pilgrim's Progress*, p. 98.
[2] Taishō Tripitaka, Vol. L, p. 256.

When he had finished dictating, he sent for Tripitaka. 'Your Majesty's style,' said Tripitaka, 'is very lofty and archaic, and your reasoning is subtle and profound. I notice, however, that there is no title at the head of your essay.' 'I made it up in my head during the night, as a token of gratitude to my reverend brother,' said the Emperor. 'How would it be if I called it "Introduction to Buddha's Holy Teachings?" ' Tripitaka kowtowed his assent. 'My talent,' the Emperor continued, 'pales before the wisdom that is inscribed on tablets of jade, my words are put to shame by the maxims that are incised on bronze and stone. As to the Esoteric Texts, my ignorance of them is alas profound. This, remember, is an essay composed in my head, and necessarily rough and clumsy. It is, I fear, not worth your notice and you have no need to thank me.' The officials who were present all congratulated the Emperor on the felicity of his improvised composition, and recommended that it should be circulated everywhere, both at Court and beyond.

'Won't you read to us out of the scriptures?' said the Emperor to Tripitaka. 'Your Majesty,' said he, 'this is no place to recite holy writ. The scriptures may only be read in a place dedicated to religion.' 'Which is the holiest of all the shrines in Ch'ang-an?' the Emperor asked, turning to those about him. 'Holiest of all is the Wild Goose Pagoda,' said the Grand Preceptor Hsiao Yü. 'Take a few chapters from each of the main Scriptures,' said the Emperor, 'and reverently transport them to the Wild Goose Pagoda. Then we'll get my holy brother to read them out to us.' The selection was made and they all went off to the pagoda, where a platform was erected and everything made ready for the recitation.

Tripitaka told Pigsy and Sandy to hold the dragon horse and mind the baggage, and Monkey to be ready to hand the scrolls to him. 'Your Majesty,' remarked Tripitaka, 'will have to have copies of these scriptures made, if you want to promulgate them throughout your Empire. The originals are far too precious to be bandied about!' 'That's perfectly true,' said the Emperor. And he gave orders that scribes of

332

the Han-lin Academy should make copies of the scriptures. These were distributed through a special agency set up to the east of the city, called the Temple of Transcription.

Tripitaka had already gone up on to the platform with a number of scrolls, and was just going to begin his recitation, when the familiar gust of perfumed wind reached his nostrils, and the eight Vajrapanis appeared in mid-air, saying, 'Recitants, leave your scriptures and follow us to the West.' Immediately Monkey and the others, including the white horse, began to rise from the ground. Tripitaka laid down his scroll and rose above the platform straight up into the Ninth Heaven. In utter amazement the Emperor and his ministers did homage to them as they receded. Soon afterwards a great Mass was held at the Wild Goose Pagoda, the True Scriptures of the Greater Vehicle were for the first time seen and recited, and multitudes of lost souls were saved from darkness. Moreover, through the labours of the Temple of Transcription their blessing became universal.

Meanwhile the four pilgrims and the white horse were carried back to Paradise by the eight Vajrapanis, and counting up the time taken by their going and coming, it proved that the whole journey had barely taken the eight stipulated days. It happened that when they arrived, all the deities of the Holy Mountain were assembled before Buddha, to receive his instructions. 'We beg to state that the pilgrims have been to Ch'ang-an, as commanded, have handed over the scriptures and have now returned to report,' said the Vajrapanis. They then motioned to Tripitaka and the rest to come forward and receive their heavenly rank.

'Holy priest,' said the Tathāgata, 'you in a previous existence were my second disciple and were called Golden Cicada. But because you paid no heed to my teaching and scoffed at my doctrine, I caused you to be reborn in the East. But now by the true devotion you have shown in the fetching of my holy scriptures, you have won great merit and I herewith appoint you to be a Buddha, with the title "Buddha of Precocious Merit".

'Monkey, because you made trouble in Heaven, it was

found necessary to imprison you under the Mountain of the Five Elements. But fortunately, when the time of your retribution was ended, you turned your heart to the Great Faith and your endeavour to the scourging of evil and the promotion of good. Upon your recent journey you distinguished yourself by the subjugation of monsters and demons, and have done, first and last, so well that I hereby promote you to be the Buddha Victorious in Strife.

'Pigsy, you were once a marshal of the watery hosts of Heaven. But at a peach banquet you drank too much and made free with a fairy maiden. For this you were condemned to be born into the common world, with a shape near to animal.

'However, when you were haunting the cave of the Cloud Ladder, you were converted to the Higher Religion, eventually became a priest and gave your protection to Tripitaka on his journey. Greed and lust are not yet utterly extinct in you; but remembering that you carried the luggage all the way, I now promote you to be Cleanser of the Altar.' 'Hey! What's this? I don't understand,' said Pigsy. 'You've just made the other two into Buddhas. Why aren't I a Buddha too?' 'Because,' said Buddha, 'your conversation and appearance still lack refinement, and your appetite is still too large. But the number of my worshippers in all the four continents of the Universe is very large, and it will be your job to clean up the altar everywhere and whenever there is a Buddhist ceremony and offerings are made. So you'll get plenty of pickings. I don't see what you've got to complain of.

'Sandy, you were a great Captain of Spirits; but one day at the Peach Banquet you broke a crystal dish and were banished to the common world, where you settled in the River of Flowing Sands and lived by devouring human flesh. Fortunately you were converted, zealously and faithfully carried out your vows and protected Tripitaka. In recognition of the way you got his horse over the mountain passes, I now promote you to the rank of an Arhat, with the title "Golden Bodied Arhat." '

334

Then he turned to the white horse. 'You,' he said, 'were a child of the Dragon King of the Western Ocean, but you disobeyed your father and were found guilty of unfilial conduct. Fortunately you were converted to the Faith and became attached to our Order. Because you carried Tripitaka to the West and on the return journey transported the scriptures, your services too must be rewarded, and I hereby promote you to be one of the eight senior Heavenly Dragons.'

The four pilgrims all kowtowed their thanks, and the white horse also made sign of its gratitude. Then by Buddha's order it was led to the back of the Holy Mountain, to the side of the Pool of Magic Dragons, into the middle of which it was pushed with a splash. After a short while, it began to stretch itself and its coat began to change in appearance. It grew horns upon its head and its body became covered with golden scales, while on its cheeks silver whiskers grew. Its whole form was suffused with magic tints, its four claws rested on prophetic clouds; it soared up and out of the pool, wreathed its way in at the gate of the Palace, and circled above the Pillar that Supports Heaven. All the Buddhas burst into exclamations of wonder at this miracle that the Tathāgata had wrought.

'Master,' Monkey said to Tripitaka, 'I'm now a Buddha, the same as you. It's not fair that I should still wear this golden fillet, so that if you choose to recite your spell, you could still plague me. Make haste and say the "Loosing of the Fillet" spell, so that I may get it off and smash it to bits. Otherwise the Bodhisattva may use it to play her jokes on anyone else.' 'It was put upon you,' said Tripitaka, 'at a time when you needed to be kept in hand. Now that you are a Buddha, it has vanished of its own accord. Feel your head and you'll see.' Monkey put his hand to his head. What Tripitaka had said was quite true. The fillet was not there.

The promotion of the five saints took place in the presence of all the spirits of Heaven – Buddhas, Bodhisattvas, Arhats, monks, local deities and Guardian Spirits. While the newcomers took their appointed places in the great assembly, multitudinous voices rose in prayer: 'Praise to the Buddha of the Past, Praise to Bhaishajya, Praise to Śākyamuni . . .' and so on through all the Buddhas, till finally for the first time they chanted 'Praise to the Buddha of Precocious Merit, Praise to the Buddha Victorious in Strife.' Next they invoked the names of all the Bodhisattvas, Kuan-yin, Mahāsthāmprāpta, Manjuśrī, Samantabhadra and the rest, ending with 'Praise to the Cleanser of the Altar, praise to the Golden Bodied Arhat, praise to the Heavenly Dragon.'

I dedicate this work to the glory of Buddha's Pure Land. May it repay the kindness of patron and preceptor, may it mitigate the sufferings of the lost and damned. May all that read it or hear it read find their hearts turned towards Truth, in the end be born again in the Realms of Utter Bliss, and by their common intercession requite me for the ardours of my task.